A Shadow ~from~ Tomorrow

Mark Streff

Mark Streff

This is a work of fiction. All characters, names, places, and events used in this book are a product of the author's imagination or are used fictitiously.

Paperback ISBN: 9798285393290

Set in EB Garamond Medium font
Cover font in Lombardic Narrow

A Shadow From Tomorrow

For Katie

A Shadow From Tomorrow

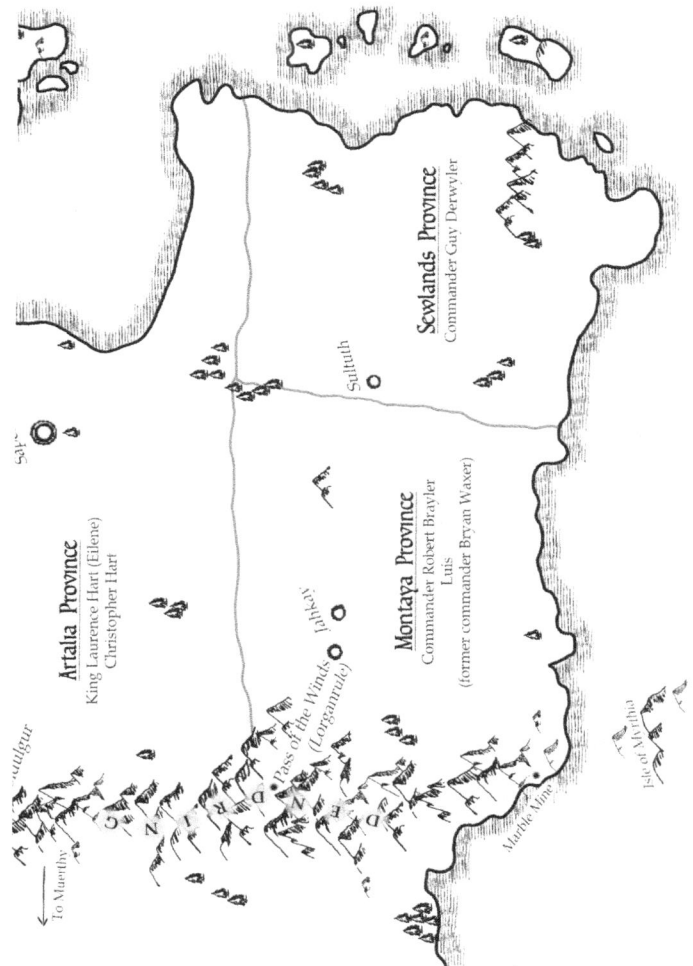

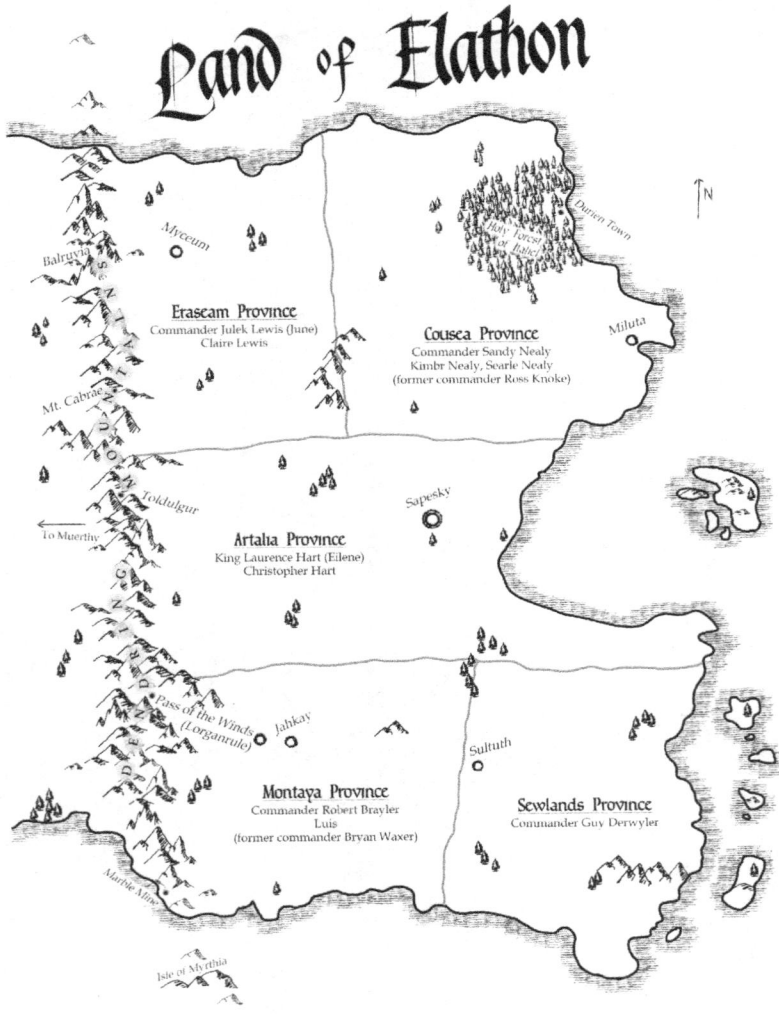

Chapter 1.

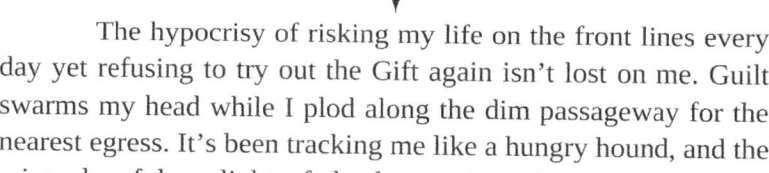

The hypocrisy of risking my life on the front lines every day yet refusing to try out the Gift again isn't lost on me. Guilt swarms my head while I plod along the dim passageway for the nearest egress. It's been tracking me like a hungry hound, and the crisp cheerful sunlight of the late spring afternoon makes me want to smother it. I turn my steps to the training grounds. I need to do something to relieve the pressure.

I walk on the trampled weeds that serve as the groundcover in front of the castle's stable and crinkle my nose. Battles can stink worse, but the acrid smell of horse stalls never seems to leave. Worse, it always finds a way to bore deep into my nose. I move through a few more narrow ways covered by ancient stone arches.

The training grounds stretch out before me around a corner. They're just how I remember them: rough, functional, and effective. I always loved honing my swordsmanship and there's always someone around for extra practice. It came easy to me, but I still put twice the amount of effort into it as anyone else. That's why Laurence Hart thinks I'm the best in the army. It means a lot since he's not just my king, he's my father.

I stop between two rings to watch different sets of fighters drilling their craft. The memories of my own untold hours in the rings brings a smile to my face. Two young men swing their swords and shields like they're performing a dance they've rehearsed a hundred times. I watch their footwork and eyes, the swings and lunges, and hold my tongue. They notice me and pick up the speed. It's fast—a fast dance. I'm not easily impressed by sword-fighting, but they don't know that.

"How am I fighting?" the closest one asks.

He's strutting around with his hands on his hips during a break. The sweat glistens on his arms and face, but I'm not near as impressed as he imagines I am.

"Like a boy," I answer.

"What's that supposed to mean?"

I want to roll my eyes but think of what my father would do, and manage. At least partially—I avoid the eye rolling.

"It means you fight like a boy. Not like a man, and not like a woman."

I didn't expect him to like my comment. He snaps back, "I suppose you fight like a god. Lesasil maybe?"

A smile curls my lips. "I can hold my own."

"If you're so perfect at combat why don't you have a go against us?" the second one asks.

The one wears a shirt with the sleeves cut off and the other's shirt is balled up near a post—it probably helps them fight better. I know their type and smile in response, then grab up a wooden sword and move toward the opening.

"You must be in training?" I ask while I take off my blue cloak and drape it across the guardrail. My billowy sleeves catch the uncertain breeze and do little to intimidate my opponents. Two girls in their late teens were practicing sword skills earlier, but evidently found our banter more interesting and paused to watch.

"Almost ready to graduate—probably as officers—and head to the Eraseam Province," the first says with a glance at the girls. "Then we get to show the soldiers there the latest training from Sapesky."

An urge to laugh them to scorn floods every bit of my body, and I hide my amusement by turning away as if I'm making sure my cloak doesn't fall on the ground.

I turn back to them. "Don't be overconfident."

"I'm not the one who came to the training grounds to taunt officers," one says.

So much arrogance.

"You asked, and I offered a suggestion," I say and walk toward them while I examine my newly-acquired sword.

The shirtless one snorts and shoots me a look of contempt. "No shield either? You'll wish you weren't so overconfident by the time we're done with you."

He lunges at me and I move aside to avoid his practice sword. It's longer than the one I have, but I'm good with most weapons.

"Wait until he's ready," the other says, and I glance up from my sword.

His face is shadowed from the brilliant sun, but I can see he doesn't care too deeply about fighting fair, despite his pretty words and the glance at the girls in the other ring.

I shake my head. "The Guldeth won't care if we're ready —just if they are."

The two men move to the center of the ring and make sure I stay between them.

"No place to clap your back against," the first taunts to distract me, but his glance over my shoulder and the crunch of gravel from behind warns me of the other.

I crouch and his thrust goes over my head. He overextends himself so I slide closer under him, grab one leg, and place my palm on his chest before I explode my body into a straight line from feet to raised hands. He careens through the air, completes a flip, and slams to the trampled dirt floor of the ring. His sword-brother is almost upon me so I take a step back while I flick my sword into the air and catch it. I trip this one with a sweep of my foot while I block his attack.

They both get to their feet and glare at me as if it'll change the fight.

"I said you fight like a boy because girls don't fight with ego," I say.

They circle me—more cautious this time. I jump to the side to surprise the one with his shirt still on, knock away his textbook defense, grab him by the shirt, and whirl him at his friend. They need to fight together to have a chance.

"Girls, men, and women take instruction when they see it's available," I say. "You haven't reached that level of maturity yet. Fight together if you're struggling alone."

I know they teach that in the academy, but it's hardest to get the young men to accept it. That's why the death rate is always the highest among the newly-graduated men. They teach that too, and I'm always surprised most don't bother to figure out why. The ones who survive the first few months have already learned it or learn fast.

They coordinate their attacks this time; one with a swing to my head, the other with a stab aimed at my stomach. I duck below the slash, bring my sword up to redirect the stab, and push through the shield one shoves. I elbow him in the ribs and move between them.

"Coward!" the shirtless one shouts as I roll to the ground to avoid his backhand slash and spring up a few steps away.

"You'd rather feel my stick on your side?" I ask.

They lunge as one and for the first time I bother to engage in what they seem to think of as real fighting. The only problem is, I don't know their choreographed moves, so I have to restrain my natural tendencies and fight poorly.

I can fight like the worst, but I refuse to give them the satisfaction of seeing me step back. I move side to side and occasionally throw momentum behind my sword to fling their own back into their faces. I land several blows on each of them while their mock blades never reach within my guard.

I still breathe through my nose while they're already panting.

The shirtless one can't hold back another taunt and, with a smirk, calls, "You must be one of the shield-fodder they brought out early."

It boils my blood, but not enough to make me lose my head.

This fight ends now. I parry the man's sword in a way that flicks it out of his hand. I savage his shield and throw it aside while I break between the two again and send the shirtless one reeling. Before his shield even lands, I raise my sword in both hands and chop it toward his head. It shrieks through the air for the fraction of a heartbeat before I rotate my grip so the flat of the wooden blade strikes the top of his head. He's down in an unconscious heap without so much as a groan.

I turn to his friend and knock his sword away. He grips his shield with both hands and attempts to hide behind it, but I reach out with one hand and rip it from his grasp. He raises his arms for shields and turns away but I grab him by the shirt again and force him to look into my eyes.

He sees nothing but anger while he looks. I know because I can feel it. Anger seeps from every pore the way it might in a real battle on the front lines. "I hate that term," I say and make sure to bite down on every word for emphasis. "Let him know that any officer in my regiment who calls a soldier 'shield-fodder' doesn't survive long."

His mouth gapes as he gains the first glimmer of my rank. He nods and looks like he's learned his lesson so I release my grip, drop my menace, and speak to him like as much of an equal as I can manage, but keep the edge of intensity alive. "You'll be good fighters if you'll learn the practical side of it. I'm Oruvian the same as you, and want you to have the best chance at the war as you can. Remember that anyone who offers you advice means well so you'd best take it."

He swallows and I walk back toward the rail to gather my cloak. That last one didn't seem so bad on his own; if only he kept better company. He'll need to bring his friend back to consciousness. I hope they both turn out alright in Eraseam.

I hear, "how did you do that?" and, "can you teach us?" almost simultaneously as I start to don my cloak. I look up and see the two girls staring with wide eyes and gaping smiles that look like the edge of laughter.

Yep, eager for instruction, I think.

Chapter 2.

I jump into the ring with the two girls who watched me demolish the future officers. The shirtless officer isn't moving despite his friend's effort but it doesn't bother me. He'll come to, and if he doesn't, then... so what. I don't have much sympathy after I see someone treat people below them poorly, especially if the one on top hopes for a position of authority. If he'd pulled that in my regiment, he would have wasted the six day walk to get there.

The young soldiers stare as I walk toward them. It's not because of muscles hidden beneath my billowy sleeves or a pompous show of pretension like the two men over on the compacted dirt. I don't think they heard me growl at the man when I was across the divider, either, so maybe they guess I'm only an officer.

"That was incredible. Will you teach us that?" one asks.

"I'll teach you what I can," I say.

I love a keen pupil. They don't need to be good—just receptive. Some of my favorite students were awful to begin, but they put in more than the required effort when I was with them and practiced on their own without my prompting. Those are the best ones.

"I watched you a little for a while earlier, but let's see where you are to begin."

They gawk at me for a few seconds.

"Your skills," I say. "Let's see them so I can make suggestions."

They ready their wooden swords and move into position. Their stance is good, but awkward—probably since I'm watching. One has black hair and the other's is so dark brown I momentarily question if they're sisters, but their height is mismatched and their faces look different enough. The black-haired one is a few inches taller than the other, who has eyes to match her brown hair.

They make tentative moves at first, like they feel self-conscious with me watching, and the initial strokes are coordinated like the boys' from the ring over. When they finally get comfortable, though, their struggle is less rehearsed, more imaginative.

"Good, good," I say.

I stride over. They lower their weapons and turn to me for coaching.

"You'll do fine when you're called to the war; you've got imagination, strength, and discipline. Still, I can teach you a few things your instructor won't be able to. What are your names?"

"I'm Shelbe Hadder," the black-haired one says.

"And I'm Elara Ronrout," the one with brown hair says. "We're from the Sewlands Province."

I incline my head the smallest amount. The war is a few years old and has started requiring new soldiers, but the Sewlands Province hasn't sent many. It's because their people are more reclusive and the province is in the far southeastern portion of the kingdom. That struggle has weighed on the king for years.

"Your moves are good and imaginative," I say to Elara, "but they sometimes get repetitive. Repetitive because that must work against Shelbe. You two practice together a lot?"

She blushes. I turn toward Shelbe.

"Enemies don't use repetitive strikes, mostly because you don't get time to learn and practice with each one. Guard against against this."

She moves to a ready position and I slowly raise my sword in an upswing Elara never used. She flinches back and barely manages to block it. She regains her balance with wide eyes as she realizes she wouldn't have survived the simple attack.

"Now you," I say as I swing a little faster at Elara's ankle. She manages to block it. "Good." I whirl back around to Shelbe and she blocks it without tumbling. "Good; you're quick learners."

"Here's another one." I jab my sword at Shelbe's ear but stop before I poke her. She swings to knock my blade out of the way but dodges at the same time and only falls on her back and drops her sword. Elara does little better. I put my sword in my belt then offer my hands to help them both off the ground. Shelbe brushes the dust from her midnight hair.

"That's fine for practice," I say and indicate her loose hair, "but don't ever wear it like that within a day of the front lines."

She nods at the reminder.

"Alright, you tried to dodge and parry at the same time. You can do that and sometimes you need to, but right now it gets in the way. If you did either one successfully, would you need the other?"

Shelbe shakes her head.

"Right, focus on one. Which comes naturally to you?"

"Dodging," Elara says with enthusiasm.

I figured. Boys usually want to parry, because they think it's cooler, but most others dodge.

"Thrust at me a few times, both of you."

They stare, and Elara looks at my sword in my belt.

I smile and say, "I'm dodging here, not parrying."

Elara screws up her face as if she doesn't want to see me hurt yet thrusts anyway. The wooden point comes for my face but I move my head aside so I feel the rush of air across my cheek but nothing else. Shelbe stabs for my chest but I turn aside.

A few fibers of the sword catch on my shirt, but only in the fickle way grass clings to clothing in a meadow.

I could have disarmed her there, but I resisted. I usually save that for when I need to teach a lesson or want to be a jerk, and the boys in the other ring deserved it. I see the one is stirring now.

I dodge a few more of the girls' thrusts and swings, and they start to warm up to the game. They're no longer afraid they might hurt me and hack like they were at each other.

Now Elara and Shelbe both swing at me so I lunge between them. Their extra enthusiasm has them follow me and they turn towards each other. I hear soft gasps of astonishment and turn around. I smile and walk back toward them to look at each of their arms. Their sleeves don't extend far past their shoulders and, as I expected, each of them has a white line across their arm where the other's practice sword struck them.

"You knew that would happen, didn't you?" Elara asks.

"Not for certain; I wanted to see if it would, though. Dodging is important to practice, but parrying is as well. Sometimes you need to parry an errant blade from your own line. They're less frequent, but worse and harder to dodge. In some ways it's easier than a duel."

They both nod, wide eyed and eager to learn more. I'm happy for these new soldiers; they'll do well when they're called into service in a year or two.

"You started a good parry earlier," I say to Shelbe, "but you didn't follow through with it. If you want to dodge, dodge. If you want to parry, then parry, but there has to be a commitment. Ready?"

She lowers her stance and I thrust, still with some reservation, but she surprises me and dodges. It's more pronounced than my dodge earlier, but she does it well. She beams and I match her smile.

"Well, I didn't expect that. Nicely done."

I thrust again, a little faster this time, and she moves her sword up to catch my blade.

"Still a flutter of a dodge there, but good. If your body flinches into wanting to move, make sure it's into a stance that keeps you ready for whatever comes next."

I think for a second.

"Yeah, try me with that," I say. "Both at once and I'll show you what I mean about the need to stay ready."

Shelbe swings and I dodge in an unnatural way. Elara's thrust follows after and takes me in the ribs. It doesn't feel good. She smiles when I rub the spot.

"Strong movement. I suppose I earned that. Okay, I dodged Shelbe's blade, but didn't give thought to what was next and set myself up for sore ribs. In combat, that *could* send you to a physician for a week, kill you, or turn the battle against us, which could kill your friends."

Sober looks fill their eyes while they nod. I can tell they're grateful for the instruction. Very different from the two future officers I left a while back. The one regained his feet, and they're both leaning against the far rail, watching us.

"Anyway, I'm busy tomorrow, but if you practice I can check up on you in two days." I lean my head toward the other ring. "If they give you any trouble, you can tell them that I'll hear about it."

"We're leaving with our company before then," Shelbe says.

"Oh, that's right," I say. "I'm leaving also—wait... Are you going with the prince?"

"We are," Shelbe says. "And thanks for the training; this will serve us well at the front. We'll practice along the way."

"Are you one of his officers?" Elara asks with a light voice to imply they might see me on the journey.

I shake my head. "No, I'm the captain."

Their eyes widen as they recognize me as the prince.

"Your Highness," they say and bow. "Prince Christopher, we had no idea."

Oh great, everyone watched before while we fought, but now they gape. This reaction is half the reason I wish I could give up my birthright and just be a regular captain. Power is a heavy enough burden, but coupled with leadership, it sometimes becomes insufferable. Then add the Gift in… and you get people who gawk.

"Please don't," I say. "There's no need to—"

"But you're the prince *and* our captain," Elara says as she straightens up. Shelbe does the same.

"Yes, but…"

I don't know what to say. Of course everything they said is true, and they do owe me the show of respect, but I wish I could leave it all behind. Leave it for… I shake my head to clear my thoughts.

"A simple salute will do if we're not in a formal setting."

They bring their left fists to their chests opposite the heart and press them there for a second.

"I've got to meet with the king now," I say, then turn to leave. "I'll be able to give you more instruction on the journey back."

The practice field seemed to swell with soldiers while I fought in the rings. They all stare at me, not because many know me as the prince—I'm not at Sapesky often enough for cadets to recognize me—but probably because rumors circulated about my strong presence against the two soon-to-be officers. I'm half surprised the crowds don't call for a rematch so they can see it for themselves.

Memories from years ago and thoughts for current practice filled my mind as I came toward the training grounds, but now I leave worried. Those girls were good—for their age— but they're too young for dispatch to the front lines, and certainly not polished enough. I don't know if I can change that, though, and thoughts slam around my head like the bottom of a waterfall.

I take a deep breath and my thoughts recede to the calmer shores of logic. At least I'm good at training those who want to learn. After all, my favorite students sometimes need practice.

There won't be shield-fodder in my regiment.

The clock on my father's desk shows a quarter after the hour. I've been here for fifteen minutes with nothing to do but sit and think. He's never late, so I know there's a good reason, but it still irks me. If I'm needed on the front lines so badly, why summon me here to pick up my reinforcements? The messenger who told me to come pick them up could have easily brought them with her. It's a shoddy, shady attempt to hide the real reason, which I can only guess at.

I sigh.

Some call me Gifted and some call me Cursed. The Gift is a curse, so I suppose the latter are right. After all, it's only damaged my life, or what's left of it. The benefits sound great, but... I never asked to have it steal years off my life.

Power is a heavy burden, and those who seek it don't know what they aim at. The Gift is even heavier, yet you can't seek it. Neither can you rid yourself of it.

I would know, because I'm a prince. I have the power that implies, and the power that being a captain of the king's forces in northwestern Artalia entails. I'm desperately wanted on the frontlines—now more than ever—but he summoned me back here. The messenger said it was to pick up my reinforcements, but I know it probably has to do with Luis's death.

I fall into a reverie, then hear voices in the passageway and realize the clock shows twenty after the hour. Dang, five minutes gone like that. I smile. I love losing myself in my thoughts; it's the safest place for someone like me.

Father says Mother used to think it could be the most dangerous.

One of the voices dies away, and I hear the sound of footsteps echo down the hall like the last remnants of the conversation. A few moments later my father, King Laurence Hart, enters. He's a well-built man, with features more solid than my own, and carries himself with the easy grace that decades of experience brings. Even his hands exude confidence as he sits across from me and places down a few papers. He looks preoccupied, though I would have thought that from the look in his eyes even if he wasn't twenty minutes late.

"Thank you for coming, Captain Hart," he says.

He looks a little apologetic, since he knows how much I dislike formal visits, but the preoccupation outweighs this feeling.

I nod, and he continues. "We have your reinforcements ready to take when you go back. How does another five hundred soldiers sound?"

My eyes widen. "That sounds great." And yet... if they're all new... "I didn't think we could muster that many experienced soldiers so quickly."

"Sometimes war makes strange things happen," he says, then lowers his voice. "You're one of the best captains we have on the lines. Between you and me, you're the best captain we have at all—better even than the commanders. I just can't be in the habit of saying that for when I'm around others."

I don't mind his awkward compliments—I just appreciate that he gives them. A shimmer of sincerity flashes in his eyes and I smile back.

"Thank you. I do what I can."

"I know you do," he says, "and I know how much you like your duties there but I wanted to see your face when you heard of the reinforcements. It's so good to see you."

"I'm glad to see you too," I say.

This is great, but it doesn't feel complete.

He turns aside to regard a tapestry on the wall. It depicts a forest scene with a steaming kettle in the center and several figures around with upraised mushrooms. They almost look magical, as if they hold a secret yet to be discovered. I hate it. It's hung there since my boyhood. I remember the first time I went to hide behind it and found a chest of drawers in an alcove. He and Mother admonished me to keep the secret—which I did, even from my best friend Claire. I try not to remember those days—they were too good.

"I don't get to see you very much," he says, still while he scrutinizes the tapestry.

"I'm busy with the war." It's a lousy answer, but it's the first one that comes to me.

He sees through my parchment-thin excuse. "Even before the war," he says, "I didn't see you very much. I'd still love you if you were a little less... perfect as a captain. You know that, don't you?"

Wait, what is this about? Does he want me to step away from the war? I just nod.

He turns back from the tapestry and looks at me. We lock eyes for a while and he fixes me with a gaze that reaches deep into my soul as if he's probing for truth. Admiration sweeps over me, as it usually does when we're together, and I hold his gaze as steady as I can. *If only I could be like him.*

"Your mother did, too," he says.

I look away and eye his desk. I wish he wouldn't remind me. He knows I've tried to block out those final memories.

"Chris, you don't need to be my best captain to have my respect. You have my respect because of the man you are. Very few people become captains by age twenty-eight, and it's not just because you're the king's son."

I look up into his eyes when he says my age. There's not a flicker of insincerity, so I nod.

"I'll try to visit more often," I say. "We never know when the attacks will come so it's hard to leave."

"If the attacks come when you're away, you can always get back in time," he says with significance. "You just have to accept and use your Gift."

It's not a gift, it's a curse. I've tried to tell him that. The officers and soldiers at the front lines understand, probably because they don't have a choice to believe me or not, but they at least act like they do. Him, though... I've tried to tell him so many times.

"I don't think I really have the Gift," I say. "You know I've tried it three times and it didn't work for me. She was still dead each time."

"You could have tried it again," he says. Tears well in the corners of his eyes. He turns to the tapestry as if it could bring him comfort. "Your life would be so different now if your mother had been with you past age fifteen."

"I wish I could have saved her," I say. "The last ten years have been awful. I think about the 'what ifs' every day. The Curse ruined my life."

"What if you could have saved her the fourth time? Wouldn't that have made it all worth it? Worth another year of your life to have a mother around?"

I thought my ire rose while waiting for this conversation to start, but now it really does. "You weren't the one to see her dead four times," I say.

It's low, but I want out. Out of this castle and back to the front lines of the war. Back to the death and distraction. The battlefield is so much more comfortable than this.

He looks back at me with hard eyes. Tears still cling to the corners, too small to fall, and I feel a twinge of fear.

"And you think you're the only one who valued her?" he asks. "You think trying three times is good enough to learn the greatest Gift anyone could be given?"

It's my turn to look at the tapestry, except I don't gaze— I glare, as if that does any good. The figures are still there around the kettle; unmoving, fantastic. I was always taught that our tapestries depicted history or at least legends, not blatant fantasy.

"Was that Commander Brayler out in the hall?" I ask to move the conversation away from our perpetual point of contention. Commander Robert Brayler was Luis's father, and I thought the conversation would go here. Might as well urge it along.

"Not him, but it was someone from Montaya Province with a message from the commander."

He waits, and I wait. I'm comfortable with silence while I stare at the tapestry. After all, I started the conversation, but knew he wanted to bring us here anyway. "It was about Luis," he said after a while. "The commander is upset about his son's death, as any father would be, but this messenger didn't blame the Guldeth. At least not entirely."

I know where this is going. Of course I'm not happy about Luis's death either. Nobody in the kingdom is, but I wasn't even there, and couldn't do anything about it. Actually... that's not entirely true; my inaction is probably the very reason we're having this conversation.

"That's been two weeks already," I say in an effort to direct the conversation away from where I know it's going. "Even if the Curse worked for me, it's too late. Am I supposed to give up fourteen years of my life so he can have his son back?"

"When did you learn about Luis's death?"

That's the exact question I didn't want him to ask. His tone is low, his voice calm. I finally tear my gaze away from the tapestry to meet his eyes. They looked collected, despite whatever threats the messenger may have brought. If only I could be more like him.

"Two days after the battle." It hurt me to say it, mostly because I knew it would hurt him.

"So it wouldn't have been fourteen years, just two," he says. "Two years of your life to save perhaps fifty of Luis's?

Don't you know how Commander Brayler and I stood even before this? This makes things so difficult."

Here we go again. The Gift always comes up no matter what we talk about. It's partly why I try to keep my distance from, well, everybody.

"Yes sir, I've thought of little else since," I say truthfully. I caught myself that night twelve days back, when alone in my room, slipping into a swirl of memories. The Gifted only need to earnestly desire to return to the time of their recent memory, and the whole world relives that day. But the price is heavy—a year of aging for The Gifted during the relived day. I stopped myself before going back and reliving the two days that led to Luis's death, but the sensation scared me. I hadn't felt it since Mother was poisoned ten years ago, when I was fifteen. And now I'm twenty-eight.

"Thought of how bad it would hurt me? Hurt us? Possibly hurt the war you're working so hard for? There's a reason I managed to muster five hundred more soldiers, and it's not because they're as prepared as they should be."

I fight the urge to roll my eyes at an absent superior, Robert Brayler, for his immaturity. "Commander Brayler shouldn't even pretend to have any authority over my Curse. I know he's a commander, but that doesn't place him in a position to determine who lives and who isn't important enough to try to save. He can come to the front lines with me if he forgot what war really is, but my Curse isn't subject to his whims."

"You shouldn't call it that," the king says. "It really is a gift. You just haven't learned to use it yet."

Now I grace the top of his desk with a glare. "I don't really want to learn it. Like we just discussed, it doesn't work for me."

"You can practice," he says, leaning forward and looking at my face, wanting me to meet his eyes.

I'm too stubborn right now to raise my eyes from his desk. "The price is too high to learn it."

"The Gift is why Captain Pullen is so loyal," he says. "June saved his family and he remembers it. What if you could learn it and do something similar? Besides, it might provide closure. You've been different since her death. I want to see you happy."

"I could be forty years old this afternoon with nothing else to show for it. Is that what you want?"

"You know I don't want that, Christopher. It might not take that long."

"But it might," I say. Such a pathetic answer. I hardly recognize myself now, away from the battlefield. I'd rather strategize a night ambush in the mountains than discuss possible implications of my Curse.

"Just once more," he says. "For me."

I shake my head side to side as if watching the ponderous motion of the pendulum on the temple clock in Toldulgur.

"I can't." Those words rarely pass my lips, but they somehow feel okay to mutter to the man I know I can trust. "The hurt is too deep, still too raw."

The king sighs, and I finally meet his gaze. He looks older now, as if my refusal to age myself aged him, but I know it's a trick of the sorrow. It tears at my closed-off heart and threatens to open the box I've built around it. My lips part to give in, but he speaks and saves me the trouble of a blundering concession.

"This doesn't change how I feel about you. I'm still proud of you." He sits straighter and says, "Thank you for coming. I hope to see you again before you go."

"Thank you Father." I stand and walk toward the door without a backwards glance. I'll visit again before I go. Maybe to use my Gift, but probably just to say goodbye. If only I could be more like him.

I crave a peaceful evening and find it by staying close to my room. I prefer peace or full on war to the mind-numbing inanities a prince suffers during a prolonged stay in a castle. I'm civil to everyone I meet, but not because I'm a prince; it's because that's who I am. Even when a day is particularly tough, I keep my head up as high as I can and act like everything's as good as cold cream. Easier said than done, but I try.

Next morning, I enjoy a brief respite from the fatigues of the field and remain in bed to rise with the May sun. The day dawns magnificent and I almost wish I'd been up fifteen minutes earlier to watch it from a higher point. From my view, though, it still dazzles my eyes as I look out on the world, aglow with life.

Cottages dot rolling meadows. Sheep are visible on some of the hillsides, but only those right outside the walls of the castle, or when they're gathered around their shepherds. The buds on the leafing trees swell with each passing day, and what used to look like snow-kissed petals have now blossomed into small versions of their coming summer leaves. The bucolic scene stirs my heart and makes me turn away. It's too dangerous to let myself imagine that life. Not now.

I turn back to my door and glance at the boar head mounted above. It's an ugly, cut up thing, but far too important to take down. Besides, it's from one of the largest boars in the kingdom. No one would have guessed an animal could almost break the line of succession. A good reminder to keep around.

Officers will complete most of tomorrow's preparations, but I still want to make sure everything is ready. I head to the seneschal to arrange food from the larder. He's surprised to see me breaking my fast early, but greets me in his frank way. I sit alone in the corner of the hall, where he brings mutton, spring greens, and fresh bread. I smile at his simple salute; I've told him not to bow when we're alone.

Once I'm finished, the seneschal reviews the preparations. I'm grateful it all looks good because I need to go see the king. I *want* to go see the king. My fit from yesterday afternoon has passed, and I know I won't age myself fifteen years to go back and save Luis. He didn't pressure me to, but something about... *me* made me slip close to the edge I swore I'd never near again.

I've walked the passage to the king's Business Room thousands of times. When I arrive, I stop myself at the rise and fall of voices from the other side. I intended to arrive first this morning, but when I hear a heated discussion through the door, I wait outside.

"It's not *his* decision to withdraw his soldiers and he knows it," says a voice I've heard before.

"He also knows we're too occupied to enforce that." I recognize my father's voice.

"Curse him if he thinks he'll get away with this. Is he going to join the Guldeth when this is done and we forsake him the way he's doing to us?"

I recognize this other voice, but can't recollect where I've heard it before.

"He's pulling his forces out of Artalia and Eraseam to guard along his own borders—"

"Everyone knows there's hardly any fighting down there. Luis's death is unfortunate, but it was an accident. Nothing more; anyone could get caught in a situation like that. There's got to be a real reason."

The king waits, and his calculated silence is telling. I should go, not because I can't handle classified information, but because they expect this conversation to be private. I take a careful step down the passageway but stop again as I hear my name.

"It's Christopher," my father says. "Commander Brayler's mad he didn't use the Gift to save his son."

"He should have," says the other man.

"That's not worth debating. He refuses to since he tried to save his mother and cou—" he stops short. *Couldn't. I know that's what he meant to say.* My heart aches with the memory but swells in relief that he refrained. If only I could be more like him.

"Couldn't?" the other voice finishes. "He hasn't practiced?"

"Not that I know. It's a heavy price to pay for practice."

"We're lucky he doesn't have it, Your Majesty," says a third voice.

Silence fills the room and I glance both ways down the hall. *Good; I'm still alone.* No chance I'll now unless I have to.

"So he's mad that Christopher won't practice and give up years of his life. What of it? How is pouting back to his province going to fix anything?"

"He wants me to punish Christopher for his son's death."

My heart skips a beat until I realize the absurdity of it.

"And you won't, will you?" the second voice asks. It sounds like a challenge.

"I would—if he did something wrong," my father says, a steely edge to his voice, "but he didn't. Nobody would convict him for such an absurd charge even if I did listen to him."

I smile at the blank wall in front of me while silence overtakes the room and hall for a minute.

"I suppose it's for the best, then. We better hope the Guldeth don't find out he's walking the edge of betrayal."

More silence. The stakes are a lot lower for whoever my father is talking to, but still the other man feels the tension. It seeps under the door, through the keyhole, maybe even through the wood. Guilt pours into my mind and joins the creeping tension to create a strange mix of emotions.

"I appreciate you bringing the new soldiers as fast as you did," the king says. I hear the dull clink of a mug settle onto his wooden desk.

"Mmm, I wanted to come myself to see the real reason for the request. We know messengers can't always bring the complete truth."

That voice. I know I've heard it before. I wrack my brain to recall anyone with the vocal pattern, inflection, or tone I hear through the door. Nothing. I try to narrow it down to only those who my father would speak to in this way, but their conversation draws me back to the current moment.

"The captain taking them to the front appreciates your muster," the king says.

The conversation ends and I hear a chair scrape against the floor. My mind and body leap to attention as I run a few paces down the hallway and turn around to face the door. I walk forward as it opens and I see who my father was speaking to. He has short, curly black hair, and a dark beard cropped too close to show the curls. An instant is all it takes me to recognize him; I grew up with him frequenting Sapesky; not as much as the commanders of the other provinces, but often enough.

"Commander Derwyler," I say and salute with my fist over my chest as I come toward him, "I understand you've brought the reinforcements I'm to take. I thank you heartily."

Guy Derwyler, commander of Sewlands Province, doesn't share a border with Murethon, yet understands his role in the kingdom. His rough manner wouldn't make one think he could manage taxes from his dukes with a careful hand, but he does. The easiest place for us to fight the defensive war is in the Dendring Mountains, and he knows it.

"Captain Hart," he says and greets me with the same salute. "I trust you'll treat them well and help most return home."

I wait for an insinuation that I need to use Gift to help our cause, but none comes so I reply, "I will bring as many home as I can."

"I was concerned about committing the five hundred I brought, but I know your reputation. Keep those casualties low. Makes it a whole lot easier on us commanders."

I nod my head as the passageway echoes his words. My father unknowingly impressed me with the importance of low casualties through years watching his leadership.

"You know how not to treat cadets after the way Rafael was treated," he says.

My face flushes hot and my eyes flutter about the commander and the stone walls. I would reprimand someone of my own rank or below, but even with the king on the other side of the door, probably willing to support me, I want the commander's good will and let the topic go. His loyalty to my father is enough to stay my tongue.

"I treat them the way they deserve," I say, meaning with respect, "unless they prove otherwise."

His laugh sounds like a sharp bark of hollow merriment.

"I've heard other captains say the same, but I don't think they meant it the same as you. Guess that's why your father insists we advance soldiers from outside noble houses too."

He leaves, and I'm grateful to see his back and shoulders diminish as he moves toward the far side of the hallway.

Commander Derwyler left the door to the king's Business Room open. I walk to it and see my father standing, staring at the faded tapestry. Seated is Eric Shutt, constable of Sapesky. He was the mystery person I only heard once. I clear my throat to gather their attention.

The king turns and Constable Shutt rises.

"Ah, Christopher," the king says. "Thank you for coming back. I'm glad it's so soon."

The constable bows to the king to excuse himself and shuffles past me. We don't look at each other while he leaves.

I help myself to the chair and sit in the still warm seat. "I said I'd come back before leaving and want to make sure I honor my word, especially to you."

My mind is still heavy from Guy's offhand comment. It's only comments that touch on my family that seem to affect me.

The king smiles and asks, "You met Commander Derwyler in the hall?"

He heard us talking, no doubt, and I nod.

"He brought the new soldiers to reinforce your positions," my father says. "I'm grateful he's committing more soldiers to the war. For the show of support as much as the actual effort."

I almost give away my earlier eavesdropping, but stop myself with only a sign of agreement.

"Commander Derwyler isn't... discrete... is he?" I say after a while.

"What do you mean? Father asks, the pitch of his voice changing a little as he moves his head to the side.

"His choice of conversation out in the hall."

"Oh." Father smiles. "He's been like that as long as I can remember. The Sewlands people, as a rule, don't care as much for social conventions as we do. I confess I wasn't listening to everything. Was there anything in particular he said?"

"He hinted at Rafael's passing," I say.

Father's brows drop at the mention of his son's death. I lost my mother and elder brother in a short time, both in tragic ways, and the memory still stings like a fresh wound. The look in his eyes shows time hasn't dulled his pain either; only distracted from it. I selfishly hope we don't talk about my Gift again.

"Why didn't you tell him not to? Father asks.

"He's my superior," I say. "And since I owe him thanks for the five hundred soldiers, I didn't want to make things hard between us."

"He means well, though he's rough," Father says.

"It still hurts the same," I respond. Misery wells within my chest.

"No, not quite the same;" Father says. "Malice would cut deeper than thoughtlessness."

It's true; his comment didn't hurt as much as some of those initial ones. The comments that made me spend countless hours in the training grounds. The comments that still stick with me when I'm in my role as captain. The decisions I make in camp, everything filtered through the pain.

"How did you know the reinforcements are from Sewlands?" he asks.

His question brings the topic back to something productive and should relieve my pain; relieve our pain, but my body tenses.

"I met a few of his soldiers at the training grounds yesterday," I say.

My skin starts to crawl. It's not a lie because I knew it, and knew it before I overheard their conversation. The only new things I learned were how Commander Brayler withdrew his soldiers from helping defend the rest of the kingdom and how he wanted me punished for his son's death. The latter one didn't bother me much since my father spoke true: I did nothing wrong by not using my Gift. If anything, it was an error of omission. Maybe.

"How were they?" he asks. "Ready for the front?"

I'm talking to my father as the king now, and the king wonders what he could expect as the fallout of the Montaya province isolating itself. Telling him of my encounter with the two future officers tempts my mind, but I keep control and tell him about the Sewlands girls.

"I worked with two in the ring," I say, "and they managed well with all the basics. They sorely lacked experience of actual combat, but took instruction well so I worked with them on that."

He eyes me while I'm speaking, and I notice his eyes dim like when I mentioned Rafael a few minutes ago.

"I heard Guy give you his confidence in bringing them home," he says. "You have mine as well."

He wants to make sure no parent shares his experience losing a child to the war. Even though I don't have children of my own, I've thought the same for years.

"I always do what I can. I..." then I stop and look up. The king sits still, continuing to look at me. He doesn't urge or interrupt, simply sits and waits for if I want to go on. His appearance is every bit like the king, but it's not the king who's looking back at me; it's my father. I couldn't say this to the king, but to the man who lost his son to a raid, I have the courage. "I'm going to march the soldiers hard for the front, but the days' travel will be a few hours shorter. I need to train them in the combat techniques they'll encounter at the front, and we'll use the evenings for that."

No words, just a look. Admiration, trust, pride, and is that—? Yes, it's love. That look gives me every bit of strength I'll need to endure the rigors of the summer. I'm experienced enough to know the highest leadership in the regiment holds the soldiers together, and I somehow know it's given me enough strength to hold everyone together, too.

We don't say much beyond this, and I leave soon after. Time to verify preparations are the way I want. And maybe work with some cadets at the training grounds. I'll be sure to spare some time.

Chapter 3.

My body wakes me early for departure. My heart flutters with a quickness I know well from years at war. This is a different quickness, though, but I know it will increase as I awake closer to the Dendring Mountains each morning. The new soldiers, if they were arrogant yesterday, will be on the edge of vomiting today.

I swing my legs from the edge of the bed and stretch while I rise from the mattress. I don't often allow myself a mattress at the front, and that's just one of the things that makes me popular among the soldiers. Bearing the same hardships they do, even sometimes more, grants me respect. That, and the attitude I've fostered in my regiment since rising to captain, helps perpetuate the way the soldiers treat me. I expect obedience and give good treatment, rational orders, and respect for them in return.

The sun hasn't yet risen, and I have some time for quiet reflections. I wander the maze of the city before coming to the gate as the first faint glimmer of sunlight sneaks over the horizon. It's far from sunrise and I smile to myself in the cool stillness that I have to myself. I leave a trail through the dewy grass. It doesn't bother me through leather boots, and helps scrub away yesterday's dust.

A stone outcropping comes into view. I haven't been paying attention to where I've been walking, but my footsteps seemed to lead me here. It's not my special place—half the children in the village probably stand on it each month—I've just stood on it many times. With Rafael a couple dozen of those, and hundreds of times after. We enjoyed staring into fires and letting the thoughts flow, but if we needed time to talk alone, we always seemed to wander to the outcropping. It was second to a fire, but we could be alone if we came early or late—sometimes that counted for a lot.

The castle's bell recalls me to my senses. I'd been staring into the rising sun without heeding it for a few moments and blink hard to clear my vision. I return with a heart heavier than I meant to carry, though it seemed like somehow my mind wanted me to wander there, as if I needed the reflection.

Blue-cloaked guards at the castle's yawning archway let me into an ever-greater frenzy of Oruvians. Most of the faces are young, and I recognize only one of my officers among the initial throng. It's Weaver Deloc, and he shouts orders over the commotion. I'm glad he has the chance to travel farther west. He and his sister were originally stationed in Myceum, but the war has pulled him all over. I smile to myself as I watch him for a few seconds. If we were a few days' march farther west, I would call him aside with the express purpose of pointing out how his blond eyebrows disappeared in the low-angled sun. There's too many soldiers to do it now.

He looks toward me for a second and catches the mischievous flash in my eye enough to know my thoughts, because when he looks away it's with a smirk and roll of his eyes. I find it best to keep the soldiers as happy as we can, and that starts with the officers.

I'm surprised to see my father among the mass of people, so I walk toward him. The young soldiers act as confident as they're able, but they feel my aura of command and make passage to him easy.

"Good morning, Your Majesty," I say

I use the full salute as an example for the new soldiers. He's my father first, but everybody else knows him as the king. It wouldn't be fair if I addressed him with familiarity in front of everybody.

"Rise, Captain Hart," he responds, offering me a hand.

He offers no reason for coming to the courtyard, and I know it's not his custom, so my interest is instantly peaked.

"I didn't expect another chance to speak to you after yesterday morning. What brings you here?" I ask.

He flashes a smile and says, "You liked the reinforcements of five hundred so much that, well, I have another gift for you."

My eyebrows rise.

"I should have told you this earlier, but Commander Brayler is pulling his soldiers from the other provinces. He wants to make sure the Montaya border stays secure." This is what I wasn't supposed to overhear yesterday. I feel a pang of guilt before it dissolves since he's telling me. I open my mouth to speak but he continues, "Yes, we all know there's not much happening at the Montaya border, but we can't enforce keeping him with us now; it would be more trouble than it's worth."

"Is that news my gift?" I ask, momentarily worried that he discovered my eavesdropping and is unloading sarcasm to reprimand me.

"Far from it. I have a real gift for my child. With the five hundred additional soldiers—more under your direct command —I want you to have another tactician with your regiment. She's arguably the second best one in the kingdom."

I smile my approval. I'll lose a few tacticians when Commander Brayler pulls his soldiers away, and I never mind another, as long as she's good.

He pauses for a few seconds and I wonder why until he says, "She's been brought up by the best one. She's had some experience but needs out on her own to advance farther."

Julek. Claire. My heart flutters for a few beats, and I struggle to understand why.

"It's your old friend Claire," the king says. "She's certainly one of the best since she's watched her father her whole life. Seen the impact a tactician can have, and the results if the advice isn't followed."

He breaks off in a way he only does when distracted. I know the reason for his faltering earlier, and I'm only one of the few in the kingdom who would: he doesn't trust Claire's father. *Didn't* trust her father, rather. Ever since the commander's wife June died nine years ago, about the same time as Rafael, the king's been better, but old humors die hard.

I perform a quick calculation in my head. He notices what I'm doing and says, "You'll need Claire for your regiment."

It's the same conclusion I'm coming to, and I'm not exactly happy about it, fluttering heart or not.

"If this is a trick to make me use my Curse, I'm not falling for it," I say, my eyes losing the glimmer I thought they held just a few minutes ago.

"It's nothing of the sort," he says. He lowers his voice yet maintains perfect control. "You're the best captain headed for the most heavily-contested crossings and you need the best tactician with you; not nobody."

It's a true observation that I don't appreciate; she and I were friends growing up, but I've drifted away over the last ten years. I've seen her since then, only a few times, and am courteous, but everything's been awkward since our mothers both passed. Rafael was older, but still enjoyed our company, too. Three family members gone from our lives—that can rock a friendship.

"I only learned about Robert's decision after we spoke about you leading Guy's five hundred back," the king says. His lined face holds far less tension than it should after everything I know he's been through. "They'll be good at the front with your guidance. Take the time to give them your style of training along the way like you said."

I leave with a little tension still between us. It's not how I want it, but we both need to resume our duties.

Weaver sees me walking away, comes over, and asks, "What's this about Commander Brayler withdrawing his force back to Montaya?"

I've only officially learned about it now, and tell him what I've had time to process. "The king told me a few moments ago. He knows it's a false pretense to flee to safety, but we can't do anything about it."

I'm not happy about the decision, and he isn't either. He rubs his light hair and responds, "Thank the gods we have five hundred fresh cadets to lead back; I just wish they were better prepared for combat."

"Nymunia smiled upon us," I say. "And we're training them along the way."

He looks confused so I continue, "We'll march by day and train by night. The king's already approved my plan."

He raises his pale eyebrows I'm so fond of teasing him for, streaks his hand through his hair, and nods. "Alright; I like it."

"You hear we're going to Mt. Cabrae?" I ask him.

His face lights up. "Really?"

"Yeah; Toldulgur should be secure enough for Captain Flamex to handle alone so we're going to reinforce Commander Nealy's position. That'll allow Commander Lewis deeper into Eraseam."

He looks as happy as I'd expected as he turns his attention back to the soldiers, and I go to my chamber to gather the few things I had brought. That done, I head to the even busier outer-tier courtyard to oversee my officers' preparations. Blue pennants flap atop towers in the light morning breeze. Weaver wouldn't have spread the word of our new destination without my approval, so I tell the other officers. Most officers don't care where they're stationed. They might desire, like Weaver, the thought of being near home. If anything, everyone will appreciate the new surroundings. None of the soldiers will notice in the least either; they'll all be far from home either way.

We travel far the first day, and stop late in the afternoon. Our plan to stop early each day so we have time to train circulated the group hours ago and excites everybody. I only have a handful of officers to break the soldiers into groups with, so it won't be as personalized as I'd prefer, but my officers all have experience with real combat.

We don't stop for our first meal, then only pause enough to eat the same rations again. The drills after the long day of travel wear on the soldiers, and their enthusiasm had dissipated before we finally stopped for the night.

The next day we rise early and resume our march west with a slight angle towards the north. Many of the soldiers complained to each other and the officers about such an early start after an unusually tiring day of travel and drills. Wait until they find out how the next day goes; I was easy on them since it was their first day out, but I can't do that today. They won't be ready if we don't push hard on training.

We walk all day with a few refreshing rests, then stop late in the afternoon.

I notice a few weary cadets near me start to unpack their cooking gear to prepare a fire and food.

"You won't need that out yet," I say as I walk by.

They pause and watch me as I reach a nearby gathering of officers. We have around six hours before the sun sets completely, and they think we'll train the whole time. I'll surprise them with one break. Hard, but worthwhile things usually are.

I assign officers to instruct the soldiers on particular points of weaknesses cadets often exhibit. Like a bucket of water on a campfire, the knowledge of how the rest of the night will go stills the last of the bravado among an arrogant few. The next few hours pass with a continual rush of spring wind. I walk among the groups with my officers. I instruct the large groups and help individuals with certain motions. I stay vigilant for both actions that need praise, or the slightest variance that could cause a unit to falter.

I walk to a hillside outside our makeshift training grounds and project my voice across the darkening field. "The Guldeth don't care if you're weary. They'll take it as a reason to fall upon us. How you train now determines, in a large measure, if you'll survive through the summer." I watch a few more drills and observe the cadet's growing confidence. "Some of war is luck, but much of it is skill," I say. "The skills you learn over the next few nights could save your life in the right circumstances, so focus well. The hardest part isn't walking in formation into battle. The hard part is knowing that if you walk off that field, you'll do so without all your friends."

The darkness grows nearly complete an hour later, so I dismiss the soldiers. They trudge back to their gear to gather materials; first for a hurried meal, then as much sleep as possible before I'll rouse everyone at first light tomorrow. I watch their slow steps and drooped shoulders with some satisfaction.

The two soldiers who thought they would receive advancement to officer soon travel with us. They never meet my eyes and instead focus on each other's moves. I had split them up halfway through this session to see how they perform against someone else. They aren't terrible now that they're open to instruction.

I know my officers well enough to notice them showing languor, though they're better at hiding it and acting through the pain. I check myself to make sure I'm projecting vigor. The new soldiers did well tonight, but it's not enough. The fatigue introduced an extra hardship and most bore up well; I'm eager to call them for an early march tomorrow and repeat today.

I sleep well and wake up grateful we're still in the Kapesky province because I notice a few drowsing guards. My sleepy inclination is to let their officers deal with it, but I realize I'd impart a more thorough lesson. I recognize one as Shelbe

Hadder, who I helped with her swordsmanship back in Sapesky. This will be good. Squatting down before them, asleep with their backs against a pile of gear, I smile grimly to myself as I resist the urge to have fun at their expense. I've seen it done, and it doesn't give the commander the respect or loyalty they think.

Each one wakes at my simultaneous touch on their shoulder. Their eyes open and faces instantly spring into an attentive fear. Before they can bluster out a terrified apology, I start talking in a level voice.

"Guard duty after the day we had yesterday isn't ever fun, but hundreds of your comrades rely upon their guards to keep them safe through the night. An early warning can be the difference between victory and defeat. What difference does that make?"

It's a silly, obvious question, but I want to make them say it.

"Life or death for us, Prince Hart," Shelbe says. "I'm sorry."

Her crimson face frames her blue eyes in a strange combination. Her friend is flushed in splotches like firelight playing across his face.

I turn to him and ask, "Who else?"

The flush grows deeper.

"Our friends in the regiment."

I nod, and ask, "What could that lead to?" They need to follow the track to the conclusion.

"Defeat," Shelbe says, "and a defeat could lead to more defeats."

I smile slightly and look at the young man.

"Every loss in battle brings the kingdom closer to the possibility we're trying to prevent. I'm sorry too," he says and hangs his head.

I'm far from happy they lost vigilance, but it's a good opportunity to learn; even awakening to their captain would be enough to terrify any soldier into remembering the lesson for a lifetime.

"The look on your faces shows me you won't forget this," I say. "but do it for more than fear of your captain's wrath. Your brothers and sisters in arms don't take kindly if this happens anywhere near the front; do it for them."

We march through the day. Noon comes and goes and I still decline to ride a horse. The soldiers notice if their captain rides when they cannot, and I'm not sure it increases their respect; it certainly didn't for my captain when I joined.

All day everyone expects a grueling uninterrupted training session, and they're not wrong, but I'm change one thing; time for a quick meal before starting the extra six hours. The soldiers eat as rapidly as possible, grateful for the short time to refresh, and the officers stop a few groups from making fires. I eat the limited meal I give myself time for and move to a side location where we'll have training. Shelbe is one of the first to arrive, along with Elara Ronrout, and the other sentry with Shelbe the night before. They're scared and anxious to make up for their mistake, but I hush my tongue; nothing can drive the lesson home further.

My officers begin the instruction and I notice with satisfaction that the groups are gaining confidence and making more rapid moves. We've taught them enough options where they have too many variables to perform choreographed dances, and I swell with pride at their increase in skill. I make my way around the scattered groups, stopping to watch different ones and admiring their growing abilities.

One particular unit stands out. The cadets are gathered in a circle as if they've already started single combat practice, and cheering as if it's getting good. I move forward to see what they're doing, and make sure I can congratulate the winner on particular points if it's a real match. It's one of my officers, Mariana Brown, and she's struggling to hold her own. Her opponent's back is to me, and all I see is long, light brown hair, with glimpses of practice swords visible at her sides. Mariana's skill with a blade is strong, yet she appears to struggle from time to time.

They fight a few more minutes, turning around a few times, but I'm at the back of the circle and struggle to see the other's face past soldiers craning their necks for a better view. Those in front let out a loud cheer and I see Mariana pump her fist into the air in victory. I start to push my way through the excited throng. Everyone's looking at the person next to them, jabbering about what they just witnessed.

I gain the front, step into the circle, and immediately notice the girl with the light brown hair. My heart flutters again and I'm sure my eyes widened the slightest bit. She has a tall and muscular, yet thin form, and the belt around her tunic, drawing it close against her waist, shows this well. Dust clinging to her tall boots make it match her light hair perfectly, which is still tied loose for traveling.

Claire. I had mostly forgotten about her coming along. The king informed me she was joining as the new tactician. My mind has been busy with other matters since we left, so I didn't bother to look for her. She's receiving congratulations from Mariana and others around her for the good stand. I'm impressed as well. I've heard of her skill as a tactician the last few years, but none of the reports ever mentioned her skill with the blade.

The cadets in the celebratory circle start to notice me, and all heads turn my way. Claire meets my eyes and flashes a smile I barely return. A greeting of familiarity almost passes my lips, but I resist, almost ashamed of how easy I manage.

"Not many people can stand up so well to Officer Brown," I say, still holding the simple smile that unintentionally silences the group.

"I've practiced the past few years, Chris." She's still smiling, but the shocked looks on the surrounding faces remind her that we're not children anymore. "I mean, Captain Hart. I've practiced with my sword." Her smile is gone, even less visible than mine, and the rapidly rising strain isn't lost on anybody.

I try to ease the tension, and say with a larger smile, "I hear you've become quite the tactician."

"I believe that's why your father assigned me to Mt. Cabrae," she says.

There it is again; she can't help her familiarity. It annoys me that she hasn't moved on as fully as I have, and withers the large smile on my face.

"We'll have to make plans before we arrive," I say. It's lame, and I turn and leave through the circle.

I walk away, holding my head high and walking with my usual commanding stride, but can't help but feel like I made a fool of myself. The laughter never dies when I walk into a group, but it did there, like my presence had smothered their joy with an icy melancholy.

Chapter 4.

"You took longer coming here than I expected. Are the new cadets slow?"

"No, but they didn't have the skill I wanted."

"They'll learn quickly."

"They *did* learn quickly back along the road. I'm not going all the way to Sapesky to bring back five hundred bodies for us to bury."

I'm not in a mood to joke or let Commander Nealy's officer continue acting like he's still the captain in my absence. Mobent is capable, and led my forces over to our new position, but I feel better when I'm in control.

The king had dispatched a group of riders to my former assignment in Toldulgur and had bade the acting captain march some of the soldiers northward. Over the recent weeks we've noticed the heavier fighting move steadily north. We expect Mt. Cabrae to see more action than Toldulgur, so I join Commander Nealy along the pass in south western Eraseam. Montayan soldiers gone, this arrangement makes the most sense. I have control of my battalion again and the officers are instructing the cadets on how we operate so close to the fighting. Everything else done, I want to speak to the commander.

I've liked Sandy Nealy since she became commander of Cousea nine years ago. If I'd been called to reinforce the former commander, Ross Knoke, I would have refused. Not that Father would have had a chance to call for that; Ross would have been executed if he hadn't died defending against that raid nine years ago. Commander Nealy, though, always treats me and everyone around her well enough. I like her children, Searle and Kimbr, also. They're captains like me, and I expect to see at least one of them here.

I intuit we arrived near the end of a battle from the heavy atmosphere of the fortress. Commander Nealy waits in her hall, and I feel reassurance that the battle wasn't large enough to warrant her presence on the field. I enter the Great Chamber and receive a greeting. It's friendly despite the anxiety of awaited news.

The door swings open. She stiffens, sees her son, then relaxes.

"We repulsed them, commander," Captain Kimbr says.

Commander Nealy relaxes even deeper into her chair. Even without knowing the details, she and I read victory on his face.

Captain Kimbr stands half a head taller than me, and carries that large head atop his substantial frame. Even when he wears a simple tunic, his wide shoulders make him look like he's wearing armor beneath. He's at least a dozen years older than me, and his muscular build gives the impression that his authority and skill with arms came easily, but I know his rise to captaincy wasn't due to his mother's influence. I'm happy for him for his leg up; how could I, as the king's son, not cheer him for the natural gifts he developed?

"Prince Hart," he says, and gives a salute with his fist. "Captain Hart as well, I believe."

"Bowing isn't necessary now," I say when he starts to dip.

"It does the soldiers well to see you earn your position," Commander Nealy says.

I can tell Sandy is smiling by her voice, and I look toward her while she speaks. She has as much reason to say such a statement as anyone in the kingdom, with two of her children captains as well.

"The morale has slipped since we first came here," she says. "You carry such a good reputation for military strategy and treatment of your soldiers that even the officers can't help but grow in excitement."

It flatters me to hear such words, but their ensuing conversation interests me more. They talk about Kimbr's battle, and it's my first serious word of the war since my departure. As I share the same rank as Kimbr, I'm allowed to hear everything between him and his commander. Their conversation done, Kimbr and I both bow and leave. I know I can omit the bow, but it comes naturally when I'm before my superiors. Power is a heavy burden, and I find willingness to bow lightens it.

Kimbr and Searle served under Ross Knoke with their mother before she advanced to her position. He was an officer when Rafael first joined. We're walking together, and it's tempting to ask him about the events of the raid, but I resist. Learning more wouldn't bring him back, and just considering asking makes me feel like I'm dragging a sore wound through gravel.

The rest of Kimbr's soldiers reach the fortress. Some are wounded. A few are bad enough where I'd be surprised if they see the next morning, but I smile to all and give a few words of encouragement since that's the best I can offer; they're in good hands among the physicians. Kimbr and I part ways, and I walk back toward my new soldiers to see how they're joining with the professionals.

The first person I meet is Claire, but I should say she met me, since I was still far from my soldiers. She's wearing her real sword this time, and the flash of the metal scabbard behind her as she walks toward me shows off her narrow waist. I glance aside then forward again as my lips part to let a low hissing sigh escape from my lungs. She's coming straight towards me and evidently wants to talk. I'd rather not talk, but I need to soon, and there's no choice with the way she's walking; I may as well right now.

"Hello Claire," I say and greet her by her familiar name, partly by old habit, and partly since there's nobody else around.

"Hello Captain Hart."

My mouth shifts into a sort of smirk. "What, I'm not Chris now that we're alone?"

Her face reddens around her constant smile, and I stare back, strangely unable to meet the smile with one of my own. She sought me out, but hesitates, so I start with my intentions. "We'll need to visit with Captain Kimbr's tacticians tonight."

She nods, and keeps looking into my eyes.

I'm not going to look away or simply stare at her, so I ask, "Are the new soldiers finding their places?"

"They are," she says. This seems to pull her from her reverie. "I'm glad to be here. I've learned a lot at Balruvia and I'm eager to try the strategies here. I'll see what works and learn what else I can."

How different from the future officers in the fighting ring. She's staring again, and I'm on the point of breaking the silence when she continues. "I hear you almost killed an officer back in Sapesky."

I raise my shoulders in a shrug. "He wasn't an officer, and it was far from a killing stroke."

More silence. Surely she wanted to talk about more than my run-in with the arrogant soldiers, but she's silent and I've said my piece.

"I'll find you before I talk with his tactician tonight."

"Chris," she says as I turn to go. It's sad, imploring, as though she's trying to break me, though I know she never would. We were too good of friends for that. "Wait. I've hardly talked with you in ten years; can we talk now?"

My heart thunders to life like it does during an ambush, and I prepare for the worst. All the warning signals tell me to leave, but she keeps talking and holds both my hands, so I guess I do have time now.

"I never wanted our friendship to end," she says. The depth in her eyes calls to me like salvation. "And I don't blame the king for my mother's death." *That can't be true,* I think. I move a few steps to the side but she still holds my hands and implores, "Can't you see I'm not bitter like my father is?"

"You're still my friend," I say.

The lie hurts, and I pull my hands free. I want to say something as I walk away, but no words come, and I leave her standing there without a backward glance. I feel even more heartless than back during our march, but there's a reason we've hardly talked in ten years.

The room for my use more than meets my needs. I have it to myself; something few in Mt. Cabrae can claim about their quarters. Solitude is exactly what I want now. I flop on the floor in the center of the room and try to exhale my frustrations. My mind keeps racing so it doesn't work. I'm worried about my standing in the regiment, if they're gossiping about me, and the possibilities for the weeks or months ahead while I'm with Caire. I'm worried about managing to hold up under my responsibilities. If I've blundered both times I've been around her and we'll be stationed together, how can I learn to manage? It's completely illogical and against the strength I've trained into my mind, but the fears threaten to overwhelm me.

I summon every bit of strength to drag myself off the floor, but I don't have the luxury of wallowing. I'm on the front lines and will be called into action any day. I *must* regain control of myself before I see her again tonight, and I know the best way. The fatigue from the past few days weighs heavier on me as the captain, yet I know this is what I need. I rush from my room and down the short passageway until I come to another door. Then I slow myself, ease it open, and walk into the sunlight. I hold it together until I reach the woods beyond the gate.

Then I run. I run like the wind is chasing me. I run faster than I've ever ran before. A cramp makes my side ache yet I run on. The very center of my chest aches like my heart is pumping blood to all the wrong places yet I run farther. As much as this feels like it's going to kill me, it feels like it's bringing me back to life. I run along the ridgeline where no trees grow and relish the cooling wind finally catching up to me as I slow for an ascent. I pick out a destination ahead, and stagger the last few steps where I reel and almost fall over the edge.

I brace my hands on my hips and rasp out gasps for breath while overlooking a magnificent view. My heart pounds as if to escape my chest and my lungs scream in fierce agony. My legs feel like they'd drop off my body if I gave them the chance and everything, up to the blood pounding through my head and swirling around my ears, hurts, yet I feel myself again. I wait here for an hour, watching, wondering, marveling. Anything but worrying.

I jog a brisk retracement of my steps that leaves my body shaking from exertion by the time I reach the gate again. Shaking, but unshaken. I'm myself again.

I slip into the refectory and start eating alone. A group of officers joins me after a few minutes. They helped bring my regiment to Mt. Cabrae when the king's riders gave notice of Commander Brayler's decision to pull away from the war. I'm usually quiet, especially when I eat, but my own thoughts distract me now. I make a few friendly comments to everyone, but let them continue their conversation without much input. Meal finished, I rise and start a slow walk around the fortress. I want to keep my head clear before I find Claire and join with Kimbr Nealy's tactician, and activity works well for that.

The evening marches in on the sonorous roll of wind in the mountains. I find Claire waiting along the main path through the fortress. I feel the cut of shame at her bowed head and perpetual smile flattened at the corners. She looks like my lack of words earlier had an even deeper impact than I thought. She rises without a word and, without looking at my face, follows me for Captain Kimbr's hall. I glance at her and see the edges of her eyes glistening in the low sun. She wipes at them when she sees me looking, but neither of us say anything.

We enter the hall. Commander Nealy and Captain Kimbr don't know Claire well, haven't even seen her recently, so they think she's fine. I know her from years back, though, and can tell. She's been crying, and I pity her, but pity myself, too. I didn't learn to run my feelings into oblivion just this afternoon; only after scores of times trying to cry them away. I've endured many sleepless nights and tortured days. I've borne the longings of loss and feasted on the ashen taste of regret. I've suffered through the same pain, so I callously act like I don't notice her sorrow.

"The rivers are swollen with the spring runoff," Captain Kimbr says. "And that's probably the largest challenge besides the Guldethian forces."

Rivers glutted on water from the high snowpack makes most things harder for our war effort. The mountain streams, usually narrow and shallow enough to ford in the summer, are impassable torrents in the spring. Going miles out of our way for a bridge, sometimes to find it blocked or destroyed by the Guldeth doesn't help our feeling of control. They have the same difficulties to contend with, so it doesn't only affect us, but we can't feel their frustrations.

"It's the same as it is every year," Kimbr continues. "Only this year, we tried to hold more bridges as winter came to an end. This came at the cost of losing a few passes."

From my position leaning against a side table in the high-beamed room, I'm close enough to see everyone and their reaction. Several of my officers sit at the table or stand to the side near me. Near me... and my tactician. I've stayed silent the whole time so far, waiting while Kimbr informed those of us who were away for a while about the recent developments.

All in all, the Great Chamber is crowded.. Mt. Cabrae, while strong, isn't large enough for the number of soldiers garrisoning it now. Years ago a hundred soldiers under a few officers held it and patrolled the lands around. Thank Lesasil they managed to hold out for succor after the Divide.

"With the increased fighting we've seen over the winter the loss of the passes is grievous," Commander Nelay says. "It would put us in dire straits without Captain Hart's five hundred Sewlands cadets. Especially with Commander Brayler withdrawing his forces."

The officers take to muttering among themselves. I pay extra attention to how Sandy and Kimbr observe the effect her last sentence produces. I've been away for over two weeks and want to know how leadership truly views every matter. Kimbr keeps a close eye on his mother. The surroundings swell in the subdued but visible way a boat on a rising tide follows the water. Commander Nealy notices the look and barely nods her head to him.

"There is one development I need to tell you about," Kimbr says.

His statement silences the room, and nobody even shuffles their feet. He's discussed this with the commander, and I doubt I've heard it so I set my back even straighter.

"We captured a Guldeth captain yesterday and he carried a message. Their moving forces northward isn't because they think we're guarding those passes less. The letter gives the indication that their latest strategy is to send even more forces against Captain Lewis's positions west of Eraseam."

I glance at Claire, as does everybody who knows who she is, and notice her face flush at the thought of the Guldeth pressing her father harder.

Kimbr looks at his mother and she speaks. "We can't know for sure if this is true. We all know it might be a clever deception; something meant for us to find so we adjust our strategy." She pauses to look around the small crowded room. "The captain was captured, not killed, so that makes the possibility of deception more likely."

We've known the Guldeth to plant messages or incriminating items on soldiers we find when we're burying bodies after an ambush. Apparently Sandy and Kimbr think it's something more than that since they're bringing it up before the group. They're both experienced enough to know the difference.

"Whether or not this specific message is legitimate," she continues. "I don't feel right doing nothing with the information. Commander Lewis lost some soldiers when Commander Brayler pulled out. Yes, we're seeing the fiercest fighting here, but we cannot deny their steady movement north." She looks at me now and many pairs of eyes follow the direction of her look. "Captain Hart, I need you and your tactician to take a company of your new soldiers to Commander Lewis's aid."

That's why Kimbr looked to his mother to finish the narrative; he couldn't presume to give orders to a soldier of equal rank who also happens to be the prince.

I raise my standing by bowing to the commander, and say, "We will leave as soon as you desire."

I want to talk with her first and find if there's any more to the intercepted message before I leave. Hearing I'm going with Claire, though, threatens to reverse my exhausting run. A run I took when I should have snatched what precious rest I could manage. I'm not having that prove fruitless. I swear I'll keep a handle on those emotions, and I raise my shields.

"We'll manage the loss of the passes alright," Kimbr says. "We've lost and retaken them before and can now." A few of his officers nod slowly. "The one we managed to retake was a success."

"Can we really call an encounter with more than a hundred dead or wounded a success?" an officer asks.

Another captain stares at the officer. "We managed what we set out to do. It is exceedingly unfortunate, but it couldn't be helped."

"The difference is the expectations," Kimbr continues. "Last year we didn't expect a major change to their conquest strategy and could align our forces to match theirs."

"But now," Kimbr pauses and looks around the room. The Great Chamber has only one fireplace, and with so many of us crowding inside, the light doesn't shine evenly across everyone's face. The windows on one side of the room loom dark above our heads. "Now their strategy is apparently changing. We've noticed it even before this message. We need to stay vigilant and ready to adapt. No more expecting tomorrow's fighting to take place along the same lines as yesterday's."

The officers murmur assent while looking like they wish he'd have told them the practical side of what that means. Kimbr gives a final admonition, dismissing the officers at the same time. "I'd like to speak with the captains a little further. Officers, remember what we can expect. This summer won't be like last. I'd like you to keep forces ready for a moment's notice."

Officers file out, and Kimbr asks Claire to remain. This dispels any doubt among the remaining captains as to the nature of the next discussion. The nearest captains close the doors, and I can see everybody's face despite the depleted sunlight.

"Now about that message we found on their captain," Kimbr starts. "Everything I said in front of the officers is true, but there is more to it."

He looks around at each of us as if wishing he could probe our thoughts, and I swear he stays locked onto my gaze the longest. I think I can read fear in his eyes.

"The message goes on to say they *are* planning to move farther north. Captain Hart, I think you need to move your soldiers to Eraseam's capitol."

My brows furrow. "Wouldn't a strong defense on the border negate the need for a reinforced capitol?"

He nods, but my mind holds far more questions than his answer supplies. I look first at his mother, and then back at Kimbr.

"There's more to that message," I say. "And I need to know it if I'm being sent to Myceum. Unless they're through the northern passes already and marching for the capitol?"

Commander Nealy shakes her head, "They're not through the mountains—at least not yet—but you're right; there is more to the message than we've said. They are planning on moving their forces north, and they are also planning an attack on Myceum."

Faint gasps circulate the room.

"How do you know?"

Kimbr answers before Commander Nealy can. "The Guldeth far overmatched us, and we only took the captain by a stroke of luck at the end. The battle started poorly for us, but after a while we turned it in our favor. As it ended, I led a squad around their flank and attacked their captain's location. His handpicked soldiers sold their lives dearly, but couldn't stand against the crush of the changing tide, which is when we came in. I don't believe this message was planted to deceive us, and if we're to trust it we need to reinforce Myceum."

His logic makes sense, and moreover, I trust Kimbr. I had no doubt about the necessity of Sandy Nealy's order, but I wanted to know why I was called to the capitol specifically. I could have asked privately, and he would have had to answer me as the prince, but I think everyone here has the right to know the full truth about the war's events. They need to know why I'm going to Eraseam's capitol, too.

We finish the discussion and leave the hall, filing into the silvery moonlight. I wait for my officers to make a few plans about our next steps. I'm not happy about heading to Myceum, but am mature enough not to show it. When I look at Claire, I do so with an expressionless face. It's an attempt to prevent any emotions. But I realize I do it because I'm half-frustrated, half-mad, so I've already lost. I'm going to the city she grew up in, but that doesn't make it her fault. I remember my run, chide myself, and try to brush it off. But she's still standing there, looking at me, and waiting for orders with the officers.

"Get some sleep. We won't all go of course, but tomorrow I'll want everyone's help to prepare. We'll split the cadets up by company and I'll take a few north. I'll leave the morning after tomorrow." They nod and all turn to walk back to their rooms. Everyone except Claire.

Chapter 5.

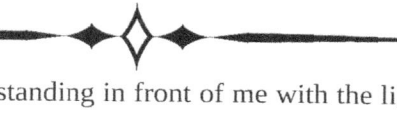

There she is, standing in front of me with the light of the crescent moon shining from over her shoulder. I glance once at her before I almost turn away and follow in the tracks of my officers. That single glance shows me her still swollen eyes, shining in the moonlight. The crescent behind her reflects silvery light across the castle's stones, but on her hair, blowing ever so gently in the breeze, it shimmers like beads of water on the finest threads of silk. Her beauty overtakes me for a moment, but then I remember my shields and start to turn.

Shields or not, my heart cries out against me for the cruelty I'm about to inflict on her. I stop before I can move a muscle or even sway in the wrong direction. She's strong and far from pathetic, but I can't bring myself to move away. Instead, I bring my eyes to meet hers, but find her looking at the ground. "Claire," I say. She looks up and meets my eyes. Pain radiates from them and tears threatening to overflow from her eyelids shimmer more than moonlight on a pond. She blinks once as we look at each other, and each eye yields up a single tear.

Two shooting stars, caressing her cheeks, streak down the delicate alabaster skin and cling to her lower jawbone before they dislodge and crash to her tunic. My shields are down enough to not be calloused, but not enough to fall for her in the moonlight. The hurt between our families is too deep, too raw, too…. I sigh. Some breaks cannot be mended.

"You... wanted to talk privately?" I say.

I don't know what she's expecting, but I need to break the silence. This won't be like last time. She sways like it takes every bit of restraint to not throw herself on me for staying. I'm sure the look on my face shows my surprise.

"I need to talk to you somewhere. Anywhere," she says. "We can't go on like this, especially if we're going to be stationed together. We have to work together for the good of your kingdom."

My kingdom. It's an appeal that doesn't work on me. If it wasn't for my mother's memory and my father's wishes, I wouldn't be a prince. I shouldn't be first in line, either; Rafael should, and I've had the audacious cruelty to resent him for his death many times. My kingdom. The kingdom I want safe for the people. The kingdom I've worked so hard to develop my skills for. The kingdom I've bled and killed for.

"We *will* work together," I say. "We need to develop strategies together, maybe not tomorrow, maybe once we can consult with your—"

"What we *need* is to stop the tension between us. It can't go on. The whole kingdom will suffer if we can't get beyond this hurt. Can't you see *I'm* willing to? I told you earlier that I'm not bitter like my father is."

"I'm willing to stop the tension, too. But it's too late to undo what's done."

"It's not your father's fault my mother died," she says. Like this afternoon, she insists, and steps closer. Her deep brown eyes widen to plead.

"He could have saved her, but he didn't," I say. "They reserved the Balm of Life for me. Me—the prince who won't even use his Gift. Your mother could have used it; *she* would have helped the kingdom. I've grown up without a mother because of someone's greed, but you grew up without a mother because of my family. Our selfishness. How could you not be bitter?"

"She knew the risk every time she used her Gift. She knew, and my father knew, that The Balm of Life was to be saved for the king and queen's Gifted son. Even before I could remember it, my mother always told me she aged herself in full knowledge there was no way back. She and father *knew* what they were doing."

"That doesn't mean they liked it," I say as she grabs my hands.

"Your father stationed us together," she says. "Maybe it's not to try to mend us; he may not have thought of that, but we have to work together."

"He said it's only because you're the best tactician beside Julek." I use her father's first name, rather than his full title, Commander Lewis, because we're alone, and the familiarity of my childhood comes natural now that I'm deep in the conversation. Saying her father's name brings a new thought to my mind, and I ask, "You're not bitter... but Julek is?"

"Yes; didn't you know?"

"I've assumed it, but the king asserts he isn't. I've not seen any signs of it."

"Well, he must do a good job of hiding it around the king, but he often would ask me why I wasn't. Either way, you and I have to work together."

The tone of our conversation takes a different feel, one I'm grateful for, and as thin wisps of clouds slide across the night sky, the moon's light darkens. She's extraordinarily beautiful, even though she just finished crying and the crusty residue still clings to the sides of her eyes. I'm not about to allow myself to lower my shields any more. They're down enough.

"Working together means we'll be in contact alot," I say. "Probably until the war ends. I want things back the way they were, but we can't ever go there. We both know that."

The storm my comment raises in her eyes shows she's far from agreeing with me. I want to draw my hands from hers, and would have no trouble doing it from a man, or any other woman, but her....

"We can *act* like things are the way they were," she says. "Your mother can't come back, Rafael can't come back, and my mother can't come back, but why does that mean we can't care for each other like when we were kids?"

"We can and we do care for each other," I say. Flames flash from her eyes, accentuated from the still-present moon glimmer, and I get the hint to put more thought behind my words. "You don't care for me anymore. You haven't had time for me since Rafael's death. I know he was your brother, but it was hard on me, too. You could have at least acknowledged my friendship with him."

I could match her anger with my own, but a heavy feeling overtakes my heart at the memory. I put a note of resignation in my voice that douses her fire. "It's not just losing a brother, Claire, or a mother. One murdered, one dishonored and little better than murdered. The way you lose them makes a difference, too. I'm glad you never had a chance to experience that."

Her features soften and the moon completes the transformation. The very picture of sorrow, a goddess of contrition, she drops her hands and sinks her chin to her chest. I can feel remorse radiating through the air between us. Her constant smile now looks like a false mask. No light behind the gentle curve. No customary warmth from within.

"I'm sorry," she says.

Far more than words reach my ears. It's every bit of her pain from the past ten years wrapped into two words. My shields still up, I feel, not an anger, but a coldness creep around my body, starting at the base of my neck and rising to infect my brain. It trickles down my spine and wraps around my chest, suffocating any scintillation of sympathy beating to life in my heart.

I nod once, and reach out my hand. I touch two fingers to her chin and notice the chill spread there, instead of the heat I could expect from the feel of her soft skin. With a gentle motion, I raise her face to mine, and we look at each other, sorrow lashing between us with a fitful intensity. "I know. But some breaks cannot be mended."

I move my hand from her chin and let the backs of my fingers slide along her cheek. It might be a trick of the light, an involuntary reaction, or a droop of disappointment, but I think I notice her head tilt the slightest angle into my hand.

What I'm saying and doing floods my system, and a rush of realization floods away the coolness. I withdraw my hand and take a step back with the slightest intake of breath through parted lips. I turn, afraid, and walk back toward my room, leaving her as I left her before; alone, but in the moonlight; much said, but some feelings impossible to say.

The next morning dawns bright and beautiful. It doesn't match my inner state, or calm my aching body. I desperately needed sleep last night, but managed little, and feel the effects as I stand on the same ledge as yesterday. After a night of fitful sleep, I slipped from the castle before the sun was more than a glow brightening the tops of the mountains. I reached the summit when the sun shone enough to stop me from pitching over the edge.

I watch the day break upon the night like surf on the shore; always here, and always gone. I don't feel as good as yesterday, yet I'm still glad I'm here. Brutal run aside, I always enjoy watching the sunrise; anyone with a few minutes can see a sunset, especially in winter, but a summer sunrise is a spectacular thing. Watching from a desolate place only increases the sense that it's all for my enjoyment. I force myself to smile from my place seated on a rock and start to feel better despite the whirl of thoughts that plagued me through the night.

As I jog back, I recollect my conversation with Claire the night before, and force myself to smile as I remember how I could have avoided it, but didn't. I've never been one to take the easy way, and I don't intend to start now. Not when I've worked so hard to come this far.

Maybe we can't mend the hurt between us, but at least we'll stop pretending that everything is perfect. Her father's bitterness toward the king gives me pause; my father's been insisting for almost a decade that Julek Lewis holds no grudge against our family, and it holds true by his actions. Julek was one of the strongest commanders in uniting the kingdom both before and after Heller White's Divide. Much of the credit belongs to his wife, June.

Julek was reckless, at least that's what I hear; I wasn't old enough to care. But, having had a Gifted wife, he could have afforded recklessness, especially since she had turned back every battle that went poorly for him. It would age her a year or two each time, but turning back the days so she could help him reconsider his tactics made him into the superb strategist he is today.

At what cost, though. Claire grew up without a mother after June tried to reverse too many days. I hear her father became more cautious just before the Gift aged her to death. I've heard some say he was frivolous with his life, and by extension hers, but only he can know that. Her sacrifice—her family's sacrifice, rather—in a large part, made Oruvia what it is today.

Julek's words and actions have been nothing but kind as far as I can tell, at least since I started paying attention, so Claire's words make me think. She said on two occasions that he's bitter, but I've never seen it, or heard the king remark upon it.

A few quick leaps from one rock to the other like a mountain goat brings me to a grassy plain. I see a dewy trail at the far end from my run the other way and remind myself to force a smile again. I breathe heavily and feel an ache in my stomach for food, so it soon fades, but the rise in spirit that accompanied the forced movement remains. The sun burned away some of the damp and only the thicker spots around trees remain.

I careen down the gentle plain and run as I started yesterday. Feeling the wind rush past my ears and spread my hair in a wild fashion recalls a smile to my face; a real smile, one that takes up my whole face and rests deep in my eyes.

Julek's wife, June, had an incredible amount of sway in the kingdom. And Julek did, too, I think as I slow my pace to a more sustainable jog. A Gifted doesn't necessarily have influence; power without any means of enacting it is wasted as noise or turmoil. She, coupled with her husband, the most powerful commander in Elathon, could have directed their combined might for worse purposes.

This thought brings a frown to my face. It's the first time I've thought about her ability this way. Maybe that's the reason I'd always thought my father feared Julek.

I always thought it odd for the king to fear one of his nobles, but noticed it less once I started paying attention after Mother's death. Perhaps that's why I had forgotten about it.

Their fealty suddenly strikes me, and I'm even more amazed at their family's sacrifice. I've always repressed any thoughts of my Gift, so it's the first time this occurs to me. Maybe that's why the king wanted me to learn it. Maybe that's why he and my mother reserved the Balm of Life especially for me. Julek and June could have taken it if they worked together, but they didn't. They could have stolen the Balm before the Guldeth did, and if they had, June would still be alive. Claire would still have a mother. The thought chills me. They've been through a lot. I've always known that, but their apparent internal struggles strike me for the first time. An ice pick through my shoulder.

I'm in a position to grant them a boon for all the suffering they've experienced in helping the kingdom. It ran through my mind last night, and now I have extra reason for it.

I reach Commander Nealy while she sits alone before the start of her full day, and lay my request before her. "Commander, I crave a favor from you."

"Certainly, Captain Hart, anything for you whether or not you are the prince."

I bow at the combination of answer and compliment.

"I'd like to recommend Claire Lewis for promotion to officer in my regiment. It's not proper for her father to advance her. Since she's already a superb tactician, I'd like her to hold the rank of officer before we depart."

"Ah, a favor for a special friend?" she asks with a knowing smile, as if she intuited much from our lingering together the night before.

The smile brings a flush to my face like I'm in the heat of a battle, and I say, "It's a regular favor for a regular friend." Then, an inspiration takes me. "Two more favors for friends if I may. One is Elara Ronrout, and the other is Shelbe Hadder. They're both apt pupils and will make good officers in time. They're still too fresh to battle, but in time I expect them to develop their capabilities as Claire has done. Watch them close for signs of merit."

Commander Nealy still smiles, but nods her head and says nothing more about the unappreciated jest. "Very well. I've heard only good reports about the commander's daughter. I'll include that in our visit this morning now that I have a specific request."

I stand to the side to wait for the others. My stomach churns as if I'm roaming a battlefield to look for survivors, and I block away the feeling the same way I do there—distraction.

Distraction doesn't last long, because Captain Kimbr strides into the small hall and takes a place near his mother with a nod of greeting to me. As if the others waited to follow Kimbr, the rest enter over the next several minutes. Claire enters and my gaze locks onto her searching face until she finds me and I look away. I don't want to seem too familiar, after all. Especially after last night's lingering second-long touch.

I glance toward her and try to act as if I've just seen her enter. She meets my gaze with a queer look in her eye. It's the brightest I've seen it since our brief reunion in Sapesky. The other times since that she's had her ready smile, but not this glow. I lock eyes with her from across the Great Chamber for a second and read—no, it couldn't be—hope.

Commander Nealy starts the conversation with most of the officers from the night before.

"There is one among us who is not an officer," her voice rings out across the central table. She looks at Claire, and everyone follows her gaze. Self-conscious but confident in her hope, Claire looks around at everybody with her customary grace. Their staring didn't jar the repose she appeared to have found overnight. "Claire Lewis, please come forward."

The crowd on one side of the table parts to allow Claire passage to the front. She sweeps forward with a gentle bob of her head and a brighter look about her face. I'm glad to see her advancing, especially since I know she would have worked hard for it. The price she paid, through watching her parents's sufferings and ultimate sacrifice, is one nobody would choose. Her knowledge of tactics came at a greater cost than anyone's.

Commander Nealy's uplifting of my childhood friend warms my heart. It stops the hungry shaking I've had since coming straight to act on my earlier inspiration. Brief service complete, the commander's next words knock my breath away like the blunt side of a hammer ax.

"You have your captain to thank for your advancement. He suggested it first thing this morning."

My mouth threatens to gape while Claire wheels around to look at me with shining eyes. One glance is enough to let me know I can't look into those big eyes and maintain my outward appearance of tranquility. The hope shines even brighter on her face now. How did my one second lapse of focus last night give her that look after the words that preceded them?

I dare to look into her face and give a curt nod and a smile as I would any newly-advanced officer. Little of the smile shows in my eyes, but to her joy-stricken breast, my mouth smile looks like it means all the world.

We go through the rest of the agenda, and it includes details of future movements; what we're planning, expecting, and committed to. The joy of going through tactics, especially when Commander Nealy asks her opinion on a matter, catapults Claire's joy into borderline ecstasy. We leave the hall, and I wish she would come to me with appreciation. I would acknowledge it, I decide, and drop hints about others up for advancement soon. She's smart, and I think that will dim the joy without squashing it.

Only she doesn't find me. After all the times we've ran into each other against my will, I can't talk to her now that I do want to. I pass the rest of the morning and afternoon in a whirl of swords, carts, and an endless series of questions from my officers. All the officers coming with me except Claire....

Night comes, and I sit before a fire in the sullen expectation that proceeds great undertakings. Only nothing big comes to mind; I'm only going to reinforce a capitol city on a rumor, and don't think I'll need much courage. This usually only comes to me on the night we're planning an ambush, one that inevitably takes a strange turn, and not something like this.

I've come to realize this presupposition as a sort of sixth sense, but never spoken about my hunch to anybody. I would have eventually spoken to my mother, or Claire's mother, but that's impossible, and Gifted people are few and far between; I'm not sure when I'll have another chance. I could speak to the king, but I avoid any conversation that could lead to talking about my Gift with him.

The feeling remains with me all the evening as I stare into the fire, mostly lost in my own thoughts. There's no way the Nealys could be working with the king to push Claire and me together. They could see us as a powerful match like Julek and June, but I shake my head at the possibility. I need to drive that thought away; Kimbr wouldn't fake an intercepted message any more than either of the others would falsify my need to move from the front lines.

My sleep is troubled, filled with unremembered dreams that keep me from resting well. I'm up before the first light of morning, and am grateful I'll soon work the unease away.

Chapter 6.

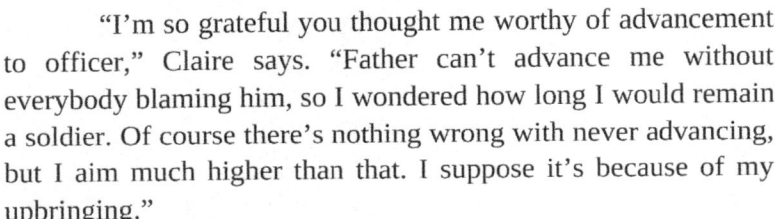

"I'm so grateful you thought me worthy of advancement to officer," Claire says. "Father can't advance me without everybody blaming him, so I wondered how long I would remain a soldier. Of course there's nothing wrong with never advancing, but I aim much higher than that. I suppose it's because of my upbringing."

She talks a lot, but not particularly fast, so my head doesn't spin. This is more like the Claire I knew as a youth. Inserting myself to set her straight on the point of favor she thinks she occupies passes through my mind for an instant. It passes on as rapidly as it came, and leaves me to hold my tongue.

"Did you ask around about me to make sure I was worthy?"

I pause, and look at Claire, who's staring back at me. She shines amid the gray fortress like a winter sun on a bleak world. It takes a moment for the question to come to focus in my mind. Although she didn't talk fast, the diverse topics and my natural inclination to let my mind wander had it doing just that.

"I didn't ask anyone," I say. "The idea came upon me the other day, and I know your father's highly regarded among all Oruvians. If you're the girl I grew up with, and if Julek and June's daughter is anything like her parents, you're ready."

The first part of my answer makes me inwardly wince, and I soften up more than I intend to for the rest, but I only realize that after speaking. My goal isn't to deflate her enthusiasm, but rather to turn it from myself. I don't want to appear to have favorites among my officers or soldiers.

Even though I do.

At least that's my latest excuse. A few days ago it was another, and a few days from now it very well could be yet another. I have many faults; a lack of self-awareness isn't among them.

My answer stops her from talking for a while, and I'm working back through what I said to see where I could have gone wrong when she says, "I want to be like my parents. Do you think I'm much like my mother?"

Oh great.

My shields snap to their full height before she even completes her short statement. That's not the response I expected, much less wanted. I wanted appreciation. Maybe, I thought, my answer might even blaze the trail for me to tell her how I recommended Commander Nealy watch a few others for advancement. It would be natural, easy, and couldn't be viewed as malicious. Nothing of the sort could happen now, and I walk beside her in dumb silence for several moments before stumbling through an answer.

"Your mother was strong-willed and loyal. Loyal to the kingdom when she, more than anyone, could have used her Gift for ill purposes. I didn't know that at the time, but looking back I never felt any reason to fear her power."

So much is left unsaid that I almost begin talking again. I want to ask her about her mother's loyalty, intrude in their family's secret conversations, and grope along paths of her memory that nine years have choked off. Paths I could have traveled with Claire beside me if I had so much as reached out my hand to give a comforting grasp. Paths I shunned.

Before I can resume, she replies, "Mother loved your parents, Chris, and the kingdom. She gave her life so that my father might help it rise to glory."

I notice the familiar *Chris* again, but can't correct her. Not after the reminder of what her family did for mine. Before I even stop to consider my words, I find myself talking. "I didn't pay much attention before I was next in line for the throne, but I've heard many times that we owe everything to her sacrifices. It's a shame they didn't—"

My mouth started speaking without the full backing of my will, but now my mind catches up and stops it. I was going to say my parents should have given the Balm of Life for June's use, but I know what a hard subject that is with the king. Father may have eventually, but it was stolen by my mother's murderer before June used the Gift her final time.

On rare occasions I've allowed myself to dream how the present could be different if I had succeeded, but three attempts was more than enough for my young mind to cope with.

Claire catches my meaning and I feel her glance at me as we plod along. The spring day has lost all joy for me and I do little more than place one foot before the other. Moving forward is enough for an army moving in the safety of its own land, but I worry that my mindset will spread across the company unless I do something about it.

"You look tired, Chris," Claire says after a long space.

My head snaps to let me look full in her face with astonishment. "How did you know that?"

"Know what?" She looks surprised.

"Know that's exactly what I was thinking about just now. Was I thinking out loud?" I'm afraid at having my feelings noticed. It's by an old friend, but she noticed. Which means others will notice it before long unless I do something about it.

"You just look tired," she says. "You're weary and look ready to drop. I've seen you up later than anyone, up earlier, and working harder, too. You can't live on willpower alone and need rest soon unless I'm mistaken."

"I'll rest once we're at Myceum."

"Is that what you said about Sapesky? And Mt. Cabrae?"

She's smiling, but with the glimmer shrouded behind troubled eyes.

Returning the smile, I answer, "You still know me somehow." We walk beside each other for several minutes, hearing the chatter of those behind us while noticing the wind rustling the treetops. I'm probing my heart for answers to our earlier conversation. It's a shame the king and queen didn't let June live. No—that's the wrong way to think about it. It's not what Claire would want me to think, it's not what either of my parents would want me to think, and it's not even true.

"Stopping now is a weakness I can't show them."

My earlier words during the extra training chafe me; after telling my soldiers the enemy won't care if they're tired, I'm the last one able to call an early halt. All I can do now is keep moving, keep it all in, act like I'm fine, and give a half-hearted commitment.

"I'll rest earlier tonight."

I feel oppressed by my reflectons, and the weariness only explains some of it. My heart is heavy, and I make a point not to walk in the downcast way of a footsore traveler. I attribute the rest to the weight of the Gift on my shoulders. I know Claire's mother could be alive whether or not I had the Gift, but right now I blame myself for having it. Since the Balm of Life was saved for me, that means it wasn't given to her, and she died sooner. I'm the reason the girl beside me doesn't have a mother. I know it's not true, I *know* it; but that doesn't make my heart accept it.

My emotion-swelled heart blocks everything but misery from my senses. I may as well be in a wintry desert. The birds and foothill scenery that usually bring me so much delight disappears. I notice nothing but the dull monotonous path leading me to yet another duty. A duty I used to scorn, and one I now tolerate. For all my cares to increase my swordsmanship, knowledge of strategy, history, diplomacy, and courtly manners, I undertake each with a repressed resentment.

Usually I keep these to myself, and sometimes I even convince myself that I'm happy, but... times like these almost convince me to throw myself into the wilds. Abandon duty, leave my country, and fend for myself. I'm young, strong, and have worked hard for what I've become. But these people around me. I love the people, yet the burden of a kingdom's worth of orchestration....

"It'll do the soldiers as much good as it will you," Claire says.

I'm on the point of asking what she means, but I stop my tongue early enough to save face. At least I think I do. She looks at me when I bite down on the words before they can issue into the world. I must have an angry look on my countenance because she unintentionally mimics my choking speech when she turns my way. "Chr—Chris, what's wrong?"

"Everything is wrong." I say it with such a savage snarl that I flinch from myself.

Claire slides closer as we walk along. Now I want nothing more than to stare at the blur of rocks passing beneath my feet.

"You can't keep going like this," Claire says. "You need to stop the company now."

I keep my face turned down, and slightly away from her. I can feel her staring but don't give in.

"Can I stop the company and give orders for rest?" she asks.

I still don't reply, but my hot heart desperately hopes she does. My silence begs for help, and I don't know how else to get it.

Claire takes the chance of alienating herself from the captain who caused her advancement to officer, and steps from my side to the closest officers. I hear her voice rise to a commanding pitch as I slow my steps.

"We're stopping here for the night," she says. "The soldiers are weary from the past weeks and need recovery time.

This is one of the highest points for miles around and easily defendable. We'll continue to Myceum in the morning."

The officers she talks to welcome the stop, for I hear them head away as I cut my steps short. Their weariness can't equal mine, and I start to consider the state I'm in, but find that too taxing. It would help, but I'm in no mood to be helped. The quagmire of my thoughts looks comfortable now, and it'll take either time or a tragedy to tear me from my citadel of anguish.

Hours pass and I find myself sitting by a fire alone. Either Claire told them, or they intuit it, but none of my officers venture to sit by me. That's fine; I don't want company. And yet... my silence is begging for help again. What I wouldn't give to have a companion. My eyes feel heavy and keeping a scowl is the only way I can prevent myself from exploding in an outburst of vehement tears.

Steps sound behind me, and they're different from the soldiers passing by to other fires. These steps grow louder with each light footfall. I don't so much as glance to the side, or give the slightest indication I notice the arrival, but *she* sits down next to me. One of the maybe two living people in the whole realm I could allow into my space in a moment like this.

I still don't acknowledge Claire's presence, but my scowl fades when she makes no attempt at conversation. She doesn't acknowledge my presence either, but I can't help feeling better with another human beside me, if only a little bit.

The silent companionship allowed my scowl to fade. It proved enough of a comfort to dull the razor edge of illogical abandonment swirling inside me. I'm in the very act of deepening my breath to ease the tension when I notice her stir. She rises, walks away. It wasn't a turn of my head which let me see her, but rather the consciousness of a general movement out of the corner of my eye.

We weren't talking, and didn't even look at each other as we sat together, but still the space she left feels unnaturally empty. The same way a dried stream bed feels more than empty; it feels unnatural.

She comes back a few minutes later and I feel my heavy heart leap with something that may border on joy if I would allow it, but nothing of the sort can pass my shields now. Relief is the strongest feeling I'll let through. Relief of the most selfish kind. Relief for what she can do for me.

Without looking toward her, I feel the wave of solace her presence could bring. It feels like my shields stop it from reaching me, though, as if I'm dying of thirst and the lapping water on the shore of a pure lake only reaches my toes, where I'm chained. Unable to move. Except in this case, unable to care. Unable to feel. Unable to... to empathize.

I notice now she brought two bowls of food and set one between us. I spurn the thoughtfulness as I hear the slight scrapings of her spoon on the one she's engaged with. I keep staring at the fire, less of a scowl now, but ready to return to the old medicine if I stumble towards weakness again.

The food she brought finally reaches my brain, and smells good. Good may be too light of a word. It smells amazing. Life-giving, in fact, and I can't stop thinking about that too now that I've scented it once. Daring to glance to the side for the first time in hours, I look to my right at Claire. She's evidently enjoying herself.

I push pride aside and take up the bowl. My first spoonful doesn't disappoint, and seemingly floods my veins with a renewed life. Mouthful after mouthful passes my tongue and fills me with some of my usual mental vigor.

Soup gone, I set my bowl beside me in the way I notice Claire does. She clears it as soon as I set it down and returns without a word. Finally feeling the smallest bit better, and because I own it to her, I finally say, "Thank you." It's such a simple phrase, and said after so long together tonight, that it would have been just as easy not to say, but I needed to say something.

Intent on preventing silence from gaining such a consummate foothold again, I stand to add more wood to the fire. Then I sit again and mimic Claire's posture. Resting on my hands out behind me is more comfortable than the hunched posture I've maintained the past few hours.

We sit there, two silent statues with the firelight playing across our features. Only now do I realize her hair is down, hanging to her elbows as she supports herself on palms spread behind her. What little wind that accompanied us during the day died away as night fell, and the ends of her hair now blow gently in our fire's breeze. It's barely enough to swirl the wreaths of smoke shining in the moonlight, but it manages to ruffle her hair into a shimmering wonder I know could take my breath away if I let it.

My fit came on suddenly, but didn't entirely surprise me. I feel shame more than surprise now that the worse has passed. When the fits of depression strike, it can pull me from a righteous pedestal to the hell of despair within minutes.

"Are you going to get some sleep soon?" Claire asks, the first words spoken around our fire besides my *thank you* since the night began.

I nod my head in a slow response. I need to rise now, and I meant to almost an hour ago, but standing seems so hard. Not the physical act, but emotionally; tearing myself from my seat to pile more wood on the fire took a superhuman effort and I only did it after a long acceptance that it wouldn't stoke itself. I know I can't sleep without first making it to the tent my soldiers readied for me, but... standing seems so difficult.

I rise, and Claire does too, then looks over at me. "You'll be alright?" she asks.

I feel like answering that question honestly, but can't quite bring myself to it. Instead, I say, "I'll make it."

A tenuous smile accompanies my reply, which I don't think convinces her any more than my cryptic words.

She gives me a serious look, one that overpowers her natural sympathy.

"You *have* to make it. For all of us."

Part of me wants to think she's referring to herself specifically needing me, but it's a small part, one almost crushed into nothingness by my last several hours. The feeling lasts the fraction of a heartbeat, and I nod.

"Thank you for..."

Words fail me. She turns to look back since we were both heading to our own tents, and her now sympathetic gaze rests on my wan face.

". . . for being with me. Thank you."

She smiles, and before I know it, I'm alone in my tent.

The wave of comfort that I allowed to wet my feet, as it were, still isn't strong enough to overpower my fabricated sense of hopelessness, but it stopped the downward spiral and even draws me closer to the surface. At least I'm no longer enveloped in the despondency I dread. That's good enough for now.

Chapter 7.

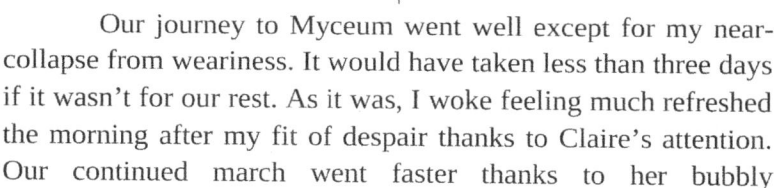

Our journey to Myceum went well except for my near-collapse from weariness. It would have taken less than three days if it wasn't for our rest. As it was, I woke feeling much refreshed the morning after my fit of despair thanks to Claire's attention. Our continued march went faster thanks to her bubbly conversation.

Eraseam's capitol looks much like that of Artalia's, but, as it's the capitol of a province, it's necessarily smaller. The reduced size doesn't diminish the grandeur, and the outer curtain wall looks from our distance like it kept the city from spilling to the countryside. Some houses line the roads leading to the main gates, but most of the gray-thatch roofs rest on houses in the walls.

Fresh yellow thatch adorns some of the larger houses, and stands in vivid contrast to the weary sameness elsewhere in the town. Timbered buildings, lovely in their own right, descend into the monotony when they're built together in large swaths.

Spring rains have come and gone, and the usual wind blowing along the mountains touches the city enough where it descends below the walls, picks up moisture from the streets, and carries it away to leave a more healthy atmosphere in its wake. The town was well-kept when I visited it years ago, and with Julek Lewis commanding over it the entire time, I expect to find the same loveliness.

A wall the same shade as the nearby mountains rises high in the air, and, though we can't see it, I know from my frequent visits as a child that the walls stand several yards thick.

Adorning the walls, like a ghoulish set of lower teeth, the slope-capped crenellations jut into the air. Half-round towers rise at even distances along the wall and have their own combination of wall-walk combined with a shallow-pitched copper roof. On the even taller keep, rounded towers topped with conical slate roofs visually break apart the uniformity of the lime-washed walls and complete the imposing look of the fortress.

With our final push to the city, the soldiers naturally regain some of the energy lost to the tiresome journey now lying behind us. I'm excited for the sight of the city as well, especially since the vague fear of it having been overthrown disappears upon sight of the fluttering pennants and farmers working in the fields.

Myceum sits on a slight hill, and we ascend to enter between two of the circular-front towers supporting the iron portcullis. A few guards atop the walls watch us, but no challenge comes. The soldiers wear the recognizable blue tunic emblazoned with the yellow design of Eraseam's eagle head across the chest.

My shame still lingers as I lead my company through the gatehouse and walk into the court familiar from my childhood. So many memories in this city. So many dreams of the past bound hopelessly here with ropes of wire.

With the bonds unwilling to break, and the shame lingering, I try to raise my mental shields to a height which excludes anything of the sort. Claire is nearby, and I hope she takes most of the conversation with the commander of the city. It's my duty, but a burdensome one now. The city's commander is, after all, her father.

The custom of Oruvia is to greet most expected guests without pomp, and I admire this custom—probably because I'm a prince and would receive a gaudy welcome otherwise. Though Julek meets us with more ceremony than I wish, my final worry for the city's safety is abolished at his presence. He's clad in armor covered with the customary blue tunic, and on his chest is embroidered an ornamental eagle head in yellow thread. The silvery hue of his glittering armor provides more for the royal look, but I see the climax of decision writ upon his face.

His bearing makes him look similar to my father. It's not the way relations of close birth look similar, but a radiating mindset. The confidence showing in his features could border on arrogance to those who don't know him, but I've heard much of his reputation and have known him in different degrees my entire life. Lines of care crease his face when he greets us with a smile, especially upon seeing his daughter.

"Greetings, Prince Hart," he says. "Commander Nealy informed me you would be here to reinforce our capitol." I nod, and the commander turns to his daughter. "Claire, it is great to see you. This is a welcome surprise."

Claire bows in turn without moving for the embrace I expect she wants. Commander Lewis addresses me before I take the chance to return his greeting. "She told me you'd arrive earlier than you did. I trust you met no accidents on the road."

"Thank you for your warm welcome, Commander." I mean what I say as I look into his face and study the aspects that show when a strong character hides beneath the features. "No accidents, thankfully. I wanted to arrive with fresh troops." I look at Claire as I say this. Though a distance away, she hears my indirect compliment and blushes that a family member heard it. I like to praise where I can. Now more than ever it helps me regain my usual lightheartedness.

Commander Lewis looks too, and says, "Ah, she's a bold soldier indeed. Hopefully not as bold as me when I was her age. It can work, but doesn't always."

This mild allusion to his late wife June's Gift and subsequent death so early in our conversation could drag my mind into a mire of reproaches. I let it pass as an oversight and follow my compliment with another.

"Your daughter is no longer a soldier. She's an officer." I motion for her to join us.

Commander Lewis beams from his average height upon his daughter. "An officer, well, that's fine. Of course I always hoped for this. Is it Commander Nealy I have to thank for the honor done to my family?"

Claire answers after a glance to me, and I suddenly become aware of an uncomfortable sensation in my ribs like that following a hard run. "My captain here requested her to bestow it."

"Well, I like that. Your playmate growing up and now your officer. Keep your head on straight, don't turn aside for greed, follow your pare... your father's footsteps, and you'll be more than worthy to rule the kingdom."

I think I notice the slightest glimmer of sadness breaking through the confidence in his eyes. It's there for only a flash as he speaks, and seems to clear away with his next blink.

"A man can only do all he can," I say. "Nothing more. It's my earnest wish to keep the kingdom as my ancestors have."

Claire enters the conversation I invited her to and changes the subject from that of the late Queen. "Why are you dressed for battle, Father? Surely a messenger hasn't arrived by another path?"

"No messenger; later today I depart for the northern passes once again. It's more important to hold a strong defense there but I come back often since it's so close. The accounts we receive after important events don't adequately describe everything I need to know."

By 'important events', I take him to mean battles or skirmishes. "Do you partake in the campaigns each time?" I ask.

"Only some times," he says, then to Claire, "No need to worry, dear. I've managed alright in the field these last nine years."

His inability to stop referring to the past nettles me, but he shows impatience to start on his way so, by way of speeding him along, I remark, "I wish you well in the northern passes. Make sure we are bored here."

"I'll do all I can," he answers, laughing.

He moves on with his few attendants. I can't shake a feeling of respect despite the many unintentional painful references he made during our short conversation. Some would say the break Claire insisted upon helped my outlook more than I realized—they wouldn't be entirely wrong—but I think it has much to do with my renewed goodwill.

Several days slide by with me hardly regarding their passing. Duty keeps me busier than I'd like, but it passes time well, and I don't mind it today. Claire is around, and sometimes I work beside her. I try not to let her see it, but it brings me pleasure to know she's near. I repeatedly tell myself it's because I want to protect her the way a brother does, and always busy myself before I can argue with my conclusion.

One day, Claire invites me aside, and I follow her before I know why. By the time I realize the thicker doors and more polished stonework on the walls betoken our arrival in the royal apartments, she's led me down paths I recognize from nearly ten years ago. If my mind doesn't deceive me, these halls lead to her family's chambers, and I hang back as she beckons me into a room I think I recognize.

"I'm fine out here if you need to grab something," I say, lowering into a frown.

The door she halfway entered was her room the last I remember, and there's no way I'm following her in now. We were inseparable friends at fifteen, but at age twenty-eight....

"There's nobody watching," she says.

My frown fully overtakes my now-serious face, forming the barrier I deem best in this moment. "That makes no difference to me, and I'm surprised it does to you."

"What?" Her face alters into something of genuine confusion; a little like my frown, but with parted lips. After a few heartbeats it transforms into an open-mouthed, full-on smile that eradicates her inexplicable expression. "No! I really want to

show you something, and I'm not bringing it out." She fully
enters her room, and I hear the door swing closed by springs. It
doesn't latch.

Disarmed and confused, I stand motionless for a few
seconds. What is it about Clarie that makes me waver? When in a
battle or commanding my soldiers from afar I'm as decisive as
any, but with Claire... I've noticed I need time to think things
through. I shake my head to clear it, step the few yards to her
door, and push it open.

Wary, but grateful for her words moments ago, I walk
over the threshold to find recollection of the room flooding back
to me. It's like a bucket plunged below water; impossible to stop
the rush, but wanted anyway. A window at the far end floods the
room with light, and her tall clothes dresser rests on one side,
while the bed rests on the other. A few prized figurines rest along
the back of the dresser, and my mind flashes back to astonish me
with the remembrance that there are a few extra since my last
visit. They're on both sides of a clock—it's made of dark wood
like the one in Father's office, but less ornate. A comfortable-
looking chair sits nestled between a bookcase and small table,
and a door opens to another room. The room is larger than the
soldiers' rooms, and private, with even a bathroom all her own.

It's still the same room I remember visiting with Rafael
as children. With no chest or shelf in front of the window, I walk
to it and see the familiar view overlooking the courtyard. Towers
rising above the wall level attract my attention, as does the city,
but the mountains beyond positively capture all focus the
moment I turn to them. I had forgotten the draw this place always
held.

I turn from the window to find Claire standing beside the
bookcase. Unpleasant memories around our last times here
together come rushing back.

"How do you do it?" I ask."

"Do what?" She moves her hand from her side to rest it
on the bookcase.

"Manage to—" I sweep my hand around me to gesture to the whole room. "—to go on in a place that used to hold so much." *But now holds nothing.* I stop myself before saying those last words, but she realizes what my question means.

"I was here when I found out about Mother's death, but why does that mean I can't find life here again? Joy, even? We have to keep living our lives."

There's the difference between us; she would have kept our friendship alive after the trauma of death.

"It's hard for me to even see this room for your sake," I say. "I didn't know it would hit me so hard. I shouldn't have come."

I can hardly claim that my losses cut deeper, since she saw hers creeping closer. I don't know which would have been worse, and it doesn't matter; it happened, and she's working through it. I think I am, but... am I? Honestly?

"Wait." Her hand returns to her side as she steps forward to prevent me reaching the door. "I need to show you something. You can leave after that."

She moves past me to the dresser and opens the top drawer. Reaching in, she pulls out a bundle of tattered papers. It takes me a few seconds to recognize them. She flashes a few before me, and I remember most of them, as if ghosts from another life.

"You kept these?" I say as I unthinkingly reach for them after a silent minute. They're notes, scribbles, and drawings from our childhood. I recognize a few of my drawings, but mostly the words when I stop to read. It's comforting, and yet... not. Unpleasant isn't the word for it. I haven't tried to block out my childhood, so why do these disturb me? "Why are you showing me these?"

"I want to see the Chris I grew up with," she says. "I'd have you return to the smiling man I knew. You're still you; why can't you see it?"

I hand the stack of papers back to Claire and she accepts them like the treasures they are. I turn back to the window. The draw is still there, and almost compels my eyes to stare out across the landscape. I notice nature holds dominion despite the mark of mankind laid across the terrain. I press more weight to the ledge so I can lean out sideways. Underneath the wood frame for the shutters, the ledge slips away. I reel forward and catch myself by crashing an elbow to the side. Claire screams as she looks up to see me teetering on the edge for a second before I wrench myself back to balance.

"I'd forgotten about that; guess I'm heavier than you."

The attempted joke falls flat and she covers her mouth with her hand. My own heart still thunders from the brush with death. Pain roars to life as the agitation abates and I wince at moving my arm.

"At least it's not broken," I say as I push through the pain and test the joint. Claire reaches for my forearm and upper arm, but I recoil. I blanch in renewed pain at the sudden movement and nearly smash it into the wall again. No way is she touching me in here.

"Let me see," she says.

"You can see fine from there." No need to touch me now. Or here. Or ever. I'm not convinced she'll keep her hands to herself, so I try distraction. "I'd forgotten about that loose brick. It's even looser than I remembered."

"I haven't been able to open it in years," Claire says. She keeps her focus on my reddening elbow. "Won't you let me feel?"

Warning signals alert my brain, but if I raise my shields high enough, it wouldn't do harm. Still not ready to give in, I ask, "What good will that do?"

"I'm trained in healing arts as well as military strategy. I can feel if it's bad enough to need immobilization."

"I'll find that out within a few hours."

"You can find out within a minute, and heal faster, if you let me feel it."

I eye her with some skepticism before relenting. "Just until it hurts."

Her first touch on my arm produces a small shiver I hope isn't visible. The arm hurts like a sword-wound, and not a rock, inflicted the pain, so it's borderline torture to have her handling the joint so soon after injury. My mind knows it's necessary and good to have it checked so early, but that doesn't lessen the pain. Forget distracting her, now I need to distract myself.

"You haven't been able to open it in years?" I growl through gritted teeth.

I only get a truncated reply while she focuses on probing my arm. Gently, I know from the soft indents her small gorgeous fingertips make, but my throbbing arm doesn't know that. "Not since... no, I haven't."

It's a movable brick on the windowsill that Claire, Rafael, and I used to pass notes between each other when our family visited. It's in her room, so not an ideal spot to exchange secret messages, but it didn't stop us from make-believing we were crafty.

"Did we jam it?" I ask, trying to think back to my last time opening it.

"That doesn't seem possible," she says. "We were always careful." She keeps her focus on my arm, but glances over at it for the first time. "I think it's good; you'll feel alot better soon. Now let's take a look."

Her eyes flash and I jump between her topics to know she's again talking about the hollow brick. It's more interesting to her than I realized. Then again, if I knew about a secret compartment in my room for years, I'd want it opened as soon as possible.

"Why didn't you smash it open?" I ask. I'm glad she didn't, because I wouldn't have been able to participate, but I'm curious.

"I almost did a few times. It never seemed right. Disrespectful, almost, after everything that passed through it." She bites her lip before continuing with downcast eyes. "I thought maybe the gods locked me from it since we didn't need it anymore."

I didn't realize this was so sacred to her. I had reached for the brick, but now step back to let her have the honor. She pulls it open, and forces it past a catch I didn't totally break by leaning on it.

A document like a folded letter takes up much of the space in the tiny alcove. Claire reaches in and reveals other oddities around the edges that make me smile in remembrance. On the front of the letter, I double-take at the handwriting; that's Mother's writing. My pulse quickens as I watch Claire open the letter with her mother's name on it.

"It's from Queen Eilene," she says softly as she glances to the signature at the bottom.

My heart resumes the rapid beating it finally quit after I almost almost fell from the window, and continues as I hear Claire read words my mother penned some ten years before.

"June,

I cannot but use this opportunity to express my thanks for your helping the kingdom. Hearing your speak of his extra care in battle on your recent visit relieves me, and must have removed a heavy burden from your heart. We probably can never understand the extreme price you're both paying for the successes you deliver, and please, please don't think that means my husband and I appreciate it any less. We value your courage and I especially value your friendship. Thank you for using your Gift for good; King Laurence and I know what you could use it for it you chose. I pray you will mentor Christopher on how to use it well.

With the most grateful regard, Eilene Hart"

"My mother wrote that," I manage to say, all the pain in my arm seemingly disappearing as she read.

"There's more, and it's in another hand," Claire says. "I think it's *my* mother's writing."

I catch the smallest glance of words written in the margin before Claire reads again.

"Claire, I don't have time to write all I'd like. I must use my Gift again. I'm feeling old. If I survive you'll never see this letter because it will never have been written. I love you Claire. I love your father. If I die, it's from that love, not Chris's father's decision to keep it all. Don't hold a grudge about the Balm. June L."

We both sit silent for a minute while the import sinks in.

"It's the last thing she ever wrote," Claire says with a breaking voice. "Father survived, but only just. She didn't have enough years left to give up so she.... She couldn't come back for the letter."

She buries her face in her hands at thinking her mother may have died minutes after placing the letter for her beloved daughter.

My thoughts swirl as well, and even the throb of my prodded arm can't draw me from the reminiscence. *Don't hold a grudge about the Balm.* Was the Balm of Life such an important part of her family's bond where June used her last precious minutes of life including it in her letter to her daughter?

I remember vividly the visit my mother mentioned in her letter, at least I think I do. It was in the fall of that year, at the harvest festival, shortly before her death. The Lewis's visited as they had often, but this time was different, as it wasn't at the king and queen's request. Not that that itself was remarkable, for everyone can always travel as they wish in Elathon.

What made it memorable was the argument between our fathers. King Laurence and Julek talked of something in private.

When they came out, their flushed faces announced their argument to everyone. Even once they regained composure, which their wives retained the entire time, I could feel the tension radiating between them. Rafael told me a bit about what took place. He heard it second-hand, at least, so my account was several people removed. He said Julek wanted the Balm of Life our parents were keeping for my use, but Father wouldn't hear of it. It was for me, Rafael said Father insisted. *All* of it.

Our mother, Queen Eilene, and June Lewis, both held on to their emotions through the discussion, and even tried to calm their husbands, with June insisting she didn't need the Balm. The memory could be mismatched, but the whole Lewis family was there; Julek, June, and of course Claire. All my time was spent with Claire back then, and I now wish to the gods I had remained with the adults for that one visit. If I had, I might be able to shine some more light if this were the correct memory.

Correct memory or not for this situation, my mind flashes in sudden realization that it enlightens the letter more. My mother wrote it right after that visit, and it reads as much like a gratified thanks for received understanding as much as a letter to a good friend.

Then June reused it for a note about a year later. Was it the most convenient paper lying around for her to pen her last hasty words, or deliberately used as a backdrop for her dying note to Claire?

June's note in the margin proves she was anxious enough for her daughter's thoughts of my family to include it in her last words in this world. She wanted my parent's wish regarding The Balm of Life respected. Of that I don't doubt.

Reusing the letter to bear the parting message, though, confuses me. June wouldn't have lacked anything, especially writing-paper, so her reusing it seems deliberate. She must have hoped Claire remembered the visit, at that point one year prior, when she added to the missive.

Claire still has her face buried in her hands when I dare to ask, "Were you upset with my family at your mother's death?"

It's so uncomfortable, especially now, that it feels like I'm belching sand as the words come into the world. She's moving rhythmically, and I think she's crying lightly until after I finish speaking. Then I worry she's sobbing in the breathless, stormy fashion of extreme emotion.

"No; I never blamed your parents." Her voice is thick. She raises her face from her hands, and I'm relieved it's not totally distorted by tears. "I told you the other night, she died doing what she knew was right. She knew the risks, and didn't expect special favors."

"I didn't know she ever really believed that," I breathe.

After all the years of holding my shields up, this simple letter from an accidental time-capsule threatens to tear them down. Nine years ago Claire still wanted a friendship with me, but I used our distance apart, my grief, the need to train, stepping into Rafael's role, supporting the kingdom, or any other excuse that didn't matter until now to stay apart from her.

"Of course she did; I've tried telling you that for years but you wouldn't let me. And when I finally did, I thought you believed me."

The still-streaming tears make the hurt she finally realizes look even more intense. I could envision us back outside Kimbr's hall in the moonlight, but instead of sadness, pain issuing from her face innundates the room.

"Just because she believed she was doing the right thing doesn't mean everyone believed the same way," I say. As much as I try to save face, it's also a veiled way to ask about her father's feelings, partly because she alluded to his bitterness before, and her answer can tell me even more.

"Other people's feelings don't matter in this case; to keep going was her decision—"

"Her decision," I say, "but it affected more than her. Other people's feelings do matter here. *You* accepted it, but Julek didn't?"

"He... he mourned her." She again buries her face in her hands.

"As a widower should, but you've said he's still bitter?" The question, only of passing importance earlier, now cuts me deeper.

"I think so," she says. It's a whimper.

She sounds ashamed, and I'm tempted to match her shame with my own. The letter wasn't even meant for me, and here I am using it to interrogate her for her family's history. History that involves me and my family, but still, I calm my rising ire. Frustrated with myself for making her feel accused, I soften my tone, and change the subject to one that seems better.

"Why didn't my Gift work?" I can't believe I asked that either, and part of me wants to pull it back, but... I want to know. I *need* to know. "I could have saved my mother if I managed it."

"I never knew my mother's Gift to fail." She looks up, afraid she said something to rouse me again. I mask my earlier pain with an impassive expression. She softens anyway and continues, "She didn't talk about how to use it much. It almost seemed like she needed to stop it from happening, rather than forcing it into action."

Waiting for the Gift to just happen matches my own limited experience with it. I stopped it after three attempts at saving my mother, before it could steal years of my life in the fruitless attempt to save Rafael, and a few times since. Never did I stop to consider a pattern.

"You shouldn't stop trying just because it's hard," Claire says. "Especially with your stock of the Balm of Life." Her anger rises in turn, maybe from remembering her mother's sacrifice. Of course she thinks it was all in vain since I'm not even using it.

"You didn't know?" Disbelief at how far our gulf spans wishes over me as we stand together in her room. The way she gawks at me says more clearly than any words that she doesn't know what I'm talking about. "You didn't know that the Balm of Life was stolen?"

Her eyes widen. "No."

"How did—" I cut myself off before I can ask how she, as my good friend, couldn't have found out. It's my fault. The theft ten years ago isn't common knowledge, and I've all but ignored her since then. "It was stolen on the same day my mother died."

"Shadow Kings killed her for it?"

Her voice is low and serious. Not everybody knows this; evidently her father told her, or let her overhear it. I nod.

"Chris, she died to give you extra chances. The Chris I grew up with and the Chris I've seen the past two weeks isn't one to avoid something due to fear."

"It's not fear of losing a few years that troubles me, it's that it didn't work three times in a row; the most important three times a fifteen-year-old could ask for. Something about it doesn't work for me. It's almost like I'm not truly Gifted," I say. I feel stuck underwater, though the birds chirp outside the window overlooking the gatehouse, and crowd my other senses. "And even if I am Gifted, you saw what happened to your poor mom; it's always one more day; one more year; a favor only you can grant; a battle only you can win. I loved your mother too, Claire, nothing like your love for her I know, but I still did, and I don't want what happened to her to happen to me." My voice rises while I'm speaking, but not from anger or defense, but because I'm slipping again into hurt.

"It'd be an honor to give that for the kingdom," Claire says, holding her own emotions down as I let mine run wild.

I shake my head. "My father's been able to keep the kingdom standing on its own merits the last nine years. If I can't continue the strong legacy he'll hand down then I don't deserve to be king one day."

"No, I mean.... I'd still—"

A horn sounds from outside and stops her comment.

We both turn aside at the strange interruption. Mounted soldiers ride down the road toward the castle.

I turn toward Claire with the question on my lips also showing on my face. "Is that—?"

"Father?" Claire answers. "What's he doing back?"

Her trained eyes must also see what I instantly notice. He's riding fast with a large company after him. It looks like everyone who rode out two days ago is in the group. That might comfort some, but I'm an experienced enough soldier to know they wouldn't ride back to the castle when their express intent was to strengthen the passes already held by his forces.

Shielded anger, fear, indignation, hope, and mortification alternatively filled my chest as we stood in Claire's room. Now curiosity overrules everything and I rush into the hall with her trailing. She comes up beside me before we reach the first door, where we meet up with a few officers. They're still discussing possibilities for the summer campaign.

The two soldiers I destroyed in the ring at Sapesky walk toward the gathering crowd. They look intimidated among the real officers and guards.

"Please don't treat him poorly for feeling hurt," Claire whispers as we walk toward Julek and his surrounding guard.

I look in her eyes for a second. "I wouldn't think of it."

Her even thinking she needs to say that irks me, but her father's early reappearance causes more consternation than any old grudge right now.

Much of Commander Lewis's company is with him, and, after gathering close, I hear what I dreaded: the Guldeth drove him back.

"We were ambushed in the foothills," he announces to the group of gathered officers and soldiers. "Apparently they've overran the northern passes already."

My thoughts overtake my ears for a moment. The northern passes overran? Driving the companies from the fortress of Balruvia there would take a concentrated effort. Commander Nealy was right; they are moving forces north.

The thoughts pass from my mind, and I listen again. "—didn't even run across a rider to warn us; their positions were outflanked and Balruvian soldiers outside the walls had to flee either north or south into the mountains."

That can only mean that the Guldeth are close on his heels. It means the enemy will arrive soon, but also that there won't be any reinforcements.

"We're on our own," Commander Lewis says, matching my thoughts. Everyone springs to attention like they each sat on a fire.

"How is Balruvia?" someone asks.

"I've only had minimal contact with some soldiers there," Commander Lewis responds, "and they didn't mention it falling. I hope Nymunia grants it may hold out until we can succor it." He clicks his tongue to his horse and it canters through the crowd.

Claire looks between me and Julek, as if she doesn't know who to attach herself to during the crisis. Her father removes any awkward accusations of favoritism by issuing me orders. He grants her a tight-lipped smile fitting for the serious occasion before riding away to find more captains.

I lead my officers to the northern gatehouse and begin assigning them to various roles. I delegate ones to amass and double-check weapons, gather their soldiers, bring basic bandages and water, and let everyone know their posts. They all know I'll join wherever the fighting is fiercest.

Claire I assign to the top of the gatehouse. With her tactical training, I'll rely on her to inform me in advance of enemy movements. In the midst of battle, I know I need eyes aloft to watch the surroundings for me. I'm a trained tactician, but I know from experience I'll lose myself in the fray more than my soldiers will need.

I leave Claire after I impart my full assurance of trust. She looks slightly nauseous, as are all who don't stay an unthinking level of busy with preparations before a battle, but I don't expect to see much fighting. It will be at least a week before they attack in any force, if this is truly their destination. Some fighting along the walls perhaps, but surely none for her in the overlook.

Chapter 8.

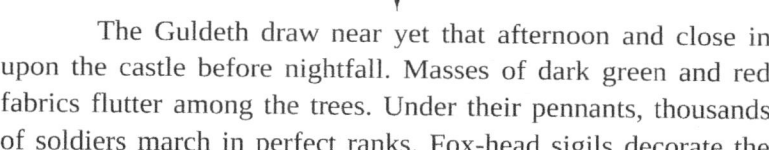

The Guldeth draw near yet that afternoon and close in upon the castle before nightfall. Masses of dark green and red fabrics flutter among the trees. Under their pennants, thousands of soldiers march in perfect ranks. Fox-head sigils decorate the larger banners and the tunics of anyone officer or above.

Commander Lewis keeps everyone almost as busy as him with preparations, no doubt the anxiety of losing the northern passes troubling his mind. He knows better than anyone but the missing captains what the defenses could withstand, and the inability to know the true fate gnaws at his mind.

He keeps a placid appearance so well that even the newest cadet could tell he's experienced leading thousands of soldiers innumerable times.

The spring evening provides us with a long golden progression to the gloaming. It's a surreal feeling watching it over the heads of an encamped army. The Guldethian force encircled Myceum as soon as they arrived and I'm scrambling to prepare for what looks like an assault planned without delay; the soldiers gather in bunches too exact for the chance groupings that naturally form in large groups of people.

My officers notice this also and send me word of the happening from their particular quarters. The storm should break by midnight. I'm extra grateful Claire had me stop for rest before we reached the city, especially since the ground before our walls is a stable place for ladders. It's a rocky ascent for them to reach our walls. When they finally do reach the wall, though, ladders won't topple easily.

I hear archers wagering down the line.

"I'll fall more than you, bet you three."

"You should bet more than that the way you missed the haypile earlier."

"The wind took it. I'll bet five."

"Looks like I'm about to become a richer man."

Once the darkness is complete, the enemy begin their assault. They weren't waiting for darkness for any reason I can tell, since they have more torches than we do; it simply seems the soonest they can manage it.

They're using the most primitive method of assaulting a castle: ladders. My heart rate increases at the bloodbath they'll endure with this tactic, but I can't say I feel sorry for them; the number of soldiers before our walls makes even me feel queasy. This isn't only my feeling; dozens of soldiers around are either hunched over with labored breathing or actually vomiting over the walls. Officers are racing between soldiers with herbs for them to chew, and I pick up a shred as an officer drops some in her rush toward cadets on my other side.

Peppermint. I chew up the few leaves, and let their faint taste swirl in my mouth to relieve the feeling. My stomach eases the churning motion and lets me think straight. Quick thinking on my officer's part to have that ready; I'm glad they had peppermint growing in the castle gardens. If you grow some, you grow too much every year after and it comes in handy now. I remember the special walled garden my mother always loved tending to in Sapesky.

Their war chant reaches a deafening pitch and drums lash the air. The sounds combine into a fearful cacophony meant to turn a soldier's blood to water.

Claire will give the signal for archers; I glance up and see her with hair braided tight and tucked in a neat coil close to her scalp. A few loose strands missed the gathering braid, and those gleam in the low sun of evening. My stomach's stopped bothering me, but now something's wrong with my heart; it's fluttering like I'm already fighting for my future kingdom.

She turns aside and meets my gaze for a long moment. I always hold a steady gaze with people. Everyone, that is, expect Claire. Over the past few weeks I've struggled to meet her eyes full-on. Not this time, though. This time feels different. I don't know what it is, but this can't be rushed, can't be stopped as much as I want to. This feeling in my heart—it's been so long since I've felt it—it's been absent for a decade.

A loud horn penetrates the shouting ranks of the Guldeth and Claire turns to face outward again. Seconds later she screams a command to our waiting soldiers and, in near-perfect unison, a hundred arms raise a hundred readied bows before them. With one motion, our soldiers draw the strings in their hands to their shoulders and pause for an instant before Claire barks another order.

"Fire!"

The rushing, hissing sound lasts for an instant before the deadly messengers slam into enemy forces with devastating effect. Chests become like pincushions, arms and legs useless. The disarray lasts only a moment, and they're coming toward us again. Volley after volley Claire calls into the evening, and some score of them fall with each, but on they come, undeterred by their comrade's screams.

At other points of the wall, I see archers called to action and start to hear cries from those directions. Thank Lesasil Commander Lewis didn't empty his castle for the defense in the mountains, I think as I turn back to give my full concentration to my forces.

Claire's calling the archers; many of the ladder-bearers fall to her direction, but we can't stop them all with arrows. The first ladders start to rise and the shouting of directions from atop our walls combine with the screams of the wounded below. It almost makes my orders blend into the confusion, but I've trained my voice from the unheard timidity of my youth into carrying a great distance over other noises.

"Fight well for your lives. An attack so swift won't leave room for mercy."

Even the newest soldiers in the regiment know my voice from the past several hours of preparations. It's met with a hearty cheer as the first Guldeth atop are sliced from their ladders.

I watch more ladders rise between the battlements, and still more. Dozens fill the spaces atop the walkway and, when knocked down, another rises into its place shortly after.

I've looked over walls after an unsuccessful attack left hundreds dead around a castle. My face, though passive as I try to block out the screams coming from all around, hides a deep sadness. It always overcomes me for a few seconds before drawing my own sword in battle. Such a waste. So much thrown away.

Officer Mariana Brown, who accompanied me to gather the reinforcements, stands beside me now, as I'm at her section of the wall. She's surrounded by her soldiers and looks as cool as I know I do. Inside, though, I'm sure she's a tangle of emotions

"Good thing we can't see far enough to know what's down there," I say.

Mariana gives a tight-lipped smile in acknowledgement and nods once; she's seen a battle's aftermath, too. "Always something to be grateful for."

"We have the walls," I say to continue her line of thinking. I hadn't realized I'd started it, and had forgotten back to the northern Spruce Duchy when we first alternated encouragement. We were both soldiers then, and now here we are; her an officer and me her captain, fighting for our lives with some of the same words we used all those years ago.

Seeing points of our line break from the initial resistance, I know this is my time to enter the fray. Mariana jumps for another enemy. I'm confident we're both better for our brief contact. The enemy pushes forward and I join the second wave of defense. I know that once they make it this far, the battle will only end when there's a victor. There's always another section of wall to defend, another soldier needing comfort or aid, or another request for reinforcements to meet.

I engage the first soldier, a thick, grizzled man with dark hair and a wind burnt face after he lands a cut on one of my soldiers. He's one of the first atop the ladder, and lived to reach us. That, and his age, mean he's a capable fighter. My soldier steps aside with blood dripping, making the leather armor a darker brown, and I thank Nymunia that she'll be alright.

He thrusts and I duck aside with the extra agility my lighter frame gives me. Then I carve up his forearm under a slip in the armor and make him howl in pain. I plow my shoulder into another foe to give the soldier against him an advantage, then spin around to meet his eyes as he comes forward again. He wasn't expecting such a challenge from an opponent my age, but I look even younger than I am, even with the Gift's effects, so he has another thing coming if he thinks I'll die easily.

I switch up my tactic and fake a few thrusts while dodging his strong swings. I'd hate to get in the way of that sword, even if it hit full armor. I bide my time for the right moment. Every second I fight him means I can't fight another, but I also know I need to show myself a continuous presence to our soldiers until the moment arrives. It comes in the form of a new soldier, hardly off the farm from my estimation, shoved between us. He almost falls across the sword and, had the last slash come from the other direction, I think it would have split him in half.

Out of pure reaction I grab the soldier's arm and continue his momentum, throwing him to the stone floor, but out of harm's way. I catch the next swing. Flecks of blood from the deep cut in his arm splatter my blue tunic. I shift my sword from the flat end to the edge and go for his throat while at the same time protecting mine from his. We both survive and he makes to draw away but I press the attack. I'm within his guard now and determined to keep my advantage.

I aim to smash my pommel to his chin, which he dodges, but not far enough; it ends with a scrape from the cross-guard across his neck. The blow knocks his breath away for a second, and I move around to finish him when something strikes me between the shoulders. It's an errant elbow from another duel, and I fall into him as he reels backward from the cross-guard slash to send us both tumbling to the floor. He's recovered his breath enough despite the fall and rolls to cover me, which I know would mean instant death. I exert all the strength my fervor gives me to continue the momentum and roll his bulk enough off me. I twist on the ground for a mere second before I bound up again, then slam my sword down into him before I even reach my feet.

Life drains from him, that battle-tested soldier, and I draw a long knife from his belt before I shove him off the back side of the wall with my boot. Good to keep the walkway clear for fighting.

I stop by the prostrate form of the soldier I saved and reach to help him up. Amazement melds with the fear in his eyes, and I wonder for a space if this is his first time seeing a real battle.

"Come on," I say with a glance at him, "there's a dozen more of those to get through."

We start to run the few steps toward the fighting, which moved on over the past minute, but I stop him short. There's something wrong with his mouth, and it's not blood, it's... green.

"You're..." I start, then smile. "You've got enough excitement now to keep you going; no need to risk choking on mint leaves."

He spits the soggy pulp out, then smiles. It's as much this reason as the actual combat that I stay and fight with my soldiers.

The tower still stands strong in our hands. I glance up to see Claire overtop the raging battle. She shouts something above the din and points. A dozen archers with her loose their yard-long arrows as rapidly as possible. She'll be okay, and it's my job to keep her free to feed information down so I can make decisions. And to keep her safe; can't let anything bad happen to her.

Several hours and grueling fatigue later, the Guldeth are fighting with such a reckless abandon I begin to quiver. It's an emotion I haven't felt in a long time: fear. Their utter disregard for their lives makes this feel like a different enemy than I ever experienced in the Dendring Mountains. They hurl themselves at me in a wild attempt to wrest my life away. I cut down one after another. I glance around in the single moment before my next foe presses on and see my soldiers under the same circumstances. Knowing I'm not targeted doesn't comfort me as much as it should, and a palpable fear makes my breath come in desperate gasps.

We have to regroup from our area after the attack grows too intense. First we crowd the base of our gatehouse, but even there our resistance crumples at the constant barrage of fresh steel. Our weary, thinning ranks can't hold. They drive us back toward the larger force to seek help from other companies.

I take an opening and rush between two foes, one of whom didn't even carry a weapon over the battlements with him. They both fall to my blades before I can register this. I've released my short dagger as it stuck in bone rather than waste time prying it free.

Their onslaught speaks of a desperate target. More desperate than if Whiteneck's whip was at their backs, I think. The natural aversion to the point of a sword and spilling their own blood seems the only thing stopping them from leaving themselves open to our blades. Not that they're really throwing their lives away, but the careless manner and brute power they send against the city makes me question the goal. Either they don't recognize me, want someone else, or... what? They can't start such a mad struggle for nothing.

We pull back again into the town, and even defend some of the castle grounds, gardens, and outbuildings, but they're pressing us closer all the time. We manage to turn the tide for a few moments as the archers still surviving atop the towers turn their fire to rain death upon groups of foes thinking buildings provided them shelter.

I doubt anybody fought harder or more desperately to turn the tide back in our favor than me. I was at the far side of my defensive area when it came, the crushing surge that overran the northern gate and allowed the Guldeth entry. A dozen times I thought my heart would beat no more, but my sword found a way to block even the most hopeless parry. The heaviest fighting always happened right where I was, or I found my way there. The breach coming in my area galled me and I risked my life more than I should have to try and check their advance.

Towards morning, with my soldiers weary enough I fear they'll drop from fatigue if not Guldethian blades, I admit something I've known for a few hours: Myceum will fall. I'm on the point of preparing to send a messenger to Commander Lewis when a soldier, a woman, young, with brown hair and brown eyes stops breathless before me. Upon meeting my eyes, she straightens from her gasping posture. Her tired eyes and drawn face show in the unsteady glare of the long-burning torch. My heart falls a bit when I see her, because the hair isn't the right shade of brown.

"Sir, it's officer Lewis."

Concern for Claire ripples through me as I glance up to the tower. Of course she's not there anymore; the Guldeth forced us from our foothold there over an hour ago. Other figures keep watch on a few other towers we still occupy, but I see few women in my hasty glance around.

Hope clings to the thread of spirit I'm still retaining after a sleepless night and dreadful butchery, then dies as the soldier continues with a face as white as those who fell, "She said she's sorry, sorry it happened in your area."

I don't make a quick enough answer, or maybe there's some look hidden on my face her nervous mind conjures into anger, so she keeps talking. "Our officer, Your Majesty. She said she was sorry for the loss."

Around us the sounds of battle still rage in our ears; rending leather armor, gasping cries for help, screams of fresh pain, and the constant snap of steel on steel. It's only now that I recognize the soldier from back in Sapesky: Elara Ronrout. I care equally for all my soldiers, and I should be relieved she's survived, but... my heart surges as I wait to hear about Claire.

"Where is she?" I ask, making my voice sound more gruff than natural so she doesn't misplace my affection, though my heart shivers inside its cage of bone.

"Over there." Elara points to the base of the last tower I saw her at. Though I can't see beyond the struggling mass of suffering soldiers, I start forward to bring a rescue, then stop, understanding what she means.

"Is she..." I barely manage to whisper.

Elara lowers her eyes.

My heart moves even slower as I relive the moments I shared with Claire over the past few weeks; recognizing her holding her own during our training sessions on the marches, seeing her across the table in Mt. Cabrae, even running from her to clear my head, as if to free my mind. Now she grips my heart tighter than ever.

"How?" I ask Elara. "And when?"

"Two crossbow bolts. Perhaps an hour ago." She hands me the bolts with a thrill of shiver. "Oh, gods, how will I ever sleep again?" she sobs with her eyes working into wide, dry, spheres with no tears unshed. She gestures to the soldiers struggling against each other a dozen yards away. "The screams. Their faces. I don't know what I even did; the training took over and I'm... here. Alive. I'm...."

She breaks down in dry convulsive tears again. I didn't want the bolts, but she needed them out of her hand. The ones that killed Claire. Her hair, her eyes, her smile. Never to light the world again. I choke on nothing.

Too overcome with nausea to take time for her plight, I grab her by the arm and start to run. My duty to warn the commander takes over and makes me move instinctively. My mind rages with an inward tempest as I race among the timber and thatch buildings to reach Commander Lewis's position.

It smells awful here, even though the bodies are still stiffening. The reek comes from blood; enough of the iron scent to intoxicate the air is the most abominable smell I've come across. It infiltrates the body, steals courage, and leaves a soldier wrecked if they dwell on it.

We come to where I see Commander Lewis's banner fluttering and I throw myself into the fray. Elara follows me, even though I released her arm almost as soon as I grabbed it. Her mind, like mine, started to clear once we had something concrete to do and we use that focused energy to find the Commander. He's shouting orders and encouragement to the soldiers in front of him, but the blood splattered across his person and the cuts across his tunic show he hasn't been a stranger to combat this night. He's losing ground as well and there are too many Guldeth within the walls before him to hold much longer.

"Commander," I say, almost shouting to make myself heard over the nearby fighting, "I've lost the northern gate and they're through; they'll be on your back within an hour."

His eyes flare in rage. I'm not a timid man so I don't shrink back. I wanted so badly to say that *we've lost the gate*, or *my officers didn't hold*, but my strong mind kept me honest in this extremity and now I see through the fire clouding his concentration that the storm will break on me.

"You've lost the gate? I trusted you, second son of King Laurence, with critical defense of *my* castle. You're even more pathetic than he is!" It's a spitting mix of fury and indignation, and all stings out in a constant volley, even the frustration I know he'd be feeling at his own failing defenses. "We're not all able to watch from our throne while others do the *real* work. The *slaughter* that *makes* a kingdom!"

He's drifting rapidly into dangerous territory, and the rage foaming up in spittle on the corners of his mouth disgusts me. He's too experienced to show complete loss of control.

"Even to the slaughter of our loved ones; ones too honorable to hide behind ranks of thousands," he says. "I hope to Xulbris that whoever let that happen fell unrecognizable with spear wounds. A burial in ravens' bellies would be too good for them."

The glare he levels on me would fix another as with the spear he calls upon so readily. His blood-splattered face and foam-flecked lips heighten the expression of madness surging over his countenance. If only he knew he said that about his daughter. I wanted to tell him of the loss, and knew this would be hard, though I expected a reception better than this.

How do you tell a man who's already lost his wife and is losing his castle that he already lost his only child? My mind stormed along channels when I rushed to his position yet managed to avoid thinking through this. I've stood against a dozen and come through, but never told a powerful man he's lost *everything*.

"Commander, Claire didn't—" I try before he cuts me off.

"She'll turn this around or be forever cursed. You Hart's can't make a big enough blunder to stop the Lewis's prowess. Your father didn't and you can't, though he *stole* my wife from me. Out with you; die as your first victim if you can't remedy your mistake!"

Conversation over, and Elara shrunk back a dozen paces with gaping mouth and face flushed with fear, I turn back to my regiment with even more emotions swirling than before. It only takes a minute of running to meet up with them. It appears they began a retreat shortly after Elara and I went with the message for Julek. It'll become a rout soon.

Blades shining like rubies hack left and right. Soldiers I've known for years fall before my eyes and they fall with heart-wrenching screams, each of which sends a stab of pain through my heart as if I'm feeling the blade there. It's my officers, my soldiers, and my friends, falling to a mad craze.

I bellow above the din and soldiers flock to muster behind me. We have a momentary respite, and I take it.

"Archers near the front," I say. "Between pikes and shields."

While the pike soldiers hold the onrush back for a few moments, the archers strain their backs, shoulders, and arms one last time on my word and a crush of arrows tears through every bit of exposed armor the enemy present as they collapse on our makeshift wall. The flash of feathers behind the arrows, the dull thrum of steel arrowheads plowing their way through armor, flesh, bone, and armor again, screams, cries, coughing, gurgling, and all manner of macabre sights. It's grim music, intoning death notes on the harp of the underworld. Sometimes cadets come to the front thinking combat is glorious, but the sensory nightmare that follows extinguishes any romantic notions of battle.

A moment after the discharge I give the order to retreat. Attempting to press our advantage would only lead to death, perhaps for all; they're a stronger force, both in number and in proportion of fresh troops. Their commanders order, and their soldiers willingly throw themselves into hopeless situations with the evident purpose of selling their lives dearly.

Our retreat leads us toward Captain Ellie Silver's regiment; she's pressed hard, but less so than mine or Julek's position, and I know the reception we'd receive with the Commander.

My soldiers and officers rush by in a flash and I follow once they're all past. We haven't run far before I hear someone running at my heels. One glance back shows me it's three enemy soldiers, and I whip around to face them while yelling "Keep going" to my retreating officers.

My sudden resistance surprises the enemy and my blade finds flesh. One down and two to go, but dozens a score of paces behind close in fast. I throw myself between them with my sword swung back so far it's near my heels then bring it around in an arc over my body. It splits them both across the face; one with an upstroke, and one with a downstroke and ends the fight as quick as I need it to.

My feet scatter a storm of dirt and I manage to outpace the surge of reinforcements. Claire's mother's private garden is around the next corner. I throw my sword over the wooden wall, jump for the top, and wrench myself, weight of armor and all, into what I think is safety. I'm in the act of throwing myself down when I notice that it's far from safety; one would think it a scaffold.

Hip and elbow breaking my fall, I land beside my sword and jump to my feet as if I hadn't plummeted three yards onto my side. I stand in readiness as I survey the scene before me. It's filled with Guldethian soldiers, all facing away from me, and then I notice Oruvian soldiers standing in a line before a man in the tunic of an enemy captain.

"June! June!" the enemy captain screams into the soldier's face. She's white from fear and trembling before his anger. "Lady Lewis or you'll get it like them!"

I see for the first time a scattering of beaten Oruvian soldiers.

"She's dead," the soldier manages hoarsely, her throat damaged by ill treatment and thirst.

"She's not dead! She can't have died already!" the captain screams and raises a heavy oak stave. His first blow hits her head and she collapses. "Ugh, it's a ruse. Bring another one."

This can't be happening; nobody fights battles like this, not even the Guldeth. I've fought them enough to know that even though we disagree, basic dignity isn't questioned. Other than the captain, the soldiers look as sick as I feel. The captain sticks the heavy club in the face of the next soldier hauled for interrogation, trying to cower him.

"Her garden; we're not as dumb as you think we are. How badly do you want out?"

"They all wanted out," the soldier says while jerking his head to his limp companions. "I could lie about her being alive, but you'd find out eventually. Then what good would it do?"

The raging captain screams his hatred. The soldier grits his teeth and slams his eyes. It's not a club this time and I hear the sickening crunch of an armored fist hitting flesh. A few more follow and the defenseless soldier collapses, still conscious, blood rushing from his mouth and nose.

It's only now the shock wears off enough that I manage to force my body into activity. I scream my own anger into a consuming flame and drive forward with my own blade ready. I pass everyone as I rush forward. It's not the soldiers' fault, not entirely, and I'm after their captain. He's weaponless, and I normally don't kill defenseless people, but in my fury I don't consider this monster a person. Any claim he once had to human dignity went with his spirit to that pile. My sword sticks into his neck and I kick his body over to speed his collapse.

The Oruvian soldiers behind me startle and, I think, grab for weapons to assist their rescue. Doesn't matter. I'd take on the score of Guldeth locked in here with me any day after seeing what they did and were doing to my countrymen. Anger burns so hot in my chest that I'm lusting for something else to kill. One isn't enough; it can't atone for the flash of what I saw. Anything. Anything I need to do to stop this madness, and I'll do it.

I wait for what feels an eternity on the once-soft green floor of June's garden, where Claire, Rafael, and I played as children, every inch of it now trampled. My vision dips in and out as my blood runs chill for a space before heating to a steaming pitch. I make a run at my first victim and my knees falter, stopping me with a dizziness that's new and yet familiar.

My vision goes again, and I feel the anger ready to spill into tears. I blink them back with my eyes unseeing the world before me, and I fall.

Chapter 9.

The falling sensation continues even after my vision comes back into focus. I reel forward and see the castle courtyard below as my body thrashes instinctively to keep from plummeting down. Close beside me I hear a woman scream, and I somehow know it's Claire. I catch myself on the window ledge and turn to look at her, standing beside her dresser with her hand over her mouth, clutching the stack of our childhood memories she saved.

What a time to come back to, I think as my elbow screams with the relived pain.

"I should have waited another minute," I say, trying a joke.

Claire looks at me, clearly not thinking it's humorous. "What do you mean?"

"Another minute to..." I start, then gesture to the window frame I'd like to decimate. The brick isn't loosened as much as last time. "If I'd waited I wouldn't have hit my arm again."

She turns her head a finger's-breadth to the side like a hawk, then glances down at my arm. "Let me see it."

"No, it's fine; I know you're a healer and all that but there's no time for it now. Your father's going to return any moment, and we need to get out of here."

"What are you talking about? He's at Balruvia by now."

"He's returning in a few minutes—" I pause, and turn to look out the window. "Yes, see him there?" I point and Claire follows my gaze into the extreme distance. They're only specks now, imperceptibly moving along the road toward the castle, but my experience proves I'm not mistaken. "That's Commander Lewis with his soldiers fleeing the Guldeth. They're going to set upon Myceum tonight."

"We've hardly been apart all day, and now you're telling me they're close enough to attack us during the night. Why are you bringing that up now?"

Her reluctance startles me; I thought everything I'd say would be taken on faith. Startled or not, I can't wait here any longer; I need to get down there to meet Julek. Claire follows me as I start from her room and catches up as I stop at a random door and throw it open.

Officers sitting at a table look as I interrupt their conversation. They're talking about plans for the summer campaign, but I need them ready for action.

"Down to the courtyard right away; this is important."

"How did you know they were in there?" Claire asks.

We pass a small group of cadets and emerge from the dim passage to the bright courtyard. The sun temporarily blinds us as we walk to the center amid the sound of a horn announcing Julek's arrival.

"I just knew."

The officers emerge, looking confused at my calling them before hearing the horn. We don't have to wait long before we hear the galloping hooves slow before the gate, then see the soldiers, led by Commander Lewis, entering the courtyard. The sight of him sitting in his fine robes, when I know they were all but mangled into bloody wrappings before my help, raises a prickling sensation at the back of my neck.

"What news, Commander?" I ask for everyone's benefit.

He sits atop his great warhorse, and I can't help but remember the words he spoke before I reversed the day. A single sentence could have swung him from a gibbet. Of course he won't remember them, I think. It'll be strange going forward.

"The Guldeth overran us in the foothills. Apparently a vast effort is taking our northern passes."

I'm in front this time, so he addresses me and I direct the conversation. "How about Balruvia?"

"With my slight contact with some fleeing soldiers I don't think so," Commander Lewis says. "They struck so ferociously our forces were outflanked and had to flee north or south. I pray Nymunia grants the fortress may hold out until we can aid it."

"You said there was a concentrated effort on our positions; is there a pursuit?"

"Yes," he says, and eyes me in a disdainful way that strikes me as how I should be looking at him after his unremembered words. "Only a few hours behind at most." His look is worlds different than the first time. As if... as if he remembers something of his words.

Pandemonium ensues, somehow more intense than last time, and I note how most officers behave the exact way as the time before. Claire's looking at her father for guidance, but he gives me the same orders as last time, smiles at his daughter, and continues assigning captains to different posts.

I head for the northern gate with all my officers following. Claire hangs close, and I can tell she wants to speak with me, so I wait to issue her orders. "You wish to talk, I take it."

She does, and wastes no time. Her face over the last fifteen minutes foretold her mind working feverishly, and I almost know the question before it passes her lips.

"Did you use your Gift?"

I nod.

"That's why you've been aching so strange; I never guessed you'd actually try it again."

I scrunch my nose a bit at her comment, but she's too happy to notice my reaction.

"Now we know you do have the Gift. Not even an hour ago you were questioning how you'd know; now you do."

I hope her jubilation lasts; mine is nonexistent. Despite all the years I'd spent ignoring my Gift, I'd still wondered what it'd feel like from time to time. The lackluster feelings I'm experiencing now don't come close to what I let myself imagine. I hoped I'd feel invincible, amazing, godlike. None of those come to my chest now; only an unexplained emptiness.

"What made you use it?" she asks, turning back to me in her excitement.

There's so much I could say. Looking back, I don't know if there was any one thing that made me try my Gift again. I wanted to save Claire's life. I wanted to reverse what her father said of her and me, and to forget it even happened. I wanted to save Myceum, and the soldiers and citizens. I wanted to find a reason for the attack. With so much to say, I don't know what I should, and decide on the most explainable answer.

"Myceum fell in the upcoming assault." Her eyes widen. "The worst of the attack came along the northern walls and that's where they entered."

"Fell? When?"

"I only came back one day."

I can read fear in her expressive eyes as plainly as words in a book. It's a short time for a mighty city to fall.

"You didn't tell Father?" she breathes, unable to fathom my withholding it when we just saw him in the courtyard.

How could I tell her what Julek said to me? My reversing the day made it as if it never happened, and yet... I can still see the bulging veins in his neck as he yelled accusations of cowardice at me, prince of his lands and sole heir to the throne; can still hear every hurtful inflection and feel the injurious emphasis used with the words; can still see all the surroundings as he unjustly tried to trample my name on the blood-splattered courtyard in the midst of a battle.

I know what he said of her. She can't know what passed, and I don't want her to. What happened that day is my burden to bear, and I'm meant to change the outcome without dwelling on what could happen again.

Loneliness has been the hardest part of the hour I've relived. Nobody else remembers the events. Only their vague emotions.

"No, I... I... It's more complicated than that," I say.

Surely her mother experienced this with her Gift. Oh, if only she were alive to mentor me, like my own mother requested in that letter. She could make the process easier.

"More complicated? If the city's going to fall he needs to know so we can change tactics. He and Mother used that strategy so many times; what else do you think she used her Gifted days for to die when she was really so young?"

Everyone's always known she used her years to help lead Oruvia to victories through her husband's influence. They worked together, with June often accompanying her husband into battles. She was trained to fight, as are all Oruvians, even those not joining the army, but never participated in combat. Her Gift was deemed too valuable to let her expose herself to danger. For a time, the king wanted me apart from fighting as well.

"For battles," I say. "Nothing else; everybody in the kingdom knows her legacy, and by extension, yours."

Claire holds a lot of sway with the soldiers, and it was partly from observing this that I based my recommendation of her advancement to officer. Officers need to be competent and effective, but just as important is their likeability. Perhaps it gives weight to the other qualities. Based on what I've seen and heard, she's all those things.

"Her great reputation holds up to time partly because of me," Claire says while her light hair wafts with each slight movement, "but mostly because of my father. The work they did together solidified your father's efforts to keep the remains of the kingdom intact after the Divide. May I tell him about it?" she asks.

Half of me wants to call Julek out for his words, but I've already decided to keep it a secret. Besides, he didn't really say them, at least not as it now stands, so I can't really call him out. I could tell Claire, but do I really want to sow those seeds?

I want to handle all this myself, but this isn't my castle, so I finally soften.

"That might be good."

"I will. You say they attack heaviest on the northern gate here?"

I nod. She turns to find her father, but stops short and turns back to me.

"Anything else I should tell him?"

If he doesn't change tactics he'll not only lose the city, but his daughter, too. Though I don't know if I can bear having her report that to him. I'm about to open my mouth when she saves me the trouble of making the decision.

"The northern gate isn't the most naturally important place to defend. Who was assigned to defend it?"

"You were." I never lie, and don't make an exception here, even though I know it's likely to lead to another question where I *will* want to lie.

"And... I didn't manage to defend it?"

It's a blow to her pride as the child of a commander, but I have to answer. "No; they attacked in a strange fashion and got lucky."

"Did I die?" she asks with an excitement that takes me aback. "I died, didn't I?"

"Yes." I say, enunciating the one syllable as slow as I can, unsure what her next reaction will be.

A look, almost happy, crosses her face for an instant before she blushes and glances aside then back at me for a moment. She doesn't say anything, and before I can register this strange event, she's left to find Julek. I watch her retreating steps with a strange feeling in my chest.

Since I don't want to sit around waiting for her to come back and the Guldeth to draw nearer, I see to my personal weapons. The officers handle their own jobs well, and I don't like to insult them by checking on their progress, so I drift. Of all places to wander, I find my steps drawn imperiously to the scene of interrogation in the garden. Two soldiers guard it for the reigning family out of respect for June, so I draw away. I could lift my rank above their heads to frighten them into letting me pass, yet I've worked hard for my reputation. Claire can enter, and even at my recoiling from having to ask her for help, I know it's what I need to do.

With my steps now bent toward Commander Lewis's Commander's Room, it doesn't take me many minutes to reach the door. I've decided to wait for Claire in the hall. After all, seeing Julek in my frame of mind wouldn't do anything to strengthen his apparently strained relationship with the king. I'd probably snap at him.

"Did he finally use it?" says a voice.

I recognize it from Commander Lewis, roughened by years of leading soldiers in combat. A momentary pause, and my mind fills the space with imagining Claire's nod.

"Curse his Gift; it's about time, that coward," the rough voice continues. "Uhhh, I suppose it's for the best, even if he should have been using it for a decade. Some people don't know what they've been given." He pauses again for half a minute and my thoughts unsuccessfully try to pierce the door to find out what's going on in the silence. "I'll let him adjust his strategy how he sees fit; if he wants extra companies just have him send word. The sooner the better so the rest of us know what we have to work with."

Claire emerges a minute later, and I startle her by my presence.

"Were you listening to us?" she whispers as we walk away together. "After not wanting to go yourself?"

"I was checking on other matters related to the attack. I only came here a minute ago to wait for you."

"What did you hear?"

"I heard everything from him calling me a coward onward."

I'm too preoccupied with wanting to see her late mother's garden to be angry with the insult. His latest comments don't bother me a bit after what he said earlier—it's more fuel for the fire of indignation—but I couldn't resist the cut at her. As if hurting his daughter will somehow get back at Julek.

Her face reddens far more than it did when I told her she died defending the northern gate. "Sometimes he speaks harsh words when he's under stress. He did say you can determine the defense as you see fit and even request more companies if you want. He trusts you, even if he doesn't always wait to filter what his tongue lets out of his mouth."

We continue with me choosing the course until we're close and Claire notices we couldn't be heading anywhere but the private garden.

"Shouldn't we return to help with preparations?"

"This is far more important than any weapons we could sharpen. Get me in there with you; I'll explain why in a moment."

Shocked but betraying nothing beyond what someone who knew her from childhood would notice, she addresses the two guards; an above-average height woman and a man who looks short by comparison.

"Captain Hart is my guest," she says. "We need a few moments alone before the battle."

The soldiers look the shock I feel, and they part from the doorway while Claire, with a flushing face, leads the way through and closes the wooden door.

"Really?" I say. "That's the best you could come up with? They'll think... never mind." I shake my head and walk to the back of the garden while looking around. I notice comfrey, sage, and basil. There's mint in a side corner probably meant to contain its spread, rosemary around the base of a tiered ornamental carving, espaliered trees along the walls like wide candlesticks, and lavender growing close to bush size despite the time of year. Flowers line the path to the far side of the garden, where a tree I didn't notice in my distress overshadows half the garden with fresh spring leaves.

"I got nervous. What did you want me here for?" Claire's still waiting by the door.

Besides the reigning family, only one gardener is allowed, and I'd feel awed at my privilege if I took time to think of it. As it stands, I want to know why this was selected as the sight of execution. I didn't think much through my emotions the night before and only had mental space for it to resurface after all my officers busied themselves with preparations.

Claire walks forward now, and I remember to answer her question, or at least acknowledge it.

"This is where they were last night," I say.

I hesitate. I don't naturally want to tell her about *anything* from the day we'll all relive, let alone this, but I need her help beyond getting me into the garden.

"Who was here?"

"The... Guldeth. I ran to hide in here after covering our retreat and found... some."

"Some... enemies?"

"Yeah. Some enemies."

"And?" Claire asks.

"What do you mean?" Me feigning interest in the bee balm doesn't distract her from pursuing the question to the end.

"Of course there were enemies here. Weren't they everywhere? Didn't you say everyone was fleeing?"

"Yes, but..." I sigh and close my eyes tight. Everyone else forgot about the battle, but I'm still holding it. Like Elara said last night; how can I ever sleep again? "You don't want me to tell you what else. Please trust me on that."

Claire doesn't look convinced as she ambles forward. I need to keep this moving.

"Really, you need to. Was there... Was there anything strange happening in here? Something that would draw their interest or any notice?"

"Absolutely nothing," she insists with the most force in her bearing I've noticed all day. "This garden is exclusively for purposes like—"

"For the reigning family and certain invited guests," I interrupt as I turn to face her, my eyes now opened but unable to meet her averted gaze. "I think they were looking for your mother," I say. She looks at me in disbelief. None of the surprise I'd expected.

"Her death wasn't a secret." She lets her eyes linger anywhere except my face, her voice cool, distant, aloof.

Of course I know it wasn't a secret.

Anger rises within me, heating my mind to a point I almost break and spew it on her in a torrent of words, but I remember she didn't see in this garden the last time. She didn't witness the night of battle, the smell of iron everywhere, the screams, the heart-stopping fear, or the beaten soldiers. I calm myself before it does more than distort my features for an instant.

"I was standing right here," I say and plant my feet, "with more Oruvian soldiers when I used the Gift and I clearly remember a Guldethian captain beating our soldiers for not knowing where she was hiding. They insisted that she's been dead for years."

"You know that's true."

"I know." My frustration threatens to overrule my natural gentleness. "I'm just wondering why they're so insistent on finding her. Could that have been the reason for such a wicked attack?"

"It's a coincidence," Claire says. "They probably wanted Julek too, but had another group working on him."

Her confidence doesn't convince me. It sounds natural that the occupying army would seek the commander of the castle —the whole reigning family—unless you were there. The brutal concentration where nobody looked over to me when I fell from the wall, the look of desperate despair on our soldier's faces, the... the bestial interrogation in the destroyed garden, everything; there's no way they were looking for the reigning family to take as prisoners.

"The way I found them in here last..." It feels like it was last night, but it wasn't. "The relived day, it couldn't have been an accident; they wanted in this garden and they wanted June."

"I don't have a clue why," Claire says. Her clipped words and succinct tone match her cool posture, and I wonder if this will lead us to an impasse.

She finally looks at me, but my frustration has been growing so I look away after a moment to avoid glaring at her.

I kick at a small branch of bee balm fallen across the path when I walk forward. This whole garden will look like the dark green ground-up foliage I just trampled if I can't come up with a better defense than we used last time. If only we knew what they wanted June and the garden for.

I wheel around a few steps later to stare at the trampled bee balm as if it called to me. Claire's looking hard at me, but a heartbeat later, when I look back to the balm again for a blink, her eyes have softened to curiosity.

"What if they were looking for a Gifted?" I ask, the idea coming to my mind in a strange inspiration. "Did your parents ever grow Dryad's Honey?"

Claire folds her arms and shakes her head with one eyebrow lowered. "I don't even know what that is."

"It's a mushroom; my father has a tapestry in his Business Room with the weaving showing the creation of the poultice paste of the Balm of Life. My mother and father would always tell me it was made from the Dryad's Honey mushroom."

Her lowered brow shoots toward her hairline. "If there's a secret here, it's not Mother's death; it's those mushrooms."

"I never believed the stories about the Balm or especially about the Dryad's Honey; up until today I didn't think I had the Gift, but now I don't think I dare question it without reason. If it's real it's... powerful."

I'm not even in possession of any Balm of Life; it's been away from my family for the last ten years, yet the freedom I feel it could provide starts to knock at the door of my consciousness.

If the stories my parents told me were true—more than stories—then the Balm of Life, if I had it, would restore the year I gave up to relive the day of battle. The tales told it can't make one younger than their natural age, but it can grant the Gifted the ability to use their Gift without shortening their life lower than ordinary mortals.

The Gift is powerful enough. Combined with the Balm of Life it could make someone unstoppable, powerful beyond measure. I've never craved power; in fact, I've neglected it by training as a soldier. I've deployed to the front despite my status exempting me from risking my life that way. I've seen myself as a man of the people; someone who tries to know their lives, their hardships, what they go through for the kingdom, and bear the burdens with them. The very thought of power swirls in my mind and seeds an unwanted lust.

"Father said the Balm of Life would have kept Mother alive," Claire says, "but he didn't know how to make it. He said the only stock in the kingdom was with your parents in Sapesky."

My mind whirs in a fresh frenzy of realization; that's what June's letter in Claire's room referred to; it's what the king and Julek's argument was about all those years ago; and it's why the Guldeth attacked unlike themselves. In a flash I see why my father feared Julek before June's death; they could have had a hundred chances to assassinate him.

I see finally why he fears me not using my Gift. The weight of power I've shunned my whole life, which assaulted my mind for a few moments, releases me again and the craving ebbs away.

Maybe that's why the Guldeth throw away their lives so carelessly for this assault; they *know* a Gifted will reverse the outcome. It's a test. A test to see if June's still alive and able to impact the war. It's too great a temptation to overcome; they need to know if we have any more.

"I'm not bitter, Chris," Claire pleads. "You have to believe I'm not. Father is bitter sometimes still, but I don't blame your parents."

"Then you fulfilled her dying wish better than he has." I take one last look around the garden in the hope of seeing a plant I don't recognize. My training's taught me many uses of wild herbs and the garden seems to be composed of the most common, though amazing cultivations of each. I put out one final appeal to Claire before leaving. "Any strange plants you know of? Please; this is important."

Since she doesn't know of any, I let myself out the wooden door. The guards look surprised to see me so soon as they move aside. Before I'm a dozen paces away I hear the guards closing the door with Claire's quick light steps eating the distance between us.

"What do you mean about my mother's dying wish?" she asks. "How do you know what she wanted?"

A trumpet blare from atop a western tower draws everyone's gaze, prevents me from answering. As I take off running with Claire at my heels it sounds again, this time to shorter answering calls from the other portions of the castle and city. Taking the steps two at a time while dodging around soldiers craning their necks over the battlements, I mount the ladder leading to the tower and emerge from the hole in the floor a few seconds later.

The officer stationed among the soldiers strides over to me as Claire straightens up from the ladder climb. She wears the same blue tunic Julek's officers all wear, with the ornamental eagle centered and larger than on soldiers' uniforms, though not as ornate as the commander's.

"Prince Hart, we've sighted enemy scouts a few miles distant." She bows. "They were to the north and moving east."

This first appearance of enemy soldiers worries me even though I know we still have several hours until their attack. There's so many variables in a battle, and the beginning stages can sway so fast, that an experienced captain worrying over trifles hardly seems worth it. Knowing how this attack ends without my intervention causes that worry to surface more than it ever did in Toldulgur.

"It can be Captain Hart today," I say. "And thank you. Keep the rest of the castle informed as more appear. Pay special attention to movements along the north side."

"Yes, Captain."

Claire descends with me and we pass word to other captains and officers rushing to confirm their suspicions. From what I gather, the preparations are well under way; Commander Lewis didn't become commander of Eraseam by disorganized habits. His wife's Gift helped him live long enough to realize his ambitions, though his worthiness kept him rising in people's estimation since his first training as a soldier.

If something happened to the Hart family line I always thought he would have made an excellent king. That was before this battle. What is a commander if they cannot take the loss along with the victory?

"It's my fault, isn't it?" Claire asks. "I'm the weak link they got lucky with."

"You're nothing of the sort. I wasn't there when you died, but them having a few well-placed crossbow shots with doesn't mean you're a weak link." This sort of uplifting bothers me. I've lifted myself up plenty of times, and still do, so doing it for others feels like an unnecessarily heavy burden. I only do it for her now because there's no extra time.

She doesn't even wince at me describing her method of death, only continues to look dejected at her feet.

"Anyway," I say. "You'll be in charge here tonight. I have something else to do."

"You're a captain," she says. "You of all people have to stay to bolster the troops' spirits. If they're bringing enough forces to breach the city within a day they'll need you near the gatehouse, not some new officer."

"You. Have. What. It. Takes," I say with an emphasis I hope lets her know this discussion doesn't need to continue. "Everyone in the camps saw your skill during training. And you were brought up in one of the best military families in the kingdom. Your personality naturally lends itself to leadership, and people want to follow you."

It works, and she stays quiet long enough for me to change the subject without cutting her off. "I need to head back to Mt. Cabrae. Get me a horse."

"Now?"

My tone leaves no room for hesitation or disobedience, yet she does exactly that. My few seconds of stewing non-answer isn't enough for her without what I interpret as insolence.

"You won't even tell me why and now you're running off on the eve of a battle only you know how to win? I still need training. It's not fair to me; to anybody here."

"Stop." My teeth are clenched and my eyes are hard as flints as I turn back to her. "You can step into a lower role if you want for tonight. The self-deprecation won't work on me and I won't be called a coward more than I know your father already will. I don't expect him to understand and I don't care; this has to be done."

I start walking again. It feels like I'm leaving footprints of flames from my simmering anger.

"Why? I know you're not a coward. What happened to make you leave?"

I turn to face her and my face softens the slightest amount. She strikes the final blow to disarm my ire, if not my frustration, at a new officer standing up to my order.

"How do you know my mother's dying wish?"

A question like that won't let me ignore it even though I'm anxious to leave. I sigh to dispel some of the pent-up emotions and answer her before I turn.

"Get two horses; I'll tell you along the way."

Chapter 10.

"Don't say it," Weaver warns me as soon as he meets my eye.

I've surprised him with a fake stern look enough times so my appearance during his preparations doesn't cause him much concern. When he falls for the bait, I always point out his near-invisible eyebrows. Soldiers, though—the new ones in particular—would assume a non-smile foretold worse.

"I need you to move your company to the northern gate," I say.

He realizes I'm here for a purpose and focuses on me for the first time. Despite the sober message I'm coming with, the temptation to ease the situation lights a spark in my eye.

"I think the lighting will be better on—"

"Knock it off," he says, then breaks into a large smile while all the soldiers around him match it.

I'm his captain, and the only one he allows to talk to him this way, but his soldiers certainly talk among themselves so I know those within earshot consider themselves privileged to have heard it happen.

"You almost had me that time."

"Couldn't be helped," I say as he goes back to lifting a few sheaves of arrows out of a loaded wagon. "But really, I do have something to tell you."

I give him time to straighten up, pass off the sheaves, and wave the soldiers off. He looks at me with two lines of wrinkles bowed over each eye.

"Matters pull me back to Mt. Cabrae immediately," I say. "I need you to take my place as acting captain at the northern gate. There will be other companies with you as captain if you accept it."

His eyebrows raise even higher into his hairline; this is the step that could lead him to a position as an actual captain, something I know he's wanted and been working toward for years.

"I'm honored you've chosen me, Captain. I'll do everything I can and wish you well at Mt. Cabrae."

A low bow dips my head at his acknowledgment. I hear two horses trotting far off.

"One more thing; Commander Lewis doesn't know I'm leaving and can't know yet. He might not understand my departure so I need someone else to tell him. Will you personally do that for me?"

He nods. Determination settles deeper into his eyes with more responsibilities.

"Wait fifteen minutes before going and also inform him I've appointed you as my acting captain along the gate. Tell him every company with you is necessary."

His poise is admirable since he doesn't fully understand the meaning of everything I'm telling him.

At this point Claire rides around a corner twenty yards away and makes for us, herself astride a great brown horse and a black one in tow. I leap for the saddle in an efficient motion. I grab up the reins and curve my mount in a few slow decisive movements and I turn to Weaver.

"Keep your head straight and fight like Xulbris. The hardest attack will come on your quarter. It won't feel like it because of the ground you overlook; you'll want to send soldiers elsewhere. Don't. The fight you show them from the start may determine the night. Don't give them an inch; don't give them mercy."

He waits for a few seconds after I'm done speaking, our eyes never breaking contact even for a blink, then bows his head in acknowledgement that I'm as serious as I've ever been with him.

My horse paws the ground, sensing our haste, before I click to it and start forward with Claire.

Unspoken authority compels the soldiers on duty to raise the gate for me despite Commander Lewis's order that no one be allowed to leave. Myceum is his city, and I'm a captain serving him, though on a technicality my birthright makes me outrank him. I'm always hesitant to play that card, and glad I don't have to, since the soldiers recognize both me and the commander's daughter. They let us out; presumably assuming we're scouting around.

Claire guides us along the least-visible paths from the guarded city before joining the main road leading back to Mt. Cabrae. We've maintained silence broken only by our horses' sounds as the castle diminished with our distance. For my part, I feel every bit like I'd imagine a thief on the run. A portion of me wants to stay in Myceum; that's where many of my soldiers are and I'm not one to run from danger. It's a battle to convince my mind that I'm not fleeing; I know I'm heading into perhaps a worse danger—death, perhaps, and willingly—but knowing it might not be viewed that way in the castle troubles my mind.

"You owe me an answer," Claire says.

She wants an explanation of how I know her mother's dying wish; I can't blame her. We slow our horses to an easier pace and come side by side on the wider road.

"Your mother's letter we found in your room. She wanted..." I trail off, not at the confused look in her eyes as much as the realization that maybe she hasn't seen the letter I'm talking about. Not *really* seen it. "Do you remember the secret compartment under your window we used to send each other and Rafael messages as children?"

"Of course. I haven't been able to open that for years. What about it?"

"We opened it. I forgot until now that it happened during the day I reversed." I stop, with Claire waiting for me to continue. Our horses are breathing easier now, rested from their gallop through the narrow paths, but we continue the slow, measured pace to allow us to talk. "There was a letter from your mother written right before the last time she used her Gift."

When her gaze moves from me to over my shoulder I know she's looking at the castle. She can probably see the portion of the castle her window looks out from, and I feel it; the longing to return, see her mother's handwriting, hold her last letter.

"You can return. There might be more danger with me."

She shakes her head to clear the thought.

"What else did we do?"

"I smashed my elbow like a few hours back and you made sure it wasn't damaged enough to need rest," I say. "Then your father arrived so we went to see the reason for his unexpected appearance. Then the battle."

"And... what else?"

"And... you died." It's strange answering her in that way. It feels like I should be more solemn, but she's here before me, alive, so any way I think of answering feels unusual.

We travel the rest of the day with intermittent conversations, usually begun when one of us feels a haunting quietness while passing through a sheltered place. We avoid a few locations perfect for an ambush and, since Claire's a tactician, the trip passes infinitely more pleasant than I thought it would when I grudgingly agreed to let her come.

Two men shout an argument up ahead. The larger of the two is leaning to look inside a wagon with the warm glow of a fire at his back brightening the last vestiges of dusk. The smaller man is beside a distant tree with a horse. I've never known thieves to use a wagon, so we're probably safe.

"What you tied in knots for? Haven't happened yet and it won't."

"It's going to break. I know it. And we need to find out why and how to stop it."

The large man sets something back into the wagon, moves around to the back.

"I know you blame me. You always blame me. Never once I remember you taking responsibility."

"Cut it out. We've company." It's a third voice, from under the wagon.

"Let's hope it's a minstrel. Or a wainwright. Get this off my mind somehow."

"Carsten mad ahead a time. Pots aren't even breaked and he's blamed me. If I break every piece he thinks I did then you would've had nothing in last wagon either."

"Having to carry everything across rough sections of road is as bad as breaking them."

"Just drop it, hun. Leave tomorrow's hurts for tomorrow."

The large man huffs, turns from the wagon.

"Now you probably think Jenny get away too. Trust me to feed her, okay, but you come double-check this knot. I'm not getting blame for this either."

Claire and I ride into their midst. Their wagon is mostly off the road and their fire is on the other side of that. The two men examine the rope together. The thin one watches the large man tie another knot with an exaggerated interest.

"Leave us alone," the large man says when he sees we've stopped. "We've got the duke's and baron's seals and everything."

"We're on a patrol to Mt. Cabrae," I say. Claire and I dismount. "Not looking for you in the least. Seen anything funny?"

"Nothing more funny than normal."

"Hank!"

The thin man sulks down by the fire.

"Beg pardon for him," Carsten says. "And myself too. Hauling the ceramics is a tricky business. We've seen more soldiers around and want to get the wares from possible fighting. Just can't drop the feeling something'll go wrong tomorrow."

"I'll bet it's the Gift-witch. Didn't really die like they said. Come back from the Sage."

Claire convulses. I grab her around the waist to keep her quiet.

"That's enough from you," Carsten says. "I won't have you talking like that at night. Bad enough during the day."

I walk up and see what he's so afraid of breaking: painted ceramics. Each piece is wrapped in cloth and packed with darkened straw.

"Shouldn't be robbers along a road this common," I say.

"Seems I'm worried about the wagon, though I don't know why," he says. "Like it's going to fall apart or something."

I'd like to help, though most of my time around wagons has been unloading supply-carts. "Did you check the wheels?" I ask.

"Of course I did. Today and before we headed out."

"Looks like this wheel's ready to drop through the axle."

The woman under the wagon scrambles from her bedroll, pulls it out behind her.

"What?" Carsten bolts to my side. "Hank! Hank; grab something. Help."

Hank and I run for the distant forest and return with some oak limbs to help brace up the wagon.

Carsten found a board under the seat and jammed it underneath the axle. He steps back to admire his handiwork. "Knew that baby would come in handy. Haha." He kicks the supported board lightly. It's not taking much weight from the axle, but he likes it. It looks like it'll be okay as long as he replaces it before moving.

"Lena's a good cook." Carsten gestures to the woman. "Hun, we have food for these two, right?"

"We do if they like coney."

He looks back at us. I nod. Claire's still too incensed to look at anybody. I've upset her before, but Hank nettled her worse than I've ever seen.

Carsten tells Hank to tie our horses alongside theirs. He mumbles to himself on his way. "Soldier probably tax twice what I make if he pays me."

We settle down to a meal of spit-fried rabbit, hard cheese, and crusty bread.

Carsten regales us with stories while Lena finishes cooking, then launches into self-praise when we're eating.

"I'm amazed I had the foresight to know something was going to break. Goes to show an old hand in the trade's got a feeling for things like that."

"Quite amazing, hun."

Carsten beams. "I'm sure I would've checked the axle before starting. We'll just repair it in the morning and be off."

"Get me up if you're up before me," I say. We need to start early.

"No trouble at all. Would you like a vase for your troubles?"

"Uh, no thanks. Your food is enough payment."

"Good. I wouldn't have given you one anyway. It'd break on your saddle. The offer was only for form's sake."

"You're not supposed to tell them that, hun," Lena says.

Silence engulfs the small campfire. After a few minutes I turn to Carsten. "You should open a tavern, man. You've got a gift for speaking."

Lena chokes on her bite of rabbit.

"Maybe. It's still impressive." Carsten muses over his bread and cheese. "I'm an old hand at this, but I don't see how it was possible if a Gifted didn't work some of their magic."

"You always mad beforehand. Always at me."

Carsten ignores Hank. "Could be the Divider, but we never know what old Whiteneck's up to."

"He might more than we think," Lena says. "And you just noticed it because you were upset if it happened."

Hank snorts.

"Could be." Carsten rubs his chin. "Wish there was a more guaranteed way to know."

"I don't," Hank says. "Everyone hates them. It's a nicer world than since she stopped using it."

I put my hand on Caire's leg to keep her quiet. I hold back a flush with an inward breath. Carsten letting Hank get away with saying it alarms me worse than the personal affront. I've known the people didn't like June's Gift, but I never knew how badly.

"Hmm." Carsten turns my way. "What's the feeling among the soldiers?"

"Better than the people; at least I think so. They don't talk about them much. Plenty of times it would be great to have a Gifted along in a battle. Maybe reverse a poor strategy. The things Commander Lewis's wife used it for those years ago."

"Guess there are reasons they're useful," he says. "They just seem like more trouble than they're worth most of the time. Keeping their friends alive at other people's expense and all that."

"At their own expense, too, right?" I ask.

"Well, yes. It's said they grow a year older each day they reverse. So there is a limit, at least theoretically. They say that's how the Commander's wife died." I steal a glance at Claire while Carsten looks at Hank. "But she was hidden away even before that. The province just got too hot for her."

"We'd have heard of her in the last nine years if she was alive," Lena says. She's under her blanket now, content to rest under the wagon again.

"I'm going to have to wake you to replace the axle tomorrow," Carsten says.

"You're going to have to find one first. I'm staying out of the damp."

Carsten shrugs, reaches for his water skin, and takes an enormous pull.

"Ahh, I always say a full bladder is better than a servant for waking you up early, ha!"

"Race you," Hank says. He gulps at least as much water.

Carsten spreads his own blanket near Lena's and doubles it over. He uses it as a sleeping mat instead of as a covering. "I'll wake you early then, hun. I brought your paints. May as well get the decorating done a little faster to get a little more from them."

Lena sighs. "I'm not waking up early to paint by firelight. I'd spoil them and they'd be wet for the ride."

Carsten tries to think of a way around it, but Lena grabs her blanket and rolls to her side. "If you wake me early I'll mix senna leaves in the next meal I make you. Then you'd be cramped up for days."

Carsten chuckles, then drifts to sleep.

Claire rises before dawn to find me awake for several hours already. Carsten and Hank are in the forest looking for a straight branch to use as an axle.

"Couldn't sleep?" she asks.

"No. Not much."

How will I ever sleep again? The question circulated through my mind all the long night, keeping me stirring with knowledge of the horrors the Oruvians might be enduring. My solemn mood around the fire before turning in reminded Claire the battle was progressing, though one who wasn't there can't understand the five-pronged assault on the senses. Her death must have been sudden since she was excited.

Despite not sleeping more than a few hours, I feel rested enough to travel the whole day.

Lena peeks an eye open, sees it's just the two of us preparing to leave, and slips from her blanket.

"Can't have him knowing I can wake before the sun," she says with a wink while she goes through their stores. "It's bad enough on the short summer days. Here, and thank you for your help."

She hands us a full loaf of bread, which Claire accepts. She smiles for the first time since she saw Hank. Her mood improved with the night as much as mine soured. Rafael used to tell me bad dreams were faeries whispering bad thoughts into my mind.

Claire's sympathy lasts as long as I let it, which isn't long since I'm not inclined for self-pity unless my mind forces me into it. Instead, we talk of her expectations in the castle fortress ahead.

"I think we'll find things as we left them," Claire says. "Commander Nealy holds a strong presence; that's why your father placed her in charge of such a strategic fortress."

My premonition isn't as rosy; with the Guldeth forcing Julek to turn around without reaching Balruvia, their possible presence around—or in—Mt. Cabrae gives me pause. They had to have gathered troops from somewhere, and the fighting along the Dendring Mountains makes the least sense to my experience. The message Kimbr captured before our departure warned us of the attack at Balruvia and now appears to show a changing timbre to the war. Sharing this with Claire doesn't do much to dim her enthusiasm, because it's not a danger along Mt. Cabrae.

"She's strong, and Kimbr, too. He was remaining there unless I'm mistaken," she continues.

"You don't think they redoubled their attack on Mt. Cabrae the same as Balruvia?" I purposely neglect to point out her father had strong captains in charge of Balruvia, but she answers that objection without me even voicing it.

"Father kept his best captains there and I'm sure that's why the fortress didn't fall. He's fought enough to not lose a fortress like Balruvia to a sudden attack."

"What makes you so certain it didn't fall?" I ask.

"What makes you so certain it did?"

Perhaps it's a good thing she's still keen on our journey and my voice of reason; with me venturing alone I would have run my horse close to death before abandoning it and running the rest of the distance myself. I wouldn't have taken a break, and probably would have made it, half dead with exhaustion, in half the time. As it is, a long-absent smile graces my face.

We trot our horses whenever they're able and so make good time through the second day. Thoughts of my soldiers back in Myceum ceaselessly assault my mind, often spreading when we're riding too fast to allow a conversation.

On the evening of the second day, as we're nearing Mt. Cabrae after a blessedly uneventful journey, I can't help but offer Claire another out. "Really, you can return to Myceum. Even before we leave Mt. Cabrae we might find a worse danger than Myceum's in."

"Where's our final destination?" She asks in some surprise. "I assumed we were going to warn them of Balruvia's plight in case they didn't know."

Our. That word isn't lost on me.

"I think," I say, feeling my way as along a dark path, "that the lack of soldiers we met along the road says enough about their knowledge of enemy movements. Your father said those not garrisoning Balruvia fled north or south so I think it's fair to say at least one made it here."

Here I breathe in the cooling air of the spring night. "Our final destination? I never meant you to come along, let along follow me to the end. My final destination is Murethon. I intend to push as far as Castle Muerthy as soon as I'm able."

"It's madness," she cries

I'm not startled in the least; it's what I expected.

"Maybe," the reply comes across my lips with an ease that, of all things lately, startles me into more awareness. "Going into Whiteneck's fortress in Murethon isn't my idea of a good time, but after the battle in Myceum I'm convinced we'll never win this war without answers. I pray they won last night and win every battle between now and the war's end, though I don't think it'll do more than delay the inevitable unless we get these answers."

"What answers? What happened in Myceum that causes you, heir to the throne, to try and venture into the most dangerous place I can imagine?"

Strange reasons fill my mind for the answers she craves, more feelings than solid facts; I struggle even attempting to articulate them. Finding out why they attacked Myceum doesn't seem a good enough answer, or possible to carry through even should I reach Whiteneck's fortress.

"They wanted your mother," I say. "And they beat soldier after soldier in your garden when they couldn't tell the officer where she was hiding. I can't explain why it's even more horrible than it sounds. Something about the certitude of finding her and the willingness to spill as much blood as it takes to wring the secret from the castle. It would have been the rest of the soldiers next, then the town. And the way they attacked; you don't remember it, but it was worse than any fight I've experienced in my years along the front. They cared not a whit for their lives, as if... as if..." I trail off here, the thought that comes to my mind too awful to articulate to someone who wasn't there.

"What?" Claire asks.

I almost don't hear her airy breath of a voice over the birdsong in the motionless trees a score of yards away from the path.

"A..." I shake my head then focus on the fortress coming into better view ahead of us. Could the same events have played out in the solitary mountain castle? "It's that... how could they be persuaded to fight like they'll have another chance to live? They couldn't have the confidence to rely on my Gift to reverse their deaths, could they? They didn't even know I was there until after the assault began."

It's like I'm there again, shaking with the remembered events while my vision darkens. *No. Not now; there's no sense reliving a day like this.* I swing my legs over the horse and almost drop to the ground. Claire winces as I stumble.

"Are you okay?"

"I need to walk. I think... I don't know."

"Was your Gift coming with the emotion?" Claire asks, dismounting as well.

My eyes go wide as I look at her beside me. "Did your mother do that also?"

She nods, "Hers was always brought on by extreme emotion, she told me. Before she died she said it sometimes became hard since she used it so much."

A smile curves the corner of her lips while she stares along our path. It's a hollow smile; sad and empty, yet full of meaning, like the headstone of the one person you know in a graveyard.

"I imagine it's hard to feel much sorrow for a loved one's death if you've witnessed it dozens of times and still have them around," I venture to say, hoping she knows I don't bear Julek any of the ill will he has for me and my father.

"She never told me that, but I was too young to be trusted with such words. Now I'm older and I look back— perhaps it's imaginings—I think she implied that."

"I need to get there to find out about Heller," I say. "If he's truly Gifted and has the Balm of Life, he could combine that into an unstoppable combination of perfect decisions. Yet he doesn't. I need to know why."

My horse stamps beside me. I turn to admire the animal with the glistening hair that's spiky even against my calloused hand when I rest it in front of the saddle. The steady clopping of feet over the ground while its head bobs in a syncopated rhythm draws my mind from our conversation enough to distract Claire as well. Her brown horse does the same and, even though it's a hand shorter, looks grand.

"You chose amazing mounts for us on zero notice," I say.

The animal stamps again. This time it alerts me to keep my senses on edge. Horses don't usually act like this without a reason so we both mount in preparation, the back of my neck rising in a shiver, my intuition of an approach several seconds behind nature's alarm.

"You should remain here," I say. "Or go to Sapesky." I wish I would have prompted her before possible danger menaced us.

"No chance, especially now." She puts her hand on her bow, strung and ready as it was for Myceum. All traces of wear have been wiped away.

After riding a few hundred yards farther we come to a rise and both spot the cause of our animal's and our own uneasiness at the same time: a soldier. A soldier of Mt. Cabrae. My pulse, which leaped to readiness at the first sight, quiets slower than it awakened. Claire and I spur our horses toward him. I recognize him from our visit with the Nealys. He's average height, well built despite his thinness, with short hair and a black beard the same length.

"Captain Hart, I believe, and Officer Lewis," Mobent calls in greeting. He bows from atop his horse.

I bow in return, surprising him, but he doesn't let it show for long before he continues. "Commander Nealy will be eager for your assistance if you can spare time for the upcoming campaign."

"Campaign?" The word surprises me.

"Perhaps not a campaign; she can tell you more. Please follow me as we're exposed out here; the castle offers a better place for talking."

Our journey to the castle impresses the importance of haste, as we pass a few empty posts, guards recalled from fear of attack. Mobent rides swiftly, saying nothing, but his gaze sweeping the sides of the road before us raises my heart rate with the expectation of some calamity.

We cross into the castle and my mind feels a bit of tranquility. Our officer escort sighs in relief while dismounting and handing his reins off to a young groom. We do the same before following his beckon toward where Commander Nealy manages Mt. Cabrae.

In the short walk, I observe how the strain of being the last officer recalled impacted Mobent. He leads us into the commander's hall, waiting by the door until a woman, hair tucked high, finishes her hurried conversation with a bow before running off.

"Thank you Mobent," Commander Nealy says.

The officer bows himself away, shoulders sinking a few inches as the weight he felt transfers to another.

"It's a surprise to see you return so soon," she says.

"I see you're busy with preparations," I say. "Hopefully you're receiving assistance from some survivors around Balruvia."

"Few enough," she says. "They arrived this afternoon. Many aren't in a state to help after their exposure in the mountains for several nights. I'd call it weakness but I can't really blame them."

"Are you planning to retake ground from the winter?"

"Indeed. We're in a position to try and retake them; and we need to. It's that the difficulty lies in doing so without endangering the bridges we've kept."

The language strikes me as funny despite its serious nature; it's commander-talk, a code phrase for 'we're short on soldiers and hoping our captains, officers, and tacticians can work a miracle.'

"And that's where we come in?" I say.

She knows I'm returning the jest she made about me asking a special favor for Claire, and flushes a little at my smile.

"We didn't expect your arrival and if you can spare the time we would all appreciate it."

"Perhaps if Claire stayed—"

"I've made it clear I'm staying with you," Claire interrupts. "Only locking me away can keep me from following you."

Commander Nealy raises her eyebrows, clearly uninterested in joining whatever Claire's willing to start. I feel the same way; I can't afford to antagonize any of my allies now.

"Suit yourself."

"Without wanting to pry," Commander Nealy asks, "do you mind telling me what brought you back here so suddenly? Surely news of Balruvia wouldn't urge you here."

"It's what happened after Balruvia's fall. Commander Lewis was leaving to reinforce the fortress when we arrived, and a few days later we found him returning with the enemy hot on his heels, hardly able to make contact with the survivors."

Her eyebrow, which settled over the last minute, raises again with the obvious realization she's too tactful to say. I continue, "You know I have the Gift, Commander?"

She hesitates. "I've heard that said."

"Well it's true; I finally used it after our unsuccessful defense of Myceum. I couldn't stop the inevitable, but strengthened our forces where the breach happened. The battle would have been fought again last night."

Composure slips a finger's-breadth. She's fighting an offensive war, worrying about her home province, and defending the bridges her forces held through the winter. She has to be wondering about Balruvia's fate, and if that affects her duty in Mt. Cabrae. Learning I have the Gift and that the capital of a neighboring province is teetering on the edge of defeat is enough. Can I burden her with knowing I intend to sneak to Murethon's most closely guarded fortress?

"Of course we don't know the outcome," I say. "They fought like fiends; I've never seen so many fall to our swords or us to theirs. It's this that makes me want to continue to..." My words trail off as something from the back of my mind flashes to life. Why is it so hard to say? She knows I'm here for a more important reason than to report a battle; a soldier—an officer at the most—would have brought that information.

"Continue to Murethon to sneak into Castle Muerthy. Wait." She opens her mouth to speak before my admonition for silence, then I continue before she can object. "I can't see a way forward beyond seeking answers there. If you were there in Myceum for the defense you'd know their intent isn't to satisfy an old grudge. They're not out for conquest, either. It's... me. Us. The Gifted. They wanted Commander Lewis's wife, but June's been gone for almost a decade. This might relate to the queen's death. We can fight a defensive war like last time but, like last time, it'll lead to this." I make a sweeping gesture at her western wall. "Everything you've seen out there. Everything Kimbr's been through. Your daughter Searle will be on the front at some point if this keeps up. We might win again, but will we next time? And the time after that? I'm not naive enough to believe Elathon wouldn't fall eventually. What are we here for if not to give the next generation a better world?"

She sits for a minute. Finally, a sentence slips from her mouth. "Does Commander Lewis know this?"

"He knows we came here—nothing more."

Tension builds in my mind while I wait for her reaction. I'm the prince; a headstrong one at times, hence my serving the kingdom starting as a soldier, and a stubborn prince can't be dissuaded by much. Threats don't work. Cajoling fails miserably. An emotional appeal might work, but has an equal chance to delay me into later, more volatile, action. Whatever her response, I'm determined to go.

"What do you need from me?"

Her words floor me. Here I was, ready for a fight, brought down by nonresistance.

Asking for help is impossible; from what I've heard and seen of the Guldethian advances I've entertained qualms about going. I know I need to go, but it still worries me. Losing a captain hurts a regiment, and this will certainly weaken our defensive capabilities, not because I'm an irreplaceable fighter, but because of the boost leadership imparts to soldier's spirits when they're fighting and enduring hardships side by side.

"Your blessing is all I dare ask for. The kingdom will suffer enough with her prince's absence even if the rest of the soldiers remain for defense."

"Kimbr has told me of your fighting abilities, Your Majesty, and I don't doubt you can take care of yourself, but even the most powerful soldier can fall to any number of misfortunes." Claire glances at me while I keep a firm hold on Commander Nealy's gaze. "You could fall to trickery, a stray arrow, or simply an overwhelming press of enemies. You are our prince and too valuable—"

"Only I can go. Only someone with the Gift, who's seen what I've seen, can go. Otherwise it'll end in needless death."

"It is selfishness to treat your life with such little worth. You owe it to your people to stay alive."

"I'm doing it for the people. They think they care who will win the war, but you and I know they're only aware of the smallest part of how life would change. Most of them don't go farther than thinking their taxes would increase and the justice system become a little less just. We know that's only the point of the sword." I stop for a breath. "People can live under any king. They're resilient and adaptable. After a space they'd even convince themselves they're happy under Heller's rule. Happy in the new routine of being subject to a despot. Happy the oppression isn't as bad as it was yesterday. Grateful their family wasn't taken by the guards. Always something to justify why they're okay with it."

"There's another way," the commander says. "I don't know it yet but there's another way."

"No," I tell her. "I've tried to think of another way and there isn't one. I don't want to go so don't think I haven't tried to find it. I'm going because I have to."

"Turn their soldiers against leadership," she says.

I give her a sad smile. This is a lot to take in and she hasn't had the time to mull this over that I have.

"Soldiers pressed into service kill morale then die themselves yet the Guldeth don't run out of soldiers willing to fight for them. I think a darned few would defect, even if I could give them the option. They grew with it and traditions die hard; even bad ones."

Her consternation might make me feel sorry for her if it wasn't for my combat-hardened mind. I can't bear the emotional weight another's position requires of them; my own is heavy enough.

"A force would attract too much attention," she says, "and leave us vulnerable at home." Her mind works the same way mine does. "If you insist it's best you go there's nothing I can do to stop you."

"I need to do this. I won't rest easy until I'm allowed to try."

She understands my meaning, acknowledging it with a slight bow. Julek knows, since I didn't tell him before I left, that I'm hoping to keep this as secret as possible. She also understands I don't want King Laurence to know.

Claire looks at me. "It may be faster to help fight our way through than go around," she says.

Commander Nealy remains silent when I look at her for a reaction.

"That makes sense," I say, unsure but hopeful.

"What of this campaign we've heard about?" Claire's held her peace since making it clear she was coming. She only leaves the role of spectator now that we've settled the question.

Commander Nealy stands straighter with both our gazes locked onto her. The personality of the commander outshines the pressure of her position. "As I mentioned, we're strengthening our hold among the passes, specifically to the southwest, but before that we need to reach them. The start of this campaign involves liberating the area leading to Starview Pass."

My brows knit together. "Leading to it? I didn't know it fell so far over the winter."

"It didn't. It was only a few weeks ago during your stay in Sapesky; I suppose nobody thought it important enough to tell you about in your short time back." She pivots to Claire. "Surely your father taught you strategies for fighting in rocky valleys? I trust we'll rely heavily upon your expertise."

The terrain I expect us to fight on, which we also call 'Giant's Ballroom', is so named for the large indentations littering the hillsides. It makes for brutal fighting. It's fine when we're ensconced in the declivities, but drawing the enemy from them; I don't like to think about it.

We end the conversation and she stops me on the way out.

"I suppose it would be unseemly for me to tell the prince I halfway hope he gets injured enough for time to rethink his decision."

Chapter 11.

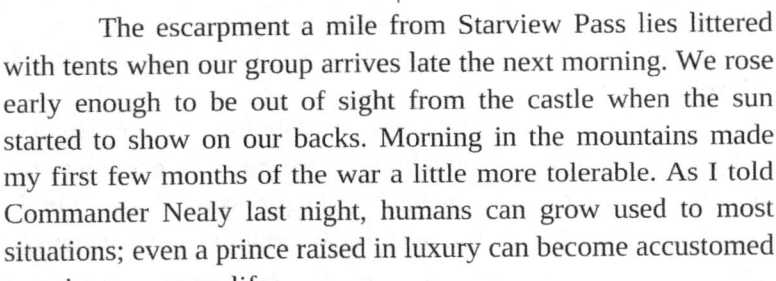

The escarpment a mile from Starview Pass lies littered with tents when our group arrives late the next morning. We rose early enough to be out of sight from the castle when the sun started to show on our backs. Morning in the mountains made my first few months of the war a little more tolerable. As I told Commander Nealy last night, humans can grow used to most situations; even a prince raised in luxury can become accustomed to a rigorous camp life.

The more contested areas of the Dendring Mountains lie west of Mt. Cabrae, the fortress built on the mountain of the same name. Most of the mountains around don't have a well-known name, so when people speak of Mt. Cabrae it's always about the fortress. We head northwest through paths more circuitous the farther we travel. Bright timber and stones show the newness of fortifications around the bridges we traverse. Everywhere close to the mountain castle is well-fortified, and the new bridges more so.

Until this spring, from what I've learned, we've held this entire area of the mountain range. And a good thing, too; a war in the mountains has unimaginable complexities. Weapons are easy when you have each soldier carry their own, with a few cartloads of arrows following to replenish the archers. Water is often abundant—sometimes we can transport it less than a mile— during most of the year.

Food is less plentiful as wild game flees as soon as we arrive. Hauling that in is an incredibly underestimated job, and one that most captains my age overlook, leaving it to chance. The older ones wisely take up the slack and work with mountain ponies and carts as much as with blades and tactics. I sometimes wonder if they're in their position because they paid attention to things like that. Destroy an enemy's supply lines and their defeat isn't far behind.

Then there's the fighting. That's where things get interesting. For every victory we win easily due to a natural advantage like getting the high ground or placing an ambush they can't easily fight back from, it seems we pay for it in a humiliating loss. We're fighting for Starview Pass, but won't see the actual Pass unless the battle goes uncommonly well. We'll fight along the slopes on our side of the Pass. That's why our forces are ranged on the edge of a plateau a mile or more away.

It'll be hand-to-hand fighting, crowding them from their positions, bleeding up hill after hill.

Despite my concerns leading soldiers into position, I can't help but look with a loathsome longing past the encamped host, dreading going yet drawn there imperiously.

"Is that Starview Pass?" a soldier asks.

Her ignorance, more than her age, shows it's her first time seeing a battle beyond the mock ones during training. She was probably with me on the trek from Sapesky. She points to a distant declivity in the mountainside behind the Guldeth.

"No. Starview Pass is a few miles beyond that. I doubt we'll reach as far as the pass today, and if we do you can thank Nymunia it went so well for us."

Nerves make her shake uncontrollably. Sometimes she masters them, managing to stay still for a while, before they come on again. Always they restart, sometimes more pronounced —more damaging—than the last. I need to help her calm her nerves or they might spill over into others.

"That's called Giant's Ballroom," I say and point out the pocked ground to everyone around me, but specifically her. "We'll fight there if I'm not mistaken. It's comforting to know the field of battle before heading into it."

It's mostly true. Knowing a field of battle, when it's to our advantage, helps calm my nerves far more than knowing we'll be at a disadvantage. A plan for an uphill advance across the Giant's Ballroom would make even my stomach churn if I wasn't experienced with far worse odds. Good thing we have carts loaded with large shields. At the best I hope we'll be near even footing. They've shown they want to advance as much as we want to repel them. That willingness could make the difference between victory and a rout.

I join the officers gathered at the highest central point. Kimbr and Mobent will be there with a dozen others I'll know from years of service together. Different ones point periodically to distant points on the horizon, making occasional sweeping motions across the vista. A few steps farther and I notice a woman with her hair fluttering in the mountain breeze. The others all have their hair wound tight.

Claire.

My heart stutters a beat, probably due to the altitude I've already grown unused to, but I wrest it under control and look up. The gathering stands out vivid against the midday sun. I remind myself they've already come up with a plan, regardless of how much experience I have. There's such an accumulation of knowledge and skill in that one space of green.

"Welcome Captain Hart," Kimbr says. "We received news of your arrival in the small hours this morning from a runner. I will be grateful for your assistance."

I bow as I continue to walk toward them. Kimbr never mentioned my future plans, or the fall of Myceum, so I wonder how much everyone around me knows. Everyone knowing Myceum's fate wouldn't usually bother me. I've reported losing battles many times, but the unknown nature and me seeming to flee right before the fight is a new feeling. Not for the first time do I wish June was alive to guide me in using the Gift.

Nobody says anything as I join the circle of gathered men and women. Other than a few glances at me, which, being so few I deem mean the knowledge of Myceum isn't general, everyone stares at a map before them. It's a small map compared to the ones of all Elathon, and not as ornate. While my eyes gather the orientation I realize Kimbr is standing at the southern end. The other captains are on his sides to have the best visual when he discusses the plans. He goes over them in full detail to benefit us new arrivals.

He points to an area farthest away from him on the map, where rough contour lines approximate the terrain we're overlooking. "Here is where I'll want you, Captain Hart. I will be flanking from their north and wish your help holding the soldiers together if it's necessary for us to split."

We both eye the map for a minute before he continues going over the other captains' and officers' duties.

He assigns Claire to his regiment and says the company she'll lead will be holding high ground, from which she's to report enemy movements to the captains. Upon hearing this, I wait a second before glancing up at her. As I expected, she's eyeing me intently, no doubt sharing my thoughts about what happened in the similar situation in Myceum. Her face looks like she's already worried about failure. I shake my head sideways, barely perceptible even for her. We don't need those thoughts overtaking her mind.

"Do you see anything needing a change, Captain Hart?" Kimbr asks.

"I'm only here to receive orders, Captain," I say. "You know this land better and have had several days advantage learning the intricacies. I've only just arrived a few minutes ago."

From the corner of my eye, I see Claire's shoulders dip from relieved tension.

"Nevertheless we have changed a few strategies since learning of your arrival." He gestures to Claire. "With another captain and two additional officers, including Commander Lewis's daughter, I feel even better about our assault."

His confidence, genuine or not, uplifts the officers; we're committed to this battle no matter the odds. I try to not feel overconfident going into battles since they can change momentum on the smallest event; a single lucky or unlucky sword stroke, someone stepping in front of an arrow, a foot slipping on a rock, or the moment's hesitation of a soldier. Early in my days as an officer I'd be feeling a deep depression leading soldiers into a fight like this; something seeming so unwinnable feels useless.

The way we're fighting doesn't lead to recklessness, which I abhor even more than before after seeing the Guldeth in Myceum. We're fighting according to a plan, under capable officers and tried commanders. Even Constable Shutt is here. As much as I dislike him, he's earned his position through decades of ingenious service. As fast as a battle can swing against us, it can swing toward our favor with almost the same rapidity. That gives me a hopeful confidence.

Kimbr dismisses the group so each of us can find our regiment, and as I wait my turn on the path off our vantage place I hear two talking in low voices.

"Favored already and only just here," says the first from several yards behind me.

"Has she ever seen actual combat?" I hear the second one mutter.

I mentally count to three and manage to avoid giving a tongue-lashing.

"That's not the behavior which will let one rise to a captaincy," I say.

My icy calmness withers her pride; evidently she didn't think a captain stood near. I stare at her for an extra second before I walk off.

My behavior could have been worse, and as I follow Kimbr and Claire I wonder what it is that always brings out the... best? No, that's not exactly right. Her presence always wrings the most passion from me.

She and Kimbr head the same direction, lost in conversation until Claire looks back at me. The look in her eyes asks the same unspoken question as earlier, *Should I tell that I didn't hold my position in Myceum?* To which I give a little smile and shake my head again. She smiles back and I feel a momentary elevation of my heart at having defended her.

Over the next several hours my attention goes to my new regiment. I need to find out who my officers are, who Kimbr's officers are, what everyone's company is composed of, how Kimbr and I will work together for the flank, and a thousand other details. We have about two hundred soldiers between us, which is large for a flanking maneuver. My soldiers consist of archers with an equal number of foot soldiers carrying shields to cover them and the archers. The archers are armed with more than their normal knives, and the swords in their belts are for once we charge into combat too close to risk arrows. Claire is with us. Shutt will lead the main force in the valley.

Since we're intent on flanking their left side, to the north, we keep out of sight more than the other regiments. We know they'll at least halfway expect us to attempt a flank and will prepare for it, but we don't need them to know the size we're planning.

The enemy soldiers forming into wide orderly ranks signals our main lines' need to do the same. While we want them to advance our way, that's assuming a strong defense meets their charge.

From our hidden overlook, Kimbr and I wait for the soldiers to begin forming up. We're vulnerable to their scouts, but so far haven't seen any. Either they're more than the normal sort of crafty, or haven't penetrated far enough to reach our hidden post.

As we rush to our regiment a few hundred yards distant, we each share the hope all Oruvians feel; that our several-mile march around will be enough to baffle their scouts. The almost four hundred foot soldiers and archers remaining behind are counting on our success.

The first several hours speed by in our haste to circle around on their exposed flank. Kimbr and a few of our own scouts, young fellows raised in the Dendring mountains, lead the way step by cautious step.

From the word going through our moving force, the young boys were forced to flee from their mountain home after returning from a day of playing to find their family home burned and their parents gone. I've heard countless stories like this and it always renews my resolve. Even if I wasn't in line for the throne with every reason to keep it strong, I'd fight for these people. As many injustices as are committed in Oruvia, we're better than this and working to improve. Ross Knoke's nonexistence is one example.

We near the end of our trek over peak and through valley, and our regiment grows silent once again. The distant sound of clashing steel and heartrending screams sobers us more than any order from a commander would. We're still a half-mile from the Giant's Ballroom by the scouts' reckoning, and as they crawl forward on their bellies to make sure the next slope is safe to summit I wait back with the soldiers.

Kimbr slides forward with his sword in one hand and the other free. He left his shield with a soldier to have better control of his movements but I know he has a knife available to hold in his off hand to balance and parry with.

"Chris. Claire," Kimbr says after a few seconds.

Hearts dropping to the lowest valley we climbed from, we rush forward in a crouching run. We reach the top and throw ourselves down beside our captain to look across the ridges.

Kimbr doesn't need to explain the situation. The sounds coming to our ears told the battle had already begun, sooner than we thought, and it had moved closer. The problem, other than their obvious lack of a second wave to send in, was the Guldethian flanking maneuver.

Our wide flank worked, yet the very ridge we plan to launch our surprise attack from is occupied by a hundred Guldethian soldiers we hadn't seen before.

The instant it took me to recognize this another thought spun in my mind. *We can fight a separate battle up here and win, or wait to come from behind and save them. Only....*

"If we don't stop them from coming down on our flank," Claire says, "they'll have a thorn in their side I don't think they'll be able to extract."

She looks at Kimbr with wide eyes, silently pleading him to order us forward.

When he looks over at me I say, "We'd beat this force for sure, but we couldn't keep our ambush a secret through it. If they can hold out against this force too, we'd be able to sneak in from the side they'd least expect an attack from."

"They can't hold out against another hundred; look at them down there already." Claire's speaking louder and faster in her agitation, risking our position, but the enemy don't notice us.

"It seems we have to surprise their ambush and join the battle the best we can once we're finished up here." Kimbr speaks with more deliberation than usual and I can tell the words cost him. We're changing his plan with only a moment's consideration. "Make ready," he says.

One last glance at their position, waiting like hungry wolves ready to strike my friends, hardens my resolve. Since we're going to overcome their ambush with one of our own, it's important to move fast so they don't spring their trap. They'd be out of reach and we'd have no choice but to ambush them after a dreadful chase downhill.

Our archers, who strung their bows before starting on the sideways path, push forward eagerly at seeing us descend.

"Complete silence on your lives," Kimbr says in words halfway between a conversation and a whisper. He turns toward the officers waiting nearby. "They're waiting in an ambush over this hill to sweep across our comrades in the valley. If we don't stop them before they swarm down there we will not have a chance. Form your ranks and crawl up the hill to be ready on my signal."

No sooner are his words out of his mouth and the officers turn to face the soldiers. The speed with which soldiers can find their officers during an important moment still amazes me. They manage it in under a minute and when Kimbr and I turn around from our overlook to see the progress, he nods at me.

"Here we go."

We salute each other as best we can from our prone position.

Kimbr sets his forefinger over his lips to admonish silence going forward, which the officers pass along. We're holding off on our usual loud roar of defiance. We'll get as close as we can before letting the archers fire a shot.

He and I rise to a crouching position and start forward, with Kimbr motioning all the soldiers along. The Guldeth are so engrossed in the battle over the final hill they don't notice our approach. We start at two hundred feet, narrow it to one hundred and fifty feet, and still no stir. I'm sweating despite the cool mountain spring. I wipe my hands on my tunic to keep them ready for my sword. One hundred and forty feet now. Still no stir.

I glance up and see the far side of their forces in the valley. They're halfway facing us, which means our forces have their backs to the Guldethian ambush. My gaze again glides across their backs. About a hundred soldiers, mostly armed with spears, crouch ready. Grim and silent, their feeling and intention matches our own.

One hundred feet now, and our archers are resisting the urge to let their arrows fly. Kimbr wants to wait for as many of our soldiers to engage with them at once as possible. If everything goes perfect and we get close enough, the archers might not use their bows, but join in behind the foot soldiers with their knives.

Despite our best efforts, two hundred soldiers can't move undetected forever, or even for long. The battle holds their attention and the sounds cover up most of the noise of our advance. It isn't enough to stop one of their hundred from turning around. It may have been from dozens of sets of eyes boring into his back. Whatever the cause, he gives a cry of alarm the same time Kimbr commands the archers to fire.

"Foot soldiers advance," he yells. "Stay with your officers."

Archers strum on their bows, together at first, before the second shot sounds a little more spread out. I'm running with Kimbr and the first of the officers into the struggling Guldeth ranks. They manage a defense by the time our sword and spears reach them, but only after a score have been killed or injured by our archers' arrows flying low over our heads.

Already going in with huge momentum, the battle doesn't last long before they break and flee downhill. Our archers joined the fight after only a few arrows to make sure they didn't hit us in the backs.

The soldiers can't help but cheer when the enemy turns and flees, though all the officers know better; our battle has hardly begun. Kimbr calls the soldiers to form up again and the celebration is cut short before it begins.

"We can crush their fleeing remnant between us and our soldiers down there. We have to act fast." Kimbr leads us over the ridge.

They're fleeing headlong down the hill, trying to form into a line with which to penetrate our lower soldier's poorly-defended rear. Though our soldiers down there noticed the engagement atop the hill, they can't properly prepare to defend from behind with how hard they're being pressed from the front and side.

With my first good view of the battlefield, I see it's far different from how the tacticians thought it would go; they've driven us closer to the valley they planned to ambush from.

The retreating ambush slows near the bottom of the valley as they have to go around more ground depressions and contend with the defense our counterparts are putting up. When Kimbr cries a halt halfway down the slope and calls on the archers to fire, several more of them drop. The Guldeth realize they have to fight from two sides as well, which distracts them from our forces.

We wanted them to focus on us and it works. A little too well. When the second volley of arrows plows down the hill it's to find them already moving sideways. They're trying to find the main army so they can join it after their failed ambush. Our foot soldiers rush forward to meet them.

They're fighting to extract themselves from the overwhelming odds we're pressing them with even though the main portion of their army is likely doing the same to our forces. With each fallen soldier they flee a little farther until they break. Several of their soldiers drop from the shield wall and run.

"Let's bring them to us, Captain," Claire says. "It's our arrows they're afraid of and if we make like we don't have many left they might advance."

Kimbr, bloody with his own and others', stops to listen. His breath comes in gasps after this last attack and he croaks out through parched lips, "How?"

"Gather arrows from behind. They'll think we traveled too light and we're desperate before we join the fight."

A light comes into his eyes which I'm sure matches my own.

"Archers!" he shouts as loud as his breaking voice lets him, "back there to gather arrows! Get what you can! Footsoldiers—pikes ready to form a line!"

The archers obey the firm voice instinctively and charge up the slope toward the fallen Guldeth. They run from corpse to corpse, darting between the struggling wounded to find what arrows they can. It's a torment of spirit as I watch their progress.

With an indiscernible order and blanketing jeer, the enemy line turns around to face us. This is what Claire wanted.

My heart beats fast in preparation when Kimbr calls, "Pikes for defense! Archers hold back and make ready!"

With lightning swiftness they're bearing down on our line of soldiers again. The speed with which they turned earns my awe since we're ready for them. They're advancing while our archers must look frozen with fear in the back.

"Fire!" Claire yells, sending the first volley of feathered death slamming into their front rank while the rest come on at headlong speed. They jump over their fallen, push past the wounded, and come impetuously. The second and third volley greet them in rapid succession before the first soldiers reach our line. Our pikes hold firm enough to give the archers time for more shots.

From my place a row back in the shield wall I can see brief glimpses of the enemy's eyes. They didn't expect such a storm of arrows. Seeing one's opponent searching for arrows among the dead and wounded during a hard-pressed battle doesn't inspire confidence in their preparations, and I stop myself from pitying their falling into Claire's trap as the soldier in front of me skewers the opponent coming for him.

Realizing the ruse, they start to retreat again. The cries coming from their line send ripples of encouragement across our soldiers. Feeling the same rush myself, I urge my portion of the regiment to follow them.

My goal isn't to crush or stop their retreat; our archers are doing a neat job whenever one of their shields falls in their mad flight. I'm wanting to drive a wedge of soldiers into their line's side, giving our companions the encouragement a fresh wave brings to the battlefield.

We charge with raised shields and lowered steel and meet their own defensive wall from soldiers on the edge turning outward. Our force strikes their side and I hack, twist, and dodge when I see an opening. We cut a section of the enemy army from their main force but not enough to make the difference I wanted. Still, it reinvigorates the dispirited soldiers who had been pressed hard for perhaps hours.

Joining with our full force, we're all together, presenting a bit more even of a fight. It'll be better for them now, but it's still far from over and the struggle could go either way. The sun dims late in the afternoon; then, while Kimbr's calling us to rally to him, the light ceases. It's because of the valley we're fighting in; the sun seems to set over the highest nearby peak before it dips below the horizon. The effect is as if hiding a fire behind a screen then suddenly putting it out.

"Fall back two hundred yards," Kimbr orders into the screamless silence. Only the cries of the wounded issue from the battleline in front of us. "Bring the wounded and fallen you can find." He means us to tend their injuries or comfort their final moments.

My soldiers hurry to carry out the order.

Breaks like this in battles can wreak havoc on morale and I go to find Kimbr, who is searching for me. "How soon will there be a moon?" I ask.

"Two hours at the most. One if the clouds stay away."

"We need to keep the soldiers busy and preparing for that moment." I say.

His vigorous agreement sends beads of sweat with a tenacious hold on his chin and nose flinging to the ground. "We'll be tending to the wounded and moving into new formations. Can you oversee the new companies?"

I nod, sending my own sweat to the cool ground of night and rubbing my forehead with the back of my arm. It's bloody, mostly dry—at least before I streak it with sweat.

"We're against the depressions now. Use them to your advantage, maybe keep us amongst them," he says through slower pants. He looks north to the way we descended, then at me for the first time. "May Nymunia's favor follow you."

My first thought upon his departure is to confirm the plan swirling in my mind with my tactician.

"Claire, I need your help." She turns to face me and I see her, for the first time since Mt. Cabrae a week ago, in the moonlight. Her hair is wrapped close now, in the same tight braid she wore when we parted at Myceum. Seeing her hair, and her blood-splattered tunic clinging tight around an upper thigh, makes me swallow a hard lump in my throat before I can speak. "I—that's not from your leg, is it?"

She looks down. "No."

I breathe a little easier even though the lump isn't completely gone. "We need to plan. For when the moon is bright enough."

"They overmatch us," she says. "We *need* the high ground. We may survive these odds in daylight with luck or skill, but at night it's different. And it's not the bright moon we need to plan for—it's before the moon comes that we're in the greatest danger."

Before the moon comes out. We don't have much time to act, and even less to plan. I suppose this is why I went to ask her opinion.

"So we're not waiting to defend?"

"Absolutely not. Waiting to defend is rolling dice for our lives. We need to either retreat or chance a sneak attack. What did Captain Nealy say?"

"He said I'm to oversee the soldiers into new formations. He's helping organize care for the wounded."

She shakes her head. "I'm not having any part of that. Let's place a force at their rear before the moon comes out and make them think reinforcements have arrived. Or burn their supplies, or make a scare among the wounded, anything. We need to *do* something."

The Guldeth have fires springing up at their camp two bow-shots away. The fires blaze, making it easier to see figures until they're a few steps on the far side, at which they're lost behind the glare. A thought enters my mind.

"Do you see tents over there?"

She squints while leaning forward. "Maybe the reflection on the flaps—yes, I think so."

"It could be a trap to make us think they're staying put for the night, or it could be real. What if we cut the ropes to make them collapse on their occupants and light the canvas? They might be too shaken after escaping from a burning tent to bother with us any more."

She smiles over at me. "Clever, but I think we'd get killed if we attempted more than a few at the edge. Maybe... no."

"What are you thinking?"

"Fire arrows, but it won't work. They're far too inaccurate."

My eyes fly wide. "It could work."

"If you think so then you've never tried firing one."

"I have and you're right; they're about as accurate as pouring water from a high cliff. Not much range either. But if we dump enough water off the cliff, fire enough arrows, we'll hit plenty of their tents. What's the worst that could happen if we keep the fires dark until we're close enough to hit their lines?"

"It's..." She stares into the distance looking like she's trying to come up with an argument to make me quiet.

"If the worst happens it means we'd have a line of pikes waiting back at our camp to shelter behind. The best result would send them flying. You saw how scared they were of our arrows earlier. It was the only thing that drove their ambush away. I've got to tell Kimbr. Gather the archers, all our oils, and make sure nobody lights another fire in camp."

I rush away, leaving with a feeling of progress—at least I'm doing something to help while I'm waiting to head to Castle Muerthy.

Kimbr sees my enthusiasm and agrees, though I can tell he'd rather wait for them to come to us. Claire's gathering archers when I return so I rouse those with pikes.

"Wait back in our line unless you hear cries from us; then rush forward to help. Cadets partner with veterans. I'll be up with the archers trying to rout them. If they chase us back, part for us to slip through and hold firm."

Claire arrives with three score archers; most bear some minor wound from the day's fighting. A few officers come with oils and animal fats, which we melt over a fire before partitioning into buckets. Between Claire, four officers, and me, we assign the soldiers to gather in even groups behind us and crawl forward in single-file toward their line.

We make slow progress as the foremost in each column carries the bucket of oil for dipping arrows. My group reaches a depression within half a bowshot from the enemy line and tucks into it. We have fire within a minute, doing what we can to keep it low and shielded. We all stick arrows into the bucket of mixed oils to saturate them.

Clouds flit over the moon like foam on the sea. The coverings gradually grow thinner as the night slides by. We need to act soon before the moon gives away our cover. I decide it's time to give the signal.

"Parley for peace?" I call. "Parley for the night?"

Behind and beside me from other depressions I hear the faint rustle of my soldiers lighting their arrows. Faint lights shine out of the hollows.

"What's that?" A gruff voice calls from behind their line of fires. "Who's out there? Show yourself."

The lights stop growing brighter. I smile as I raise my own lit arrow and draw the hempen cord of my longbow. "For Elathon!"

My string twangs as it sends the arrow forth in an arc, leaving a shower of sparks cascading to my feet. A glance beside me shows the night flare with a million specks which last a second. Turning my dazzled eyes to the beams soaring into their camp, my heart beats in what feels like slow motion as I wait for the effect.

Like the first rattle of hailstones from a thunderstorm, the arrows fall intermittently at first, then increase as if they're been going on forever and will never stop. When they do stop a few seconds later, it's to a growing sound of cries and yells from their camp. We're all lighting our second soaked arrows as the noise increases, followed by more fires springing up in their camp. I raise my eyes to sight along the arrow and see a tent suddenly flare like a beacon, lighting the camp around it in a lurid glare.

An enemy soldier thrashes from what I can only assume is inside the flaming prison, the scream seeming to pierce through the tumult and come straight for me. I push that image aside, tilt my bow toward the largest mass of tents still standing, and release.

With the release of our second and third volley of fire arrows, they come under some order and begin to scatter in every direction. We use regular arrows to quickly drop those that come toward us, but behind them we see the blazes in their camp light up their assembling spear soldiers.

Our attack began a minute ago, but with their determination to charge us we need to move back to our lines. Our own pikes are waiting back to give us a safe retreat.

"Back to the lines!" I yell three times to make sure everyone hears me. The enemy are coming faster than I anticipated and making a cry almost drowning my voice.

We turn, bows in hand, and almost fly back up the slight rise to our waiting line of pike soldiers. Rushing between the gaps they've left us, we reach relative safety and turn around.

"Archers steady!" I bellow across our line.

I breathe heavily and fit an arrow to my bowstring. Over our soldiers's shoulders, we see the distant camp. The tent-fed flames have already starved out.

The flurry of movement lasts a few seconds while the archers each assume an almost identical posture.

My attention flits from their camp to our pursuers in the space of a breath. I hold back bile threatening to plug my throat. The speed with which they managed to prepare and empty their camp lets me know they didn't wait for our arrows to make ready; we forced their hands into an early rush.

"Mark your targets well. We only get one first greeting. You've fired the wasps from their nests, now show them the sting of Oruvian steel."

A rousing call echoes around our line from archer and footsoldier alike.

"Raise and draw for your homeland."

Sixty bows point skyward, straining under the tension.

"Fire!"

Loud shouts of rejoicing erupt from every throat as the arrows fall in and among our foes. Muffled cries of despair reach us as their uninjured rush past the fallen.

"Teach them to invade our land with hard vengeance."

Officers in the ranks have the pike soldiers and shield bearers ready to meet the charge. Around me bow strings twang while arrows hiss over the heads of the pike soldiers. As much of a surreal experience shooting over helmeted heads is, hearing the hiss when you're in the line is almost more dreamlike.

Moments later, the line of rushing Guldeth reaches our shimmering line of pikes. They're lowered to chest-height, the metal tip with long shaft supports reflecting the dull mix of distant firelight, stars, and a pale shaded moon. Their onrush knocks some of the pikes away. Sometimes it's deflected into the path of a following warrior who receives an impaling without warning. Wings just behind the point like boar spears stop some of the advance while the rest of it rushes through the openings created.

Our shieldbearers lunge forward with drawn weapons while the pike soldiers fling down their weapons and grab up their nearby spears. Pushing, parrying, lunging, cursing, sweating, and screaming all reach my ears as a soldier in front of me goes down. It's too early to tell how the battle will go.

I hazard a glance at the sky to see when we can expect a moon. Now that it's come to fighting hand-to-hand again, a moon would help. It would help our enemy as well, so we wouldn't gain an advantage beyond taking luck from the scales.

Before long it becomes apparent I made an error in judgment. I shouldn't have chosen to rush into a wide line, and now they're making the most of it; they've almost pushed through in a place. My call for reinforcing the section comes too late and they're in, striking down the last shieldbearers even as they defend themselves valiantly.

The soldiers drive themselves into the gap like a wedge, separating a quarter part of our force from the rest. With the soldiers in the other company forced back, and my own fighting their own defensive battle, the aid I'm able to give doesn't turn the tables back in our favor.

When the moon emerges from a thin place in the clouds a few minutes later, I see they've organized into a group. The enemy struggle after them, hampered by arrows, but making good progress against the few archers my eyes pick out.

Turning back to the battle in front of me tears at my heart, but the soldiers here need me as well. A group that size would have at least one officer to emerge as leader, maybe even Kimbr if they're fortunate.

Even with a portion of my force separated, the priority remains driving the Guldeth away. If I were to concentrate my forces upon rescuing the smaller segment it would leave our wounded vulnerable. As it stands it appears the retreating Oruvians are only slightly overmatched; it's about twice as many enemy, but our force is backing toward the high ground.

The shining moon lets me survey the main field for the first time since the fight began, and it doesn't show me a pretty picture; lines of soldiers still wait behind those already locked in the death struggle. My mind whirls as it processes how we could have had almost equal forces earlier and now they have some waiting in reserve. Could we have that many more wounded?

Then it hits me—they must have received reinforcements during the break. I step from the line and sweep the whole area in one slow spin on my heel.

Our force with theirs meeting it; Kimbr running from the wounded camp with the rest of the soldiers who can be spared; the sloping ridge with our small personnel retreating up it; back around to what's left of my regiment.

My tongue is sticking to the roof of my mouth through fear as much as parched with exertion.

"Kimbr," I yell.

He changes his steps to come up with me.

"They have reinforcements. We need to move the wounded and get to better ground."

"Many will die if we move them."

"They'll *all* die if we don't."

My words make him look over the battlefield again. He sees for the first time the detachment pressed by twice their number. Steel clashing against armor and thudding into shields punctuates all our words.

"We *need* them moved, Kimbr. You know our position wasn't meant to hold against reinforcements."

He gulps, nods, then rushes back up the hill without saying a word. We could use him down here, and I wish he'd have sent a scared first-time soldier with the order. He's a much better fighter than—nevermind, the soldier just took a nasty slice across his forearm. I rush forward and yank him back so I can take his position.

"Wrap that and get back here," I say.

The next fifteen minutes pass in the blink of an eye yet as slow as eternity. A thick-chested commander steps before me and I end him quickly while he's distracted by another. Fighting in the hardest-pressed parts doesn't give me the chance to think; I just do and hope I survive to take the next stroke.

When Kimbr sends a soldier to tell me he's finished moving the wounded, I waste no time.

"To me! To me! To me! Back up the slope orderly and quick."

Within a minute the fighting has all but ceased as we disengage to retreat. Kimbr has moved the wounded to behind a naturally defensive outcropping.

I see him rushing to our aid, sword drawn, shield at his side, and helmet clapped over his large head. His physical strength and the intensity of the cause burning in his chest both make him a fiend in a fight.

"Where do you need me?" he snarls upon reaching my side.

"Down along the right. We've been weak there since the split. They won't know what hit them." I slap him on the back, feeling like I'm hitting a double layer of armor. His shoulders and back, hard as rocks from a lifetime of training or combat, let him swing his oversized arming sword with ease.

A calmness overtakes the night, giving me the chance to look into the scattering of stars. There's still the tramp of the enemy soldiers drawing ever nearer, against whom we won't all survive—no matter which way the battle goes. We still hear the sounds from the smaller section on another ridge. But here our soldiers are formed up, silent, waiting. Looking across the compacted mass of soldiers, I try in vain to pick out Claire, if only to give her a word of encouragement.

The enemy arrives minutes later, and we're at it again. Through the rest of the night it's unclear who will win. We hold them for an hour before their reinforcements push them forward enough to force us back, but then, fighting to defend our wounded, we rush down upon them in a final despairing effort.

A horn sounds repeatedly, and the breaking sun glow shines upon our night-blinded eyes.

The tide of war goes in and out countless times during the night until it becomes clear that despite their reinforcements, the Guldeth will have to flee or be slaughtered.

When they turn their backs to us we cheer the way only a once-hopeless army can. Fagged spirits bolstered by the indescribably amazing sight of them rushing to their camp and beyond, we shake our weapons while cheering the cheer past hope. A pardon at the gallows.

Blood smeared across my face makes it hard to find a place to wipe my sword so I settle for the tunic of a fallen enemy. All sorts of colors covering my blue tunic make it look anywhere from a darker, shinier blue than normal to the dry and cracking brown of dried blood.

I walk to the largest man on the battlefield and salute Kimbr with my curled fist over the right side of my chest. His helmet is off and he gives the same salute back. To me, equal as a captain and sole prince of the land.

"You fought like a devil," I say, gripping his free hand.

His mouth folds to a flat line; eyes shine red, almost like he's been crying. He doesn't show a single wound.

"Rue."

"Dead?" I ask.

He nods. "When we moved them." A choking sob dies in his throat, strangled while struggling for release.

A horn sounds over the peaks; it sends my mind cascading in dreadful fear; I haven't seen Claire since the initial stages of battle, and don't know the fate of our separated soldiers.

Kimbr shares my realization. I'm off like an arrow despite my wounds. Despite the fatigue of riding from Myceum to Mt. Cabrae, sneaking through miles of passes and fighting all night, I run for her. My mind neglects everything my body needs.

Despite the fear drawing around my heart like an animal thrashing in a snare, I run on.

Even my tunic, soaked heavy with blood, doesn't slow my run up the hill. When I crest the summit, I stop.

And stare.

I scramble over boulders and tear around rocks, heart slamming to bruise my ribs. Everywhere I see a face I recognize. Pale faces, covered with blood, mud, or both. Enemy lay thick as well, and I avert my footsteps a few times while scouring the ground. She *can't* be here. She had to have been missed down below.

I want to believe that, but I can't. I can't wait when she may be lying out here—dead, or dying alone. Either one would kill me.

A slight shock to my system would do me good, but none comes. More dead. And more.

I run along, skidding on the red grass but continuing my mad rush anyway.

Spying a ledge, I make toward it. She might have retreated up here with her small squad. I know she didn't leave. My heart tells me she's close.

Enemy lay thick around the edges of the ledge, many stuck with arrows, and my heart bounces the slightest bit as I feel the least twinge of hope. I climb around the ridge, step over the fallen, and observe with horror that the bodies are now mostly Oruvian.

Ugly barbs of dropped spears and the sickening red yawns of wounds contrast to the white death-pallor overtaking the stiffening corpses of my countrymen. I climb higher and rush to the back of the ledge where the survivors would have hidden.

They would have hid there, at least if there were survivors, but my search yields no signs of life. Not a spirit left in a man or woman. All soldiers ended.

The promise of a new dawn feels like a twisted mockery of life. Such a hard life, and for what? Years of monotony punctuated with moments of tragedy, and for... nothing.

She's gone, my heart tells me, and I can't even find her body. My reflections gain the upper hand for a moment before I scrape the dew off my eyes and run to check the front of the ledge.

My heart plugs my throat as I see a small patch of brown. Light brown, wrapped tightly around a small head. Hair. Innumerable people have a light brown head of hair, but my whole body feels sick as I lurch forward to look at the greatest dread in my world. My steady disregard for Claire didn't work on my subconscious mind, for I somehow know it's her hair I'm walking toward.

Enemy corpses fill the spaces I want to walk, and I have to pick my footsteps with care.

Kimbr and his friend Drake crest the hill and help. Other Oruvian officers and soldiers now search the crags and hollows, running and shouting to each other, but my mind focuses entirely on the person before me. I move aside for a fateful view and see her, unmoving, surrounded by fallen enemies, and covered in blood. It's Claire.

Bodies of a few Oruvians who apparently stood by her side until the end lay around her, but mostly she's entrenched with the remains of her fallen foes.

The battlefield gives signs they knew the defense would end in death. Oruvians fell beneath the crush, but not without pulling dozens down with them. The thought of a single officer with a small squadron against so many inflicting so much damage for our cause makes my blood run momentarily cold.

I kneel beside the body and look and feel in vain for any sign of life. A stiffening, cold corpse is beneath my fingers, but it's more than that; it's my... friend. The temple of her spirit, and instrument of good, I look with a special kind of reverence on her dirty face.

I didn't realize until now what a chance Claire took in giving that order to stop on our way to Myceum. She risked the honor her parents gave her through her last name. Risked the advantage and head-start many would have given an arm for. A wrong reception would have taken the officer title from her, negated part of her mother's sacrifice, and set her back decades or longer.

She knew that, and yet swiftly gave the order to stop. She risked everything for my sake, and now I sit here in the bloody mud after the battle. A battle she should have survived.

I didn't realize until now how little I appreciated her risk.

I'd give anything to have her back. My heart feels a crushing sensation from all sides, as if I'm having life squeezed from it. I've had friends die in battle before, sometimes many all at once, and witnessed some of their last breaths, but none of those come close to this. This is more like... reliving the nightmare of my mother's death. It's even worse than Rafael's. Bad as that was, I heard about that days after the event. Only three other times have I felt such a heart-wrenching hopelessness drain my will to live.

Anything, like with my mother, no price would be too high to pay. Just let me have another chance with her; a chance to tell her how I feel now that she's gone; a chance to return her affections; a chance to... to love her. My vision begins to fade, and I try to blink away the tears I know are causing it. Nothing happens, and I move the least bloody part of the back of my hand to wipe my eyes, but still my vision darkens.

I realize what's happening and do nothing to stop it. I want to whirl out of control. My torso sways from kneeling beside Claire's body. I could consider it a fainting-spell, but I know better.

This feeling has overtaken me before, and I've stopped it all but four times.

Not this time.

Lower the shields.

Let it in.

Take whatever price I need to pay.

It feels overwhelmingly like I'm being dragged underwater. The crushing calmness I imagine in the depths of the sea feels as one with me, and my mind and body don't resist. There's no pain anymore, no loss; just the peace between worlds.

Chapter 12.

My horse saunters along as we round a bend halfway up the mountain. I see the rough pocked face of a granite wall rise above me. The other side shows an expansive view of a valley with the tops of the closest trees level to my eyes. It's first light and this is the path Mobent, Claire, and I took with another squad of soldiers the day before.

Claire. It *is* the day before. I whip my head to see her and almost upset my horse. One of its hard feet scrabbles down the cliff face. The sturdy-footed quarter horse adjusts without rearing or tumbling, letting me focus on Claire's astounded face instead of plummeting to my death.

"What?" she asks.

"It's.... I mean, you..."

Everyone stares at me after my near tumble. It's Mobent, Rue, and Drake. Mobent and Drake survived the battle, but Rue died of wounds. Meeting their stares shoots a shiver up my spine.

"I need to talk with you," I say to Claire.

I slip from my horse, take her by the hand, and lead her along the path we came. "Make sure to take a force to outflank their flank. Don't wait for us," I say to the others, and pull her into the forest. The effort to turn it into an order comes across halfway through my message, making them still stare at us as we disappear among the granite boulders and spires.

"What is it? Where are we going?" She ducks beneath a fir branch.

"Just here. Right here." My eyes shine as I turn round to look at her.

The bittercress is just past its prime, the arnica almost ready to burst into a carpet of yellow flowers, and the first of the columbine are spreading their five colored spurs back for the fingernail-shaped petals to accent the delicate colors extending behind. The greens of the flowers and leaves contrast well with the solid trunks of aspen and pine trees, but especially her hair. I hadn't noticed it until atop that outcropping. It looks even better now that it isn't covered in blood.

"You look different. You look ol..." Claire's voice trails off as her eyes widen. "Did you—"

"I had to. Like last time they... they..." *Who am I kidding?* I think. I didn't do it because they didn't leave anyone alive; I did it because I lost Claire, the song in my soul.

"We won. We won with you, Kimbr, Mobent, and all the others. It was great and awful fighting through the night. I've never really used fire arrows until the secondary ruse. They really are as bad as people say, but they worked well enough. We fought until the evening. Our second attack, the one we used fire for, drove them from their camp—thank Nymunia—or we never would have stood a chance with their reinforcements arriving right then."

Claire's smile matches mine and I go on.

"In Myceum we had fires and moonlight. And walls to hide behind. By Starview Pass we didn't have stars half the time. No moon for the first bit of last night. I mean, tonight."

The smile gracing Claire's face grows bigger until her lips part.

"What?"

Claire laughs. "You're doing a year's worth of talking now to make up for lost time."

I can't help but match her mirth. The battle I remember seems distant, a vaporous nightmare. The possibility of losing Claire again doesn't cross my mind. I'm totally enraptured with having her back. The woman I didn't know I loved so much.

"I... I..." Words fall from my smiling, quivering lips. It's too much, having her here, having her back.

I squeeze her to me. "I can't be without you."

She stays rigid a moment, then relaxes into my embrace. With my face buried in her neck and her fawn-colored hair falling around my ears I can't hear what she says, but the relaxation and firm grasp across my back tells me more than any words could. I could stay like this forever.

It was worth the pain. Worth the year of my life. Worth a decade. For this one moment.

With my face bent into her neck, my hand combed close to her scalp, and our bodies pressed close against one another, it seems there's only now. "I can't be without you," I repeat.

Moments pass, or maybe an hour.

"That's why you came back."

I nod, if it can even be called a nod with my face doubled forward almost over her shoulder to get as close as possible. Of course that's why I came back. Two years of my life Gifted to her and I'd give the rest to keep her safe.

"You died again," I say and hold her at arm's length as my jubilation recedes into blind realization. "You were separated with a squad during the night, and they killed you. Gods that was awful; seeing you there covered in blood and knowing I'd never hold you again. Never hear your voice. Never see your eyes or get to feel your touch."

Her expression makes me stop short.

"I wasn't there—not to remember much, anyway. I sort of know what you went through—since I saw Mother in the same situation with Father, but it's different from this side. It doesn't really feel real. I know I'm not heartless but, like you said yesterday, the emotion makes it happen."

"They killed you and I wasn't even there to stop it. I only found you after the battle. One among a hundred."

"A hundred?" Her eyes go wide. "And I was in the smaller party?"

"They didn't leave any of you alive. It looked like you were the officer in charge. You killed at least as many before your squad was overrun."

"How did I do it?"

"I don't know. Lesasil can't you be a little sad you died and put me through that?"

Her curiosity the two times I've saved her definitely overpowers any sorrow for what I felt. I suppose I can't blame her for that attitude. After all, she went through this dozens of times already.

"I suppose your father's glorious deaths in battle were common topics of conversation at your dinner table?" I say with a hint of sarcasm dripping from my sincere smile.

"Actually, yes. Mostly when Mother was still around, but Father reminded me of them. He'd use examples to supplement my training."

A laugh breaks from my lips, as if I can hardly believe I'm talking to her. I take her in my arms again and she hugs back. The alternating emotions keep me reeling.

"Well, I need to go to Castle Muerthy." I say after a silent minute. "Are you still planning on coming?"

"Absolutely." She releases the hug and we look at each other from arm's length again. She smirks with a little dimple appearing aside her mouth. "You couldn't be without me, remember?"

I smile in answer. "We're leaving now."

I hold her fingers lightly. They slip from my grasp when I begin the short walk back to the path.

"We can't just leave Mobent like this," she says as I start up the path we just descended.

"I told him not to wait for us." I spin around and walk backwards to keep making progress. "And I told him the strategy they'll need. I can't risk you again there, and we have to keep moving."

"But we left our supplies with the horse. We have to get them anyway."

"No we don't," I say and stop in my tracks. "We'll get some at the outpost by the bridge a mile back. C'mon."

She follows when I start walking again. Her rapid steps bring her beside me within seconds.

As a captain and the prince, it's easy to secure provisions, arms, and other supplies from the bridge outpost. To ease Claire's conscience, we give instructions for the next party journeying toward the Giant's Ballroom to carry notice of our safe appearance.

We cross the bridge immediately after leaving the outpost and turn away from Starview Pass. It'll be a slightly longer route, but less frequented and, I hope, not the sight of a ferocious battle.

Reaching Murethon, like I said to Commander Nealy, isn't what I consider fun. Even so, it's what I need to do. Kimbr can handle the battle at Giant's Ballroom without me. For my part, we need to get to the bottom of what's happening. We need answers, and I hope those answers can be found in Heller's castle.

"Why do they call Heller White 'Whiteneck'?" Claire asks during the first day of our trek.

"It's a play on his last name," I answer, "but it goes far deeper than that. It's rumored the Balm of Life, made from Dryad's Honey, turns your skin white when you apply it. Not any sort of white, mind you; the whiteness of flower petals, or the color of some birds' eggs. Haven't you heard the legends?"

"I've heard about the Balm of course, though I never knew it turned the skin white. That's ironic."

"I think it must have to be applied to the neck. It's just speculation since I don't know if anyone's seen him since the Divide."

We walk in silence for several more minutes, our minds wandering in their own channels. Finally I ask, "Have you ever seen a dryad?"

Claire continues to swirl a sky-blue columbine she plucked from beside the road, moving it in her fingers to see every side of the delicate flower. For a few minutes I think she didn't hear me, but then she answers. "I can't be sure. They're meant to be so secretive I may have imagined it."

A minute passes before I press, "You did see one."

"Maybe. Yes. It was after my mother died, up in the Holy Forest of Italiel along the Cousea coast. Father and I were there as part of an excursion. After the Dividing War and losing June, he wanted away for both our sakes."

This time when she pauses for five minutes I keep my ears open, waiting for her to offer more.

"We were only there for fun. I wanted to practice my archery so I cut a wand from a tree to make a bow. It was an ash tree. I could still walk right to the spot and point to the limb. After I removed the smaller twigs, smoothed a place for a handle, and shaped the ends to fit my string, that's when I saw her. It was out of the corner of my eye at first. When I snapped my head to look I got the surprise of my life.

"It was a dryad like you hear about in the old tales. She had skin like treebark. Not the thick rough bark on the outside; the bright, glossy inner cambium layer. Her hair," Claire pauses and shudders. "On her head there was half hair, half twigs and vining branches. One of the branches was severed and it bled. It wasn't sap; it was real red blood. And it dripped from the severed end, evidently where I cut it.

"She didn't look in pain, or even sad or reproachful. She just looked as if to make sure I knew what I did, that my action affected more than myself. Her face was... peaceful, and yet solemn and knowing. Everything about her radiated youth except the eyes. They looked as old as the forest, darkened with wisdom.

"Her clothing was vines and leaves; bright, pliable leaves of spring. Her legs looked like tree trunks the farther they went to what would have been her feet, and it looked like she was planted in the ground, though that couldn't have been the case since I know she hadn't been there when I arrived. We looked at each other for ten or fifteen seconds without saying a word before she moved back into the thicker forest."

She pauses her story, walking with eyes on the path.

"Father said it was my imagination, but I was too old to make it up. I don't make things up.

"When I returned to the spot later that day to search for her, I found the tree without trouble and searched until sundown. Her tracks were visible at the start but faded as the miles went on. It wasn't even on a rocky place I lost the track. It was like she slowly vanished."

Minutes pass while I run her story back through my mind, trying to comprehend it. Not exactly what I expected, since I've seen the same woman in a swirl of mist.

"She came because you needed healing?" I venture.

"Maybe." She tosses the flower gently to the ground. We keep walking side by side. "Can one ever know why things like that happen?"

Several more minutes pass, each of us lost in our own thoughts, before she says, "It could easily have been a fancy; they're just old legends."

"I think I've seen the same dryad," I say.

Claire looks over at me. The gravel-strewn dirt path crunches under our feet as we bob along.

"It was years ago in a forest outside Sapesky. Rafael and I were hunting boars a few months after the queen passed. We hadn't seen anything all day so we grew careless and split up.

"Of course we split up the hounds too. About an hour later mine started to go crazy. At first they charged ahead, then they came back whimpering. I was inexperienced and thought they just wanted me among them. It appeared to work since they charged forward again. We were among the thick grass and dense fir trees. I could hear something rustling in the trees and grass beside us for a few minutes and kept on hoping to find a clearing to stand my ground.

"Three boars came at us in a rush, but my two short-haired greyhounds were ready for them with warning snarls before they broke cover. They were so hairy I thought they were dogs at first, but they were just massive hogs. It looked like two of them turned around to go back into the trees, leaving one visible.

"The nasty thing eyed us as it circled, my dogs barking to keep it back. When it did charge, I dropped to my knee and couched the end of my spear on the graveley ground. The spear skid away from the impact of the beast landing on the cross-guard. I got lucky and it died soon after.

"I heard the other two return while I pulled my spear out of the first. One was upon me before I was able to even stand, much less move out of the way. The dogs had kept their barking constant since the first and streaked past me to intercept the next one. The impact of the second boar's charge knocked me over. I tried to scoot away, kicking and yelling, but it's mouth and tusks only moved from by my legs to my abdomen.

"My yells turned to screams and somewhere in there I remembered my knife. I don't remember it, but I must have blindly slashed at its face enough to accidentally stab through an eye and strike the brain.

"After that it's weird—she was exactly like you described her. The dryad came and—I don't remember much—I think she touched my side and leg. They were torn and gaping from the tusks ripping through them. The wounds didn't miraculously heal and I passed out right after she left.

"Rafael's dogs found me a few minutes later and led him to me, with my own dogs torn and whimpering as they limped around the small clearing. He carried me a few miles until a patrol found us, then they took us to the castle. I didn't come to until the next day. The royal surgeons were surprised when I was walking a month later. They had said I'd never use that leg again. I think they were upset I made them wrong by surviving.

"Rafael told me he was about a mile away when he heard me start yelling for help, crying. It was some point in there I saw her." My brow furrows as it does every time I recollect this. "She saved me."

"And you never told anyone how you lived?"

"They said I was raving about forest dwellers before I came to. The surgeons insisted I was at least temporarily insane. Again, I think they were mad I proved them wrong. Father and Rafael were kind but clearly didn't want to encourage my talking about it."

We walk for another mile, descending into a valley along a steep path that makes us run before we reach the bottom. Around a corner we both stop to watch a small waterfall, cascading to the smooth rocks before moving along the valley's bottom, water ceaselessly flowing since our ancestors first ventured to create a path along the winding course.

We turn away from nature's majesty.

"I never knew you and Rafael had that happen," Claire says.

Guilt plugs my throat for a minute, just like it does so often around her. Only this time, I'm man enough to acknowledge the reason for it.

"I'm sorry. The king kept it quiet for fear the people would think he let his heirs roam alone in what could be viewed as dangerous country."

"You could have told me. I wouldn't have thought you a fool for seeing a mythical being."

"It's not a good excuse, but my head wasn't right after the accident and losing Mother."

"Did you want to use your Gift when the hogs were bearing down on you? I mean—you probably had an extreme enough emotion."

"Didn't even cross my mind. It was too soon after three bitter failures." My mind makes my mouth punctuate the last few words, moving them from a statement to a defense. "I'm sorry," I repeat a moment later.

I stop, face Claire, and pull her into a light embrace. The hair she's left down caresses across my check and lower neck. When she wraps her arms around me in return, I squeeze tighter and crush her to me. "I don't ever want to lose you again."

Chapter 13.

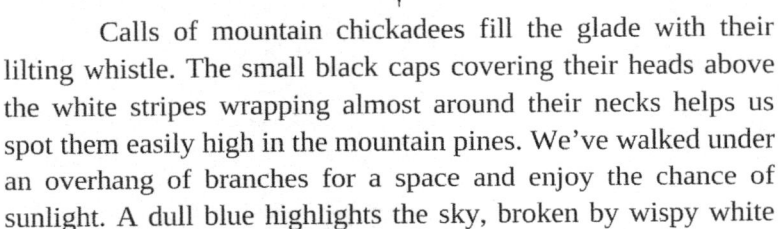

Calls of mountain chickadees fill the glade with their lilting whistle. The small black caps covering their heads above the white stripes wrapping almost around their necks helps us spot them easily high in the mountain pines. We've walked under an overhang of branches for a space and enjoy the chance of sunlight. A dull blue highlights the sky, broken by wispy white clouds that look like trailing gossamer webs.

The birdsong grows fainter when we reenter the cover of trees. I use the change of scene to bring up a recurring thought.

"Did your mother ever regret using her Gift?"

Claire hesitates, then answers with deliberation. "I don't think so."

"No, not about saving Julek," I correct myself. "I mean did she ever regret using it for other reasons?"

"Not that I know. She always used it for reasons close to her heart. She loved Elathon as much as any soldier does, and gave her life in her own way."

"How about changing the outcome of a battle? Sure she could save Julek by employing other strategies, but what about the soldiers who wouldn't have otherwise died except for those strategies?"

Our boots on the forest floor create a gentler sound than the harsh grating of gravel stones.

Julek tried to keep June's Gift a secret, but by the time she started using it to reverse battles, it was too well known. In the end they simply stopped announcing when she used her Gift. Since no one could completely know of its use, it worked fairly well in stopping public discourse. But those who had a loved one die in battle often remembered her Gift and held hushed conversations about the possibility of it being the commander's fault. As much of a help it had been in bringing peace to the kingdom, it left a festering boil deep in Eraseam's subconscious.

"My... my mother's Gift was for the kingdom's benefit," Claire answers. "Who can say a commander surviving a battle isn't for the good of everyone?"

"Yeah..." I say. The thought has occurred to me more than once, but never bothered me until now. It's good for everyone except those who die in their place.

"She used it to bring down the casualty numbers overall. Often she managed to save entire companies from walking into a trap."

"If a hundred die in war but none are related to you, that's a lot less of a concern than if fifty die with one being your son or daughter."

"Well what should she have done?" Claire says, responding to an attack only in her imagination. "It's your kingdom they were helping after all."

"It's not like that. You know I used my Gift in Myceum and at Giant's Ballroom. Who am I to say it was for the best?"

"You saved me both of those times."

Her timbre shows she still feels attacked. I pause a few seconds to make sure I'm not drawn in to really attacking her. "I know. I'm not questioning that either. It's just—how do I know there wasn't a single soldier who survived Myceum the second time around who might turn traitor. Big windmills spin on small axles, and they can turn anything into dust."

I fall silent and, while I hope she responds, I'm grateful for the space to think.

"I suppose that's the risk we take in doing anything, or doing nothing. The horses we took from Myceum might have been needed in Mt. Cabrae to carry an urgent message. Maybe our actions today will have an effect fifty years from now."

"True," I say. "I'm grateful I don't decide what the outcomes will be; who survives and all that."

"It's all up to chance; directed chance, but still chance."

Before long we find ourselves climbing a gentle slope along a winding path through the mountains, leaving all traces of streams behind for the occasional glimpse of water gurgling down at a sharp angle. This leads us to where the trees grow thinner, granting our first uninterrupted view of Murethon. It's been years since I've traveled far enough to overlook the land. The war mostly keeps me fighting in the mountains, and now that we're on the western slopes, we're no longer in the province of Eraseam, or in Elathon for that matter.

The thought lends a sober moment to my undertaking, and I feel a strong inclination to reach for Claire's hand. She doesn't have to be here with me, I remind myself. She's strong and capable. Compromising between reason and desire, I look over at her. Her light brown hair, still down despite my frequent reminders that I'd feel better if she braided it high, blows in the breeze. A strand across her nose makes me catch my breath.

"Let's go."

Early in the afternoon, we're walking amongst massive granite boulders. Spirited trees grow from small fissures, sometimes looking like they're perched atop the sheer-sided rocks, other times growing sideways before shooting skyward. The ground beneath our feet is a slippery coating of long tan pine needles shed from the lower branches. Stones, both loose and fixed, lie hidden under the covering.

Usually walking, occasionally scrabbling, we make our way up what we think is the last of the large hills. The peaks here are low compared to in the Dendring mountains, but the western foothills are vastly different from those on the Elathon side. As we reach the top, the boulders grow smaller and look more like natural formations that are a part of the mountain, rather than parts broken free from nature's incessant advance.

Breath comes harder now, so we're less inclined to speak. I point this out to Claire. She smiles and says, "If the hill wanted us to stop it would be like the tale of the sun and the wind trying to force the traveler to remove his cloak; gentle force proved more effective than aggression."

We don't stop with the coming and passing of the noon sun. As at other times, we eat a small meal while walking easier terrain. A few hours after noon, during the warmest part of the spring day, Claire stops. She's walking ahead by a few yards which I easily cover in a matter of steps.

"What is it?"

"I thought I... saw something," she ventures, then shakes her head. "It was probably nothing. Just an animal or a trick of my eyes."

I'm too experienced of a soldier to take her words lightly, though. With my hand on my sword, I step before her. "We can't be too careful. After all, we're not in Artalia or Eraseam. The wolves prowling these mountains can be almost as bad as the two-legged predators."

It's a party of Guldethian soldiers, at least twenty of them, and they don't look the sort of pleased to see us I'd like. Pack animals, just like wolves, but the look on their faces pales my face more than a hunting howl would.

"Who are you wandering the wilderness when everyone else is taken up with the freeing effort?" The foremost calls. He's average height, with a face scarred heavily enough for me to see it from the distance. A small shaggy robe of animal hide rests on his shoulders, extending partway down his back. One weapon stands out against his well-fitting tunic: a sword stuck in a faded leather belt. The man's appearance doesn't warrant any special consideration. His face does. Clean-shaven, serious and intelligent, it gives off the impression he knows more than he lets on.

"We're traveling south to see our relatives. They were displaced by the war and we haven't heard from them all winter." It's a long shot, but worth a try.

A smile curves his lips, and men and women behind him laugh. "Nah; just as you're not who you pretend, we're not the same as we look either. You can take us for a band of robbers, but you'll be mightily mistaken." He stops to snicker. "And you —you two look too self-assured for Murethon peasants. Our boors are so smitten with the Grand Overlord they can hardly look anyone in the face."

Okay, I think, *so if he isn't a common robber and he's astute enough to recognize us as outsiders, that makes him someone from Heller's inner circle. At least his army.*

"I'm with the Grand Overlord's special force."

Soldiers. My first guess proves correct.

"The testing grounds for his shadow force, you might say."

Shadow force, shadow soldiers, shadow warriors; where have I heard of them?

"Enough talk, though. You're not who you say you are and that's enough for us to bring you in. There's no need for boasting about your friends following behind; we've been watching you for a mile and know you're alone. I recommend coming quietly." He draws his sword halfway while the others follow his example.

A quick glance at the other faces tells me they're used to being obeyed yet unafraid if there's a struggle. It doesn't look like this force would let itself get into too many struggles.

"You won't find me easily cowed." The damage I've inflicted on their army over the years lends my courage wings. Fighting the temptation to boast of it, I content myself with drawing my own sword as well. The sound of Claire doing the same lends a harmonious, almost musical ring to the sound.

The soldiers before us part to go around their leader, motionless, as he allows them to fan out. Claire and I have thrown our packs away from our feet and taken up the most sure-footed spot we can find, bracing ourselves shoulder to shoulder as we watch them pick up speed.

"Aaah!" I yell as I parry the first sword-thrust aimed at my chest. Following with a rapid riposte, it sends the soldier off balance, but before I can press my advantage, another soldier swings. It's a swing like Elara and Shelby tried on me in Sapesky, but with killing force and practiced skill. Ducking between their blades isn't an option since I'm essentially guarding Claire's back so I take one blade with my own and flash up an armored elbow. It works, deflecting the blade at the last moment. The space I needed opens up and my sword slides into and out of a soldier so fast he's moving into another attack position before he knows he's been impaled.

"Alive! Alive! We need them alive." I hear the man shouting.

The words bolster my spirits as much as I imagine they catapult our foes into action. It'll be easier to defend since I know they want us captured. Hopefully unharmed.

Them not trying to harm me is a risk I'm willing to take. I throw myself in the midst of an unwinnable battle, asking Lesasil to keep me safe, trusting the same for Claire. If their leader's words weren't true, Lesasil will have a hard time sparing my life.

The next fraction of a second makes it clear they truly want me alive, but I have no such restraint as I slice my sword across a few blocking blades, throwing my off-sword arm out for balance, helping me finish with a lunge.

"Rrraaah!" The noise escapes my throat in a loud cry as I brace my abdomen before a particular heavy slash.

"Chris!" I hear. It's Claire's voice, and she's the only one who knows my name anyway. After sidestepping a swing that threatened to remove my arm, I glance toward the sound. A full dozen yards from where I stand, she's fighting with the final desperation before capture.

Did I move this far or did she?

The thought steals my breath as I shove through a soldier, running to her aid before it's too late. Minutes ago I knew they wanted us alive, but upon seeing the red sword wrenched from her grip all thoughts except saving her life flee my mind.

Leaping over bodies strewn between us, the short distance to cover feels tremendous and I fear not reaching her in time. Her hands are behind her back, her hair tangled in a Guldeth's fist, a blade near her throat.

"No," I yell from instinct.

The thought of them wanting to capture us alive floods my system again, nerving my resolve. With a dreadful gamble I ignore the soldiers holding Claire, and throw myself in the midst of others. They scatter, knowing it's an uneven fight. Loss for me means capture; loss for them means death.

Their leader rallies them with a call. "Kings in mind! Kings in action! Take him for your prize."

Prize indeed. The leader recognizes my kingly spirit, but there's no way he can place me for the king. No matter; they'll regret paying the exorbitant price for a prince.

With the rallying call, they press with the best order they've shown yet. Combined with losing my battle partner, their new strategy lends their overwhelming odds the easy opportunity to disarm me. I fight like a wildcat, though, even once my sword is gone; scratching, punching, and tearing until they control my hands and wrest them behind my back.

Captured at last, I have time to look around. My survey shows a red mess of trampled grass scattered between the fallen soldiers. Claire downed three, and I'm responsible for five lying in the dirt, at least two of which I know fell to killing stokes. Still, it wasn't enough to stop their overwhelming numbers from capturing us.

"Get us out of here!" Claire yells as they bind her hands roughly behind her back. They're doing the same to me while the leader actually rearms us. It doesn't help; in fact not reaching the weapons so close to our hands adds to the chagrin of capture.

"Why? So we can sneak in another way?" I'm not happy about it either, and my shields automatically seem to raise when someone tells me to use my Gift.

"I suppose this is as good a way to enter as any," Claire says. Her voice is raised. "If I knew you were going to walk us into their hands I may not have come."

"I tried to talk you out of it."

"You could have told me we'd follow a reckless *lack of* a plan. That would only have been fair to me."

My mind screams at me to point out Julek's known recklessness and how unfair *that* was, but a cord burning into my wrists as it's drawn tighter draws a repressed grunt from me and takes away the need for restraint.

Pain as a distraction; how lovely.

"Enough of your lover's dispute," the leader says. "We're taking you to the Grand Overlord for questioning. Ordinarily we'd have killed you without you even seeing us, but you seem halfway worth the trouble of taking there."

"Who are you to take orders from a man like Whiteneck?" I say and try to rile them to lose their heads.

He only smiles. An evil, malevolent smile, filled with foreboding.

"I'm part of the best force in Murethon. Shadow Kings take suggestions; not orders. We weren't ordered to bring you in; we thought it would be advantageous." His smile drops. "So no, we aren't ordered to do anything. I'd suggest you mind your tongue if you want to keep it past questioning."

"Huh," I scoff

I look significantly at the several dead or wounded on the ground.

"They didn't make the cut," he says, then leaves.

I'd almost have preferred a slap across the face to his emotionless retreat. His cold silence is something I'd do to an enemy; very different from a common robber.

The moonless part of the night has already passed, and we see it light up the eastern sides of Castle Muerthy's towers as it swings above the horizon. The dark green and red pennants look black in the shadowy moonlight. Our captors surround us on the walk over the stone bridge. They tightened into a formation as we neared the castle, holding us in a way I, and I assume Claire, can't help but admire.

They lead us past guards, through the yawning gates, and under the watchful eyes of sentries who stare at us from damp stone walls. Inside, the whole castle gives the impression of a fortress far older than Heller's Divide. Crude buildings with small patches covering the original layer of patches lean against the castle walls, as if but for the stone supports they would have fallen decades ago. As a lean woman opens a door, revealing a flicker of firelight for a second, I think I notice the structure quiver.

Children gathered by the well stare blankly as we pass; their protruding cheekbones catch enough moonlight to cast shadows on the sunken parts of their faces beneath. One clutches the bucket, which I only notice since it's hanging by a chain, not a rope. The soldier standing in the courtyard keeps an eye on them, as if worried the bucket will disappear again. She seems fed well enough—at least she has real clothes, not loose-hanging threads that ripple in the cool night breeze.

Open-air steps leading to a lower courtyard slow our progress, giving me a chance to look over the scads of buildings clustered in confused disorder. Few of the buildings have bright roofs: I can almost smell the dark thatch heavy with mold or see the sagging, spongy, flaked-off boards of old shingles.

Down in the lower terrace of the castle, we turn a hard left, this time entering a door set in the retaining wall. Occasional torches light our way. We've left over half our guard behind now, yet I still can't do anything to try escaping with my hands bound. Also, the guard behind me wouldn't allow the effort.

Warmth relieves my body as we pass lower into the castle. A turn when we reach the bottom shows a narrow passageway behind heavy bars. If hearts could sigh in dejection, mine would now. Rattling coughs interspersed among the low droning of moans reach my ears from ahead.

Our escort says a few words to the guard on duty before we're let inside. Hearing the sound of the bars clank back into position relieves my ears from moaning, but now we pass through the gauntlet of curious stares. It doesn't take glances into many of the cells lining the passage to convince me of our guard's wisdom in keeping their faces straight forward. If seeing the starving, lice-covered prisoners could help them, I would look, but I'm in no position to do anything.

"In here," our guard says, motioning us into a larger cell at the end. "We'll come get you in the morning if you're wanted."

A slam echoes in the stone space. The hurt to our ears is a final signal of our captivity.

"That was weird," Claire says seconds later.

"What?"

"They didn't take our weapons. We can try to escape."

"Our best option is to stay here."

"What!"

"Captors never tell prisoners anything; since he said they might come get us in the morning it means they will."

"So we have until morning to escape," Claire says. She pivots around to place her sword hilt near my bound hands. "We'll figure this out as we go."

After a half-hearted attempt to reach her sword, I say, "We came here to find answers. I think now that we're here we'll have as much success being taken before Heller as anywhere we could sneak."

"How do you know we'll be brought before him?" she asks, one eyebrow lowering as she turns to face me, tossing hair out of her eyes.

"The soldiers. You've got to admit they weren't ordinary enlisted men and women. It's true they made a poor showing of themselves until their leader rallied them. It didn't take them long to capture me after that. He said they were Shadow Kings in training. I've heard of them; Heller's secret assassins." Moments pass, the ear-blistering sound of moaning again filling the air. "And he's right, we're not ordinary citizens. We stand out in this dungeon like two peacocks in a flock of geese."

"Peahen. I'm a woman."

Her serious expression combined with the words stuns me for several seconds before Claire starts chuckling, breaking into a full teeth-showing laugh. The anxiety still rests in her eyes, though now it has to make room for a possibility. The possibility of success.

My bewilderment melds into a grin. Despite being surrounded by wailing, tormented prisoners; despite being thrown into a cell at the end of the dungeon hall; despite the realization that only one person knows my intended location with a war raging between us anyway; despite everything, that shared moment of laughter wraps a bandage and applies pressure to the cavernous sore of my belief.

Anguished cries continue through the night, often cresting in cackling shrieks of deranged laughter. Exhaustion aside, my heart bruises for their sufferings. I've heard stories of life in Murethon since Whiteneck's Divide, but like all stories of seldom-visited lands I didn't know how much to believe. It appears I should have believed them all.

Disrupted sleep comes eventually. I sit against the wall and allow my head to lull into a corner, resting my head against a handful of soiled straw meant for bedding. Claire stretches out on her side with her head resting on my lap for a pillow. I long to free my aching hands, if only to better cover her ear and let her have a more restful night.

Morning comes—at least I assume it does—when a guard's footsteps chink down the hall. They stop by each cell for a moment, tossing what I notice to be a moldy piece of bread between the bars of each. At our cell the guard stops to stare at us. We're both awake so I clamber to my feet, fighting to keep my tingling legs from shaking.

"I need an audience with your Grand Overlord," I say.

She tosses a piece of bread to Claire. Then she stares at me until I think she's going to leave. Before she breaks the stare, though, she reaches for a bowl I hadn't noticed on the tray.

"Extra for you two." She passes the bowl through the bars. "We'll come for you soon." She turns on her heel then stalks back up the terrible corridor. Pleas for release follow her from more than one prisoner.

A slight smile overtakes my lips despite the sigh I breathe out simultaneously. I crouch, then slide the bowl out the opening and push it sideways.

"For you."

Moments later I can hear scraping and scrabbling, like a large rat pushing its way through a hay pile against the soggy corner of a barn. A knobbed, emaciated hand reaches through the bars, coming into my view long enough to see the tremble as it draws the bowl back. Gasps meet my ears seconds before a slurping, sucking sound tells me the soup was put to better use. My stomach turns, making me glad I'm near the ground.

Claire holds out a dark lump.

"At least our bread isn't moldy."

The sun's position marks the time as about noon when we emerge from the dungeon, flanked by four guards, still with our hands bound, still armed. The maze toward the higher spires of the keep winds through buildings mostly made of stone. These look better than the houses, but far from the well-kept workmanship of Elathon. Everything drips from a mist the night before.

Wooden doors painted green and flanked by a pair of soldiers bar our passage.

"The two he requested," says one of our guards.

The other soldier nods. "Soon."

A rapping noise reaches our ears, the signal for the guards to admit us.

"Enter," the soldier says. She opens the doors.

After the light from outside and in the relatively bright corridor, the open doors look like they barred the entrance to a cave. Heavily shadowed and quiet, the throneroom startles me. I'd thought we were being brought before Heller White, Grand Overlord, but this dim edifice looks nothing like my expectations. Our silent footsteps let me know we're walking on carpet. After even one night in the dungeon, the carpet feels luxuriant for my legs.

The inability to see far into the room disturbs me so I pretend to trip, causing my scabbard to clap against a spot of armor on my leg. Two audible cracks meet my ears a breath of space later which my mind uses to interpret the room as a large mostly open space. Candles flicker at intervals, giving an ominous air of walking toward cultish secrets. Only the narrowing tunnel of candles and the backs of two guards guide us through the room, making footsteps feel labored, useless, like they're leading nowhere.

Our guards peel off and motion for us to continue toward brighter candles lighting up the outline of a human. It's only a shadowy form, sitting on an ornate throne, wrapped in the shrouds of a heavy cloak.

Vague imaginings of torture instruments lining the room begin to form in my mind. As I will my eyes to adjust to the dim light, a face begins to form. A cunning face, with features tight as a lead coffin except the open jaw. Ridges as pronounced as a well-drawn map appear to cast shadows on his lips. When I look at where the eyes would be, the firelight still plays with my own, showing dancing shadows. In the grim darkness, without visibility, the feeling of focus washes over me. It's the focus I find in my father, Julek, and others of high station. The kind of bearing I strive to command. The feeling in the unseen eyes tells me more than a placard on a door.

It's Heller.

Chapter 14.

"Remove their bindings," a soggy voice commands.

Heller White, Grand Overlord of Murethon, sits on the throne before Claire and me, cloaked with shadows in addition to his robe.

A guard steps from our side to cut the bonds. Unspeakable relief makes me forget I have weapons on my person, so focused do I become on massaging life back into my hands.

Silence fills the space between us for a long moment, letting me stare continuously up and down Heller's form. I see hands, fingertips protruding through sleeves where they rest on the worn wood of the chair. Smaller details start to become visible when I stare at the dark form and not at the candles.

Heller turns his eyes on me, causing the hair on the back of my neck to bristle. I resist the urge to place my hand there, to withhold that satisfaction from him.

"You, son of my old friend. Tell me; how fares His Majesty?"

His tone makes me want to wring his neck, but I'm too smart for that; too well versed in interrogation methods to show anger now. His voice is slimy, like his tongue is a salamander.

There's no reason to deny being the prince; he seems to know so much already. "King Laurence is well."

A short answer feels like enough to his sickening person. Words drip from his mouth like he's drooling them rather than speaking.

"What an incredible stroke of good fortune that brings you both here. I'd almost believe it was fate if I wasn't too smart for such inanities."

Something holds me back from speaking. I'm not sure what. Normally I'd have some answer when standing before the enemy.

"But they say you were brought from in my lands," he continues. "That is a strange place for a prince to wander without an army at his back. Without guards even. I'd expect Julek's daughter to have her own guards rather than serve as one."

Claire starts at his recognizing her.

"Oh yes, Ms. Lewis, I know your father well."

"Julek? You might have seen him on a battlefield but he's never hung around scum like you," Claire says.

Maybe there's a chance he falls for her lie.

Heller's pale fingers emerge farther from his too-long robe, tapping rhythmically as he turns his head aside to regard Claire. Her tongue stills, leading to a silence deep as death.

"Careful what you say, girl," he croons moments later. "Make sure you know who you insult before speaking."

"I kno—"

"Hush. No, you don't." A wicked smile peels across his lips. "And that is what will make this fun."

Candles flicker on the numerous tables throughout, providing an uncertain light my eyes are finally used to. While it's far less grand than the state rooms in Sapesky, or any of the provincial capitols, the room still holds an air of solemn majesty. The thick carpet we walked in on runs a short distance to each side, ending in a white border. It extends all the way from the door to Heller's throne, giving the room a ceremonial appearance. Elsewhere on the floor, wide boards stretch end to end in neat rows. Rich muted arches matching the floor vault into the ceiling, disappearing in the darkness before they touch. These numerous pillars of wood give me pause for their ability to conceal more guards. Even though we weren't disarmed I have little doubt we're being watched. Maybe, though, just maybe...

"What makes you think you know who I am?" Claire asks. She's seething with curiosity.

Heller sighs, raising a hand to scratch his neck. The robe folds back a little to show an arm with strange markings on it.

"I know your father, or knew him, rather. We haven't seen each other for years. Maybe it's been decades even," he says, stopping to cackle at his own joke. "Yes, years and decades all at once. I know June also, though I haven't seen her in even longer. You have the same personality as your father with the looks of your mother when she was your age. You probably never saw her like that thanks to Julek. She had higher cheekbones than you may know her with. Tell me, how is she?"

He licks his lips like a prey animal moving to the kill.

"I haven't seen Commander Lewis in a while," Claire answers. "His wife died many years ago."

"Come come, you can't honestly believe that lie. One with her power can't have been brought to an end so easily. How is your mother?"

"She died nine years ago and I'd appreciate you not bringing it up, bat-livered whiteneck."

I groan. *Nymunia we're dead*, I think. She's looking daggers at him.

"Claire Lewis," he says, stopping to wet his pale cracked lips with his tongue. "Young woman with the feisty eyes, kin to the kingdom's most sinister murderer."

Claire stands more upright while I join in glaring at our host.

"Oh, you don't know—not a big surprise, why should he tell you, after all? Such a coward, *such* an unworthy coward..."

His voice trails off, leaving his words echoing back. My mind swirls with a fog, almost like his voice is enchanting me. I'm silent, mute, while I wait for his next words like a bird before a snake. It's revulsion, not fear, that holds me staring at him.

With all his ghastly appearance and loathsome mannerisms, it takes all my concentration to move my hand ever so cautiously.

"Well, you don't have to tell me about June. I'll find her sooner than later." He shifts in his chair, hiding the arm markings I noticed earlier. "Those who pretend to walk in the light are more careful to hide their actions than those they accuse of walking in the dark—no, no, I'd hate to be forced to have you killed." I move my hand away from my sword, where it's been gliding.

"There's archers with strings drawn waiting to end you. My Shadow Kings. Believe me when I say they don't want to. Some saw you ten years ago, now that I think of it. They said you weren't in the state to accept a greeting, and I know they're honest. Oh yes, honest, and oh so reliable."

He breathes through his mouth, never letting his tongue rest from either playing over his lips or talking.

"Now where was I? Hmm, it was the, um, oh yes— murderer, murderer. The nobility are quick to point out where others go wrong. They don't point out their own defects, though, do they? They hide behind their screens of perfection by throwing dirt on those they place below them. Too much mud in the eyes makes it difficult to see."

A cackling laugh escapes his mouth while he continues to lick his lips, eyeing us. His allusion to the arrows trained on us doesn't escape my notice, though after surviving everything Claire's said I don't fear to say much.

"You say that about Oruvian nobility but what about your Shadow Kings?"

"I'd expect a son of Laurence Hart to say that. But what are kings except wielders of power. Trusted with life and death of those they've convinced are worth less. They can set themselves up as kings with as much right as anyone. If we took tallies I'd wager fewer innocents have died by all my Kings' hands together than from the one on Sapesky's throne."

I open my mouth to speak, then clap it shut. Innocents do die at the hands of kings. I, a prince and captain at once, understand that more than most. War decisions made in Sapesky's Presence Chamber certainly lead to civilian deaths.

"Those who die from our war would only be the tip of the spear if we didn't defend our land."

"Yes, that's what they teach you over there." He almost sounds sympathetic. "It hasn't changed. Has it ever occurred that you might not have every side of the story? That your wisdom is limited by your experience? By your life?"

His head listed to the side while he spoke and, now even more like staring into a snake's eyes, I feel my will ebbing.

"All that is where you're wrong, I'm afraid, Christopher. You see, I don't set myself up as a king. I let my subjects with kingly qualities join the order. The Kings follow me since I know how to direct their energies. All I do is lend them my experience."

"Your Shadow Kings killed my mother so you could weaken the kingdom and get closer to rule over Elathon."

"Dear dear," he says, glancing at Claire, who is standing a step beside and behind me, her hands off her weapons. "There is no limit to the deception the nobles will throw up to protect themselves. So noble. So noble..."

As his voice trails away he extends a tattooed hand up to his throat, then scratches it with a single bony finger.

"Why did they tell you I 'divided' the kingdom, isn't that the word?"

He sits and waits, staring into us and yet not at our eyes. It's an uncomfortable feeling almost making me forget to answer the question.

"You were a captain in Montaya. When my father promoted Robert Brayler to provincial commander, you surrounded yourself with officers loyal to you—not the kingdom. Since you couldn't take the province from him by force you fled over the Dendring mountains with your loyal subjects, tempting them with rich positions in the event of your success. We've heard from those returning to loyalty; we know what it's really like."

"Is that really all you know? I'd think a prince would have learned the full truth even if it was repressed from the commoners."

"That is the truth. It has enough details."

"It lacks details, and they matter very much. Many times they matter more than the broad actions. Would you go into battle against my forces without counting your arrows or learning how many companies are in your regiment? Broad actions are important. What about their food and water? Bread or cheese? How much of each? Stored in sacks or crates? Is the food up to each officer? Each individual? No. The newest cadet knows that's absurd. So what do you do? You focus on the details, or make someone else do it. Details, details."

"For war, yes; for your treachery, no. You took the weakened half of the kingdom, details and all."

A chuckle emerges from his whitened throat, then manifests into a cough.

"Oh Christopher, it's a pity you're held back by conventional thinking, or I should say lack of thinking. The convenient timeline is a place I erred. I regret how easy I made it for the throne to cover up the true nature of my disappearance. Not that I give Xulbris's ear for my reputation back there; it's their false ones that burn me."

"False reputations?"

"Of course, of course," he says, stopping to wet his lips. "Remember when I said to watch out for the nobility of nobles? It's nonexistent. Surely you knew of Ross Knoke?"

My blood heats, rises to flush my face. Heller notices and gives a sickening smile, stretching his cracked lips to resemble lifeless snake scales.

"Oh, you do your future kingship, do you? What do you know of him?"

I clench my hands. "That traitor would have been hanged if you hadn't beaten the king to his death."

"Glad I was able to serve my old friend even from over here." Heller's smile lingers through a rasping laugh while he scratches his white throat again. "Commander Knoke was one of the reasons. The act was too grievous to pass over, hence his bad reputation. He committed many more offenses before Rafael's death, always tucked away. If you've ever wondered why the king was so willing to condemn his dead memory to the mud it's more than because he was an easy scapegoat; he had much against him already.

"Then there was the queen's murderer, though he hadn't yet done so. I thought he would. It pained me to hear, though I confess I was relieved to have been right about that... noble.

"I could tell he was jealous; wild with it. I was only surprised how long he managed to restrain himself. June's influence helped with that, I'm certain. That part is only a guess, mind you, yet he did it for her."

His gaze is directed beside me now, and I look over. Claire wrinkles her brows in angry disbelief.

"Yes—he did it for her as much as for himself. He thought the pleasant end would scrub his spirit clean from the black phantasm. It almost pained me to keep all the Balm of Life when the Kings brought it back, but Julek and June live by the forest and easily got more. Pathetic, but I suppose he's convinced himself the effort was worth it. Hopefully she doesn't know about his attempt..."

My face mirrors Claire's now. We both stare at Heller in mute astonishment. There's so much neither of us understands.

Heller groans. "Xulbris you're more ignorant than I thought. But I like you, Christopher; you're smart with potential. Potential to be a King sooner than otherwise. Regardless," he says and shifts in his chair again while keeping his sickening smile mostly on Claire, "I said this was going to get fun and I was right."

He turns to me. "Think back, Christopher, if you can to the night your mother met her end. Describe it to me. Every detail you can remember."

Panic floods my system, threatens to shut me down, so I raise my shields as I've done so often over the last ten years. Even with a decade of experience, it's normally hard enough to shut out the memory; but his provocation, his eyes, make it so much harder. The memory is seared too deep from seeing her dead each time and failing three times. She was already dead each time I got back. Three times, three failures; it's too much for a fifteen-year-old boy to endure. It's too much to bear; I clamp my teeth and stare at the ground.

"No? Well I know all about it," Heller says. "After all, my Shadow Kings were there as you pointed out. They took a different part in the matter than you seem to think; it's true they arrived to steal the Balm of Life from Sapesky; it's true they were near Queen Eilene when she was stabbed; but it wasn't them."

"It was them," I say through gritted teeth. I don't dare open my mouth or move my eyes to my captor-turned-tormentor. "It was them with a Velvet Breath dagger; I saw them carrying them."

"She was killed that way, and the Shadow Kings do carry weapons misted in Velvet Breath, and you are correct in thinking you saw the red glow, but those weapons are for—how shall I say it—dispatching themselves if they need an escape. No, my Kings didn't kill Eilene because they didn't need to. They are experienced enough to only hit their targets. Someone close to you was there out of sight."

His gaze slides over to Claire, moving cooly as his lips curl around his teeth, appearing yellowed with their proximity to his neck.

"This is where the fun begins, Christopher, my future acolyte. Imagine, from a lowly prince to a Shadow King. I can teach you much, but we will discuss that later. For now, know that my old friend, the king's friend, and the queen's own friend murdered the queen."

He pauses, grinning wickedly upon us.

"Julek."

The name stutters my heart.

"Hard to believe, I know. The nobility of nobles. Those sort of people are why I left. I tried to warn your father but the idiotic bureaucracy wouldn't let me get a word with him. Dividing was the only way I could fulfill my oath of honor."

Honor. The word jams into my mind like a splintered plank. An hour ago my eyes would have gone wide and my mouth let out a raucous laugh in disbelief at Heler White, leader of The Divide, thinking himself honorable. Now, though.... Now I remain silent. Have I not lamented the nobility of nobles many times?

"They're not all as bad as you're telling yourself," I say. "Ross was ego-driven and vengeful."

"And Guy—" Julek asks "—not ego-driven?"

Tactless, but loyal, I think.

"How about Julek—vengeful?"

There it is again. My heart does another backflip.

"Shall we ask Ms. Lewis?"

From the faint gasp beside me I guess Claire's does several backflips.

"Do you know what happens when someone uses a Velvet Breath dagger?"

She stays silent. My eyes are locked on Heller's broadening grin. It almost makes him look elated. My eyes widen while I put significance to the stain on his cloaked arm for the first time. Honor indeed.

"There's a permanent mark on the hand that did it," I say.

He catches my glance, then raises his hand to let the robe drop back. "No," he says, "this wasn't from Queen Eilene. You're right, though—this is what happens. Several of my

Shadow Kings have markings from their use, so I can't prove it wasn't one of them. I have a better way."

"The punishment for its use is death without trial," I say.

"Who made that law?" he sneers, licking his cracked lips. "Oh let me guess; nobility!"

Speech abandons me for a moment while he sits cackling to himself. The flames licking up the loose-spun candle wicks dance side to side from their own faint air currents in the sealed room. The rich carpet beneath my booted feet feels like it won't support my weight, or maybe it's my trembling legs.

"Don't tell me you think they abide by their laws; no level of deception can hide that from a prince unless you're the worst hypocrite, which I doubt."

He turns his gaze to Claire and I follow. She's white, almost as pale as Heller's neck.

"The fun is only beginning," Heller states, holding up his arm to let his markings show full in the glistening candlelight. "Claire, have you seen Julek's hand and forearm in the last— what was it now—ten years?"

The dreadful look on her face as she turns my way tells everything. She has; she must have. My heart sinks to my feet, to the soft rug, but it feels like it's dragging across every available sliver on the wooden floor. Julek, Eilene's murderer? Impossible.

"Those markings—show up from what?" Claire asks. Her unbelieving voice is a choked whisper, her eyes like unlit beeswax candles viewed from atop; large and round, with a single dark speck hiding in the center.

"From... from using a Velvet Breath dagger. Have you —" I cut my words short, not wanting to finish them, though I can't tear my eyes from hers. Deep hurt registers in mine, with the same reflected in hers. She also harbors fear, terror even, at the revelation. There's dread, fright, a swirling mass of emotions storming through her shining eyes.

"This is even better than I thought," Heller says. "The truth hurts doesn't it?"

"Shut up you awful, flea-ridden, snake belly!" Claire screams through coming tears. "You're a half-rotten rat chewing... chewing a..." her voice quavers then falters completely as tears stream from her eyes.

Her outburst doesn't sting Heller the way she wanted; he licks the deeper crevices on his lower lip with the tip of his tongue.

Yesterday I would have launched myself forward to comfort her. Now my head is swimming with unexpressed hurt. How could Julek have done this to my family? Claire drops to the ground, sobbing in great gasps at the outrage laid upon her. There's no way it's possible. She's mistaken, drawn down by the circumstances, the night in the dungeon, the tormenter before us. Her reaction can't mean what it seems to.

"Sorry to have spoiled a lifetime of illusions, Christopher," Heller says, his focus on me, "but you really needed to know sooner than later. You could continue on the path to become a worldly king, but a Shadow King would suit someone with your reputation better. I've been watching you from afar through my informants for years and I can promise you it fits a man of action better.

"Think about it—never caught up in court politics, no listening to some imbecile prattle about superfluous gripes. We both know you think of the king's associates as little more than large children so inflamed with their own self-importance they can't see beyond their own desires. If you become king of Elathon you'll become nursemaid to dukes and barons, seneschals and chancellors. Commanders would be the least of your worries. As a Shadow King you could direct the world in a meaningful way."

"No!" Claire screams from her position on the floor. "You're filth!"

Heller looks over to Claire. She's collapsed in a quivering heap on the floor. Her sobs come in episodes.

"Aww, look what you've done by bringing her along. You must feel awful. Your lover if my Kings' report was correct. Can you believe your best friend's father killed your mother? I love to think what that will do in Sapesky."

"You're lying." My mouth feels like it's stuffed with cotton. Somehow I know he isn't, but my mind can't believe this of Julek. "He couldn't have killed the queen; he's too loyal; fought too hard for the very thing the queen's death brought about."

"She didn't take much convincing," he says, glancing over.

I gulp. Claire's reaction stops my mind's resistance more than any logic ever could. "What are you trying to do?"

"Trying? I'm succeeding. I'm establishing rule by those with merit, not birthright. You happen to have both, and King Laurence does too despite everything he has to go through in his position." He pauses, takes a deep breath, and speaks in a tone a friend would use. "I didn't want your mother dead, Christopher. Believe me it would have happened a lot sooner if I did, and it wouldn't have been when her son was near enough to stumble in on the assassin. I hate sloppy workers. No, what I'm doing isn't against you, your kingdom, or even the collective nobility, but many of them"—he shudders—"have the lowest honor you would imagine. All I ask is for you to open your eyes to the possibility—only the possibility that there is something you don't understand behind the functioning kingdom you've been raised in."

He shifts in his chair, presses his feet to the ground, and slides himself back for an upright posture. It matches the hardened edge his voice assumes as he alters to seriousness.

"Now that you've seen the truth you can't unlearn it. Claire can, and will, if your honor is as upright as your father's when I left; if it's as upright as my Kings'."

"I can't remove mem—"

"Take away the day and you take away the memory; only some emotion remains; learn, observe, and recoil in horror; come crawling back to tell me I'm right." His eyes widen and he stares into me, makes me want to turn away yet I can't. His ardor continues: "It means nothing to me. You'll think the worst of me for a space and try to talk yourself into thinking you haven't been living in the center of a lie your whole life, but you'll come around quick with your true heart. You've always been apart from the others for a reason."

Heller looks at Caire, shoulders shaking from her position on the floor. She's bent forward, almost curled into a ball with her hands cupping her face.

"Looks like you're the only one who can save her from the mental anguish," he says. "That or she'll have to go her whole life knowing Julek murdered the queen. Her best friend's mother. There's no pinning it on the Shadow Kings anymore. Not for you, anyway. Maybe not for her. Not for anyone you choose to tell. Do the right thing."

It should be so easy to laugh in his face, to tell him to do his worst, that he'll never break me. Yet when I open my mouth to speak, other words come out.

"The right thing. You're letting us go?"

Heller smiles, one half of his thin crusty mouth curling up.

"You want me to use my Gift so we can escape. Is that it?" It doesn't seem real.

"You're a forest fire; flaming here and there for no real purpose. If June was willing to teach you my informants would have let me know. I still don't know why she's so hidden. No matter; we'll have Myceum soon, answers after that. What I want is to see you find your Gift, benefit from it. I can train you. Embrace it and when the time is right you'll come back, and take your place as my acolyte."

He's trying to convince me, use me, test if I'm obedient. He doesn't know I've discovered it already.

"No," I say. "I'm not yours to throw around. Use your Shadow Kings, and do with me what you will, but you won't humiliate the prince of Elathon with his consent."

Heller sighs while keeping his eyes on me. The disappointment resting there is mixed with something I've only seen on a battlefield. Instead of feeling successful at reproaching him, his dull expression fills me with a sense of foreboding.

"Bring me an expendable," Heller calls.

Soft sounds from behind a wooden pillar reach my ears before an unseen door opens and closes.

"I shouldn't be surprised," Heller says. "After all, you're well-bred and grew from your own merits as well. That's what I find fascinating about you. But everyone does have his limits."

Foreboding fills me as I await whatever Heller has in store for me. I straighten my posture, mentally rehearsing how I'll react to different threats he'll put before me. Thumbscrew, knee-splitter, strappado; stoicism seems my best option for anything. If they try anything on Claire, though—I glance at her —I may draw my weapons.

Limiting my glance to only her on the ground, not scanning for hanging hooks on the rafters or checking my weapons tests my willpower, so much rehearsed over years of camp life. The unseen door opens a minute later and I hear footsteps coming closer over the dark wooden floor. Candlelight falls on the features of two men as they near the rug.

"You'll find me persuasive," Heller says as the two draw near.

But I'm not looking at Heller. A soldier leads the least foreboding man imaginable toward the dais; he's appallingly thin, with bones showing through the shrunken skin covering his upper arms. A sand-colored shirt hangs loose over his frame, little more than a skeleton from the gaunt, haunted look in his face and deep-set eyes. The shirt covers almost to his knees, and there's no breches, no boots, nothing besides his long shirt.

The soldier shoves him in front of Heller, hiding our captor from my view.

"What have you done to this man?" I stammer, horror stricken.

The man with his back to me shakes, and with the small threadbare shirt hanging about his shoulders, I can see the bones sticking out like they'll break the skin if he makes too quick of a move. Shock and anger at this sight crowd all the fear I hadn't quelled.

"Is he even a man?" Heller asks as he stands up and prowls closer, still hidden from my view. "He's lacking any quality that would make me think so. No muscle. No fight—not even in his eyes. You'd break my white neck"—he chuckles in a sickening, gurgling way—"if my Kings weren't so close, but this... mudlark, outcast—nothing."

The prowling continues and I may just call Heller's bluff if he comes close enough.

"Spirit broken with the simple withholding of food. I'll bet he won't even defend himself." He raises his hand and brings it across the man's face. His head swings sideways from the slap, then falls back into the resigned hunch.

"Stop." I order in a tone so tense I detect an instant of fear as Heller glances at me. A heartbeat later it moves to contempt.

"Am I getting close to your limit? I told you you'd find me persuasive, my spirited acolyte. You'll be a good prize."

With a motion faster than I would have thought him capable of from all his time in the chair, Heller whirls toward the man. With my sight blocked, I can't see what's going on, but it looks like a fist to the stomach. That isn't my limit, but I can't sit back while he continues to torment this man. I leap forward as a flash of shining steel draws back into the thin shirt and Heller shoves him spinning into my arms. The man collapses forward with eyes wide as I catch him.

A warm spot spreads across my chest.

My eyes go wide at Heller's dagger. His look of unconcern floors me. He throws the dripping blade to the side. I look back at the emaciated man expiring in my arms and see relief in his eyes. Relief, resignation, and pain. His eyes flutter closed as he exhales his final breath against my neck. He was so frail, so wracked, his body welcomed the release without a struggle. The seconds it takes me to lay him on the rug emphasize his wasted condition.

"Not on the rug, please. It's so hard to clean."

Fire flashes in my eyes and my hand goes to my sword, stopping short of drawing it on him while my eyes cloud in anger.

"Am I finding your limit?" Heller torments me with a smile. "It's fun to break a man to your will like a fractious horse. Even more so a prince."

I'm halfway on the floor with the corpse, beside Claire. She gasps through her heavy breathing, tears still streaming down her face. My flaming eyes snap back to Heller's face.

"I'll never join you."

"Do I need another one?" He returns to his seat. Something inside me knows he isn't joking. "Everyone has a limit; I just need to find where yours is. Something will make you obey me. Remember Commander Knoke's shield-fodder—is that enough for you?"

"Why do you want me to escape?" I say; my tone is laced with hatred, my eyes starting to cloud.

"I told you earlier. I want you to find your Gift. You'll come crawling back, and *that* is what I'm after. A quick path to Kingship for you, and a prince of Elathon for my acolyte. The order we can impo—"

"No," I yell. "You'll never get me to join you."

My mind seizes up at the torrent of pain coming my way. As my eyelids blink across them, salty drops cascade onto the man's thin covering, soaking in, mixing with the growing stain of his blood. All I feel is the sharp knife of misery driving into my heart, twisting to sever every connection with the world of joy. My face contorts into a grimace, and tears flow without the least obstacle.

Claire disappears from the edge of my vision as it darkens. It feels like I'm pitching forward, and as my body seems freed of the present, the half-formed thought swirls in my mind: *there's nothing wrong with fleeing this place.*

"Well done. You'll be back."

I hear the vague echo before the world disappears into a moment of peace.

Chapter 15.

Around me, the world swirls into clarity. I realize my surroundings and I fall in stride without a hitch. Claire walks a few yards ahead just the way we had been before we were captured by Heller's Shadow Kings. None of the peace accompanying me during the first trek over these hills remains, only a powerful urge to—

"Wait," I say.

Claire stops. The usual smile on her face fades to a look of worry as she sees my eyes. The next instant has her wheel forward, looking for foes.

"What's wrong?" She runs back to where I'm waiting. "You were just so—oh Lesasil you... did you? Chris what happened?"

The onslaught of questions hardly registers in my mind.

"What is it?" She reaches my side and takes my hand in hers. "What happened where you used your Gift again?"

Claire stands breathless before me so I ramble: our fight, the capture, night in the dungeon below Castle Muerthy, and Heller's throne room. I tell her about the man he murdered before our eyes, how we kept our weapons the whole time, and Heller's baiting me to join him.

I tell her everything except Whiteneck's accusing Julek. When it comes time for relating that, I stumble, my feelings for her dissipated. I'm as unable to bring myself to recount the experience as I am unwilling. When it comes to the end I realize I'm trembling all over, cold, sweating with the recollection.

"You did the right thing," Claire says. She brushes my one-year-older cheek with her soft hand. Yesterday I would have leaned into it. Now I flinch. "Did you get the answers you wanted?" She asks.

"No. I had to leave. You... you don't know what it was like in there." Nothing more descriptive comes out. How can it? She didn't experience the full day leading up to the visit, didn't walk bound for a day, attempt to sleep leaning against a stone wall with bound hands, didn't listen to the incessant moaning in the prison, or smell the rank straw, or fetid castle grounds, have the man die in her arms. She didn't bear Heller, whose very presence made me sick.

She was there, but lost all but the emotions with the passing of the day. I can't grudge her for that, yet there are other reasons for a grudge.

She winces like she remembers some of what happened "Did they torture us?"

I don't even know how to describe what happened. "No..."—I start, then correct myself in a rush—"yes."

"Yes? What did they do?"

"Heller... talked." I look away so I can't see her reaction. When I chance a glare back, she has her eyebrow lowered. That, with the look on her face, transform it into a strange mask of incredulity. I look away again, angry at her interest.

"Talked? We talked with him, he wanted you to join his secret warrior cult, you refused so he killed a prisoner, and you used your Gift to save the man and us. That's got you so worked up all of a sudden?"

"That's not the half of it," I say.

"What then? I was there and feel something of it still. I have a right to know. You wanted to talk with Heller. Sounds like it couldn't have been any easier."

"Quiet," I say.

She looks around as if the ambush I told her about is upon us, then turns back to face me. Only by now I'm turning to face east again.

She bounds to my side. "What is it?"

"I can't talk now." It's all I can do to keep my eyes off her because if I do, they'll blaze irreparable fury between us.

"But—"

"No. I cannot talk now." I can't talk to her. Not without devastating consequences.

"You can tell me," she says.

"Leave. Me. Alone. I'm protecting you from my anger. From—" I stop short, cutting off the words forming on my lips.

Every word I'm forced to speak in this wild state of anger feels like she dumps another brazier on me. Heart seething worse than a stormy sea, I long to ask her for help. If only June were alive—she's been through this. Even though I can't imagine she ever went through a Curse this deep, I imagine she could help.

Maybe Heller could— No. There's no going down that road. I know where it would lead, and there's no way I'm even starting a journey into quicksand.

My foul mood infects Claire. Somehow I'm not in the least ashamed. It's as if I'm punishing her for Julek's actions. Like I'm treating her as my mother's murderer. The blatant suffering I'm experiencing feels like it belongs to her. Let her share it.

Not surprisingly, her carrying the sorrow with me only makes the total burden heavier. Still, it doesn't bother me. Temptation to tell her almost overwhelms my reason, keeping me on edge for the next several hours.

Cold clouds pass overhead and bring a mist which overwhelms the sun's rays even before night. If anything, the soaking raises my mood a little. Having something outward to direct my frustration toward cools my head a little. I'm relieved I've managed to not take out my anger on Claire for this long.

We're far from safety on that account, and far from Elathon, but this is the least awful I've felt since coming back.

Fire flickers to a precarious life nestled on a pile of tinder. Claire gathered it from beneath some thick trees surrounding our clearing. It's fallen pine needles, what looks like rabbit fur blown out of a nest, and half-rotten leaves. A good find on a night like this, to be sure. It's the same weather we endured our night in the dungeon.

"It's a cruel twist having the Gifted remember the day they wanted away from," I say to try breaking the silence as we eat.

Claire takes a long time to answer. When I doubt she'll ever respond, she says, "How else could they know to make it different?"

"I don't know. It's just... did June ever feel tormented by memories of the previous day?"

We both stare into the fire, and I poke a glowing log with a stick. The pressure causes it to collapse. A shower of sparks rises into the mist, where they're extinguished.

"Not in my memory. She always felt happy at her ability to have a second chance, to make the world a better place."

We sit in silence, hearing nothing besides the crackling of the fire and the drone of insects all around. I chance a quick glance at Claire, wondering if she's thinking about our conversation after we left Mt. Cabrae. I had asked if June ever regretted using her Gift, though this feels different.

"Did she worry about having reversed a day she may not want to change after all?"

"She never let on about that. I was young at the time, though, so she could have simply wanted to hide it from me; keep her young child from mirroring her worry."

After another ten minutes a tentative voice slips from between her lips. "I feel desolate too. You feel it wasn't worth a year of your life?"

An urge to defend my actions riles the back of my neck. She didn't ask about the details I left out earlier, so I'm able to control my still-wild emotions.

"It probably was," I say. I stop to think about Luis Brayler. I didn't use it to save him but I brought back the man who is again alive to rot in Heller's dungeon. "Actually I know it was. Why is it so hard to live with it?"

"The right decision doesn't mean it will be easy to live with," she says and draws her knees to her chest. "You changing the one day back to change even one action can alter the fate of the world. Imagine if Mother never saved Father the first time—he couldn't have continued leading Eraseam. Mother would have but what if something like in Montaya with Heller White happened about the same time as his Divide? Where would the kingdom be today? What about all your people? The Gift is a gift worth using. I..." she trails off for a second, then looks at me, raising a delicate hand to brush my now-one-year-older face. "I'm glad you've decided to embrace it. Hard as it is."

"It doesn't feel like a gift," I say. "More like a curse. I didn't count on the mental anguish. It was awful the first time before I used it, and I can't say it's been a blessing any time since. I know I saved you, but we may not have even been in that situation in the first place without the Gift."

Claire understands what I'm saying. She bites her lips, probably thinking about her mother's experiences.

"It's a heavy burden. One Mother didn't always like carrying. Since I was young she didn't confide much in me, but her heavy heart wasn't lost on an empathetic daughter."

"I don't want to embrace it," I say. "I want to give it up; live in peace on a small tract of land where nobody knows me as the prince. I want to rise early, raise a family and animals on my farm, work hard, and grow old in the comfort of a home I build myself. I want to spend my days reading, wandering the forests, and improving the land with a wife and children. Uhh!"

Stop it, Chris, I tell myself, *it's impossible. Wanting that is worse than a waste since it also makes me miserable.* I lay my head in my hands.

"But who cares what I want," I continue aloud. "Being the prince sounds great to everyone who *isn't* next in line for the throne. I never envied Rafael his elder status, yet here I am, cursed with leadership among the nobility. I understand the life you can't lead always looks the best. A broken plow in the spring would be annoying, but it can't be worse than listening to squabbles among the nobility. I've heard Father placate a baroness because a neighboring baroness used a public road through her family's land without explicit permission. That's the life I have to look forward to. As much luxury as I want to drug myself with between days dealing with adults less mature than some children in their territory."

I interrupt my train of thought, force myself to stand, then pace before our fire.

"They're so smitten with their own importance most of them can't see the needs of others. As a king I should be free to impact the world in a meaningful way," I say, an echo of Heller's words. The realization of twisting toward his mentality, even in this small matter, stems my rant.

I collapse onto my seat. I pull my knees toward my chest, wrap my arms around them while staring into the fire. Firewood rests drying near the heat, so I pick up a thin log, and place it atop the small blaze.

Minutes go by, and I want to charge through the forest in a reckless run. It always makes me feel better, yet I can't do it in a strange country. We really shouldn't even have this fire going, but after growing used to the light I can't bear to put it out.

Swirling thoughts of Heller's words ring loud in my mind. Saving the man felt like the right thing to do, but what other fate did I send him to? The haunting look on his face makes me think he almost preferred the swift death to endless years of everything about him ebbing away. He looked like there was hardly anything left; body, spirit, dignity—all gone. I saved him for a dubious fate, saved Claire from dreadful memories as well, and... fled.

I fled at Whiteneck's bidding. No matter how many times I tell myself it was forced, Heller coercing my will lances my princely pride. At the time I thought it was the right thing to do, yet now the consequences gall me.

I try to change the subject.

"The weather hasn't changed; this is how it was when they brought us into the castle."

"Would you expect the weather to change based on where we walked?"

"Not really; it's just—I... never mind."

I just want to talk. I think. *I want to forgive you for Julek's action. I want you to help drag me from the depths of my mind.*

"Much of the world can change on the smallest decision," Claire says.

Like the murder of a queen. My lifting mood sours again despite my efforts to buoy it. Claire notices the change and remains quiet.

After a time I'm at least able to feel the slightest bit of gratitude for her silent companionship. The same uplifting presence she gave during my near-collapse on our trip to Myceum.

Hours later I'm on the point of thanking her for staying with me through the inner battle when we're surprised on all sides. Weariness flees my body, replaced with surging adrenaline at my instant recognition of the Guldethian dark red and green clothing.

"Halt for desertion," orders a voice behind me.

I flip around and see firelight glinting on arrow points. The voice came from someone tall and proud with hair cut shorter than mine. The build and facial pattern show the woman in charge of this group isn't used to being disobeyed. The style of her tunic with the gold cloth strips at the shoulder seams announce her as an officer.

Harsh voices don't command my implicit obedience—I've been around fighting for too many years to fall for that—but the words she spoke stop me from drawing my sword. *Desertion? They think we're deserters?* Anything else and I'd have cut my way from their encircling trap or died trying by now.

Claire shares my confusion. Though she doesn't remember the difference of our ambush yesterday, she refrains from drawing a weapon.

"What company are you with?"

My gods can she really not see us? The dim fire at my back shouldn't be making it too hard to see past a silhouette. The soldiers ease their bowstrings, unable to hold the massive tension any longer.

Maybe since she's asking about what company we belong to she's an officer, I think. Maybe she hasn't seen my blue cloak. This is the perfect chance; perhaps the only one I'll get. It's worth a shot. "The *companies* I command answer to me —not the other way around. I need to ask you what regiment you belong to and what you're doing here."

My commanding voice comes forth for the words, but she's evidently spent much time in battle as well, as she doesn't flinch at my higher rank. She may not even believe it. With an inscrutable mask shrouding her reaction it's impossible to do more than guess at her next intention.

"If you think you're a captain we better take you to our commander to sort this out. Wouldn't want you to have to deal with an underling like me." The sneer is like Whiteneck's only somehow more maddening. It's probably because they're binding our hands as they disarm us. So different than when we were brought before Heller.

The plan didn't go as well as I'd hoped, yet I keep my sinking spirits inside. They don't deserve the satisfaction of seeing discomfort pass my face. As I see my sword handed to a soldier to stow away, I wish I'd have used it on them first. Then again, if they didn't recognize me even after my show of authority, perhaps it's best we didn't fight to escape. Killing me probably wouldn't distress her too much.

"They're from Elathon, Scintia," says a soldier who had been rummaging through our packs.

She turns on us, half a smile hidden in shadow as our fire is kicked out behind us. "Elathon. I should have known. This is a good prize indeed. Maybe my best night's work ever if you're really a captain." Scintia turns from us, raises her voice, and calls to a different soldier, "Berlee, what's the perimeter?"

"All quiet."

"Good." Then in a louder voice meant for everyone, she says, "We're heading for Commander Headon."

She's an officer in Heller's army, but she won't remain an officer for long with her ability to command. I'm halfway honored, halfway chagrined to think my capture might launch her to captaincy.

Gruca Headon, commander of Heller White's army, was an officer of Oruvia before Heller's Divide. He was stationed in the Montaya province, where they met. Gruca had a promising career as a soldier, almost as good as Heller's, but the advancement didn't come fast enough for either's ambitions. Robert Brayler, current commander of Montaya, petulant as he can be, was equally deserving of the position Heller sought. The king took his extra length of service into account when deciding on the next commander, and Heller started his Divide soon after. Robert Brayler controlled the initial rebellion in his province well enough until the main forces of the kingdom could be mobilized. With King Laurence leading the largest force ever assembled under his reign, the Dividers contented themselves with flight over the Dendring mountains.

The king couldn't safely take his soldiers through the mountains with winter coming on. The country was unprepared, the army ill-equipped, so preparations occupied the winter months, making the lack of decision easier on everyone's conscience. By the time spring came, few enough people had connections strong enough to make them want to pursue reuniting with Murethon. The region wasn't as resource-rich, they argued, and proved a drain on Elathon without a costly war. Why fund a war to regain a poor country? If Heller wanted it, he could take it. Debate reignited around the necessity of the once-certain expedition.

In the end, the debate dragged out for weeks. As a child too young to be involved, I sometimes listened to Mother and Father talk about it in private. My sentiment, if it was even mine since I was so young, mirrored the king's: we have to take it back on principle. The natural separation of the Dendring mountains made it easier for the nobility to think the war that would ensue wouldn't be worth the cost. Principles can and should be fought for, they said, but the benefit of showing our belief must be weighed against all costs.

Voices were raised, friends became adversaries, and political alignment shifted. Besides the hard glances among disagreeing nobility which the next issue would reverse again, the only outward change was the construction of defenses at the main mountain passes: Balruvia and Mr. Cabrae in Myceum, Toldulgur in Artalia, and The Pass of the Winds, also called Lorganrule, in Montaya.

The trek to meet up with Gruca lasts through the night. Thankfully my adrenaline at our capture lasts until the first glimmers of sun poke over the Dendring mountains. Flashing banners greet our eyes less than an hour after sunrise. Faint hope glimmers in my heart for an instant before my tired reason catches up. The fluttering banners, even from our distance, show up a dark green set against the outline. Red borders flap continuously in the steady western wind, outlining the color which might have been lost among the background of fir trees.

Several banners show the sigil of a fox. A combination between affront facing with the slightest dexter tilt, the posture shows something of the animal's profile while maintaining a view of both eyes. All except one banner shows the same animal sewn in the matching red fabric of the border, set out from the dark green field. Black thread adds details to the ears, eyes, and teeth.

This one banner boasts the fox, alike in outline, but with greater detail. Different shades of red and black embroidering highlight the peaks of the ears, shadowing on the eyes, and the mouth. Long canine teeth show up well against the background, and the incisors look almost realistic. Our guards lead us to this banner.

A contingent of guards surrounds it, milling about like they're breaking camp.

"Looks like you have an excuse for being late," a middle-aged man says to Scintia. "Let's hope it's a good one."

"Tell Commander Headon our prisoners act superior to any we've yet encountered."

"Hmm," the man grunts. "We'll see about that. I hope they're valuable for your sake—he's almost left without you once already."

Scintia shoves us toward the new guard, a man I take to be a captain. I think I killed him in Giant's Ballroom, but can't be sure with the poor light we had that night. He's broad-chested and thick-stomached with bare arms, a red tunic hanging loose over his armor. His arms are large though round, and the lack of cording visible don't strike me visually, but I've been at war enough to realize a man his age and size can't move himself around a battlefield without ample muscles.

I'm small, thus my arms show strong definition when I've used them recently. It's easy for a young male soldier to feel cocky when he has these traits, but again, I've seen too many die at the hands of soldiers like this to underestimate him if it comes to that.

I notice all the soldiers watching us. Most wear dark green over their armor, and some have red foxes sewn onto the chests, though most of these are different. The varied patterns and intricacy of the uniforms gives the impression of a company assembled from volunteers, or that their army is struggling. I've always seen uniformity among their forces.

The stocky man leads us to a shelter leaning against some trees. It's a rough shelter they'll be able to take down in minutes; even more simple than a field tent. The only portion remaining serves to block the wind. Our guard grabs our shoulders to march us around the final tree.

Behind the shroud is a man, about the same age as Heller, though he looks far more healthy. Bright armor linked by heavy leather straps glistens out from under an outer layer of fabric. The leather is so dark it's almost black, possibly from re-dying it dark green many times. Buckles holding his sword at his side and daggers across his chest shimmer as he moves to see us more clearly.

Instant recognition covers both of our faces. Mine is darkened while his brightens. The man's features aren't so different in age than Robert Brayler's, whom he served under, or rather served beside. He would have served under Commander Brayler if he hadn't followed Whiteneck's Divide. He looks exactly like the man I've met on the battlefield several times, though never close enough for swordplay.

"Prince Christopher," he says in a pleasant voice, eyes flashing bright with delighted surprise. "I wouldn't have thought you were the rat sneaking around behind my lines. When you weren't at Giant's Ballroom, I thought you might be in Myceum. Guess my forces left to garrison that area won't have surprises."

"I'm wherever I'm most needed."

"Hmm," he mutters, looking like he wants to thank me for being his prisoner, as if I'm needed here. He doesn't, and instead says, "War drives us all in strange directions."

He turns to Claire, saying, "You look vaguely familiar, though I can't say I know you, girl."

She stares at him.

"Bodyguard doesn't make sense; there would have been more of you..." He wrinkles his eyebrows. "A wife or a—"

"I was needed behind your lines," I say, breaking his line of thinking.

"Indeed, and I confess I'm ignorant as to why you were here alone. It's so strange I may just let you go on your way. Will you tell me your intent?"

There's no way I'm telling him I sought to meet with Heller and succeeded; he's smart enough to question why we were roaming in Murethon after the visit rather than locked in some remote prison. I merely shake my head, hoping against hope that he'll really let us go.

"I suppose not," he says, matching my slow head shake. It almost feels like something my father would do. "Can't say I'm surprised; I wouldn't either if the roles were reversed."

He watches us for a while, tapping his heel on the ground and his long thick fingers on the armrest. Mouth drawn to the side of his face in a look of concentration, he leans his head over his shoulder, says, "Break camp."

Over the next several minutes the sounds of packing gear grow louder. It looks like most of the camp was ready.

"I've wanted to say, Prince Christopher," Gruca says with courtly manners, "how much I've admired you from afar. I knew your father well before the Divide and always knew his children would grow up like him. Like both your parents, I should say. You fight like a cornered badger yet command your regiment with honor. Many nobility only act with honor when it's convenient." He stops, reaching for a glass half full of amber-colored liquid on a small table at his elbow, then smacks his lips once after draining it. "My, that's good. Not that I care very much about the new soldiers—they're too untested to grow attached to—but early on in the war I remember a squad of a few dozen reported being surrounded by soldiers. I didn't know you by sight at the time to check their description, but their reports show it was you who could have butchered them. Instead you turned your force aside." He motions a nearby guard over to take the glass.

"If we were closer in age I may have stayed in Elathon for your sake," he resumes, pulling his thin eyebrows into a minor frown. "Maybe knowing a man like myself in Sapesky would have kept me around. But as an ambitious young man I needed to make my own way in the world. It was nothing against the way King Laurence ruled; I simply wanted a faster path to the top, one that was more sure. Waiting was alright, but after I saw waiting didn't always work I grew impatient. After all, there's only so many provinces to command and a blessed few roles suited for me in Sapesky, all desirable enough where the men and women in them wouldn't leave until feebleness forced them out."

"You should have stayed," I say. "It's not too late to return."

He lets a half-smile overtake his lips. "You know the people would never allow me back. It would be political suicide for you or the king to suggest such a thing. Maybe if I were in a lesser position over here, not one of the original Dividers, they could consider it. But they won't now." He shifts in his chair. "Not that any of that matters. I like my position as Supreme Commander of Field Forces in Murethon. Your father can't offer me anything to compete with that. I could even set myself up as King here."

"A King," I mutter to myself.

Gruca looks at me for a long moment before he stands. Following his gaze as he looks around camp, I realize the last vestiges of outside comforts have been disassembled. Only his small area of repose remains.

"We'll talk later. For now we need to get moving."

Soldiers swarm his area, snatch his chair, table, and canopy from the ground, break down the pieces for transport.

"You're letting us go, then?" I venture.

He smirks then leaves without a word.

Gruca's soldiers treat us well enough for prisoners. Stares of awe intermingle the more common ones of hatred, yet they don't touch us or cause the undue hardships they easily could. One lets us know Gruca ordered them not to touch us. It's a small gesture I should feel grateful for.

The sun rises on our right while we wind through mountainous paths. The tracks are narrower here, and not as well-groomed. Before we've walked an hour, it becomes clear the paths were expanded more recently. They're not as worn-down to show gravel as ours in Elathon. The regiment weaves around mountain stones projecting from the path. In Elathon, these smaller stones were leveled to make the trail easier for animals and wagons.

Though we're bound, Claire and I are allowed to walk together. I feel little inclination to communicate, but she sidles a few feet closer when the soldiers appear engrossed in their own conversations.

"Did you notice how Gruca said he expected to see you at Giant's Ballroom?" Claire asks toward noon.

"I did. It troubles me too."

"Does that mean he was there?"

"I think so." My answer is clipped. I'm in a far worse mood after hearing their conversations over the last few hours. My frustration over our fire last night has returned with greater violence.

"And if he expected to see you," she continues, "it means there was a battle. That was Gruca's force you saved me from."

I've been berating myself since he said it. I kept it hidden in front of him, so I don't know if it was a farce meant to intimidate me into submission. I'm inclined to think it was real and that his intent, menacing as it was, didn't go as deep as I'm making it out to be. He would love to know how deep those words cut.

"Chris?"

"It was one of his forces, yes."

"There's more here than what we fought?"

I nod.

"So since part of his army remained... we didn't win the battle—I mean the second time around—did we?"

The blow almost crushes my spirit. It would have if the vestiges weren't already huddling in the deepest corner, ready behind a face masked by smoldering anger. A friend saying the words unintentionally doesn't make them hurt less. More soldiers died the second time around, some would be the same as the first time, some different. Each one would have impacted the world in a unique way, a way I'll never know. I suppose the effect would have been the same if I'd been able to save the queen; a kingdom different from the one we have now. Better? For me it would have been, but what about everyone else? I'd never pondered the question this deep until the last few hours. It's bothered me, but at least I could live with the illusion that Myceum's plight couldn't have gotten worse. If years in combat have taught me anything, it's that something else can always go wrong. Somehow I'm hoping Myceum won the second time around. At the Giant's Ballroom, though—there's no illusion.

"What does our loss mean?" Claire asks in a subdued voice. She senses anything beyond that won't receive an answer.

"It means more soldiers died than last time. More widows and widowers were made on my account. More children growing up without both parents, more parents growing old without the comfort of the children they worked so hard to raise. I may as well have killed them by my own hands."

A moody silence envelops me, unshed tears mercifully clogging my throat to block the flow of words I don't want to say. I will not say I regret turning the day back; not to Claire; not to anyone. I don't even know if I regret it. Maybe I wouldn't have succeeded in standing before Heller. Maybe we wouldn't be here. *Correction, Claire* certainly *wouldn't be here.* I wish the thought bothered me. The truth is, right now it doesn't. I'm too numb to feel anything beyond frustrated rage.

"You didn't kill them,' Claire says. "You wanted to make the day better. My whole company was slaughtered last time and you gave the chance for that to not happen."

"Sounds like it went worse for our forces than the first time around."

"But you tried. You can't control how the second day goes."

"Your mother influenced it. The difference between the first and second battles was you and me. We made strategic decisions and I knew what those decisions were. I should have passed more information along through Mobent. He could have carried vital information to Kimbr, but I was too focused on my selfish goal to bother telling him everything. I could have saved a hundred lives with a few words. And I failed."

My rant descends to a whisper, as if I can't bear to tell myself the truth. Claire doesn't have time to respond before Berlee, the soldier from earlier, wanders over to keep a closer eye on us. I'm glad, since any word I speak to Claire in this state could lead to wounds. Emotional scars like I'm struggling so hard to move past.

The easier walk for the rest of the afternoon has got nothing on my lousy attitude, and I'm thoroughly exhausted by the time we're allowed to halt for the evening. Other than Gruca and his captains, we're the only ones allowed to sit right from the start. Everyone else is either making a fire, gathering wood, finding water, stashing supplies, or unrolling tents—or guarding us.

The big captain from early this morning lounges on a chair an officer brought him, munching on white bread while doing his best to act like he hasn't noticed the very prisoners he's guarding.

Officer Scintia walks to his side, bringing a pewter plate with roasted beef, two halves of an onion, and more white bread.

"Looks like they were worth enough after all, huh?" she says.

"For now at least," he says casually, flicking a bit of beef fat onto the ground beside him. "We'll see what Gruca wants to use them for when we're closer to Balruvia."

This makes me perk my ears up. I've been listening to conversations around us as much as possible. Most of them have been about Giant's Ballroom, fanning the flames of my anger. The new information interests me a lot more than their war stories against my kingdom.

"He's really the prince?" Scintia asks, talking about me as if I can't hear.

"Yeah. Kinda pathetic, right? Gruca says he knows him from during the war, otherwise I'd doubt it."

"Watch yourself, Werlek, he could be dangerous if he ever gets an army back," Scintia mocks before walking back to her fire.

Werlek, the captain, still acts too important to notice us. The plate of food takes all his attention, except when he reaches around to wipe his hands on his red cloak. Good thing it's dark red, or the grease stains would be even more unsightly. A long rumbling belch finishes his meal, whereon he grabs the nearest soldier, transferring guard duty to her. It's Berlee. Disgust wrinkles my nose as I watch him leave. The soldier doesn't appear to like him much better, which lightens my mood more than it should.

His mention of Balruvia still worries me. We've been heading north, and after a victory by Mt. Cabrae, there's little stopping them from reinforcing their army up higher in Eraseam.

I look at Berlee, who breaks eye contact for a second before looking back. Her gaze hardens the second time she looks, as if she's trying to prove she's in command of the situation. Training in the Oruvian army has made me far more experienced than she thinks. I've seen young soldiers try to prove themselves before they're ready. A quick judgment makes me think she's lucky she's here and not in a battle.

"Were you at Giant's Ballroom?" I venture.

She looks surprised at my question, then shakes her head. "I was with Commander Headon's force."

"Gruca's a fine Commander," I say. "I wish he'd use his abilities for Elathon."

"I'm sure he'd wish the same for you," she shoots back.

Dead end.

I try something else. "What brought you into Whiteneck's army?" I ask.

Her eyes widen at my use of Heller's derogatory nickname. "The Grand Overlord *allowed* me a spot in his army. Not every family is so lucky to have soldiers chosen."

"What was your training?" I ask, genuinely curious. I don't expect her to answer since she's so young, and probably scared half to death, but maybe she will. I've answered questions from prisoners from time to time as long as they're amiable ones, surprising myself how I can prattle like the nobility.

She's taken aback by the question, and looks around to see if she's receiving any signals to end the conversation. "Uh, it's thorough. A little rushed now since we're—" she stops, looking afraid of her words.

"You're short on soldiers, I know. We are too." I say. Claire doesn't even react; she knows it's basic information their scouts have surely already reported.

"I... wouldn't have guessed," she says.

A smile graces my face. It's strange how a willing conversation with a pleasant person, even an enemy, lightens the spirit. "A war lasting years tends to do that to a kingdom."

She smiles as well, though it's guarded. "Have you eaten yet?" she asks.

When we shake our heads she calls to another soldier walking by, sending him for two meals. The rye bread, crispy ends of the beef, and cups of cool water from the nearby brook refresh us after the long march.

"So," I continue, trying another conversation path as we eat, "Captain Werlek said you're going to Balruvia?" I lift my tone toward the end of the sentence, and it appears she's in a giving mood, since she nods despite her surprise.

"They say we're close to capturing the fortress." Her eyebrows, elevated from her shock, drop now, like she's unsure whether to show her relief at their success, which also means our hardship.

Then it hasn't fallen yet, I think. *Them holding out this long is a relief.* Then I continue aloud, "I hope Barevia holds. It means alot to my country."

"I just hope the war ends soon," she says, looking aside as if she'd like to move to a fire.

"We hope that every day also," I say.

"You're really the prince?"

"I am."

"Then surely you have some control over when it does end. Can't you broker peace?"

A smile curls my lips, though it's dark enough I doubt she sees it. "It's not that simple. I wish it were, but there's too many factors for it to happen like that. Maybe they told you

you're invading us to avenge an ancient wrong, or to keep Whiteneck alive."

Her eyes narrow. "I'm not so foolish as to think that. We both think we're fighting a just war. I'm not convinced it will be a better world if one side or the other wins. *My* world is worse because of the war. My *friend's* worlds aren't any better from it. I'll do whatever it takes to end this soon. The only—" she cuts herself off, and I think she was on the point of insulting her leadership.

Claire's surprise at Berlee's outburst shows she's surprised by the sudden change too. We were enjoying the conversation until I let our guard steer it in an unproductive direction.

"Why is it an honor to be chosen as a soldier?" I ask.

"Our last names are enrolled in the Register for extra protection, and our family receives a share of our wages." The flame in her voice cools a level, making me think we might be able to continue this.

"Extra protection from what?"

She looks around like she's afraid of being watched. "Why do you want to know?"

"I'm interested because that land should be mine."

Her fear lifts to a smirk. She wants to rag me for what I know she'll think a useless wish. "Protection from..." She trails off and looks like her anger already burnt itself out.

Berlee stares into the growing gloom. Night completely overtakes the sunless day and leaves our fires the only light, blinking and dancing among the soldiers like a group of forest spirits. The blanket of clouds obscuring the stars helps keep some of the warmth at our level, making our lack of fire easier to bear. Berlee feels the lack despite the clouds and draws her heavier cloak around her legs. The way she glances between her comrades and us, it's clear she's not happy about duty holding her from the companionship.

"Protection from... taxes? Laws? Whims?" I prompt minutes later.

"What? No," she says. Her eyes snap over my shoulder. My eyes narrow at her lie before footsteps announce someone walking up from behind.

Someone stomps a booted foot into my back. I sprawl forward; rocks and pine needles cut into every bit of exposed skin.

"That'll teach you to try 'n' sweet-talk your way out," says a rough voice from overtop. Werlek is back. I hope he's had his fun.

Berlee jumps to her feet and leaps back amid gasps. Hushed chatter slowly resumes as I roll to my back, taking the long way to sit up because of my bonds—thankfully tied in front.

Claire dares to help and defies Werlek with eye contact before she speaks. "It's good to finally see evidence of your courage."

The captain looks like he's going to attack her as well, so I'm on my feet in an instant. Even with my hands bound, I'm certain a kick would drop his first attempt. My back flares with pain, but I shove it aside; this is how I fight.

"Wanting a better view for the next stomping?" he asks. His breath reeks of liquor.

"I've heard it takes a strong man to beat a tied up woman sitting at your feet in your country," I say. "Can't miss this."

Pockets of chatter drop like a ram under the butcher's mallet, filling the night with nothing more than the fire's crackle and insects' drone. Werlek is twice my age, which means at least three times as much fighting experience, and half a head taller. The fire reflecting in his eyes must not match the intensity he sees in mine, because he scoffs and says, "Watch your back if you know what's good for you, scum." Instead of anything against Claire, he spits on me, then turns away and disappears among the soldiers without a word to anyone.

Berlee slips into the crowd. I sit beside Claire and try to wipe the blood from my face.

"Here, let me," she says.

"I can do it."

"Chris, you're shaking."

She reaches for my face without interference. When I try to look down to pull rocks from my hands, I get a shower of pebbles and realize she's doing more than wiping blood away.

"I don't think Gruca would allow this," Claire says.

I laugh. "Doesn't look like the captain cares."

Berlee returns and hands Claire a bucket. "I'm done guarding you. Just don't try to escape." She walks to sit with the nearest group of soldiers, who alternate glancing between her and us.

Claire draws a rag from the bucket. She wrings it out the best she can with bound hands and daps at my face. The water is pleasantly cool against the rising heat. All of a sudden I'm glad for the chilly night air.

"You realize he would have won, right?" Claire says. "Eventually. And that you would be traveling with broken bones the next few days as a best-case scenario?"

"I'd land a few good kicks on him. Besides, the odds don't always matter. I fight on principle when I need to. If he'd tied up Berlee and attacked her I'd have stood against him the same way."

"You're a fool," she says, using her bare finger to dig out some sand ground into my cheekbone.

"An unarmed fool with enough intensity to make an enemy captain back away."

Despite the kick and radiating pain, I'm smiling. It feels good to do something again. I may regret it in the morning, but hopefully there's enough discipline here to prevent captains from beating prisoners once it's known. I don't have much faith in it, but I'm going to relish this victory while I can.

Stirred into wakefulness by seeing or hearing a rumor of me standing up to their captain, the soldiers remain around their fires longer than I'm used to. The pain of my jarred muscles and burn from scrapes across my front tries to keep me awake, but two days and a night of traveling have me worn past exhaustion. I'm grateful the interrupting cut of a lash isn't across my back. Before long, the drone of insects lulls me to sleep.

Chapter 16.

Werlek looks daggers at me as we set off. From his unrested appearance it looks like he's been watching his back all night, yet something in his eyes tells me I still need to.

Scintia walks near us, and I mentally prepare myself to defend against any insults she could fling. Instead of coming our way, she walks farther ahead without a glance. She couldn't have missed seeing us, yet she passed up the chance to toss a rude comment.

Berlee lets Claire tend my wounds, which are thankfully more a nuisance than dangerous. She brings a rag soaked in wine the first morning and oil the next. The wine was for cleansing; the oil to help with scarring.

Each time I see Berlee I'm surprised with her distance and lack of communication, especially after she seemed so willing to talk when we first met her.

"She must have been threatened after talking with us too much," Claire says. "It's probably why Werlek came over in the first place."

I shake my head. "He's too lazy. If he wanted a soldier to stop talking to the prisoners he would have sent an officer. At least if he's half the bully I think he is."

By now the soldiers have dropped enough hints for me to pick up what I surmised: that we'll arrive at Balruvia before nightfall.

When I woke the second morning without a knife in my back, I began to think Gruca held a just discipline over his soldiers; that he retained the influence of an honorable Montayan upbringing. This afternoon, though, the regiment slows and I see the reason; there's a man ahead surrounded by four soldiers. He isn't blocking the path, but each soldier slows to see what their companions are doing.

"No, please! I've paid my taxes—even the third levy last year," the man begs. He's wearing a dusty sand-colored undershirt woven from hemp, held closed by square chunks of leather used as buttons over a ragged blue top. The boots look like they were made years ago; probably from his own animal's leather and wood nailed on for soles. The straw hat flops over a scared face as he watches an officer move in.

"Take the cow," the officer, Scintia, directs the others.

It's a highland cow, a rare animal in Elathon, but more prevalent in Murethon if the two still behind the man are any indication.

"No," he begs. "My daughter is fighting by The Pass of the Winds. Vianney Vall; she's as feisty as any. Check the Register. Have mercy on me, please!"

The man is pawing at the first animal, afraid he'll lose it. I can only imagine what it cost him to feed the animal through the winter, and seeing him losing it now hurts like a fresh wound.

"Take a second also," Scintia snaps.

"My family will starve," he wails. He abandons the first animal, tries to back the remaining two away.

We're almost abreast of him now, rapt with interest. Scintia grabs the old man by his shirt, rips him closer, slaps him across the face. "You want to lose the third too?"

He whimpers, scurrying away from the soldier as she releases him. When he reaches to grab the halter around the final animal's neck, he flinches even though no hands raise against him now.

My face heats and my back hurts again, as if Scintia's beating me too. This can't happen to an old defenseless man; not even in a schismatic country.

I take a step forward.

"No," Berlee says. She steps to my side with a hand on my shoulder.

I whip my head around to face her. "Is that the sort of protection you've offered your family by being selected to Whiteneck's army? Is that the honor you crave?"

"He'll be okay," she says. A flush creeps up her neck.

The man's slumped form retreats with a single cow in tow.

"Unlucky for him, but lucky for dozens of us," Scintia says to soldiers around her. Most take it as a joke, though several look like they're imagining their father or grandfather in the same situation.

Uncomfortable laughter soon dies into the usual chatter of an army marching within its own borders. The man's plight would soon pass out of memory if it weren't for the highland cows. The soldiers are leading the docile animals by their rope halters to our next campsite. Experience tells me the animals will help fill the soldier's bellies tonight. The event with the passerby makes me wonder how far this regiment lacks discipline. For it to happen in the Supreme Commander's regiment erodes the respect I've developed for Gruca.

Though my mouth waters thinking about the beef they'll be eating, I have zero expectation I'll taste any. Receiving food more than once every few days is more than I would have expected from the Guldethian force.

"That man might have a family at home," Claire says. "These soldiers are every bit as awful as we've been taught."

"Gruca might not be that bad," I venture.

"How can you say that? Didn't you see what he allowed to happen?"

"He can't know everything going on. What if that officer's captain is Werlek? Do you think he'll discipline her if he gets some? Or allow the information to reach the commander if the animals weren't supposed to be taken? Maybe this is common. Maybe there's a reason Berlee could bring us meat the other night."

The thought silences her for a space, thinking through my comments. "No way," she finally says. "That poor man acted surprised. If the war has been going on for years he'd have heard of something like this happening to someone before."

"That's exactly my point. The man was surprised because this isn't systematic. I think it was an act by this specific company, intentionally hidden from Gruca."

"Someone would rat if this happened now and then."

"You can't be sure. Lots of soldiers looked upset, but people who disagree are often cautious to the point of doing nothing. Most didn't cheer Werlek to fight me the other night, but some did. Absolutely nobody sided with me. It takes incredible moral courage to redirect a group you're part of. Even with words."

Claire huffs. "All the more reason to win this war."

She's not wrong about winning the war, but I'm not naive enough to think we'll change that by the simple expansion of Elathon's borders. At the least it will take generations for change to occur. We may not even win, let alone free the citizens from this treatment.

The more I think about it, the less importance I attach to winning the war. So what if we defeat Heller? His government will be replaced by my father's, with me likely at the head west of the Dendring mountains. Being in a position of power is one thing, the ability to wield that power is another. As bad of light as we see Heller's reign in, it's light to his people. One they're familiar with. My brief interactions with soldiers over the past few days demonstrated the people hold Elathon in low esteem. Experience has shown me people would rather have a dim light they know than an unfamiliar bright light.

Perhaps a better solution would be to support a man like Gruca in a bid for the throne. My one interaction with him showed him as reasonable, discerning. After only a few minutes' conversation he allowed me the confidence that he could set himself up as king, if only a Shadow King. Impatience to rise to a high station—not a quest for control as far as I can tell—fueled his participation in the Divide. That, and he ordered our good treatment. It didn't appear to work well, but it was there. Maybe he doesn't know about the captain's attack. Everything leaves me wanting to propose backing Heller's assassination, but... no.

"What?" Claire asks. I look at her, realizing I'm shaking my head.

"Oh, nothing."

"You were muttering."

"It's just—" I drop my voice. "I was thinking replacing Heller on the throne might be enough to steer this country in a better direction."

"What are we fighting this war for if not to replace Murethon's throne?"

"Replace it with someone internal, I mean."

Claire scoffs.

"What?" I ask. "You don't remember anything of the day we met Heller. He's clearly not good for this country. What if he were replaced with someone less bad?"

"Less bad? You've cursed your Gift so many times I don't think you can pull it as an excuse now," she says. "And why are you so infatuated with Gruca? Is it because he gave a toothless order to treat you well?"

Her comment annoys me. "It's not about returning a favor. I appreciate his gesture, but we both know it was little more than that. He's far better than Heller, and the people would probably accept him."

"Remember how he said he doesn't care about the newest soldiers," Claire says. "You of all people should hold that against him."

"He cares far more than Whiteneck."

A disturbance in the ranks ahead cuts our conversation short. Stopping an army at midday is a slow process. As the soldiers in each successive rank realize their comrades have stopped, the formation compresses. Since this is the day we're supposed to reach Balruvia, anxiety propels my emotions to try and discover the defender's plight. Presently a murmur whispers across the halted soldiers like a wind rustling fall grasses: "Balruvia. Fighting outside Balruvia now."

Officers and captains rush forward while the rest of the army stands speculating. Claire and I exchange glances. I can't tell if mine—let alone hers—is hopeful or fearful.

Minutes later soldiers split to the sides of the path while the returning officers rush down the narrow space. Each stops before his or her company to deliver the same message: the battle around Balruvia has already begun.

Minutes later we're lost in the frenzy of battle preparations. Only this time, we have no part in it. Packing slaves unload weapons from the occasional mountain pony and hand them to officers who, unlike common soldiers, don't carry their own weapons. The sun sinks past the hottest part of the day and within the hour even we can see the fortress.

Balruvia sits between two peaks. A river still swollen with spring melt flows in the bottom of the valley before the castle, overtop of which a stone bridge extends west.

Constructing the bridge provided contention in the already-tumultuous time after the Divide—several politically powerful people wanted to cut off all contact with Murethon. But lack of a bridge, some argued, more than encouraging reconciliation, would make contact harder and serve as a monument to Elathon's self-assured virtue.

Contributing to its defensibility, the fortress was strategically built on the edge of a steep ravine, as all the fortresses in the Dendring mountains after The Divide were. Since its completion, the only serious threat to the fortress came this spring when the Guldethian army swept from the north to surround it in their press for Myceum.

At points of its short history, Balruvia was whitewashed with lime to provide a more intimidating obstacle. With recent years of war slowing the ability to do more than care for it structurally, I know the appearance has suffered.

At our distance it still gives the impression of being carved from a single piece of stone—a third peak chiseled away to provide an impregnable bulwark.

A horse jumps into view, Gruca atop shouting over the noises of excited soldiers. "Captain Honsten, down the southern slope there. Captain Kafter, take your soldiers around north. Werlek, you and your troops will be with me." With that he whirls the animal around. A mare, I notice.

The animal's dark brown coat glistens as it moves, matching Gruca's partially-armored form. Curving plates of armor cover him from the waist down, with patches of mail guarding the open joints. His loose dark green tunic waves as he rides the jostling of his mare. A fox head, the same elaborate one from his banner, decorates the back as he returns to the front.

With nothing to do except attempt an escape, Claire and I are borne along by the company we're part of.

"Everybody's guarding us," I say with relief. "Which means nobody is."

She whispers back. "Now we only have to worry about someone looking for an excuse to linger behind."

We haven't been with Gruca's force enough to know what to expect. If the whole force were fresh, which I doubt after hearing about Giant's Ballroom, I'd expect a certain number of desertions. What I'm hoping is that nobody's fresh enough to let terror hold them back.

"Guarding us *would* be the perfect rationale." All we can do about that is pray we're forgotten about for even a minute.

Shouts before us increase as the masses of soldiers see the distant battle. Craning my neck finally yields results as I get my first good view of the fortress. Knots of soldiers line the walls. Many are moving in formations with even more running alone. From my perspective they look like ants scurrying on a thousand different missions.

Claire and I both know what's going on down there, and we look at each other. She's revealing more fear than I am, though it's just as prevalent behind my eyes. I can't help but voice what we're both thinking: "this force will turn the tide."

She swallows. "Against us, I fear."

It's true. Our practiced eyes see the patches of blue and dark green on the battlefields and make an instant judgment. A captain can't say how a battle will go with as many variables as individual soldiers, but numbers count for something. It looks like they're on the edge of overrunning Balruvia even without Gruca's reinforcements.

A shout far ahead is lost in the return shouts around us.

"They're heartened," Claire observes. It sounds like she dredges every word from her sick stomach.

Gruca and his captains split into the three segments and rush forward on their separate missions. My heart rises to my throat at their easygoing manner; they know they'll crush our forces.

To our dismay, some soldiers remain behind to guard us. We're bound, and the dozen cadets pace back and forth while their comrades prepare to engage.

Claire and I join them. It's a distraction from the real fighting, as they let us watch beside them.

"Gruca's leading the main body to the gate: it's weakening already." I say in the form of commentary. They don't seem to mind so I continue. "They might push through it within an hour even without him, but he'll turn the tide your way. Who was the captain going down the southern slope? Anyway, they'll land against hard resistance based on the body count there. I think it's from the archers. There's plenty on the main wall-walk but second rank on the higher towers behind doubles their power. Those ones aren't harried by close fighting yet. Ouch—yeah, that was an impressive volley."

They don't stop my commentary even when I'm cheering their comrade's deaths from beside them. I move a little aside for a better view. "Your other captain—the one who headed around north—will find the easiest time unless our defenders find a way to spare soldiers up there. I hope to Nymunia they do. See the blue banners there?"

I go quiet. Watching the battle gives us all a heavy heart. It pains me to watch as a captive instead of bloodying my sword as a participant. There's so many soldiers I care about down there fighting and dying without my help. I know I couldn't turn the tide, but I'd certainly leave a trail of carnage as I fled.

Giving commentary on a battle I can hardly bring myself to watch over the next several hours gives me an idea on how to treat high-ranking prisoners in the future. At times I'm interested, at times horrified, but my frustration rises as the sun sets. Moved almost to the point of tears, I continue my pacing, forgotten by the Guldeth in the monotony of their watch.

Night has almost dropped, and the Oruvian trumpets have sounded the retreat. The fortress has all but fallen, with the remaining soldiers fleeing in a desperate body from the eastern gate. A glance to our guards shows me they're too interested in watching the final bloody resolution to notice us for a while.

"Get up. Let's go." I say to Claire. She takes the earnestness in my voice to heart and belts after me through trees and over rocks.

A mile later I hear a scrabble on stone with a muffled fall. Looking behind, I see Claire lying on her side, struggling to right herself with bound hands. I reach her side in seconds.

"You could have used that before," she says as I produce a short knife from inside my boot, sawing through her bindings.

"Wouldn't have done any good." I drop the knife and move to where she can cut my ropes as well. "Alright, come on."

Ten minutes later we're confronted by an Oruvian soldier. She looks more intent on running with us than bothering to check our identities. Her uniform is perfect.

"Who are you?" she tries to demand as she retreats.

"Follow us and ask questions when we're safe." We rush past the surprised soldier, who joins our mad flight away from the fallen fortress.

"Now who are you?" the soldier gasps as we walk for a rest.

"An Oruvian captain," I say, thinking it best to not use my name. "Claire here is an officer."

"You're not wearing Oruvian tunics. How do I know you're not scouts looking for our nearest muster?"

"Because we don't even have a blade long enough to stab you," I say through heavy breaths. Running the first mile with my hands tied was as tiring as all the other miles combined. "We'd have brought weapons if we were scouts."

She looks convinced, though still leary.

"Which way to that muster?" I ask.

She points, and follows when we start running again.

"What company are you part of?" Claire asks at our next stop. It's nearly dark and we haven't found anyone.

I interrupt. "I think we're off course. You said the muster was this way?"

She looks like she wants to nod, but refuses to meet my gaze.

I walk a few steps closer. "The Oruvian muster. You said it was this way." She shakes her head, still looking anywhere but in my eyes. Her behavior flares doubt in my mind. "What company are you with?"

Fear clamps her mouth, making me think she's a spy leading us off course. I grab her shoulder. "Answer me. What company?"

"Officer Broadwine's, sir."

"We were prisoners for the whole battle," I say, "and only escaped before we found you back there. What's the status of his company?"

"They're good. Strong and hearty soldiers. Probably few casualties in the ranks."

"Chris," Claire says. I look over and notice her eyeing the soldier's uniform. My eyes widen when I look back to see its complete lack of stains.

"What's your name?" I ask.

"Ann Flune." Her voice is little more than a whisper.

"And you didn't see battle?"

"No, sir."

Claire steps in, "You're the stablemaster's apprentice, aren't you?"

Ann nods.

"Was that your first sight of fighting?"

"Yes—actually, no. I was at Myceum, but my company was one of the few not called upon. We were stationed as backup to the southern gate."

A blush deepens on her cheeks as she talks, afraid she's incriminating herself beyond the obvious desertion. My face flushes as well, though it's not from fear. Dealing with a deserter after a defeat is always a lot harder than after a victory. I'm glad Claire is doing the talking now.

"Seeing fighting in a battle is a lot different than practice, isn't it?"

Ann nods. She looks ashamed. *Good.*

"You've seen it twice now," Claire says. "What do you think you'll do next time?"

"I'll stay and fight. At least, I hope I will." There's no mark of decision in her tone.

Claire puts her arm around the girl's shoulders. "What you'll do is you'll make yourself proud next time. I know it."

"Yes," she says, decisive for the first time since we first found her. "I will. Thank you, Officer... Claire."

Claire opens her mouth to speak. *Oh, no,* I think.

"Officer Lewis," Claire corrects, then realizes her family name might not have been the best choice.

Ann's eyes go wide. "Officer Claire Lewis, as in daughter of Commander Lewis of Eraseam?"

"The same."

"Oh, I—please don't report me. Unless, of course, you're bound to—then do what you need, I suppose. Of course you will. Pay me no heed."

My scowl drops to a mask of detachment.

Claire jumps in to smooth over the slight. "Don't worry; he's too busy to deal with something like this. I won't even inform your captain. I don't think Captain Prince Hart will either, will you?"

Leave it to Claire to drag a smile from me in this hour. My cheeks bunch a little at seeing Ann's jaw drop. "I think having us find you is enough punishment."

"Yes, Your Highness," Ann says meekly.

Claire chuffs quietly, causing Ann to flinch and look at me, but I pretend not to notice.

"As I said earlier we were prisoners and only just escaped. Do you have extra weapons on hand?"

"Indeed," she says, so eager to help she starts to draw her sword. "Ah, I'm sorry," she says, then puts it back in the scabbard. She unbuckles it and holds it out. As I reach for it, she has an inspiration, drops to one knee, and holds it up. It's meant to be formal, especially when she repeats "Your Highness" with head bowed.

Claire can't stifle a laugh and almost snorts with the forlorn effort. My smile broadens while Ann looks up at me, reddening. "Thank you," is all I manage.

"Let's stop here for the night," I announce, changing the subject. "It's dark enough we might eventually travel by the moon. For now, though, I think we're better off waiting for daylight. Especially since we evidently ran miles in the wrong direction."

Claire agrees, and I turn back to Ann to make sure she doesn't take my last comment as a personal rebuke. She's still kneeling on the ground. "Um, rise, please," I say, then, "You don't need to worry about that out here."

When we've all cleared spaces for sleeping, we gather in a circle. I've dragged branches for us to sit on, Claire found some small twigs, and Ann had means to light a fire. We keep it as small as possible, only feeding enough twigs to light sticks the thickness of a man's thumb.

"What happened in Myceum?" I ask. Ann said she was stationed there during the battle. Since she's alive, I'm hopeful we were victorious the second time around. The events I reversed from the first battle didn't leave things looking good for prisoners.

"It was a victory," Ann answers. "My company was stationed in the southern end of the courtyard so we didn't see much fighting."

"They attacked the other gates?"

"Yes. Ours as well, but the northern one took the heaviest assault. It's funny—before the battle Commander Lewis"—she glances at Claire—"he stationed so many soldiers and reinforcements there it's like he knew they'd attack the seemingly-strongest point. After the battle we heard the older soldiers saying it was almost like he had his wife back with her Gift."

Claire's gaze feels hot against my profile. Continuing to look at Ann, I ask, "What sort of victory? I mean, was it close?"

"Not very, at least not that I could see. We were in the courtyard—never called anywhere—so it couldn't have been that close, I don't think."

Now I meet Claire's gaze. She's smiling—really smiling —and I should be as well. Something stops me from moving beyond a cadaverous mouth-only smile. There's no reason not to smile at having saved the provincial capital from the dreadful fate of mass executions. Maybe it's fatigue, maybe it's knowing different soldiers died than would have without my interference. Either way, the knowledge which should lighten my heart anchors it to a bedrock of weariness.

Ann goes to lay down while the fire still dances in the charred patch of dirt. I hear her breath change to a deep, rhythmic drone.

"What's wrong," Claire asks.

I sigh. "I would have saved some of our soldiers' lives if I'd been there."

"Would you have?"

I turn to Claire with indignation spread plain across my face. "Of course I would have. I'm incredibly adept at weapons if you haven't—"

"That's not what I meant, Chris," she interrupts. "If you were down there don't you think you would have held on longer than anyone else? Led troops into more dangerous gambits? They might have killed a lot more enemies with your leadership but you probably would have lost soldiers. *Different* soldiers than if you hadn't interfered."

I open my mouth to speak, but close it a second later. It takes a moment to process a reply. "I pride myself on low casualty numbers."

"I know you do. Everyone knows they're impressive, especially your father, it's just you can't throw yourself on hot coals for every fight you're not a part of. The fight is over and you couldn't participate. It isn't your fault."

"The crown bears ultimate responsibility for everything that happens in the kingdom."

Claire pokes at the fire. "Don't make me blame you for getting captured earlier. You know I want to do it again, but you can't stop something like this from happening. Like you said earlier, so many possible outcomes can result from a single change."

"It's Ann, too. If it were a victory all her friends would shame her for disloyalty and that would be the end of it. Defection is so much harder to deal with following a loss."

"She's punished enough, Chris. Yes, the battle would have gone differently, but not by much. You know as well as anyone that her returning to her company will be harder than facing down an enemy."

The fire's dance settles to a glowing flicker. Claire slides from her place by the pile of coals to sit against my side. The miniscule heat from the embers doesn't radiate far, and her warm body next to mine makes me relax for the first time in days. She puts one hand on my arms and her lips close to my ear.

"Chris, even if we lose the war—even if Elathon falls—please don't blame yourself. You're doing all you can. I wish you could see yourself the way I see you."

She stands, stretching her arms to the million stars above, then picks her way a few steps back to the space she cleared earlier.

I stay seated, unmoving, for hours. Long after both wandered to their sleeping spaces, long after the coals gave up all pretense of light or heat, I'm still sitting. The moon has risen now, casting a soft silvery light over everything. Somehow the only way I notice the passage of time is the stars, first rising, then twisting through the heavens.

Claire rolls over behind me, then a few minutes later I hear her stir. "Hey," she says softly, resting a hand on my shoulder. "You need some sleep, Chris. We'll make it okay"

I nod, then stand and briefly wonder if I would have sat up all night if she didn't urge me to sleep. How I'll manage to tell her about Julek's treachery has invaded my worried mind enough over the last several hours that I can't bring myself to look at her. I stumble to my sleeping-place on numb legs, now questioning if I ever will. Seconds after my head rests on a bed of leaves, I'm asleep.

When the sun rises the next morning, we've already been walking for two hours. With nothing along to eat, I grab up a few green strawberries to try.

"Phew," I gasp after swallowing one. I toss the rest at Claire. "I realize I'm not very hungry after all."

Claire smiles in return. It's my attempt to bridge the gulf between us. She's aware enough to recognize it's there, but there's no way she can realize how wide it is.

"Ann," I say, "there's one more thing I want from you to make up for your desertion yesterday."

Claire tries to meet my eyes. She looks worried at what I could say.

Ann visibly deflates at the chafing of a raw wound. "Yes?"

"You might be dealing with mockery from friends for a while. That's plenty of punishment, along with running into us last night." I stop to laugh a little. "I can't help with your friends and comrades, but I have some advice I want you to follow. Are you ready for it?"

"Yes, Your Roy—I mean, um, yes. I'm ready."

I turn to face her, making sure she meets my eyes before I smile and say, "Have some confidence. You're good enough to do this."

She glows. It looks like I removed a double-weight marching-pack from her shoulders.

Chapter 17.

"I'd like to speak with you in private," Julek says when he sees Claire. She's bobbing toward him with me in tow.

Finding the Oruvian muster wasn't too hard once we realized Ann accidentally led us away in her fright. Traveling light, with empty stomachs goading us on, we three caught up to the retreating force by the next evening. Ann disappeared soon after we made it past the guards, no doubt looking to blend into the group.

"Certainly, father," Claire says, beaming at seeing him for the first time since riding out of Myceum.

Julek leads us into his tent. It's the largest one in the camp. His armor, no doubt scuffed and scraped from the battle, has already been shined almost to castle perfection. The soldiers in the rest of the camp haven't yet found time to do more than essential repairs like replace broken straps or bend back the rare jagged dent.

Julek holds up a piece of chain mail covered in flaky red and brown splotches. "A turn in the sand barrel and this mail will be as bright as ever." After he sets it beside the rest of his armor, he continues into the tent. It's dim inside the tent—a faint pink light illuminates everything inside through the west-facing canvas with a single spot showing a sinking yellow ball.

"You took Merry and Ironfoot," Julek says from his spot on a collapsible wooden bench.

Claire stands before him. "We needed quick travel to Mt. Cabrae. Excellent mounts for such a ride."

"Huh." Julek chuckles. "You have your mother's face and my soul behind it. I didn't notice for a few days. Not until we left to liberate Balruvia. Too busy starting to clean up the damage from our successful defense."

Julek turns to me. Until now I've been glad he's limiting his attention to Claire—I feel anything but warmth toward him. "I understand I have you to thank for the victory—you and Weaver Deloc."

Hearing Weaver's name jolts me from nursing the resentment I feel. "I trust he delivered my message."

"He did. I didn't understand why you left so suddenly and I think he was as genuinely confused as me, but we had too much to think about. After all, you both can take care of yourselves. You've proven that many times. Speaking of which, where have you been?"

"We went to Mt. Cabrae, as I'm sure Weaver told you, then made a foray into Murethon before Gruca Headon captured us near Starview Pass. They hauled us along as they went to further the assault on Balruvia."

"Ah, the battle by Giant's Ballroom," Julek mutters. It looks like a cloud casts the smallest of shadows on his eyes, as if in dim memory. "We just heard today about the defeat. What can you tell me about it?"

His eyes flicker between us until I speak. "Probably nothing more than your messenger. We learned about it from Gruca after our capture. Apparently some of his force was present at the battle."

The camp around us feels on edge. Maybe it's that I've been through so much worse lately, but I'm feeling more threatened by Julek's stern affability than any unknown enemy.

"You figured it out then?" Julek says, interrupting my thoughts. "I mean your Gift, since you left us a perfect strange strategy to win at Myceum."

"It happened in an extreme of emotion, yes."

"I'm glad it finally manifested. If only June were here to teach you..."

Claire pipes up. "I told him many things about it."

"I've no doubt you did. But knowing it second-hand as a small girl is different than passing it on after scores of personal experiences." Julek turns to look at me. "This battle—the one at Balruvia—it was *extremely* important to our cause. I'd like—"

"No."

"What do you mean, no?"

"I mean I'm not going to use my Gift to reverse it. Another chance wouldn't have mattered anyway with the odds what they were. End of discussion."

"There hasn't been any discussion. It's only two days. For you. For your people." He stands, and a vein bulges in his neck.

"No," I repeat in a tone that doesn't leave any possibility of moving forward. As soon as the word leaves my mouth, though, I realize I'm arguing with Julek—not exactly someone known for giving up easily.

"Piss on you, boy, it's not like I'm asking you to reverse back as far as The Giant's Ballroom, too! You could give up two years to save countless lives. What would your mother think of —"

"I'm *not* doing it," I say. "I'm the prince and there's no use trying to force me into it." I take a step forward, my hands curling into fists, "And you'll leave my mother out of this if you have any sense."

He moves to start pacing, then stops and faces me, finger thrust outward in a threatening gesture.

"We've lost both passes into Eraseam and you won't do anything about it? You self-cent—"

"Father!" Claire interrupts.

"It's a shame to lose both passes the same week," he continues. His voice is more calm now, but it carries the same menace mine did. "More shameful to not change it since you can."

I meet his glare with a blazing stare of my own.

"Do you know how many soldiers died back at Mt. Cabrae?" Julek asks.

I don't, so I keep staring at him.

"Over half of them! Captain Kimbr had a regiment and over half were killed."

My jaw drops the slightest bit, opening a space between my lips. My eyes don't lose their edge. If anything, they're more flint-like than ever. He of all people has no right to ask me to use my Gift. Not after what he did to the queen.

"He's already reversed the Giant's Ballroom to save my life, Father," Claire says. "And Myceum, too. He's saved my life two times. You can show him a little gratitude for that."

"Reversed Giant's Ballroom?" Julek breathes. He keeps his eyes on me but speaks to Claire. "You fought there before?"

"Yes. He reversed a victory to save me. He only owes loyalty to the king but he did that for you."

My heart dropped at Claire's words, but I don't let him see it. Eyes gleaming a new lively fire, he takes a breath to steady himself. "Well, I suppose saving a man's only daughter twice counts for something." His gaze dances to Claire, then back at me. "I suppose that's the two years I was asking for, isn't it?"

He walks past me and exits the tent. I glare at his back until long after the triangular flap falls into place.

"You really said that," I say to Claire.

"He does owe you gratitude. I wouldn't be alive otherwise."

"About reversing the Giant's Ballroom."

"I don't see why where it was done makes a difference."

I turn from the tent opening. "He's already furious about me not reversing a battle we lost. Then you told him I reversed a battle we won. What conclusion can he possibly draw from that?"

She looks uncomfortable. "That... you wanted his daughter alive for some reason."

"What? No I..." I run my fingers through my hair in frustration. "It can't ever be like that between us."

"Then what was that at Starview Pass?"

"It was... just a wish. Just another hope I can't ever live."

I leave Julek's tent and resist the urge to kick his armor as I pass by. "Another curse of power," I mutter. "Giving up your life for people like him."

Julek's guards look at me in surprise. I don't know if they heard what I said, but I don't really care. Claire follows me, too.

"What happened?" she asks. "Was it something in Castle Muerthy?"

Oh, how badly I want to tell her. Looking at her makes me think of everything I've wanted my whole life. Makes me think of everything that could have been if I wasn't cursed with knowing my mother's killer. The farm, the home, the children: it all flashes before my eyes. Tending the animals, working the fields, hunting the woods: all the work shows in my mind like play. Walking down a dirt lane, Claire and me swinging a laughing child between our hands; waking early and walking miles in the dark to the highest hill to watch the sun rise on Midsummer's morning: the play threatens to clog my throat. It might kill me to hold it back, but at least this way I'll be able to keep myself wondering if it could have worked.

"You'd hate me for telling you," I say. "Better to have you only hate me for not letting you know."

"I won't hate you for it. Whatever it is can't be so dreadful as all that."

"I'll make sure we're in different reg—"

"You can tell me," she implores.

"Different regiments. I'll sort it out when we're in Myceum. You stay with your father and do what he wants. I'll be somewhere far away."

"Don't do this to me, Chris," she says.

I turn around, place one hand on her shoulder to keep her away and close my eyes while looking down—away from her appealing eyes.

"Please tell me," she begs. "Please."

"You don't know what you're asking for," I say. "Please just trust me."

"But I've stayed by you through so much already. How can it be worse than what you told me we've experienced?"

I turn to walk away. She stays between her father's two guards, her voice growing fainter.

"You don't have to hide again," she calls. I'm not far enough to stop from hearing the plaintive desperation. It rends my already overflowing soul, but I simply shake my bowed head and continue walking.

Night passes in a haze of sleep and fear. For the rest of the camp, it's worry about the possibility of scouts alerting them to a pursuing force. For me, it's second-guessing my decision to distance myself from Claire. Horses leave an hour later. It looks like they're all traveling different directions.

Stars blink overhead and fires crackle in the distance. The combination makes my thoughts flow in channels of recollection. Like with the fires Rafael and I used to sit beside, memories pile one atop the other.

I remember back to shortly after Rafael's death. The queen had been murdered the year before, and Rafael's death cut King Laurence another abominable blow. I was trying to accept the responsibilities a future heir to Elathon's throne must shoulder, but my anger would get the better of me. I went to the king's Business Room after he confronted a livid foreman, expecting to find him rattled. His mood surprised me. After the discussion for an aspect of design on The Pass of the Winds, he answered my timid question as if he'd only just come from a pleasant stroll through the royal gardens.

"Will you do me a favor, my young man?" he had asked.

"Of course."

Then he had said: "You seemed unsure of yourself after the foreman left. Don't let mistreatment sway how you think or behave. Doing so gives the other person power. This is more than being King one day. It's about you as a growing man." He smiled and his eyes showed he meant it. I had bowed and turned to go, but he called me back. "And by the way, Chris; I liked your idea for a name. We're calling it Lorganrule."

Night's chilly air and the recollection makes me clear my nose, breathing the fresh mountain smell better than I've done for days. I should be giving Claire the advice to retain her pleasant personality even though she can't be with me. She's giving me power to make her miserable as much as I've given myself license to dispirit my own mind. Again it's power, and I've abused it.

Wrong as it is to use that power against someone I love so deeply, the effect I've had on myself startles me more. At my worst times, I've used it willingly, so I know it's been there. Used against myself, though, the damage I've caused hasn't occurred to me until now.

I smell again, feeling the familiar scent of a dead fire wash over my mind like the sea over rocks. Every bit of me wants to rekindle the fire and sleep beside it.

Chapter 18.

Relief washes through the camp at sunrise. I see it overtake everyone from my self-appointed place on a hill as the regiments move out. I've stayed apart since my arrival, moreso now that I've distanced myself from Claire. I'm still not convinced our separation is the best solution—only the easiest—but I'll have time in Myceum before I leave.

The rest of the journey to Myceum goes well, lasting until the sun shines straight down. The sight greeting our eyes is a less dismal display than I would have expected at seeing the first assault break the walls. We approach from the south west, so we can't see the northern gate with the associated damage from the fierce fighting. I'll be sure to visit the site of repairs and talk with officers to learn as much as I can about their victorious tactics.

Since I'm avoiding Claire, I need to avoid Julek as well. That makes it easy to visit the northern gatehouse. I spot several soldiers I know before I find Weaver. He's holding a straightedge and greets me with a broad smile.

"Well met, my prince," he says. "I'm glad to see you made it back from wherever you ran off to."

"I take it you're extra happy to see me since you were victorious," I chide. His enthusiasm helps lift my spirits.

"Rather. It went exactly like you said: forces against all the castle, other officers calling for reinforcements, and me wanting to give them. I would have, too, if you hadn't specifically instructed me not to. They came close to overwhelming us a few times as it was. In the end we held them off as you can see. It was strange, though; they practically fled when they realized we were too strong to breach."

A soldier rushes up to him. "Captain Deloc, the commander will be wishing for an update on the progress before long."

I let out a long whistle. "*Captain* Deloc. Has a nice sound to it."

His grin takes up most of his face. I know how hard he's been working toward becoming a captain. It feels good to have put him in a position where he could finally prove his capability.

"The commander advanced me after seeing the assault we repelled. Several were advanced to officer as well." He rests the straightedge on the ground and continues, blond eyebrows high into his hairline. "I appreciate you trusting me to lead the defense in your absence. And for your guidance. I wouldn't have been advanced if it weren't for you."

I wave my hand. "Not everyone with a good opportunity takes advantage of it. I wouldn't have put you in that position if you hadn't taken initiative over the years."

He smiles again, then presses his left fist to his chest with a slight bow. "Thank you my prince. I better go report to the commander. We've made much progress. Feel free to look around."

With Weaver heading to report to Julek, I wander the walls and descend some scaffolding on the outside. The damage was severe on a few merlons. The soldiers and workmen laugh when I step onto the rickety scaffolding.

"Careful there. We can't build this too strong or we might not be able to take it down in time if an enemy shows up."

It's a good precaution, one I'm glad they bothered to take. There would be enough turmoil in the castle without worrying about removing a veritable ladder.

Late the next afternoon, the castle grows astir at the approach of a large party. I was planning to leave the next day, and on the point of venturing a visit to Julek so we both would know which soldiers I was going to take. Officers rush to warn the commander, who appears pleased.

"She's here earlier than I expected. What a pleasant surprise," he says with a glance at me. The look deep in his eyes after his outburst doesn't feel right.

When the party nears the southern gate, even Julek's face turns a shade surprised. The ranks of mounted soldiers, flapping sapphire banners, wagons behind, and sun flashing across more armor in the rear trumpets the king's presence. "Well now, *he* is much earlier than I would have thought," Julek says. The glance my way looks a bit worried this time, and I don't know why. Surely the king's traveling party on the road can't concern him.

Julek leaves the keep's upper balcony with his focus narrowed on the brick walkway before him. Telltale signs of trouble well within my chest. It's unexplainable, but reaching Father before Julek seems... important. And yet Julek's passing comments make it feel like something he wants. A statesman can manipulate another with well-timed glances, so I'm not falling into his game.

I make my way down to the courtyard. My thoughts run entirely on telling Father what I've discovered. I somehow need to see Julek's forearms before the king departs. Father—the king —could order his commander to bear his arms, but that would be going off Heller White's word, and could be politically dangerous. Not only that, it's also impossible to accuse Commander Lewis of murdering the queen unless I give the king and his court an account of my adventures in Murethon. No— that could spin out of control.

The king listens to Julek. His presence, utterly unexpected by everyone, makes me wonder about the condition of Sapesky.

From atop his regal mount, the king makes an imposing figure bearing down on the commander. His face is knitted in a consternation bordering on anger. Whatever Julek is telling him, I hope, is something he's opposed to.

"That's a deep gamble, Commander," I hear him say as I draw closer. "Wandering the slippery edge of a crevasse is more dangerous in the rain."

Julek makes a profound bow. He waves several pages forward to care for the king's horse, and my father finally dismounts.

"Captain Hart," he says, his expression lightening a little. "I've missed you, my boy."

"It's good to see you as well, Father," I say. "I was on the point of leaving for Sapesky tomorrow to ask you for further orders."

"Looks like I saved you a great deal of trouble. I was on my way here when Julek's rider met me along the road." The king's eyes darken a shade as he hands off his horse's gold-colored bridle and leads me away from prying ears. "This soldier was apparently coming from near Balruvia all the way to Sapesky with a message for me. He told me many new developments. Some I hope aren't true."

My steady heart quivers at his words. I want to steal a glance at Julek. "I'll be happy to tell my version of any story you're questioning," I say. My guarded words are chosen so I don't have to lie later. I'm happy to tell the king anything at all—anything that doesn't have to do with my conversation with Heller White or reversing our victory at Giant's Ballroom.

"Perhaps we'd better find a council room." He turns back to the group. "Refreshment for two in an available chamber."

Squires and stewards, eager to please, jump at his words as if they just upset a basket of eggs.

Julek tries to join us, and it's a huge relief to have Father around to turn him away. "This visit is between a father and his son. There will be time for a wider council tonight. Please prepare for that."

Julek bows, places his fist on his chest. "As you desire. Commander Nealy should arrive by then."

The king's brows furrow. "Indeed." He leads the way into the nearest door. I follow with my usual commanding step but feel wholly inadequate to trace his powerful footsteps.

He knows his way around the castle from years of diplomatic visits. I know my way around from playing hide-and-seek with Rafael and Claire on those years of visits. He guesses at a room and finds it empty. Minutes later two stewards enter with platters of food.

"Quite a spread," he comments as he reaches past the fruits for the meat. It's smoked venison with a knife and two-pronged fork sticking out.

"Allow me." I grab the serving fork. The knife makes a grating sound when I scrape it on the pewter beneath. I place the first bit of meat in my mouth, generating a laugh from the king as he turns to the narrow window.

"I don't think you have to worry about Julek poisoning me."

My head jerks up to stare at his back as he leans into the window casement, avoiding the thick oak shutter. *Oh, if you only knew*, I think.

The king continues. "He's brash but helpful. Harmless, really, though I don't mind everyone else thinking his bite is as bad as his bark."

I force the venison down my throat without remembering to chew it. He turns to look at me and catches the end of my distressed swallow. "That bad?"

"I think it's fine. We'll see." I pour a cleansing drink from the decanter on the other tray and down it.

"Well I suppose we'll find out if that's poisoned, too," the king says. Then he steps from the window. "What's gotten into you, Chris? You've never insisted on being my poison tester before."

My erratic behavior catches up with me, and I shake my head. "I'm sorry. There's been a lot going on."

"I know. That's why we're here."

"No. You don't know the half of it."

King Hart cocks an eyebrow. He gestures at the chairs. "Then we better start now."

He helps himself to the venison, some wine, fine white bread with cold butter, and an apple. "Do you need to try the rest?"

I look up to see the glimmer in his eyes. I shake my head then grab the same assortment plus a limp carrot. "Preserved remarkably well since last autumn," I say.

A few minutes into our meal, he asks, "Now what's this about you figuring out your Gift?"

This conversation is normally difficult to have with anyone. Especially with the king, since we've started it so many times. Me feeling guilty over the queen's death is entirely my fault. Even when he has asked me to try and discover my Gift, it hasn't been with blame at not having done it sooner. We both lost someone precious that day and we both know I tried.

Guilt pangs my chest again. "I've heard it said June could only use her Gift in a surge of emotion," I say. "I realize I did use my Gift at Mother's death—it's the same sensation I experienced then. Only.... Only I didn't know it at the time. I didn't change the events leading up to it in the proper way. This time Claire died and Myceum was overrun. I'd never seen a battle like that; so much senseless violence. It was rage beyond anything I've seen—like taking the castle was their secondary objective."

He's stopped eating now, hands resting beside his plate with a morsel of venison on his knife.

I talk down toward the table. "I reversed the day of the battle, let an officer know where the attack would come, and left for Mt. Cabrae. I needed to get to Castle Muerthy to check a hunch I had. Claire insisted on coming with me and we ended up in a battle west of Mt. Cabrae. I... *we* won the battle, yet I reversed it because Claire died. Now I heard they lost the battle the second time around." I have to say this. As incriminating as it sounds, he needs to hear it from me.

"We were captured, taken with Heller's commander Gruca Headon to reinforce Balruvia where we escaped to join Commander Lewis's retreating army. It's.... I should have reversed Balruvia to give him another chance. I'm sorry, Father."

Raw emotion makes it impossible to look up from my plate. Though I'm unable to feel a glare on the top of my head, I still don't want to meet his eyes. I can imagine sorrow as fierce as any anger piercing the depths of my soul.

"My appetite has fled like geese before a hound," the king says after a while. "Julek's messenger brought news of some of that. Mostly about you reversing the victory at Giant's Ballroom."

"And Balruvia?" I ask.

He hesitates. "Somewhat. It seems you'd have known the size of their reinforcements, though. No sense wasting a year if the result couldn't be anything but the same."

My eyes close involuntarily.

"It's a strange set of circumstances," the king says. "You're trustworthy enough to have made the best decision at the time."

When I don't look up, he asks, "Do you think you made the best decisions with what you knew at the time?"

I shake my head.

"No? Then you doubt the discernment your mother and I instilled in you?"

"I doubt myself in those matters," I say. "I want out."

"We all doubt ourselves when something goes poorly. The Gift always operates after uttermost pain. Situations like that make it hard enough to exist, let alone think through all alternate futures. June realized that using her Gift didn't guarantee anything. Sometimes there's events outside our control.

"Excellent penit blanega, by the way." He remains silent until I recover enough heart to look up. He's holding a cup of white wine; his eyes are kind, the ones I'm used to. He sets his knife full of venison down and says, "Chris, you have to realize that no matter how it turns out—each Gifted instance or however the war goes—I'm proud of you. Your value doesn't lie in victory, but effort."

A deep breath graces my lungs, calms my heart. I know how many people would give up years of their life to hear words like that, yet I received them free.

"I know a mess like this makes it hard for you going forward," I say. "I'll try to reverse back to Balruvia if you'd like."

"No." He drops a brow and scowls. "I'm not going to make the mistake of trying to control your Gift again." He stands and walks over to my place. My downcast gaze sees his cup of penit blanega lowered to the white linen tablecloth. He places a hand on my shoulder, and I allow my eyes to drift upward. "There haven't been many Gifted in the kingdom, and none as loyal as June was," he says. "It's a hard burden to learn how to carry at all. June had a teacher. I prayed she would live to instruct you in its use—evidently not enough. I should have allowed her use of the Balm. It was a jealous stinginess that held me back."

"She used it too much," I say.

"For our benefit, yes."

"She used it at her discretion."

A mirthless mask of a smile overtakes his face. "Either way. Now she's dead and there's nobody to instruct you."

"How many Gifted do we know about?"

He shrugs. "A few in our history. The citizens may have Gifted among them but they're usually too busy working or paying attention to other things to notice."

"Any nobility with it hidden?"

The king shakes his head. He grabs up his cup of white wine and meanders around the room. "Heller has it. He didn't learn much—said June couldn't teach him well enough after a few short lessons." He swirls the cup, staring into it. "Other than Heller there's nobody I know of besides you."

Heller could *teach me after all*, I think. *More than to be a Shadow King. He could teach—*

"Did you ever make it to Castle Muerthy?" the king asks.

I shudder. In that instance I wish the Gift would have taken my memory as well. "Yes. We were captured and taken there. It was so awful I reversed the day of capture to lead us away."

"My gods, you've been busy practicing. Makes me even more sorrowful Heller's Shadow Kings took the Balm of Life. Here I thought your aging was from hardship and captivity."

The recollection pulls at me to call Julek out despite my uncertainty. The king sits down, takes up his knife again, and eats the piece of venison. "He's probably been using it without our knowledge. Maybe that's how he managed to take Mt. Cabrae and Balruvia."

"We can't be sure they took Mt. Cabrae," I say. "It was Starview Pass and maybe the Giant's Ballroom. And they didn't need Heller's Gift; it was my fault."

The king raises a hand in warning, yet he can't say anything as he swallows. It's my turn to press a comment.

"I didn't know you knew Heller before the Divide."

He gives a wry smile. "'Knew of him' is a better way to put it. I know all the captains but few of them well. It's my job to work with the commanders, who in turn work with their captains. In Montaya's case, it was difficult to appoint Brian a successor. Everyone needed to accept I made the best decision possible. Unfortunately, Heller White and his friend Gruca didn't. Heller's discounting of June's instruction carried hard against him. Hence I chose Robert Brayler; despite his loose tongue he can be taught."

"Gruca's not as bitter as Heller. I think he may be reasoned with."

He stares at me. "Who told you that? Was Gruca poisoning your ears when you were his prisoner?"

"I spoke with him after our second capture. It seems we may be able to ally with him in overthrowing Heller."

"Second capture?" the king asks, latching onto my slipped tongue instead of the intent.

I stare at him as he takes another bite. My plate is still entirely untouched. "Yes," I finally say, forcing myself to start eating the carrot. "We were captured and taken before Whiteneck the first time. It's when we escaped with my Gift that Gruca caught us."

He looks at me in a *tell me more* way. His appetite returned.

"Heller wants me to join him. Says he's going to force me to join his elite Shadow Kings."

The king's eyes darken. I know it's anger directed to the apostate Whiteneck. "Did he say how he's going to cause this?"

I take another bite of the carrot to cause a delay. "He was intent on forcing me to use my Gift. He... he tortured Claire with lies and murdered a man in front of us."

It's hard to not tell the king about Heller's accusation of Julek. The way he treated me during Myceum's first battle, the things he said about my father and me, and the accusation—true or not—make me think he deserves the indignity of a false accusation even if he proves to not have the Velvet Breath mark upon an arm.

Returned anger welling from depths of forgetfulness boils over, moving from a bubbling pot to seething cauldron. If they were real tears, they would roil water to the hot fire beneath and make steam billow.

"Tortured her with lies?" the king asks as he finishes his meat. "You're not one to exaggerate, Chris. This had to have been pretty serious for you to call it that."

The war in my soul overcomes the rest of my body. It makes me drop the remainder of the carrot and cradle my face in my hands. Shivering takes hold. It's a shiver of rage. Of wrath.

I hear the king's chair legs scrape the stone floor and footsteps as he walks toward me. "Dear Lesasil what happened?" There's as much anger in his voice as there is concern.

"Your..." a servant opening the door stops short. "Your Majesty, the Commander is prepared whenever his Highness is disposed." He closes the door without a sound.

"Let's go," I say, suddenly in control of myself. I stand and shove my own chair away. "I have a few things I need to say to Julek."

"Do we need to discuss this privately first?"

"I'm going now," I insist.

The king follows a few steps behind. The rage inside burns so intense I'm sure he can feel the heat. Walking to the Commander's Room serves to intensify it. I almost wish I could challenge Julek to trial by combat. As skilled as Julek is, surely the gods would smile on a man avenging a wrongful death.

Claire sits beside her father in the hall, pale yet upright. My anger stings too deep to allow her beauty any sway over how I'm feeling. Commander Nealy sits on Julek's other side, with Kimbr beside her. They look as serious as I feel, and it arms me even more for a fight.

"King Hart," Julek begins, "I'm pleased you came immediately."

"We came because it suited us," my father replies in clipped tones. The room turns icy.

Julek continues as if he didn't notice. "When I sent a messenger to Sapesky I also sent one to Mt. Cabrae. I never imagined you'd arrive the same day Commander Nealy did— before her, in fact. I'm glad for it because we have much to discuss."

"We have indeed." The king speaks in a slow, menacing tone. The grandest chair is unoccupied, yet not in the accustomed spot at the head of the table. The king motions to a servant to move it into position. The gesture of it being among the other chairs certainly isn't lost on him. "I understand our position in western Eraseam grows more precarious."

"It does," Julek says. Sandy and Kimbr nod along. "Losing the two fortresses along both main mountain passes in the same week opens the entire province to invasion."

Kimbr remarks, "No longer do we have a concentrated war, but a sprawling one. They can go wherever they want."

"They reached Myceum before either fell," the king points out. It doesn't make a difference. As he takes his seat, and I beside him, I can't help but feel he's on defense right from the start. At least I'll be able to regain us the upper hand any time I accuse Julek. Wait for the perfect time.

Commander Lewis looks at Commander Nealy and Captain Kimbr, receiving a nod from each in turn. "I believe I'm speaking plainly when I say the Oruvian presence is growing precarious in *all* of Eraseam *and* Cousea because of one young brat."

The king's eyes ignite as my spirits collapse. "Do you realize what you're saying?"

"Perfectly. It's not something we say lightly, either."

"Betrayal is measured in blood, not weighed by scales."

Julek cocks his head. "What are you saying?"

"This castle is by rights mine," the king says. "All soldiers in the kingdom recognize me as sovereign. I could have you strung from the highest tower by sunset. Large decisions in the kingdom will ultimately be made by me and *all* my soldiers will carry them out."

"You don't have much choice in the matter," Julek says. "With Montaya's transgressions this is the last thing you need. As for your soldiers out there, would you care to look?" He motions to an open window.

I slam my chair back to join the king in looking over the courtyard. It's partway cleared since our arrival, with fewer bluecaparisoned horses of my father's guard taking space on the matted-grass below. A few soldiers stand in groups—far fewer than those who arrived—but the way Julek's soldiers surround them, it's clear they know they're holding a precarious welcome.

"How dare you threaten me," the king growls. "Commander Brayler is loyal. You know his reaction to Luis's passing is one of his caprices. Let him rest for a while while the war is in the north and he'll emerge twice as strong."

"Let's not play that game," Julek says. Commander Nealy and Captain Kimbr look resolved, yet glad Julek's the one speaking. "We want something you can grant us, and grant us easily."

"And that is?"

Julek looks at me, and the fight I entered the room with sputters in my heart.

"Put the prince on trial. He's slighted three of your other four provinces by either lack of action, or worse, open betrayal."

"That *open betrayal* saved your daughter's life," I say. "How could there be a trial against me based on my own words?"

Commander Nealy and Kimbr glance at each other. The commander speaks. "Commander Lewis told me it caused The Giant's Ballroom to fall. One break in the armor can let a limb be severed."

"Damaged armor doesn't mean you put the blacksmith on trial," I say.

Commander Nealy's frown deepens. "But sabotaged armor calls for such measures. The people there are furious. The soldiers are more forgiving, but their patience has limits."

It's been my defense for a while, and I look at the king, standing beside me in the Commander's Room.

He can't give up the Eraseam and Cousea provinces with Montaya already openly flaunting his orders. As effective as a bucket of cold water at quelling lust, their unification takes the wind from the sails of my anger. Accusing Julek now wouldn't do any good. Since he's managed to threaten mutiny with another large province during a time of war, he's in a secure position. Even if Father were to cut him down or degrade him to a lower rank, his soldiers could be in on his threat.

From wrathful ire to floundering helplessness and back, my face flushes scarlet with impotent shame. Julek doesn't know I was going to accuse him of anything, yet his brief gaze in my direction shows some sliver of understanding, as if he's suspicious.

For the fraction of a second I look at the king, I pity him the decision. He shouldn't have to make it. It's my fault. It's my —

"I will go on trial," I say.

The king looks at me, surprised. I hear a young woman's gasp from the line of my accusers.

"I have nothing to fear from justice. Using the Gift without a teacher leaves me open to mistakes—mistakes of which I'll bear the consequences."

I take a step back toward the table. I look pointedly at the Nealy's then let my gaze linger a second longer on Julek. "Justice will be done upon all. An accusation of a prince doesn't mean revolt, but an unfair trial can turn the mind of the people. It's up to the ministers to keep the throne from toppling."

Kimbr starts to speak. "Of course the king has the last word after the court makes a ruling—"

"Binding," I say, my eyes flashing away from Julek for a mere breath.

"Binding it is then," the king says. "I want the Lord High Justice of the Sewlands province to administer the trial. Since you all clearly bear a grudge against my son, and we're to hold this as a binding trial, I'll declare as impartial an administrator as possible. Someone not associated with any of you."

The king glares around the room. Kimbr's mouth snaps shut. I look at him and he drops his eyes, then averts them to a side wall. He's ashamed, even refusing to meet my eyes.

The king continues, "We'll hold the trial when the war settles down for the winter. For now, Captain Hart is too valuable to draw from the lines."

"He can damage the effort if he's allowed freedom before," Julek says. "Not to mention this would give time to sway opinion of the facts. Distortion over months would damage the kingdom's view of fairness, not to mention, should he prove guilty, he would defect for an unknown reception rather than face justice."

"Hold me as bail, then," my father commands. "I can't leave the kingdom. Nothing has been said against me this whole time, and I'm surety enough for his cooperation with the trial. I have complete confidence in his honor and want it known."

The king's booming voice quiets the room; Commander Nealy now looks almost as regretful as Kimbr.

"Fine," Julek says.

The king glares at him, taking a step forward. "I wasn't asking your permission if it was okay. The prince submits to a trial so I say there will be one. Your opinion as the accuser means nothing in this matter."

Julek bows his head. He doesn't break eye contact, instead he brings his fist to his chest in salute. It's flawless; nothing insolent detectable. "Consequences of the prince's actions aren't publicly known," he says. "We all know what such knowledge would mean if it were to become public. I volunteer to keep the prince safe in Myceum."

Silence falls on the room like a veil. There was a reason June's Gift was hidden after a while; the families of soldiers fallen in battles influenced by her Gift often clamored to have her punished as a murderer. Most had no way to know if the death was different from the first time around, but the argument didn't work. Just as logic didn't work on grieving families back then, thousands of people thinking I let the Guldeth through the Dendring mountains would be a nightmare as bad as the war itself.

There's a subtle threat obscured in Julek's generosity. He could tell anyone he wants about me using the Gift. It would be on my word, but grieving people would believe a rumor of my self-incriminating word. A rumor so insidious wouldn't matter if it were true or not.

Fear trickles up my spine. I look at the king, doing my best to hide the dread I feel. He's glaring at Julek, who looks mildly back as if he doesn't know what he's doing. My father nods. "Very well. Christopher will not leave Myceum. Thank you for your hospitality."

The king steps from the room; I follow close behind. We tramp through wide, tapestry-hung corridors, and I notice my father nodding at the servants and making sure they know he is willing to move from the center of the passage as well.

We emerge onto the courtyard and the king strides across it with a baleful measure. We're walking toward a group of soldiers—Julek's soldiers. This could go well or ill. I sense for the familiar slap of scabbard against my thigh, taking assurance in feeling it.

The soldiers look from one to the other of us, unsure what to do, and glance at each other like they each want to be the lowest-ranking in the group. We close the distance in firm strides, me planning to follow my father's lead.

Julek's soldiers part so the king can access his guard. They're as confused as anyone, and show signs of recent anger despite their obvious relief. In the safety of an Oruvian capitol, they weren't expected to remain with the king the entire time. I can see the relief in their soldierly faces: they were blaming themselves for not having foresaw the danger.

King Hart appraises his guards. "You seem to be missing some of your equipment," he says, gesturing to their belts. "Do you know where it is?"

"Yes, Your Majesty," replies one.

"Go get it now. The king's guard shall not be lacking for anything." He turns to Julek's staring soldiers, draws one of their swords, and gives it to his own. "Take this in the meantime." He repeats the procedure with each of his guards as they file past, until he and I are alone with Julek's soldiers, over half of them disarmed.

"Have a care," the king menaces around. "You don't know how close you were to having your heads roll."

The soldiers take a step back as one body, leaving us a wide path to follow the king's guard. Soldiers committing treason, even under order, are found complicit. Harrosh led many soldiers to this, and Heller would have done the same if he hadn't escaped fast enough.

"What brought you to Myceum?" I ask once we're alone.

"I came to provide support for the rebuilding after Myceum's successful defense. Commander Lewis's messenger met me along the road telling of your... misjudgements, shall we say. They didn't sound completely true, but I was coming anyway. I wanted to make sure."

We swing around a corner back into the castle, making our way to a large tucked-away room.

Several of Julek's soldiers, differing from the king's guard by the relative plainness of their uniforms, pass us by with bowed heads. We're on the right track. A few quick strides past wooden benches and heavy doors has us before an open door. Through it we see the glimmer of brighter uniforms moving in front of windows. Everyone turns to face us when we enter.

"What happened out there?" the king asks the group in general.

It's a much larger group of guards than was out in the courtyard. Some of Julek's soldiers remain; it looks like they're handing back the last of the guards' confiscated weapons before they scurry from the room.

One guard steps forward. It's Scott Pullen, Captain of the Mounted Division of the King's Guard, a man I know from growing up. His hair, once a dark brown, sparkles silver in the reflected light of a shield lying on the floor.

"Forgive us, Your Majesty," he begins, going to a knee. "The garrison caught us unawares and surrounded us. Fearing for your life, as we knew none of us were with you, we surrendered our arms without a fight. Many of us they herded here." He bows his aged head and it's only now I notice his rugged hand gripping the pommel of his returned sword, resting tip down on the stone floor. "Had we known it would set you free we would have died gladly for you."

"Rise," the king commands. "There is no fault here. The Commander and I had a misunderstanding. Nevertheless, this cannot be overlooked. Captain Pullen, you'll accompany us and discuss this."

"Yes Your Majesty," the captain responds, rising to attention.

"Everyone else, get comfortable while you wait."

He turns on his heel, followed by Captain Pullen and me. We flank him in the halls as he leads us to a room reserved for his visits. It's near Claire's room and therefore Julek's. We three enter. Captain Pullen goes right to work ensuring the room is secure. I haven't seen him inspect a room in a while, but he performs it with more care than I remember. He looks in the wardrobe, under the bed, and behind the drapes. Even the window doesn't pass his scrutiny; he leans out and looks up, down, and sideways.

"I would recommend you have guards in your room tonight, Your Majesty," he says.

The king sighs. "So be it."

In the same room as I spent weeks of my life over the years, I can almost see my mother's spirit take up her place beside the high window. My hands curl into fists without realizing it. Knowing Julek is nearby boils my blood. Even though I haven't seen his hands or arms since Heller's accusation, his attitude, his bearing, his insolence, his kindness, his very presence bothers me. The fight which left my system during my accusal returns in full force.

"Why were you checking my food for poison?" the king asks.

After a minute of waiting for my reply, he turns around. I glance at Captain Pullen. He follows my gaze, then says, "Can you give us a minute?"

Captain Pullen salutes. "I will wait outside."

"This must be important," Father prompts once we're alone.

I nod. "I don't know if it's true, but it would affect everything."

"How much everything?"

"The bedrock of the kingdom sort of everything. Julek's insolence back there would be child's play by comparison."

The king turns his head part way aside. "You're trapped in Myceum now, yet you act like you have the leverage. I see no benefit in that. The only upside is we didn't determine when the Lord High Justice of the Sewlands would come to administer your trial. Hopefully that delay lets us clear the air before it happens."

"With any luck the Lord High Justice won't even make it here," I say. "Julek doesn't know it yet, but I've got as much blackmail on him as he thinks he has on me."

"I wouldn't call it blackmail; that would signal intent. Julek can be imprudent, but I wouldn't put blackmailing the prince past him."

"Would you call what he did to your soldiers back there loyalty? Or threatening to leave you to fight the war with only the Sewlands backing you?"

The king stares at me for a few moments. There's a hard expression in his eyes—not anger, not pain—it looks like resolution. "The poison-testing?" he asks.

Changing the subject feels like a dagger slipped between my ribs. It stuns for a few seconds while I gather my wits to respond. He didn't even know he did it, yet it hurts. A simple twist of the dagger by giving an angry glance would drop me to my knees.

"It's just... I don't trust Julek as much as you do."

"You were of the age you spent time with his daughter instead of joining us in council. That was good for a boy, though I wish you wouldn't have given up her friendship. It's been making my relations with him difficult as well, though I never wanted to say it."

I snort. "Is that why you made sure she joined with the reinforcements you had me take back?"

"That was a small part of the reason. Hardly more than an afterthought, really. The commander wanted her to see real combat outside of his regiments and he sent her to Sapesky for me to place. I sent for you, she arrived, Commander Derwyler arrived with his five hundred, you arrived, and I sent you back. I didn't scheme, though I probably should have."

"I hope I haven't made governance hard," I say. Usually I'd mean it, but this time I feel much less sincere.

"It is forgiven. I'm grateful you weren't given the chance to poison-test the food in front of our host."

"You've changed that view since we left," I say.

"As I said to my guard: a misunderstanding."

"Then what was that you did out in the courtyard? The *your heads will roll* threat to the guards?"

"An overreaction."

"Overreaction? Misunderstanding? They were nearly complicit in treason. They—"

"There was no treason," the king interrupts. "It was a mistake. I overreacted and need to see Julek to make things right."

"He's not—"

"He's offering you protection after you committed a grave indiscretion. It's one thing to use your Gift poorly, another to proclaim it."

"There's nobody to teach me how to use it." It feels flimsy when it comes out of my mouth, and the king takes the advantage to prove his point.

"I tried to have you use it many times. You'll recall June lived a year after your mother's death. You could have learned a lot in that year. Could have grown." He takes a deep breath and runs his fingers through his gray hair.

Humiliation and shame flush my face crimson as the king makes to leave. The chance I wanted to voice my concern against Julek is gone—evaporated like morning mist. A face full of shame and a heart full of bitterness, I can't look him in the eyes.

"Earlier you said you were proud of me," I say. It's a plea, though I use a hearty voice in hopes it doesn't break.

"I am," he replies with a gentle smile across his face. "But that doesn't mean I'm proud of all your decisions. Actions have consequences. I can help you out of some but other times you need to endure the lesson."

He leaves the room, probably unaware he's desolated me to my self-tormenting thoughts.

Chapter 19.

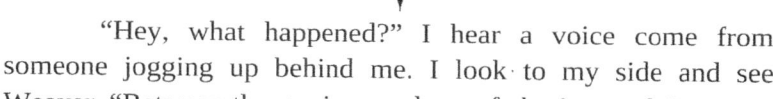

"Hey, what happened?" I hear a voice come from someone jogging up behind me. I look to my side and see Weaver. "Between the garrison and your father's guard, I mean."

"I don't want to talk about it." I wonder how much he knows. Since it's the next day, gossip could have spread like wildfire.

He walks beside me in silence for a while. Finally, he asks, "So you're not to leave here, huh?"

I shake my head, sighing. "How much do you know?"

He becomes defensive on the spot. "Very little, okay? They told the captains and officers to keep an eye to make sure you don't leave. Said it was for your protection as well as the kingdom's. Nothing more."

"Sounds like politicking to me," I say. "Commander-talk for *I want this done but I don't trust you enough to tell you why.*"

We're walking around the outer courtyard, and I glance up to see the tower Claire defended during the first battle at Myceum. If we keep the current trajectory we'll walk by the reigning family's garden, so I change course.

"Yikes," Weaver says.

I look over at him. "Think I'm too hard on the commander?"

He thinks for a few minutes while we walk by soldiers, citizens, and a monotonous stone wall rising high into the air. "I don't think I can answer that," he finally says. "I owe you both loyalty. If I say you're too hard on him I'm not thanking him for my advancement. Then again, you're as much responsible for my advancement as anyone." He falls into silence. "I really don't think I can answer that."

"I'm asking you as a friend," I say.

"As a friend, I want to say you aren't too hard on him, but I don't know why. Yet I think the commander is just and knowledgeable despite his strict visage."

Endearing characteristics, to be sure. That's why it's so hard to think ill of him. Even after my father's top commander humiliated me in front of him, the king started feeling alright about him minutes later.

Weaver continues, "I want to be loyal to you both."

I look at him. "What makes it hard to be loyal to us both at once?"

He starts, and I can sense his confusion. This is what makes it so hard to even think Julek is a traitor for more than a few minutes at a time. I have emotion to drive my accusation, but everyone else feels the powerful man's personal magnetism.

"I guess I don't know," he says after a while. "Don't know why I said that."

"What do the soldiers and other officers say about my confinement?" I ask.

"Not much. They don't understand it any more than I do, but they're probably as nervous to ask questions as me. Nobody going for advancement wants to be thought of as taking liberties."

That's right—almost nobody knows why Julek decided to 'offer' me protection. I suppose it's good I didn't make my blunders more well known, since public outcry could shift our already uncertain position along the Dendring mountains.

"Is there anger over the lack of communication?"

He shrugs. "A little frustration, but it's nothing the commander doesn't do from time to time. He always tells us in the end, and that makes the troops trust when he deems a secret necessary."

I kick a rock in my path, then drag my gaze from the ground. A turn to the right would have brought us to Claire's mother's garden. The memory brings the taste of bile to my throat. I'm glad I paid enough attention to not have taken that route: recollecting that senseless scene hurts my heart and head.

Try as I might, I can't seem to shake the memory from my mind. I felt the fear so strongly after entering the garden that I used my Gift for the first real time, fled, reached Mt. Cabrae, and continued into the heart of Murethon. I had a single-minded confidence I'd talk to Heller no matter the obstacle. It's like the way starts calling to me, and I stop. Weaver waits for me a few paces ahead, then looks around while I stare at the garden door.

"What?" he asks.

I start down the broad gravel and dirt route. High stone walls interspersed with towers line my sides, but I'm making for a small walled section with southern exposure.

Weaver catches me as I stop before the guards. They move into a more erect salute as they recognize me

"I need inside."

They look at each other. Neither wants to be the one to deny the prince entrance. One moves aside while the other looks like he wishes I hadn't come this way. "Yes, Your Highness."

Weaver slips in behind me, looking a little bashful at entering the garden yet letting his curiosity get the best of him. "I've only ever seen this from the towers," he whispers. "It's far more stunning in person."

"Chris?" a voice asks when we're wandering up the path.

I whirl to face Claire in the entryway.

"I wanted to have a few moments alone to think," she says. Weaver looks like he wants to dive into the lavender to hide. "Looks like Nymunia wants something different for me."

She looks resigned to our presence; while I certainly do not relish her showing up, even if it is her private garden.

"Perhaps she does. I'm looking for answers."

"More than the first time you made me let you in?" She leaves the shelter of the entryway and steps onto her garden's lovely path. The bee balm and mint at her sides show up in vibrant shades against her contrasting uniform. I notice the late-blooming daffodils and early sprigs of rosemary for the first time.

"Yeah, more than vague theories this time." I look aside, and when I look back, I see Weaver disappearing through the closing door. "There's..." I trail off in frustration, and only speak when Claire draws near. "It's that— There's got to be something they wanted here beyond finding out about your mother.

"If Whiteneck threw his soldiers at the wall, confident we had a Gifted in the castle, how would he have known? Yet I can't see any other reason for him to allow such a reckless attack; he's never been one to value his soldiers, but wanton waste isn't like him. He had to have been in the attacking party the first time or at least had another Gifted to report back to him."

"It wouldn't have done him any good," Claire points out. "I only have a vague remembrance when you use your Gift so he wouldn't remember it either. It'd be wasted no matter what."

"I'm told the second battle lasted only until they realized our defenders were using an illogical defense," I say. "But the Gifted couldn't have been Heller since we saw him in Castle Muerthy shortly after; he would have still been with the attacking force for the second battle."

"They wouldn't have needed a Gifted with the strategy you're pointing out." Claire looks out over the garden, perfectly manicured, nothing out of place. "Jacob tends the garden well," she comments. "He puts pride in every plant here. Even the mint stays in its corner as if it knows spreading would be a waste with him to watch it. You asked me if there's ever been strange plants growing here and there hasn't; leastwise nothing stranger than oranges. I asked Jacob if we've ever grown Dryad's Honey mushrooms, and he denied it. Father doesn't remember it ever growing here either; says he'd love to, but it can't be cultivated."

"You asked your father?" I ask, my eyes widening.

"Certainly; he said he wanted to grow it for Mother, but couldn't even find some growing wild to attempt transplanting."

Fear from her indiscretion grips my heart. I try to remind myself she can't be held liable for mentioning something she wasn't aware of.

Claire takes a step, bringing us closer than we've been since the camp outside Myceum. Since my humiliation and accusation.

I know what I owe her, yet for her sake I don't think I can give it.

"I'm sorry, Claire, for how I acted that night. That wasn't right. I'm tired of how I can't make up my mind. With everything else it's easy to be decisive, but I've mistreated you."

I look across the garden at the ornamental tree, various bushes, and terraced beds. Imaginary sounds of children playing, animals lowing, and gentle breezes filling apple trees reach my ears through my mind's pure desire. Nothing in years has felt so important yet so far away.

"You know I love you." She reaches a hand up to brush the side of my face, and I exert every bit of willpower I have to not grab it for a kiss.

I shake my head and pull away. "This can't last. I've seen the past and it's too terrible to let you know."

"There has to be some way. Nothing you could have done would make me want to spend my life apart. Everything we talk about for our futures that we want—I still want all of that. I want you forever."

"I want nothing more than to have our futures intertwined," I say, "but it just can't be. Please trust me that it's better we stay apart."

There's too many tears streaming her face for me to look. I bow my head and fight back my own.

"I'll tell you if you want," I say. "Then you'll hate me for a reason, and I can live with that."

"You know I never could," she whispers, nuzzling into my shoulder. "Please."

I back away and brace myself to tell her. I can handle an icy glare, just not her going stiff in my arms. The garden door creaks open. The guard who let Weaver and me in earlier says, "Your Highness, the commander would like to see you immediately."

I sigh and bow to Claire with a salute. When I rise, I meet her red eyes with a flushed gaze of my own. It lasts a second before I turn.

A soldier escorts me to the commander's private cabinet; a sitting-room connected to his bedchamber. Works of art line the walls: paintings of prim ancestors and artistic representations of Lesasil; tapestries of hunts, legends, and landscapes; wood carvings of exquisite animal specimens; and sculptures of soldiers locked in combat, the uppermost always bearing a remarkable resemblance to the commander. Mounted animals above the doors and fireplace draw my eyes upward; a hawk seemingly captured in flight soars along one wall, while an elk's horns hold up a bow and the two parts of a broken arrow. I've seen his cabinet before, but Julek doesn't know it: Claire, Rafael, and I snuck in here when we were children.

"Thank you," Julek says, nodding and smiling to the soldier as he closes the door.

He's removed his ceremonial armor from earlier, and has on a well-cut jacquard coat in shining blue brocade, his crest embroidered across the front. Deerskin gloves compliment the tan hose on his legs. Black boots with blue trim complete the look.

Being alone in the room with Julek doesn't bother me; as good of a fighter as he's rumored to be, he's practiced little since his wife's death and I know I could hold my own even without my blade. The stone bust beside me seems like a good makeshift shield.

Him wearing gloves indoors with no apparent cause seals my determination.

"You should thank me for offering protection," he prompts to start the conversation while pouring an amber liquid from a decanter at his decorative table. He picks up a tray with two clear glasses and extends it. I take both glasses, pouring the liquid into one, swirling it, and redistributing the contents. He sighs, rolling his eyes as he sits.

"I'd only need protection if you spread the word," I say. "I consider myself a blackmailed political prisoner."

"You have full reign of the castle," he says. He tips his glass sideways until the liquid touches the rim, stops before it spills, then sets it on his knee. "Either way, political prisoners are treated well."

He turns his head aside, and while lounging in the plush chair, looks suddenly tired.

I struggle to keep a hard expression in my eyes. It seems impossible that my mother's suspected murderer sits across from me. After I almost bring the glass to my lips, though, I set it on my armrest.

Julek sees the arrested motion and takes a deep drink from his own. He makes sure I see him swallow it. "Satisfied?" He stands and pours more to sip on. He gestures to the decanter. "Help yourself."

He sits, saying, "I don't like to think of myself as taking political prisoners. After all, word would leak of your improprieties sooner or later even if I didn't say anything."

"You're holding it over my head just the same. What do you want?"

"You've grown suspicious of late, Captain," he says, toying with a decorative chest on the walnut end table opposite the decanter.

Concerned with treading lightly, I say nothing and only swirl my drink around the glass.

"I really wish you'd try the beverage. My brewer has been experimenting with fermenting barley and wheat off and on for years. They started off with a few leftover grains after making bread, and liked it enough to try again. I've sampled it a few times and can tell you this is their best yet. Almost good enough to offer the king."

He takes a sip, and I mimic him. The bite on my tongue makes me inhale through my nose, which makes me cough, almost asphyxiating. Sputtering into the glass erupts the liquid over my cheeks, and I'm in a coughing fit for a few moments.

Julek grins, standing to grab a towel for my face. He stops by a statue of what I assume is him and June.

"Like brandy but it tastes like fire," I say as I wipe my face. "If I didn't mix the glasses myself I'd think it was poisoned."

He ignores my subconsciously rude comment, falling into his stern but amiable visage. "Do you prefer penit blanega? I sent most of the castle's store with your father's train since it's his favorite, but I have a private reserve." He moves a tapestry of a nymph aside to grab a key off a hook, and my eyes flit to the side of a cupboard. Julek continues to the cupboard, unaware I've known where the key was stored and what it opened for over a decade.

My eyes darted sideways, but my mind is a world away. "You said the king's train left?"

"Perhaps an hour ago," he says, pulling a bottle from behind upright decanters like the one on his side table. "Here we go. I sent the barrels with him—they travel better than these."

My mouth feels dry, and it's only partially from my choking fit. If the king left, that means his Guard left also. I'm alone.

"What do you call that?" I ask as I set the original glass down, trying to ease the tension I'm building within my mind.

"That? Haven't thought of a name yet. Might name it after the brewer; it would serve the family well for their hard work. Anything else would be shameful."

We make eye contact as he works his knife into the stopper. The way an iciness takes the room, we must both reflect on the Oruvian muster; that was where he last used the word shameful with me.

"That was a slip on my part," he says. "Let's not talk about my loss of temper. Saving Claire helped me more than you know."

For a moment, it looks like his eyes flicker indecision. As quick as it appeared, it leaves, with only a stern look for the wine bottle. It glugs air as the sun-colored liquid floods around a cup. When done filling it, he pours some off the top into another glass, then makes sure I see him swallow it. When he offers it, I take it, and have a sip.

"It's where you got the foothold for my imprisonment," I say.

"Only if you view it that way. Protection for your own good is how I see it—that's how your father sees it as well."

"Did he tell you he was leaving?"

"Of course. He came to see me and apologized for overreacting. I thought it was strange he'd leave this time of day, but maybe he just wanted away from what may soon become the front lines."

Julek calling Myceum the front lines makes me want to roll my eyes. It's a subtle dig at my unwillingness to use my Gift to give him a second chance in Balruvia.

"Of course," he continues, "he said leaving you alone would let you learn to extricate yourself from your own difficulties. Something he called a kingly characteristic. It was probably only that concern that bid him leave so swiftly."

My mind falters at him wording something that way. I realize I'm holding the glass too hard moments later. A look down shows me my hands, but also Julek's gloved fingertips gripping his drink.

I drain half my glass and ask him for more of the wine. He says, "Help yourself to however much you'd like," then follows it with a gesture.

I expected him to reach for it, but this is just as good. Darting my hand to grasp his, I hold tight enough to grab his glove and yank. The movement draws us both to our feet in a shower of liquid and glass. He curls his hand into a fist and pulls, but I've drawn the glove down enough to see his wrist. Holding fast and pushing his sleeve up, I see even more. Black swirls ride the natural curves of his lower forearm, twisting around every variation in muscle bulge. As he fights to free himself for a second, it looks like the designs change with every movement.

I force my eyes to look into his and read fear for an instant, then see them harden into steel. They could be mirrors of mine.

"I knew it," I say. "You were there that night. You were in Sapesky on another matter but you weren't really interested in funding watchtowers."

Pointing to his chair leaves no room for discussion. Most people wither under my commanding stare, even before they recognize me as the prince. But Julek isn't most people; living through the worst of Eraseam's battles, he's seen more than his fair share of strife. He returns my glare, as if to say *make me*, but he sits nonetheless. It's only after waiting long enough for me to know he's sitting because it suits him. Without him cooperating, I still hold my air of authority.

"You killed the queen with a Velvet Breath dagger. And you've been hiding under our noses since."

"I can explain—"

"It was a lie and everything since has been a lie. Loyalty, good will; all lies. The love you've shown my family has been a farce. I've had a bad feeling about you for years without knowing why. Only now I know, and the kingdom will all find out. June's Gift protected you during her life, but there's nobody here to rescue you now. Claire and I visited Heller and he told us. She was devastated and I used my Gift to get us out as much to wipe her memory clear. I would have thought you were more honest than Whiteneck."

His eyes go wide. "Let me explain."

"Why?" Emotion threatens to overwhelm my reason, but I don't care. There's been too much pain building into this moment for restraint. "Are you insane where you think you can sit there and explain away why you murdered the queen? You can talk yourself into thinking it was for the best, or whatever you've been telling yourself the last ten years, but not to me. You'll do good to remember I'm the prince, and I'm her son. Remember? Didn't you hear the stories? I was there—and now you're staying to justify yourself to me of all people."

"I didn't want to," he almost shouts. "And I'm not a Gifted who could have turned back the action anyway."

"Your wife could have. Did you ask her to?"

He nearly spits his words. "You fool, it was nigh a fortnight before I was back in Myceum with her. And didn't you refuse to help Luis Brayler after only two days? Your own people in Balruvia? You saw the defeat happening; it would have only been one day. One day for possibly how many lives? And you would expect me to ask her to likely give up the rest of her life to repair my one folly. I should have asked her that but nobody can ask you to use your Gift? I've said it before, Prince —you're selfish. You don't know the ways of the world. We all make mistakes and your birth doesn't make you impervious to the consequences.

"I've tried to make it up to you. I've thrown my life into protecting your kingdom, protecting something my heirs will never inherit. My life in service to your father's ideals both before and after the incident with Eilene has to count for something."

Agitation writ upon his face, I steel myself for a confrontation. That bust beside me looks sturdy enough to block any weapon he could draw in here.

Julek's words keep flowing. "June's life was given for Elathon—for your kingdom. Every bit of her Gift and every waking moment of our lives was spent trying to strengthen your family's throne. When it would crack, we would throw ourselves to act as supports until the foundation could be rebuilt.

"All I wanted was the Balm," he shouts, crying now. "I wanted her to live. Yes I made bad decisions I couldn't reverse, but I've lived with them ever since. Regardless of what you think of me, you know deep in your heart I loved your mother. Loved her for June's sake, and your father's sake. I didn't want to kill her. It was a moment of fear, a moment of panic atop years of dreading when she would be taken from me. Is that so bad? Wanting more years with my wife? It's the same thing your parents sought to give you when they withheld it even though you showed no desire to try."

Hard creases show on his cheeks and the corners of his swollen eyes. "It was wrong; I admit that. Only in my dark imagination of sleepless nights did I ever deny it, but never when thinking rationally in the light of day. Deep in my soul I've known it was wrong ever since the stroke fell. A hundred times I've almost told your father, a hundred times I've taken up quill to write him, but to what cause? I've always bitten my tongue or burned the confession. Fear at first, but then I convinced myself it was for peace because he shouldn't know.

"I've suffered enough and won't any more. The king didn't need to know then and he doesn't need to know now. Not ever." His voice comes shrill. The look in his eyes as they wander over his shelves unnerves me. I have my hand poised to grab the stone beside me. He threatens, yet he doesn't move.

"I didn't want it to come to this. Really I didn't. As much as your father didn't need to know, I never meant you to either. I'm so sorry, but I cannot have someone wrecking everything I've been through. If I'm discovered now the last ten years of suffering will all have been for nought."

He turns inflamed eyes to concentrate on me. "I know you may escape using your Gift, and I wouldn't remember this day. Not much, anyway. Bear in mind you'd give up a year of your life for revenge, and that's not your way if I know your family. And you'd have to accuse yourself of going to Castle Muerthy. None of the populace would see that as anything besides working with him; not after all they've been through. I didn't want it to come to this, but you leave me no choice." He grimaces.

The faintest noise imaginable sounds behind me. An instant later, pain explodes in the back of my head, and I slump from my chair.

Chapter 20.

A splitting headache, like my brain is leaking from a gash in my skull, greets my waking. I lift my head from the cold rest; it totters, threatens to crash down again. Waves of nausea overtake me, and with the taste infesting my mouth, I realize I've been sick through my daze once already. Deep breaths push the worst of it away, and I let my head fall forward.

The cold stone registers as comfort to my throbbing face. *I must have hit it on the floor when I fell,* I think. Uncomfortable cold soon works its way through my clothing. Only now do I notice the pressure, but since I feel it against my face and knees I can't understand it. I tilt my head back, lose control, and it hits something behind me. Waves of pain radiate to every nerve in my body; I let out a low moan. Finally, able to open my eyes, I see a loose grid of black poles. It's a metal window lattice, the kind in the lower floor of a castle that needs to hold up to assault. My viewing angle feels strange, though, since pressure holds me from the front, back, and under my feet.

With a chill worse than a plunge in a mountain river in spring, I realize it isn't a window lattice at all: it's an iron grate. Panicked, I struggle to move. My hands are free, but my feet are shackled together with a straight bar between. Memory of Julek's cabinet floods my aching head. I had the smallest sip imaginable of his new brew, and sputtered most of it onto my chin, and the wine he tasted as well. I move a hand to the back of my head; it doesn't hurt from hitting the prison wall.

Attempts to shimmy up the shaft they lowered me into lead to torn clothes and aching joints. Damp walls and shackled feet don't lend themselves to a climb, so each time I clatter down the few feet into the mixture of mossy water and vomit at the bottom. An hour of this finds me exhausted, bleeding, and more angry than I've been in a while. Trying to dull my misery by plotting revenge leads me to imagining Julek in the same situation, but it flames out at its utter ineffectiveness.

A day passes—at least I think it does. Without room to sit or even turn around, what I take as night from the darker grate above passes in a haze of wretchedness as I continuously shift from one slumping position to another. Taking some weight off my feet always seems to jam my knees into sharp stone. All I have left to occupy me is the icy wait for a certain death— forgotten and alone.

When I'm about as thirsty as I've been in my life, I hear the welcome scraping of a door latch. Flickers of light seep down the grate. My eyes blanch at the dull reflection. When I look down, there's an older man staring at me. Myself. Aged by the Gift. Two voices above draw my eyes up.

"He's been fine. No eat or drink like you said."

Another voice answers. It's a deep voice, one I recognize, one I hate. "No sense wasting it on him now."

Julek steps at the edge of the grate, and I can tell it's him even from my low angle by his gloved hands. We stare at each other until he speaks. "Don't look at me like that. I already told you I'm not going to have you ruin something I've berated myself over these last ten years. You wouldn't be in this mess if you hadn't been so insistent on sneaking around and finding out things not meant for you."

"So you're going to make up for killing the mother by killing the son?" I ask. "How does that make any sense?"

He clicks his tongue. "I'm not going to kill you. Might be hard to believe since you're in there now, but if you're good I'll move you to a better cell—something fit for a political prisoner, hmm?"

"I could have had you killed upon grounds of suspicion. I gave you a chance and this is how you thank me?"

"I appreciate you not doing that—like I said, especially after what I've been through this past decade. A tormented conscience is the heaviest thing in the world."

"I struggle to see how that's my fault," I say.

Julek's eyes flick up, and I hear the other voice again, though I can't make out the words. I think it said *just in case.* Julek smiles in return. I see hands exchange something round, then Julek calls down again.

"Bearing yourself with dignity will make your move to the other cell come more quickly. You're deep in the castle—so deep nobody could hear you, though your voice sounds fine. I'm glad you're not screaming yourself hoarse like most do in there."

"The king will hear of my disappearance and know my last location," I say. I'll do anything now except give him the pleasure of thinking his offer for a better cell is any different than how he offered me protection from my own people.

"I've thought of that, of course. Only a few of my guards know your location and they're paid extremely well." A glance to the guard on the other side of the grate, just out of sight, brings a pained smile to his face. "And they share in whatever fortune chooses to send me."

"Like a kingdom?"

He shakes his head sadly. "You read me wrong. I never wanted it to come to this, but one bad decision led me to another. The queen's unfortunate death led me to this in response to your searching."

"You don't have to follow the path you started down; you can walk back up the path and choose another."

I can't tell from my spot below, but it looks like he rolls his eyes.

"Spare me your superior virtue. Until a few weeks ago you wouldn't even use your Gift and now I'm supposed to manifest it. Please."

"I didn't mean the Gift. I meant you can walk another path any time with willpower."

Julek lets out a frustrated sigh. "You're too young to give lectures on choosing your own path; too naive. Your experience in the war instilled maturity, but time must pass for it to bloom; give it a few more decades and you'll see you can't always determine your own path. Think of the peasants. Are they all forging their own road? Do those in the dust stay there because they don't want to climb?"

"That's beside the point," I say. "You don't have to keep me in prison for life just to keep me silent. I'll swear an oath—forswear vengeance—just let me out."

"You were doing so well at keeping your dignity," he says, clucking his tongue. "What comes next? Offers of gold? Then what: threats?"

"You know I'm a man of my word."

"You're doing a poor job of convincing me," he says with a shake of his head. "I wish you were better, but as good as I am at convincing myself of what I want to believe, even I can't find another way forward."

My neck aches but I keep looking up. There will be ample time later to stare at the wall inches from my face.

"You can't keep me here, you know. I can escape with my Gift."

He winces, or maybe it's a play of the firelight. "Let's say you did, and managed to tell your father what you suspect of me. Who did it seem he believed? And to indict me you'd have to tell the whole kingdom you visited Heller, and we both know how that would look. Besides, do you know how long you've been down there? Has it been one day or three? Were you unconscious? And what would happen if you Gifted back to a time you weren't thinking?"

He stares at me for a long time. I stare back, forcing my mind to remain calm. It being a test of outlasting the other crosses my mind as a possibility. If it's a game, I'm not willing to play with such high stakes as my life.

Julek raises his head after a while. "Food once a day. Water twice."

"Yes my lord," the guard says.

Julek shifts to leave, then looks at me. "I know saying I'm sorry it came to this doesn't make it any easier. I only hope you can come to understand it in time."

"I suppose this hurts you more than it hurts me?" I ask. It's bold, and I'm in no position to taunt, but it may be my only chance.

Julek comes back to the grate and draws something from inside his doublet. "You see this?"

It's a knife—a dagger—and it's glowing. Red light seems to come out of a blade as if it's made of hot coals.

"Velvet Breath," I whisper. They disintegrate after one kill, so he has more than the one that marked him Branded.

"A Velvet Breath dagger," Julek says, apparently not having heard me. "It's a wonderful weapon; useful, as all weapons should be. Imagine how different warfare would be if all weapons killed with a scratch."

"It's an illegal weapon," I say.

"And why is that?"

"Because it's permanent."

"Hmm, permanent. Now isn't that interesting. Aren't all weapons permanent?" He taps his upper lip with the flat of the blade in mock rumination. "Oh—you mean permanent for the Gifted. Strange how your definition of right and wrong aligns to your unique needs. You're okay with us killing each other with regular weapons since you can save the people you find important but not with illegal weapons?"

"I wish you'd prick yourself with that," I say.

He laughs, then cautiously sheaths the dagger.

"One more time," Julek says. "As badly as I'd love to let you go and have this all behind us it cannot be."

Before I know what he's doing, he tips the round object in his hands, revealing a bucket on its side. Water hits the grate, splitting to cascade as it falls through the narrow shaft. I duck and crack my forehead into the wall. The water still rushes over me.

"That'll be the morning water," I hear Julek say. The guard chuckles.

Echoes from two pairs of feet die in the distance behind the locked door. Why they bother, I don't know, since I couldn't get through the grate even if I could reach it. The day drags by in dull monotony broken only by my thoughts. In the beginning, they're repetitive—often violence against Julek—but as that leads nowhere, I concentrate on banishing them. Fear holds me captive as often as indignation. Nobody who cares knows where I'm being held, or even that I'm a prisoner at all.

The light dims and my keen ears pick up the sound of boots on the other side of my door. A minute passes before the guard stands atop the grate.

"'Yer supper," he says, and drops something.

I catch a piece of bread in my cupped hands. A breath later I hear water spilling through the grate again, and I tense, not slamming my head into the wall, but not protecting my supper. The guard laughs, and I hear the wooden bucket thumping against the door as he locks it.

The water smelled awful all day, but I'd grown somewhat used to it before it drained lower. Now with the fresh deluge, the stink is higher around my ankles again. Worse, my bread is soaked. Bread soaked in water is terrible, but the taste from the new water as I begin to munch is abominable. After a few tries of plugging my nose, I give up and shove the whole piece down my throat in a single swallow.

Day runs into day. I learn to catch my meal then cover it with one hand to keep most of the water off. When the guard dumps the bucket the morning after the first time, I tilt my head up to try and catch a mouthful. It's putrid, but I do it each morning and evening to keep the thirst from overtaking me. The daily dousing helps dilute my own filth; is a further attempt to break my spirit.

Routine keeps me sane. I pray in the morning, exercise, catch a mouthful of water, lean on my right side, then spend a few hours hoping for release, alternating to lean on my left side at some point. Praying usually comes again to stave off despair, followed by thinking about battle tactics and imagining strategies before supper. Exercise is limited to flexing my calves in the morning. In the evening, right before I've come to expect the second dousing, I jump in place—at least as much as my ankle shackles and the filth squishing at my feet allow—it's the lowest level at this time of day. Eventually, through a deep stomach rumble, I laugh to myself at how readily I eat whatever food the guard offers me each evening. Days before I'd been worried about being poisoned while a guest, now as a prisoner I'm borderline grateful for each stale morsel.

More time passes, and if I hadn't been forcing myself through the routine I set—forcing myself to hope, to pray, to exercise—I'd have fallen into the despair of thinking my life has always been this way. I just finished eating a mostly-dry crust of bread when I hear a noise. It sounds like the guard is coming back, only they've never done that before. I wait, tense as I think Julek came to taunt me. I refuse to ask him to move me to another prison; I've reminded myself each day that he saying I lost my dignity doesn't make it true.

By the time I notice the noise, the door is opening. It's quieter than the normal careless crashing the guard makes, and moments later a light shines through the grate. With such a bright glare, I close my eyes even as I hear, "Here he is!"

The voice is exultant. It's a man's voice.

A skidding noise rushes across the floor. "Chris!" Even without my eyes I'd recognize that voice anywhere. It's Claire.

"Here, cut the lock," she says.

Scraping sounds from above, then Claire moves the lantern aside. She looks down. "We're getting you out; hold tight."

The admonishment brings a smile to my face. "I'm not gonna run." Then more serious, I add, "What are you doing here?"

"Almost got you."

The scraping stops in a loud *clang*. A shower of metal shavings hits my head. They raise the grate on rusty hinges, the lower a looped rope. Thankfully I wasn't in the prison too long, and my muscles still work, though only under focused strain. My other rescuer does most of the hauling until Claire grabs me under the arms to help. I catch myself, then roll sideways. Another soldier I recognize pants beside me, already coiling the rope.

"How did you find me?" I ask, baffled at seeing my captor's daughter and my recently-advanced friend Captain Weaver Deloc.

"Father's held political prisoners here before. I happened across the door years ago and never told him. I've heard Captain Flamex tell Father there's even a tunnel in a granary in Toldulgur."

"You knew he did this to me?"

"Figured it out. He told me not to ask questions I shouldn't, and that you'd be back from Toldulgur when it suited you." She gives me a hopeful smile. "I knew after you decided to tell me your dark secret that you wouldn't leave without saying goodbye. And I told Weaver I'd report him being in my garden if he didn't help me find you."

Realizing my chance wandering into her garden and her casual meander to the same place is all that stood between me and life in prison, my mouth goes dry. When Weaver moves the light to shine brighter, I shy away. Unaccustomed to light, my eyes are as hurt by its suddenness as theirs are to its lack.

"Sorry." He turns the light around.

"So you two have gone and released the commander's most secret prisoner?" I ask.

"Don't remind me," Weaver says. "I should've taken the punishment for entering the garden."

"I'm not worth the risk?" I smile.

"Ah, I meant, um..."

Claire saves him further embarrassment. "With any luck he won't know who did it. I never told him I found the entrance."

Weaver has the rope wound, the lantern in his hand, and the grate lowered into position. "We've gotta go."

I do my best to stand, then collapse onto Claire's shoulder.

"Easy," she says. "Give your legs time to remember what they're for. Do your guards normally come during the night?"

I shake my head. "Only morning and evening."

Claire lowers me to the floor, then looks up at Weaver. "Help me rub his legs."

He drops beside us, cuts the shackles from my ankles, then busies himself on my calves. Through pants soggy from my recent dousing, he squeezes and rubs a burning sensation starting at my toes.

"So I disappear without saying goodbye," I say, "and you immediately think your father is holding me a secret prisoner. Why?"

"I saw what went between our fathers and you. I saw your father leave, otherwise I'd have suspected something sooner, but when his son went missing, it sounded strange. After all, you weren't supposed to leave and he didn't seem to care. When you didn't turn up and Father claimed you left, I started thinking. I didn't need to stretch my imagination far to think you'd be a target."

Claire says it like she isn't bothered at all. She's taking everything well. Well enough where I need to tell her. She can handle it.

"Claire, this isn't the only treachery he's committed. Julek—he..." my voice trails off like the light of Weaver's lantern into the shadowed gloom of the small room.

"Tell me," she says.

I take in a deep breath as I stretch my legs. "Do you know why I was locked away?"

She shakes her head.

"What I know removes him from his position. Removes him from Eraseam." I take a breath. "He murdered... the queen."

Claire stares at me for a minute; I stare back.

Weaver asks, "Wait, your mother was murd—oooh." He shuffles a few steps away, looking like he'd rather have bitten his tongue off.

Claire stays focused on my eyes, her own unblinking. Finally she moves as if to speak, but the words catch in her throat. She swallows, then says, "I—I thought it was Heller's minions."

She doesn't remember our visit with Whiteneck.

"I did too," I say. "Everyone did based on my word that night. But I never actually saw her stabbed—only walked in afterward."

I've spent so long contemplating this, my ire doesn't grow at the fresh mention. I suppose digging into an old wound creates a scab so thick it can't break.

"Everyone thought it was Heller's doing—the secret force he calls his Shadow Kings—because they use Velvet Breath weapons in some missions." I pause. "Do you know what Velvet Breath is?"

Claire nods. "A mist you hold a weapon in to infuse it with instant-killing ability."

Weaver is shaking his head, muttering, "Rare and deadly."

"Right," I say. "And it gives the user an indelible mark —a brand, so to speak—on the limb which wielded the weapon. Julek is Branded."

Claire pales further. The lantern light shines across the small room easier than a torch, but its flicker plays across everyone all the same. She turns her face to the floor. She simply stares—no tears, no emotion, no denial.

"We need to go," Weaver insists. He offers me his hand. I take it and he drags me to my feet. Once I'm steady he does the same for Claire.

My legs struggle to propel me, and I only stay upright from Weaver clutching my arm like I'm an elderly man. Claire locks the door behind us, and we travel through a narrow corridor, proportional in size to the small room we came from.

Ahead, another wooden door stands as a barrier. Weaver moves to it, followed by me, then Claire. He lowers his free shoulder to the center, braces his feet against the stone floor, and pushes. The door moves inward in perfect silence, then twists on hinges, and we step through. We're in a dark room in a flash, and I'm looking at chairs, tapestries, busts, and carvings I recognize while Weaver closes the door. Julek's cabinet. I do a double-take before the door closes. The combined mechanism of hinges and track for the door to close on hides the door behind a heavy bookcase. As it slides into place, every vestige of a door disappears, leaving a bookcase perfectly filling the space it yawned moments before.

"I should be able to—"

"Shh. I hear something."

Soft footfalls, like feet on thick rugs, reach us through the inner door. The door leading to Julek's bedroom.

"Oh gods, you said he didn't come in here at night," Weaver says.

"Stop moaning and hide," I say.

A heartbeat later we hear the door latch open. With no time to hide, we stare at the opening door. Firelight from the chamber beyond amplifies that from Weaver's lantern and shines a ruddy glow on Julek's surprised face as he enters.

His eyes lock with mine as he asks, "Captain Deloc what are you—and Claire? I don't know what lies he's been telling you, but I was on my way to escort him to better accommodations."

"Accommodations?" Claire asks, all signs of apathy gone from her tone. "That's a prison no traitor should endure. How could you!"

"Traitor indeed. You saw his accusation but not what came after." He fumbles at the door; one more barrier to our flight. His rattled nerves recover as fast as they departed. He speaks to Claire, as if she's the only one he needs to bother convincing. "You shouldn't have intruded in my chambers. I assure you I was coming to move him."

"Assure me! What good is that after the lies you've been telling me the last ten years?"

"There are no lies—"

"Let's see your hands, then." Claire watches as Julek remains motionless.

Julek speaks in a level voice after a strained silence. "Lies of good intent, like the ones your tender friend here tells."

"If my word is good enough to indict me," I say, "It's good enough to testify what transpired when you had me locked away. You are under arrest for treason against King Hart of Elathon."

I realize I lack a weapon to draw for effect. My posture and tone speaks for itself, though not against someone as headstrong as Julek.

"Absurd," he says in his own imperious tone. "Protecting the kingdom from a short-sighted featherbed prince gone rogue is commendable." He turns to Weaver. "Captain, arrest this man. You'll be demoted for your part in freeing him, but nothing scandalous will spread. In time, you'll realize you didn't entirely throw your life away and can even gain back your advance."

Weaver almost looks like he wants to obey. His torn countenance prompts Julek to continue his tirade. "Claire, I'm ashamed you let your heart overrule your head, but a turned heart isn't as bad a non-repentance. You and I still have a path forward. Come." He extends his gloved hand, which she neglects. Seconds tick by on his gilded weight-driven clock.

"I'm siding with the kingdom," she says.

My mind whirlpools at her meaning. Her support now would mean more than it should. She just freed me from prison, but that wasn't defying her father face-to-face. My breath stalls as I wait for her to interpret what that means as if I'm waiting for the hangman to pull the lever.

"Then come," Julek says immediately, interpreting it the way he wants. "Help the kingdom as your mother and I have our entire lives."

"No."

My heart thunders alive. During the dreadful moment, I realized I was the only one unarmed. Now, at least, I have an ally. It nerves me to daring. "I have to arrest you, Commander. Don't make a scene." I gesture to Weaver, who seemed startled into compliance after Claire's resolution.

Julek backs against his door. "You can't arrest me in my own chamber. In my own castle. What would everyone say about your reign?"

"Your daughter said you lied to convince everyone else I left. After offering protection, then changing to let me leave, I know you never intended to give me a trial. What would it have been? My mysterious death or disappearance in Toldulgur? That would have made not presenting a body easy. After months of a carefully-cultivated story, few but gossipers at winter hearths would question the source of the lie."

I know I'm walking a dangerous line, but Claire's as firmly with me as a daughter can be against her father, and Weaver's given signs of support.

"Claire," Julek says, almost threatening, "the harder a decision is to reverse, the more time you must spend debating it. It's what your mother would want."

Speaking about Claire's mother seems to make her think of mine. "Did Mother die of grief? Did she realize you murdered the queen?"

Her voiced resolution steels Julek as well.

"Have it your way then," he says. "You children can't see past your petty ideals of black and white. But when you torture yourself over irreversible regrets for a decade you'll come to realize the world doesn't operate the way the minstrels tell you."

I move aside so the chair Julek sat in a week ago sits between us. "We justify death in war, but never in peacetime; never against innocents and never after the fact."

Julek snorts his contempt. "Why do you persist in this? I've said a dozen times how I never intended to kill her—I never even wanted to see her that night."

"You still need to face justice. Committing a crime is a poor coverup for murder, as is allowing a decade of lies to flourish."

Julek rolls his eyes. "Even if you hadn't accused Heller's Shadow Kings of the queen's murder, they would have been blamed—it was too easy of a scapegoat to pass over. As many people as the Divide affected, the kingdom needed another reason to provoke hate for Heller's Guldeth. You should have spent your time learning statecraft, Prince," he sneers. "Maybe then you'd have survived longer than you will now."

He draws a glowing dagger.

"Look out!" I warn. "A scratch will kill you."

Julek lunges at me, and I sidestep. I intended it as a jump, but manage little more than a collapse on my reawakening knees. Fortunately, the shock jolts my body into wakefulness, because he rounds, making me leap aside.

"The dagger is only good once," I shout. I swing Weaver's lantern like a well-timed club.

Julek dodges back. "I'll have to make sure I stick the right one."

He snarls, lunges for my neck. It would be an easy place to block if I had a weapon and didn't have to worry about the smallest scratch ending my life. I reach for his forearms as he comes toward me, but another collides with him first, going to the floor in a tangle of arms and legs. Small tables and glasses shatter atop them.

"No!"

It's Claire. She's screaming. For a moment, my heart skips to my throat. Falling to the floor it would have been so easy for the knife to prick her skin. She and Julek leap up, then both realize the dagger is lying on the ground between them. They lunge for it; Julek is quicker. Claire retreats to Weaver and my sides, and the movement reveals her gambeson scored from stomach to thigh. Her arms and hands bleed from glass cuts. She flicks blood to the ground to shake away the pain.

The dagger didn't touch her, because the blade remains glowing. Julek stumbles back in shock at what his behavior almost caused.

"Claire. Claire don't side with someone who will disgrace our family name," he falters.

I glance at her. She shakes her head, eyes welling with tears. "I can't do that; I won't."

Weaver and I move towards Julek. The look of defeat on his face tempts me to trust, but I know he's more dangerous than a cornered badger. He has everything to lose and a Velvet Breath dagger in his hand.

A sudden scream, a flying end table, and smashed lantern as I block bludgeons us into disorienting darkness. Our eyes adjust to the faint firelight still coming from the commander's chamber. The door is reopened but Julek is nowhere to be seen.

"Come on," I say.

I scoop the stone bust from the floor and enter Julek's room. Drapes hang floor to ceiling on the two windows, and his stout canopy bed bears matching curtains, tied back from the untouched covers. A slamming echo makes me look to the main door.

"Are there any more secret doors or cabinets?" I ask Claire.

She shakes her head. "None I know of."

"Door it is then."

We rush to the door, but it opens and I stumble to a stop. Two soldiers whirl into the room.

"The commander—where is he?" I ask.

It's a man and a woman. They race forward, and my eyes go wide. I recognize the man from my daily dousings. They lunge for Weaver and Claire, seeing as I have no weapon. Claire raises her sword to catch the other's, brightening the room with a scatter of sparks. Weaver kicks the woman's feet from under her, but she rolls, springing back to her feet at the foot of Julek's bed.

Claire fights the man; each gives and takes blows. In the seconds since the fight started, it's too early to determine who's the better fighter. They're between me and the fireplace, or I'd go for the poker. As it is, I refuse to wait.

Instincts kick in, causing me to throw myself weaponless at the mans' legs. He moves his short sword at the last second, and I spring for his face. His sword isn't glowing, and Claire stands ready to help, or such a move against an armed soldier would be suicidal. I crash to his side and claw desperately like a cat to a tree. Claire uses my momentum to topple him.

"Go," I shout as I wrestle the sword from his grip. He's strong, but I'm still a match for him despite my imprisonment.

Clashes of steel from the other side of the room reach my ears. They remain outside my consciousness. The man is disarmed, and I've wrenched his arms where he can't move them. I feel like I have him pinned when, with a mighty twist, he struggles around. He willfully snaps his shoulder joint to break my grip, then lunges for his boot. The hilt of a boot knife protruding takes my attention; I try to grab it before a glow startles me back. In a flash, he's drawn past his leg, cutting through his light armor. Blood seeps from the wound even as the glow extinguishes and he begins shuddering his last breaths.

"No! No!" I shout.

I look over at Claire and Weaver. They have their opponent down and it looks like she's going for the same motion.

"Hold her hands—they have Velvet Breath!"

Claire and Weaver lunge for her hands before she finds her weapon, and I spring for her feet. I tie them with a leather strap then move to the bedroom door and close the bolts. Weaver binds our struggling prisoner's hands.

I look back at her dying comrade. I've seen that same calm gasping before—when I was much younger. Seeing him takes me back to the stone passageway. It's the same; from his inability to speak, to the unfought muscle paralysis, and to the profound sense of calm settling on his face.

"Why did Julek send you after us?" Weaver asks. It recenters my thoughts.

He's hauling the fearful woman to her feet. Her pale face is red from exertion; through panting breaths she looks terrified.

I stride over. "Julek?" She attempts to mask her fear by scowling. One glance at her tells me everything I need to know.

"We're not getting anything out of her, but we're keeping her for questioning," I say. We may eventually convince her to talk, but now we need speed.

"Shall I summon guards?" Weaver asks.

A reply comes to my lips, but Claire speaks my thoughts before they're uttered. "No; not yet. First we need to find out how deep this goes."

"That would be easy if she would talk," Weaver says.

Her weapon comes to my mind; I rummage in her boot for the suspected dagger. A hilt matching the man's unbladed one meets my fingers. She kicks out as I draw it in an effort to make me slice into her leg. When she doesn't succeed, her pretense of resignation returns, looking like real surrender.

"We don't have that luxury now," I say. "For now we need to find the one who *will* talk. The one with something to lose by this."

"What if there's more guards?" Weaver asks.

"Given how Julek fled the three of us, I don't think there will be more coming. More important than that, we have to keep this quiet until we have proof against the commander."

"We have ample proof," Weaver says. He gestures to the guard slain by his own hand. "Him with no wounds besides that scratch on his leg, the bladeless knife beside him, all of our witness, her."

"If we don't get them all at once they'll scatter like thistle down in the wind."

"That's not a good reason to withhold the cry. The commander could do some serious damage on an unsuspecting castle."

The same thought troubles me; he could spin a story with the soldiers and I'm desperate to prevent that.

"He kept me in that prison for a reason," I say. "It doesn't justify the treatment he chose, but my standing with the people would be precarious if they knew his reason. I have private reasons he can't be brought to account publically."

Weaver looks incredulous yet changes the subject. "Earlier you said you didn't think there would be more guards."

"There's probably more with him now, wherever that is." I glance at Claire, uncertain how she'll be taking this. She stands firm, with clenched fists and a fiery shimmer in her eyes. She's an ally for sure.

"Right," I continue, "if there's one hidden area in his castle there will be more. Claire, where do you think we would have gone?"

She thinks, feeling the pressure from our stares and the voices of guards nearing the door. "Usually his cabinet, but not now of course... maybe the closet behind the Commanders' Room."

I rush for the door, throw the bolts, and rip it open. Guards nearing the door slow and ready their weapons for a second, then stop for a salute. Recognizing several of them steadies my worries of further treachery.

"Get in here," I order. "This woman committed treason by attempting to murder me. See to it she's held." The guards nod. I want her alive for when I come back so I continue, "Her hands and feet must be bound and separated. Gag her if she speaks. Is that clear?"

"Yes, your Highness," the officer says, then bows. "We thought you had left for Toldulgur."

"Everyone did. Good thing I was detained, because we have another murderer to catch. I'll need a sword."

Claire, Weaver, and I charge the straightest path for the Commander's Room and barge through the doors. Candelabras with a few long-burning tapers give the faintest illumination; both ends of the room are shrouded. Weaver kicks a door at the far end and draws back while it swings open. The moment it gives with no signs of a barricade, I know we're in the wrong place.

Brief search confirms this, and we're heading back across the shadowed room. Pillars in the corners make it bear a remarkable semblance to Heller's throne room.

Weaver eyes them and asks, "How are you with throwing knives?"

I shake my head. "These are far too valuable to throw."

A Velvet Breath weapon is worth a substantial-sized landholding on the black market. Since the penalty for making or possessing one is instant death, only outlaws with nothing left to lose attempt making or trafficking them. It's known a trade persists, though the law never has to deal with a case. Occasionally word reaches Sapesky that a Branded outlaw was found dead—presumably thieves' justice dealt from a deal gone wrong.

Back in the hall, I ask Claire for another idea.

"Maybe the temple?"

Our search there yields a dozen or so supplicants staring at the statue of Lesasil. Resinous incense, invisible elsewhere, swirls in smoky tendrils around the candles. To much indignation, I pull the hoods from those with their heads hidden. Irritation grows in my chest like a tumor. The temple was on the other side of the castle, and we've wasted valuable time. Even now Julek could be organizing loyal Oruvian soldiers against me.

I turn a corner at a run, careen into a soldier. Going down in a tumble of arms and legs, I have a moment's sensation of blonde hair whipping around my face.

"I'm so sorry," says a woman's voice. The soldier jumps up to offer me her hand, but I'm as fast as she is.

"No harm done. We're—Ann."

Startled into recognition at my tone, the soldier smiles, reddening. "Captain Hart. It's my pleasure to see you.

Ann Flune stands in our midst. Claire smiles at her, receiving an awkward glance at me in exchange.

"You recognize me, don't you?" Claire asks.

"I... I just thought it was strange."

"What was strange?"

Ann shies away, then stands straighter as if remembering my charge to her. "It's just... I would have expected you to take the message to your father."

My heart stills. "What message?"

"I don't know. The commander said he had an urgent message for the king."

"The commander? Julek?"

She nods.

"How do you know?" I demand.

She flinches, taken aback from the force in my tone. "He had me help prepare horses for himself and two guards. There were three ready; said it was urgent enough he took the ones already saddled, though they weren't the best for a long fast journey."

"No," I mumble.

Weaver pales. "They have over an hour head start," he says.

"We can't let him reach there first," I say, desperation invading my mind.

It feels like I'm fighting for my life in a despairing battle. Outnumbering the enemy makes no difference in this situation, and their tactics make me lose ground with each merciless drive forward.

Fighting a defensive war without worrying about civil strife bears enough stress. More than that, of all generals to abandon their province, Julek is the worst. Such a desperate move means he's cornering himself. With no way out, and every ability to gain an audience with the king, I have dreadful confidence his special dagger is meant for a single individual.

Making matters worse, it's irreversible. No matter how skilled I am with my Gift, a death from Velvet Breath can't be undone. I witnessed that with my mother. Seeing it happen to Father would be more than I could take. Unless we hurry, he'll be waiting for us with the dagger at his throat. At that point, no amount of my Gift would save him—I'd be an older man attempting to ride faster.

Julek's only hope of honor is the death of everyone who knows his secret. The king hasn't found out yet; as far as Julek knows, only the three of us from his cabinet discovered him.

"What guarantee does he have we won't tell everyone in Myceum the real reason for his flight?" Weaver asks.

"None, probably." My heart is sick in my chest, feeling like I've taken a beating with a blunted war ax. He could be planning to hold the king hostage. If he did, and allowed me to take the throne, holding the king as assurance would guarantee his safety. "I think that's why he's playing a bold hand," I say.

"So he thinks everyone in Myceum will be against him already, and he's going to Sapesky while he's welcome?" Weaver asks.

"I think so. I can't imagine a commander abandoning the entire province without a dire reason. He probably sees it as life or death..." I trail off, realizing how such a sentence would sound to Claire.

"Holding the king hostage?" Weaver asks.

"Perhaps."

"Perhaps? Not absolutely certain?"

I take a deep breath, and gently let it out my nose. I nod, only meaning it for Weaver, but it draws Claire's and Ann's eyes too. Traveling with us has to be beyond difficult.

The sun settles into the horizon, and we travel for another hour. As the waning light illuminates the clouds less with each minute, the trail becomes precarious.

"We should have a bit of a moon later," I say. "Let's give the horses some rest. And sleep yourselves; I'll take the first watch."

Claire's been quiet ever since our ride from the Myceum stables. As we loosen our saddles, she comes toward me on the other side of my horse.

"Thank you for freeing me," I say. It's the first time I've acknowledged her act. Until the last hour, the full weight of her choice evaded me. Here I am: freshly freed from her father's prison by her own hand, and working on bringing him to justice. Nobody in our party is deluded—we say *bring him to justice*, but that really means put him on trial for treason. Claire knows how it would end as well as anybody, and I feel for her despite my thirst for what I tell myself is justice.

Claire gives a slight smile then helps with my stallion's billet. We loosen it to give him confidence he'll have time to rest. He throws his head as Claire steps around him and she flinches; her mare was a hearty animal, though not as large as a stallion. "You're welcome," she says.

I can tell it cost her to say the words. The very act of pursuit with her in our company makes me uneasy. Justice, not revenge—that's what I need to keep telling myself.

Claire speaks again while I grab a blanket from my horse's side bag to use as a cushion, "Do you think he'll be holding the king when we arrive?"

"I hope we're early enough to prevent that," I say. The thought has been weighing on my mind since the second we decided pursuit.

"What would you do then?" Claire asks in a small voice.

I can't bring myself to look at her. Her voice tells me she's probably near tears. Concern and anger welling up together has to be creating a storm of emotions. I'm no stranger to conflicting emotions, but I'm done being hard on her.

Gentle.

"Plan an arrest. Have him follow through the process with impartial justiciars."

She nods vacantly. I look at her now, and she's staring unseeing at Weaver's horse. In the distance, the animal's coat looks sooty. Claire doesn't look mad, or even sad; she has to know what would happen if he's caught. Her face shows signs of fatigue.

"You need to rest," I say. "We'll be riding as soon as the moon rises."

She takes a deep breath of the night air, nods her head once more, and moves to settle onto her sleeping pack. She rolls to have her back to the rest of us, and I stare at her sleeping form, thinking a multitude of repetitive thoughts.

Justice, not revenge.

The night's ride continues after a few hours. I didn't wake anyone else to relieve me from watch since I wouldn't have found sleep anyway. We hardly say a word until sunrise many hours later—just four figures riding single-file through seldom-traveled roads. Early in the morning, we pass a flock of sheep with a young boy and two young girls as their shepherds.

Riding near Mt. Cabrae would have us traveling on the main roads and let us swap our horses for faster overall speed, but at the price of a longer road. In the end, I decided to lead us on a gradual south-east route.

Since we don't stop for breakfast, we eat while walking beside our horses. As much as the animals appreciate the break, my legs do as well. We're all good riders, especially Ann, but time walking away potential cramps feels like bliss.

Claire is walking near me, and I try to start a conversation with her. "Julek said he was going to move me to a new prison. Why that instead of leaving me there or starting me out in the other prison?" I ask loud enough for the others to hear, and she answers.

"That cell is for breaking one's spirit. The threat of returning there dissuades escape attempts."

"You've found prisoners there before?"

"A few times; I never frequented it since I wasn't supposed to know it existed. Even the upper room is small. I think it's so nobody notices and probes for whatever is in the wasted space."

"And you've never questioned him about it?" I ask. It sounds too unlikely to be plausible.

"I figured it was something necessary. The first time I was scared; the prisoner spoke with a golden tongue despite being thrown down the pit. I ran and didn't go back for years.

"Guess it's good I delayed telling you," I say. "You wouldn't have needed to come find me otherwise."

It's meant as a joke. She smiles but doesn't look happy. "I would have believed you anyway," she says. "The prison just sort of made me guess it before you said anything."

We're all silent; even Ann, who we had to bring into our confidence to have her along. She's learned our adventures, and feels a little ashamed at what we've been through while she defected.

Weaver breaks the silence. "Never seen you with a beard, Captain. I like the look if only you'd clean the edges a little."

He looks significantly at Claire, as if expecting her to comment her opinion. Her cheeks redden.

"I like your beard as well," I interrupt. Weaver gives me a surprised look. "Oh wait," I say," I thought I saw the glimmer of an invisible one."

Weaver's gelding snorts and stamps as if joining our laughter.

"Well we know the prison didn't break your spirit," Weaver comments, laughing also.

When the laughter dies, Claire answers Weaver's earlier pointed look. "It looks good, but I like Chris' face even better without a beard."

Her blush deepens.

Chapter 21.

Days pass in the same blur as night. With only a few hours of sleep each night, and either walking beside our horses or bouncing along in the saddle, we're all drained. I'm in a tempest to reach Sapesky despite my nerves. My mind tells me Julek couldn't have possibly made better time than us, but his worse horses do little to calm my anxiety. He has as much reason to hurry as we do, and desperation could drive him and his escort as hard as it does us. Despite the exhaustion, I never once have to urge my company along. I'm halfway upset by this—at least if we're too late and if Julek has the king in his power, I'd have someone to blame. So many *ifs*, but no, that's my exhaustion asserting itself.

The spires of Sapesky castle flutter blue pennants high on their conical roofs. Square crenelated towers hold the same flags, and every one is immaculate: the first good sign. Unless Julek's single handedly crippled the whole guard with the king at the end of a knife and demanded outward appearances remain the same, we may be in time. My heart soars at the possibility.

Weaver leads us up the main road to the gate. His animal senses an end to the journey and belts a final effort. Claire fell to the rear as soon as we could see the castle. My heart leaps to my mouth from anxiety. Guards roaming the tops of walls and circling the towers buoys my hope that everything is as it should be.

We slow enough for the soldiers to recognize we're friendly, or at least not a threat, before we enter the first courtyard. Weeks ago Weaver and I stood in this same place between towering walls while waiting for our journey to Mt. Cabrae. Now, with so much water under the bridge, a feeling of homesickness gnaws the edge of my mind. Soldiers, silver-tipped pikes in hand, come to greet us. They're friendly enough considering they didn't recognize us.

"It's the prince," shouts one.

A murmur goes around the assemblage as I dismount my horse. I stride to the nearest guard, who snaps to salute. I don't have time to wait, and I ask, "Where is the king?"

My voice is hoarse and my knees threaten to buckle under any movement, but I stand as upright as possible. She takes a step back once she rises, scared by the wild look in my eye. Little sleep will do that.

"The king, your Highness," she says, bowing again, "left on a tour of the kingdom with the mounted division of his guard over a week ago."

"And where is he now?"

I don't relent at her frustrated look. An officer coming from the wall steps to her side. He answers for the soldier., "The king? I'd imagine in Myceum by this time. He meant to stay a week or so to bolster the spirit—"

"He left Myceum—we came from there," I say.

He stops for a moment, considering. "If you came from Myceum after seeing the king, didn't you know his travel intentions?"

My mouth goes dry as I know the answer, yet I ask the question anyway. "He left in a hurry a week before we did. He should be here by now."

"Your Highness; he meant to visit the Montaya province after Myceum."

A club to the stomach wouldn't have dropped my mouth open farther than his words do. Consternation blinded me to Father's path. In my rush to save him, I never stopped to question where he went. Sapesky seemed like the logical choice, but Montaya makes as much sense after Commander Brayler's withdraw from the war.

I study the officer's face to see if there's a wordless plea hidden behind eyes of emotion. Nothing; only concern.

"We need fresh mounts," I say, fingering the Velvet Breath dagger in its sheath as I receive a deluge of tormenting thoughts.

"Your Highness, anything in the castle is yours, especially with your father visiting elsewhere." He turns to look at the others. They're stumbling from their horses despite every effort to appear casual. "Are you sure you don't want a few days' rest before embarking again?"

I shake my head. "There's no time. I must reach him."

"Shall I call the constable and have a force escort you? He came from near Mt.Cabrae and would probably welcome another journey."

"Balruvia and Mt. Cabrae have fallen," I answer while I shake my head. "Keep the forces ready here."

"But your safety, your Highness," the officer persists.

I've turned from him to address my companions. I call over my shoulder, "An army can't do any more good than a few on this mission." Then to my friends, who've heard every word of our conversation, I say, "You're under no obligation to follow me. I need to know."

Ann stands a little taller; Weaver tilts his chin up; Claire sets her mouth, takes a step forward. They're with me.

"Your Highness?" the officer asks.

"Four horses," I repeat, and he issues orders to nearby soldiers. I hear their feet in the dust as they scurry away, sounding like my heart. This time, the rapid beat isn't from fear or exhaustion—it's from a sense of union.

We leave Sapesky on fresh horses an hour after arriving. Different saddles, the hour moving our legs, and knowing we have ample food does much to refresh us. Nothing takes away the full effect of saddle-weariness, though, except time out of a saddle. Ann is taking the riding best, standing in her stirrups less often than the rest of us, though the fatigue weighs on her as bad as anyone.

The trip into Montaya should take half a day less than our journey to Sapesky.

Since our mounts are fresh and the best Sapesky could offer, we ride through the night, taking turns sleeping in our saddles. It's a miserable experience, with our heads tipping enough to wake us from falling. A rhythmic pattern of sleep, collapse, and jerking awake plagues us each in turn.

During my time awake, I worry what use I'll arrive with my head lolling side-to-side. Hourly attempts to keep my upper body stretched loose enough to use a sword make me feel like I'm doing something.

Morning on the second day out of Sapesky breaks late due to rain clouds at our back. A dark mass along the horizon, the summer storm grows through the day.

"So," Weaver says as the wind dies to nothing. "Any idea where we'll find the commander?"

I notice he avoids using Julek's name. It could be respect for Claire, or habitual deference to his former commander.

"He could be anywhere in the province," Ann points out.

"He's in Lorganrule," I answer.

"Why not the capital, Jahkay?"

I shake my head. "Lorganrule. He's meeting with Commander Brayler, and he'd be there for the summer."

They would have met by now. He left Myceum a week before Julek, so I hope desperately that he completed everything with Robert, then left. Gritting my teeth and riding harder as a cold wind overtakes us, I pray the storm won't be bad enough to stop our travel. After a dreadful detour, the last thing I want is another delay.

Lorganrule, named after Captain Lydia Spruce, received its name in the king's Business Room shortly after Rafael's death. My recommendation, based upon the captain I heard who fought well defending the province, received the king's blessing, conferring the moniker on the already named *Pass of the Winds*. Put together, the two names fit the fortress perfectly. A distinct feature noticed even before the Divide, locals knew when their trade caravans were returning from across the Dendring mountains from the sound whistling through the crags and ledges of the pass. Perfectly sculpted by the gods, it funneled the prevailing western winds in a roar through the pass, hitting rocks in such a way where any irregularity could be heard by those familiar with the area. Old shepherds claimed they could hear a sleeping wolf a half-day's walk away.

The dim outline of Lorganrule looms before us. It's morning, though the persistent mist makes it feel like it's near sundown. Rain dogged us through the night, but with the brightening day it's as if the sun burned away the edge, blessed us with mist. Rain no longer drives from the east and the prevailing wind intensifies.

"What is that?" Weaver asks.

It was a high continuous sound coming from the main pass before Lorganrule. We had been hearing it for minutes before it changed.

It was a slow change. I may not even have noted it past my ardor to enter the fortress. Now that I do, though, I can't not hear it. The sound is musical, pleasant and deep. It does what the rain couldn't; it makes me shiver.

"There's a change in the landscape," I say.

Weaver's never been south of Toldulgur, yet he's heard legends. Everybody has.

Known for centuries as a myth to all except the locals, it took the decimation of Captain Lydia's regional force to convince the king it was worth moving the planned construction of Lorganrule to The Pass of the Winds.

"Landscape," he says. "You mean someone walking in The Pass."

It's a question, and my eyes struggle to pierce the mist.

"Yeah."

Ann shifts in her saddle. "I've never been here; isn't it supposed to be hard to hear the differences?"

"I think so. I didn't expect to be able to hear it."

We ride through shrouds of wavering mist. At times it completely obscures the fortress, at times we see differing patterns around. The ominous sound continues to quaver through the air. Like a sunrise, it changes imperceptibly, but all of a sudden I notice it's even more subdued.

"There's got to be something there," Weaver says.

A cool breath of wind across our cheeks clears enough mist to see the fortress clear as night. We're over a mile away, but along the ground before the distant fortress we see the ground as if it's moving.

Soldiers.

The frenzy I've held myself in to reach the fortress reignites. My desire—my need—pulses to the front of my mind.

"It's a death-trap," Weaver says.

No. He can't be right. Even with their surprise, we won't fall so easily to this force.

We. I can't help from outside, especially the king.

My blood runs cold. Now even more than reaching the king before Julek threatens him, I need to make it inside the fortress.

"None of you have to come," I say. It's all I can manage through the tempest of my heart.

I spur my mare faster. Claire stays beside me. She's remained silent all day and most of the previous. Though I'm worried for myself, I spare thoughts for her. I can't imagine what she's feeling now.

Everyone stays with me. Responsibility for their fates tries to rest on my shoulders, but I'm too distracted—riding too fast—for it to settle there.

The Guldethian army is close, but not impossibly so. They don't seem to notice four riders streaking to the fortress.

Their advance remains steadfast through the returning rain. Wind shifts, and the sound dies back to the high sound of whistling into the pass.

Another few minutes of hard riding shows the size of their force.

I shake rain from my eyes. Loose hair whips around my head like my cloak in the wind. I'd kept the cloak tight during the night, but enough rain seeped down my neck that I eventually gave up the struggle. I was half-drenched anyway and riding fast enough to keep thawed.

I dismount my mare and scrabble up a slide of rocks.

"Hey," I yell. "Hey down here."

It's a risk, but having an archer spot four soldiers sneaking below the walls is worse. A fullered tunic-clad soldier looks over

"Oruvian," I say. "Let us in."

More soldiers step to the archer's side.

"Let us up. Please."

One soldier ties off a rope and throws it down. I insist Ann and Claire climb first.

Weaver and I tie the reins slack and slap the horses on the flank. They'll be fine. Hopefully they wander to some poor serf's land before the enemy find them.

We follow up the rope and receive help when we near the edge. I slip, hit my knee on the battlement. My soaked skin breaks easier than it should. Rain makes the blood run free. Only now I realize how cold I am. The chill makes it hurt like I'll never walk agian, but I push it aside as a nuisance. For at least five minutes. Making it into the castle is a miracle unto itself.

I was too worried to acknowledge it before, but Weaver's assertion of our position as a death-trap becomes clear when I climb a tower.

At first glance I agree with him. The Guldeth are sprawled across the stony backdrop of the mountain pass. I knew the play of the wind didn't really mean they stopped coming earlier; they kept coming and still do. But the pass is narrow and clogged with arrangements of soldiers. It isn't as many as I thought.

It looks like they're trying to skirt the fortress. They knew of the weakness and chose a night with an eastern rain to advance.

An officer hears about my arrival and joins us atop the tower.

"Prince Hart"—she bows—"your father arrived a week ago."

My heart stops. "Is he okay?"

"Certainly. Commander Lewis arrived this morning and they're—"

"Take me to them."

My urgency surprises her. "Yes, Your Highness."

She leads us from the tower. I urge her to run over the level places. There's no way she can understand my haste. This is beyond the army outside. This is everything.

She stops outside a corridor. "He's in the Receiving Room."

I'm through the door before she finishes talking.

Urgency gives me wings. I barrel down the hall and lunge for the closing door.

"What?" cries a voice inside the Receiving Room. "Help me!"

Weaver, Ann, and Claire lend their strength to mine. We push through the door to find Captain Pullen with a sword coming for my head.

He stops. "Chris. What in Lesasil's name took you so long?"

"Where is he?" I ask. A wild look around the room shows me the king isn't there. Commander Brayler stands over a dead guard. He's dressed in the same clothes as all Oruvian guards, but his pale skin matches the assassins in Myceum.

"He ran," says another voice. It's Commander Brayler.

"Where?"

"We don't know. Just ran when we found him out. His guard distracted us."

They're talking about Julek, I know it.

"But the king," I ask. "Where is he?"

"Ran also. Don't know where."

I notice Commander Brayler has a nasty cut on his forearm. "You just get here?" he asks.

"Yes. We went to Sapesky first. But the king, he's safe?"

"He was when he ran," Captain Pullen says.

A cry for help rises through the room. I blench at first, then realize it's a general cry from the walls.

"They're trying to go around," Commander Brayler says. "We can't let them get past to other villages."

Captain Pullen looks up from the assassin. "Is Julek going to sabotage our defenses?"

I shake my head. "I don't think he's working with them. He came here when we pushed his hand. Which way did Julek go?"

"That way," Commander Brayler says. He looks at Captain Pullen. "I need to lead the defenses."

We sprint through the door and split up. Weaver follows Captain Pullen and Claire hangs back. Ann follows me.

The hall spits us into the rain.

Water-filled footprints lead for a staircase. We nearly reach it when a rock crashes among some low buildings. The battle has begun. Horses stomp and whinny to be let out. One sounds louder than the others. Injured.

If we need them, we can't have the animals working themselves into a panic. Ann's face is pleading.

"Go," I say.

I ascend the steps alone. I hope Captain Pullen and Weaver find Julek: there's two of them. More than that, I want anyone to find him before he finds the king, even if it's me.

Shouts reach a crescendo along the walls. Outside, the soldiers set up their hand-catapults. They're not enough to take down walls, but shots aimed at the wall walk keep soldiers on edge. Even missed shots land inside the walls and wreak havoc like that among the horses.

I drag my focus from the larger battle. My own one will be enough.

I grab a spare shield from against the wall.

"Julek!" I yell.

He came from a door and stopped when he saw me. I hadn't been sure it was him until he responded to his name. He doesn't look any different; if Lorganrule's garrison saw him they'd bow, not knowing he tried to kill their king.

My sword is in my hand. I shift the grip and run up the nearest rain-soaked stairs. He looks like he'd like to run, but draws his sword instead. The dousing rain did nothing to take away his noble bearing. It's too ingrained in him, like it is in Father.

"Made it here at last, huh?" he asks when I come up with him. The sneer is enough to make me want to brain him.

He still looks himself, but feels changed. He's a different man than I remember growing up. A different man than the one who raised Claire.

"Thank the gods," I say. "You're too late."

He has a hand on his sword hilt as well. It's a full measure of confidence to match my own.

"Late?" he asks. "You're here aren't you? I'm not late. I'll only change my objective. The father or the son—it doesn't really matter."

I'm one of the best swordmasters in the kingdom. Only... he has a Velvet Breath dagger; he has everything to lose if I survive. I've upheld my confidence enough times where it upholds me now.

"You messed with the wrong family."

"We'll see about that," he says. "I was swinging a sword before you were born."

He draws his sword, plants a foot behind, and waits for my charge.

Sounds of mustering soldiers meet my ears, then drop as my concentration narrows to Julek. I test his guard, feint for a reaction. He's good. As adept at combat as I am, I'm unused to serious duels. I'm no stranger to fights within a larger battle, but a solitary duel feels different. I calm my mind and mentally take myself back to the rings in Sapesky.

I prod his defenses and Julek springs forward. He slashes where I was standing a moment before. I return it but he's fast.

The armies are forming up outside the wall we're on. The Lorganrule garrison is making it so the Guldeth won't be able to pass without an encounter. Battle-chants begin amid flying arrows.

I had thought all their soldiers were out of the mountain pass, and Commander Brayler did too. The rain lets up enough for the wind to announce that's not the case. More companies emerge and Loganrule's castle is virtually empty. Our force is vulnerable outside the walls.

Julek swings for my arm. I pull back before it dents my vambrace.

Chapter 22.

I return the stroke on Julek's arm. He lifts his hand, dagger poised, and catches the blade, then swings his sword toward my neck. I intercept the blow with my shield in a deafening crash as the metal over the oak turns the blade. It shivers my arm, but it's nothing I haven't felt a thousand times before. *I'll complain about the sting in five minutes,* I tell myself; I never end up indulging in crippling self-pity when I adopt the delayed-complaint strategy.

Julek recovers, slices up with his sword, and follows an instant later with his dagger in the same movement. Noticing his left hand hanging back, instead of joining into the momentum, saves my life as I anticipated the feint. My shield deflects his blade while my sword bats his glowing dagger away. I jerk my blade back then swing for his wrist. It glances off his vambrace. A faint trickle of blood rewards my effort as we draw away to gather breath.

"I don't want to hurt you, Julek. There's no way you can escape. Just surrender and you'll go through trial the same as anyone."

"Foolish boy," he says with a snarl. "Isn't it enough that I avenged your brother's death? He was never shield-fodder in my regiments. Couldn't you leave it at that?"

"Save your honor and stand down," I say. I raise my sword and move forward.

"You wouldn't be offering a trial if you thought you could beat me," he counters.

For a moment, it looks like he contemplates throwing his dagger at me. I hope he does, because then I feel it would be an even fight. As it stands, a scratch from the Velvet Breath dagger would end me before I could throw myself on him in an attempt to bring him to the afterlife with me.

Instead of throwing the dagger, something no seasoned soldier would do, he lunges at me with a yell. I meet him with my blade swinging around, then lay into a short charge which threatens to off-balance him.

Below, I hear the battle rage on. The Guldeth swarm in the courtyard and even on some of the walls. Atop a few towers, hand to hand combat sounds like a storm. Julek and I parry and feint in a sort of bubble, hemmed in by a tower beside us, a dropoff on the other side.

My charge makes him lurch backward, flailing his arms to keep from falling. A second too late to incapacitate him, my next lunge sends him dodging, fleeing into the door behind him. Quick but weary, I approach the door. I can't afford to give him time to find a weapon like a crossbow, but I don't want to rush into a dark room.

Knowing he won't risk throwing the dagger makes entering easier, and before my eyes adjust, I see the glowing blade arcing around. His effort to get beyond my shield failed, and with an ordinary dagger I'd trap the blade against my chest and batter him to the ground. This time, I slide my back against the wall, then spin, now being deeper in the room than he is.

"We shouldn't be fighting like this," I say. "Your honor should make you take a position along the walls to defend your country."

"A lot of good that did me," he says and rushes at me. "A dead wife, a daughter enamored with a coward."

I dodge. "You brought her death on yourself with greed."

"No," he says. "You know nothing of the real world, sheltered brat. I've noticed Claire's feelings for you. They wouldn't have lasted this long unless you've been giving her *some* hope. Tell me; if you ever have a wife, would you kill for her? Would you dare?"

He slashes at me. I step away.

"Would you risk everything to keep her alive?"

A feint, a stab, another slash. I parry.

"No reply? Not even counter-attacking any more?" Julek taunts. "Dear me, looks like I've rocked your foundations again."

I counterattack, ushering him toward the far wall. Sheaves of arrows hang from hooks below ash bows. Most of the hooks are empty, as are the armor stands.

Unless I'm careful, I'll overextend myself with anger and let him in my guard. I take a deep breath.

"We should've had this battle ten years ago," I say.

"You'd only have forced me to kill you as a child rather than as a man," he replies.

Shouts, screams, rallying cries, and the clatter of arms reaches me from the open door. I press an attack, and Julek vanishes through a door deeper into the castle. I rush through with my shield raised.

"If the kingdom ever finds out the truth, I think I'll be the hero," Julek says from a landing halfway up a flight of stairs. "A man trying to save his wife from a tyrant king—a despot she propped on the throne for years. In the end that king didn't think her life or service worth a medicine only she could benefit from. I suppose gathering dust in his palace was more important than her life; after all, she wasn't useful once we won the war for him."

Fury overwhelms me, clouds my vision. Maybe it's the tears mingled with the lurid glow of his dagger, but the world narrows to our contest.

"I did what I had to do, Prince Christopher," he says in a tone meant to cut through a skull. "Tell me; would you have done differently? If you were in my situation would you have tried to steal the Balm of Life?"

I lunge and throw all my weight behind the blow. It causes him to teeter. The top of the stairs gives us even footing.

"Would you have done it?" Julek screams while he stabs at me, enraged at my silence.

Speaking would be a waste now. I feel his same rage, and the Gift wells up. I could use it now, go back and find a way to kill him quietly, but I'm too focused on the fight. I push it away, and the feeling recedes to the edge of consciousness. Fury-driven, I don't need additional emotions to get in my way.

"Yes, I killed your mother," he says. "And I'd do it again to save myself. I didn't want to, though it was noble. Keeping blame aside from the champion is worth it. Noble. Noble!"

He stabs again, and I roll aside. It's a dumb move, and I drop my shield. Quick as thought, I take up a chair in one hand and press my foot on the back of the seat. With my hand and foot pushing in unison, I send the chair careening for Julek. He takes it with a thump, and falls to his back.

Risking everything, I scream and rush for him. Kicking his hand doesn't break his grip on the dagger. He swings his sword around and goes for my head. I block and could go for his head or neck, yet I don't.

I stomp on his forearm. I feel his armor bend under my weight and do it again. I just want him to drop his dagger. He tries to pull away, making my foot land hard on his curled hand. A scream of pain erupts at the impact, and I grab the dagger from his deformed fingers. He swipes at me with his sword, drops it, and tackles my legs. I break his grip and scoot across the floor.

Julek follows me to my feet. "Don't you leave now, you coward," he says.

He frisbees the discarded shield at me, misses, then throws himself forward in a frenzy. He reclaims his sword. I dodge and parry his cuts.

"Bastard princeling, stay and fight. Kill me to save your honor. Kill me!"

He's not opening his guard to let me in; I've already told him as much that I want him kept alive. Instead of facing me as an opponent, he's trying to make me kill him.

"I'll mark you Branded," Julek yells. "How will that look for the prince?"

He's managed to cut himself on my blade, but my eyes widen at the strategy his words reveal. He's not trying to make me run him through: he's trying to cut himself on the Velvet Breath dagger I'm holding. I step back.

"Come now, it's what you're doing to me—I only want to repay your family for the way they've treated mine," he says. His stomped left arm swings loose, and I see the pain in his eyes. Behind the fury, an intense agony lodges, and I can only imagine how distracting that is.

"Even in defeat you're trying to harm me," I say. "What would June want you to do? Sure, she probably should have been given some Balm, but let go of the hate. Become yourself again. Meet challenges with courage and strength. Redeem your legacy."

"It's not that easy," he says and moves to a position where he'll be able to kick the chair back at me. "So what if I've lived a lie for the last ten years? You were too foolish to spread the word accusing me. This is saving my legacy."

He kicks the chair, and I block it, barely in time to meet his sprawling lunge. His sword takes me across the right shoulder and I twitch back involuntarily. The movement pulls the dagger from his reach, where he's attacking the blade with his bare wrist. I smash my sword into his side, screaming with effort and the pain in my shoulder, and he totters to the floor.

An awful moment follows as I look at the blade. In his chamber in Myceum, the blade disintegrated as soon as it drew blood from the assassin, and I expect the same here.

He's watching it too, and my next heartbeat feels like it takes a minute. The blade glows in my hand; evidence he didn't manage to cut himself.

"I'm through with this," I say. It's too dangerous to duel a man with nothing to lose when you can lose your world.

"No!" he yells. He moves to his knees and comes for me while I navigate to the door.

I kick him in the shoulder; it sprawls him back. He lands on my shield, then slips to the floor.

"I hate you. Curse on the Harts and all your bloodline. Kings of death! Waste of a throne! I hate you!" I smash another shield onto his chest to incapacitate him further. His screaming follows me as I run from the room. Pity washes over my mind at seeing him rave like a madman. I shake my head. I need to focus.

The hallway I emerge into leads me through The Pass of the Winds' bedchambers and guardroom. The next door has a small barred hatch visible behind an open shutter with light streaming in. I leave the guardroom and find myself disoriented for a second.

Sounds of battle echo from the walls behind me. I find the rope from earlier and descend, sore and weary, yet confident I can help. Cheers, shouts, joy: the sounds change as I start to run, which is strange since I can't see anybody yet. Surely they're not rallying to me.

I slide down the rocky hill at the base of the wall. Soldiers fight in clustered knots by the fringes, and I see the king in the center of the heaviest fighting. Shouts emanate from the group, and I follow their gazes. Through the darkened sky, I see another force marching to the castle. My eyes haven't adjusted to the greater distance yet, but it's clearly Oruvian soldiers cheering.

Rain picks up, washing blood from the rocks before it dries to flakes. The cool touch stings my shoulder, reminding me of my wound, yet feels like the brush of a goddess. I tear a strip of fabric from my cloak, wrap it around Julek's dagger, stuff it in my boot, then throw myself into the fray. I need to reach the king.

Hacking, cutting, and chopping, I wield my sword with both hands. My skill makes the single goal of reaching the king possible in a short time.

"What force is that?" I shout over the battle's din.

"I don't know," the king says. "The men say it's ours."

Overwhelmed as we are, the sight puts heart into the soldiers. As long as we last long enough, that force could break the attack. I push my body to fight harder than anyone. I fight because it's my kingdom and because the people behind these walls rely on their prince. I fight because it's the right thing to do.

The struggle intensifies and I feel the tide, overwhelmingly against us when I first joined, begin to turn in our favor. It's like turning a ship; slow at first, slow in the middle, but then all at once it moves. It moves, but it looks like they're pulling back to regroup. We regroup as well to face off against a larger force. I feel the energy within our ranks.

A murmur sounds from soldiers to the side, punctuated by several gasps. I avoid the urge to look, instead focusing on the enemy to determine points of weakness. When their heads begin to turn, however, I chance a look to the side. It's two men—both soldiers, and the one in a blue tunic is bleeding from the wrist. His fingers are twisted like old branches.

Julek stands in front of the other man. The other is clearly a soldier, yet he doesn't look like the other Guldeth. Despite this, I can't help feel like I know him. It's not so much sight as it is a feeling. I've felt his presence before. The way his solid black clothing melts into the swirling cloak about his shoulders, along with how he holds Julek, should scare me. I look on with interest, hoping he betrays how I know him.

While everyone stares at the two on the high tower above us, I see the man move the knife he was holding. I catch a red glow where it frames against his cloak before he slams it into his sheath. He draws another knife, pushes Julek off the ledge, then flogs the blade into his neck. It bears the mark of a master, like a potter scoring a decorative line on a thrown vase. As Julek falls, his momentum pulls against the knife the assassin holds stationary. He hits the ground with a thud, though I'm sure he was dead before he landed. Screams in our ranks rise above thunderclaps.

The assassin still stands atop the wall, and he meets my eyes with his. In that instant, I know where I've felt him before. Sapesky, as I knelt beside my mother; Castle Muerthy, as I watched Heller murder the man; and in the keep while I dueled Julek. Still holding my eyes, the man brings his fist to his chest, and salutes. Unthinking, I return the gesture. Soldiers around me gasp. I blink, and see him run for the edge. He leaps and flies through the air, looking like he'll slam into the wall of the next tower over. He does, yet catches himself on the ledge of a window. He releases himself, lands on a platform. He jumps easily and leaves the fortress behind.

Sounds of battle all around draw our stunned forces to reality. I lead a V-shaped wedge through their ranks. As we saw our reinforcements arriving, they did also, and now fight with less heart. My fervor spills outward, inspires our troops. Our reinforcements attack their rear, and soon the Guldeth are on the run.

Bloody and exhausted, we don't pursue. All around, it seems the battle goes the same. Half of our force follows the king and half follows me. We help where we can, but the forces are mostly recalled by their commanders. As desperately as they wanted past the castle, now they want to secure their retreat.

Chapter 23.

It's hard not to look at uniform color when tending the wounded. Weaver told me, when his sister first joined the Oruvian army, that she was part of a prisoner swap. He told me they tended her wounds. Samantha; a young, injured, terrified soldier held by the enemy, and they helped her. I've always tried to look past color after a battle, but since then, I've tended to focus on the enemy soldiers. Not that I neglect my own—their comrades seem eager to help them and reluctant to those they drew blades against. The enemy are treated with leftover supplies unless we captains take the lead.

I walk toward a body sprawled on its back. There's blood splattered on her arms, her black hair is tossed around her face, a few strands dangling into her halfway-open mouth, and her green quilted jacket is torn in several places. She could be dead, or faking it so I remain vigilant. I approach her sword arm, held loosely around the hilt. As I bend down, she flinches as if coming back to life. I kick the sword from her grip. "Easy there," I say. "I've seen that a hundred times. Show me your wounds and I'll help."

She snarls, gripping her hand. I know kicking the sword from her hand sent it throbbing, though she meant to kill me so I can't force myself to care. *Some thanks for helping.*

"Your wounds," I repeat less kindly. "Anything you need cared for?"

She mutters an indiscernible threat; the swear is all I need. I turn and gesture to soldiers nearby; they noticed the commotion and are nearly here already. They drag her to her feet and start to bind her while I turn to help others. We'll arrange a prisoner swap, probably in exchange for our soldiers captured in Eraseam.

The next few soldiers I check are all dead, their weapons still limp in their grips or dropped beside them. I hear a cough carried on the wind, and the minutes I spend straining my ears feel like ages.

When the wind carries another cough from around a rock, I sprint for it. I backtrack, thinking I must have overlooked a soldier. This person must have been wounded badly enough to not try for my attention. *Comfort the dying*, I say to myself, *not only care for the wounded.*

As I round the rock, I see a few soldiers from earlier, but a second glance now tells me there's another. What I assumed were two soldiers tumbled together turns out to be three. A rattling inhale makes me grab the top soldier's ankles and drag him off. The third soldier, an Oruvian, looks ashen. Nothing of his appearance makes me think he'll live until tomorrow. Dried blood coats the outside of his helmet and the front of his neck like he's been vomiting or spitting. The instant sight of it drying instead of glistening gave me hope, but as he coughs again, he shifts, revealing the side of his neck. Blood shines bright there, covering the top and bottom of a slice in the gap between his armor. Something about the soldier has me feeling uneasy.

There's no way this poor man has long to live, I think. Not using his name does little to reduce my anxiety. I reach for his helmet, gently unclasp the buckle, and lift it off. As I lift, I tilt the helmet toward the wound so I don't stretch it, yet he groans. Moments like this make me wish I had something stronger for pain reduction than a decoction made from boiled willow bark and clove. It'll have to do. Blood from his helmet drips down the side of the man's head as I raise it.

I freeze upon seeing the man's face; through his helmet I only saw the shadowed frame. Now I see the eyelids, the set of his jaw, the cheekbones, eyebrows and hair. It's Weaver. He coughs and opens his eyes.

Like his eyes struggle to focus, he looks around before seeing on me.

"Hey Blondie," I say, struggling to repress emotions. "We won. Let's get you patched up."

"No," he mouths, and I stop.

My mouth quivers around the edges. I often think the soldiers performing these tasks need the medicines worse than the dying, but so far I've resisted every time.

"But we won," I say. "You're still captain and Claire's alive." I stop to laugh and cry at the same time. "And I'm alive too. Stay with me."

My voice breaks. I tear some of his tunic, ball it up, and reach for his neck. The bandage pressure causes him to flinch, then a gurgling fit of coughing overtakes him. Long blinks make me think I've lost him more than once as I squat there talking, distracting, trying to give him something to live for. Give him comfort.

As certain as I was of the poor man's fate, I now know who he is and desperately think there could be some way to save him. If only I'd pray long enough, wish hard enough, or stay here until my arms give out, then maybe he'd survive.

Prayers flow through me like water in a sieve; as soon as I formulate one to Lesasil, a wave of misery washes over me. The best I can manage is an intense throb of desire, hoping all the suffering surrounding us will somehow bless him with endurance.

His coughing goes from intense to fitful. Though it feels like hours have passed, the sun is in the same position. Around the battlefield, soldiers and officers scour the ground for survivors. The same thing is happening in every area of the castle —shouts rise from all over.

"Chris," Weaver gasps. I snap my head around to him, uncertain if I'd heard him speak. A mouse rustling through a green field of oats would have made more noise.

"Look after..." he starts, then draws a breath which sets him coughing. "Be a brother to her."

He's talking about his sister Samantha.

"I will," I promise. I'm here to comfort the dying, and try as I might to pretend he'll survive, deep down I know he understands what's coming. I've convinced new soldiers they'd heal from serious wounds, that their feelings were hysteria I'd seen before, and it comforted them for their passing. Not for Weaver, though; he's comforted too many dying soldiers to let me convince him otherwise. I repeat my words. "I'll look after her. I'll take care of her."

Peace masters his bloody face, washing away the despair death can bring to the unprepared.

"You fought well," I say. I didn't see him fight today at Lorganrule, but for years gone by, I've always been able to trust him standing beside me. I pause, then continue, "Thank you for helping Claire break me free. My trust was never misplaced on you."

He smiles, showing red lines between his teeth. He coughs once, then lets red bubbly spit dribble down his chin. A shudder wracks his body, and I remove my hand from the compress. It's not long now.

My heart seems too big for my chest and I feel its every beat. I grab Weaver's quivering shoulders to ease him back for comfort. Only now do I notice the soldier still atop his legs. Guldethian armor with the red fox head outlined in black adorns the tunic.

Weaver tries to take a deep breath, but it comes in a gasp, which chokes him. My tears have subsided. For now, I'll help him as a sturdy shelter.

"You are strong and good, my friend," I whisper. "You'll be okay in the next life, and Samantha will be okay in this one." Then on an inspiration, I add, "Give the queen my love."

He smiles. Seconds later, he goes limp in my arms and breathes his last.

Returning to my duties means I leave Weaver's body in the battlefield. Since he's a captain, he'll receive a special burial at a later ceremony, but for now he lies there with all the others, friend and enemy, and I have to walk away. My heart grows heavier as I step around bodies already gone over; I wonder if they're the lucky ones. If the soldiers checking the battlefield for the dying want the willow and clove for themselves, what's to stop them from wishing to change places?

A soldier in blue rushes toward me. "Prince Hart," she says. "The king wants you in the Receiving Room."

I nod, glad for something to take my mind from the grim surroundings.

Few notice my return to the fortress since I navigate servant's staircases. The king is there, along with Captain Pullen. The king wears a rich blue ermine-edged cloak. Thick silver embroidering over the length, decorative from both sides, matches the shining coap clasp and brings out a faint shine from the white fur. Crisp trousers tucked into polished leather boots further the disparity in how our duties have had us spend the hours since the battle.

He smiles when he sees me; I know what he assumes when the sad line plays across his lips and he extends a cup.

"No," I say, waving my hand. "I make it a point to abstain when I'm upset."

"It's water."

I smile. *Leave it to him.* He hands me the cup, which I take.

My soiled clothes make me grateful my father stands apart from the gold-inlaid chairs.

"A few hours ago I didn't know if we'd have another chance for these talks. Thank Nymunia you escaped." A few moments go by; he sips his own water. "I wanted to talk with you before we mention any of this to others. Some of it may never leave this room."

Father beckons to Captain Pullen. "The Nealy's know some of what's transpired," he says, "but they are discrete."

The king nods. "Commander Lewis held me at knife point before I realized the tables had turned."

I was afraid of that. It was the exact situation I rushed here to prevent. "Held you hostage to force my imprisonment when I arrived, no doubt?" I say, since Julek appears to have told him about my imminent arrival.

"Indeed. Once Julek told me you'd be on his trail I thought you were a little slow until you showed up with Sapesky's reserve forces; making it there and then here in almost the same time Julek traveled to one place means you rode yourselves into the ground." He looks marveled. "And that's part of what I wanted to ask you—their arrival couldn't have been more well-timed, yet you didn't know they trailed you?"

"You must know more than me in that matter," I say as I finish my water. "I only thought of your safety. Someone else must have brought forces from Sapesky unprompted. To my mind, Julek and possibly a few picked traitors were the only ones threatening your safety. Heller's forces were concentrated so heavily along Eraseam's border I never considered an attack in Montaya."

Captain Pullen shifts his stance. "The Guldethian attack couldn't have come at a better time. A minute earlier or later could have toppled the kingdom."

I raise my eyebrows to urge him on.

"We can discuss their arrival later, I suppose," the king says. "Along with the Constable's arrival. More water?"

He saw me eyeing it and reaches to pour more.

"The way we parted in Myceum pained me most of the way here," he says with even more eye contact than normal. "And it was my fault. I hadn't meant my words the way they sounded. Once Julek arrived I was forced to imagine what could have happened. Every breath I took pressed the dagger against my throat and each time I questioned your fate. He seemed afraid of your arrival so I assumed you were alive, but knowing one of us would die terrified me."

"It would have been me," I say. "I came here for my father; for the king was a secondary consideration."

He has a hard time looking at me, instead averting his eyes over my shoulder while nodding.

I know there's nobody there so I say, "Captain Lewis held me in a secret prison after your departure from Myceum." I speak for Captain Pullen's benefit too. "His daughter rescued me after a week, saying he'd spread word I'd gone to Toldulgur. This dagger," I say as I draw the one from my belt. "We wrested from an assassin he sent to silence me after the escape. He tried to stop us himself, but almost killed his daughter by accident and fled, leaving the two assassins. One took his own life; we managed to stop the other for questioning—and confiscate this dagger—but left on the commander's trail immediately. After a week in prison, I erroneously led us to Sapesky while Julek evidently came straight here."

"I suppose we can talk about the Constable's arrival now since you brought it up again," the king says. "He arrived right after you because he was chasing you; said he was worried for my safety."

I open my mouth to speak. I'm indignant and glance first at the dagger, then to my father.

"I know," the king says. "And Captain Pullen knows you'd never raise a finger against me. Constable Shutt, though, heard you had a Velvet Breath weapon. He used that as an opportunity to chase you here. Now he's hoping to put you on trial for possession of an illegal weapon."

"That mongrel. He's known me for long enough to know better."

"Indeed, but his son Drake was killed in the battle at Giant's Ballroom—the second time around—and he *seems* to think he survived the first time."

My angry countenance melts like new beeswax in a chandler's pot.

The king continues, "Don't underestimate the evils one can work when mired in grief."

"And I'm in Commander Brayler's fortress," I say. "Do I need to leave while I'm able?"

"I'm going to help myself to some wine if you don't mind," the king says. When I don't shake my head, he walks to the decanter. "My intent after visiting Myceum was to visit the mountain fortifications, then on to Jahkay. It was simply good fortune when Commander Brayler happened to be here in The Pass of the Winds. I've cleared things up enough where you're— if not welcome—at least tolerated."

"I'm no more than tolerated in many places," I mumble.

"It's the same for us," the king says. He chuckles and looks at the captain.

"Especially after being seen with a Velvet Breath Dagger," Captain Pullen says. "If anyone needs punishment for possessing a Velvet Breath weapon, I say Commander Lewis bears that penalty. Posthumously strip his title and let the populace know his treachery."

"No," I say. "We can't spread that more than it already has. His daughter rescued me and doesn't deserve the ignominy carried through that last name."

"Do you really think she'll retain her last name long?" the king asks.

I feel my cheeks redden.

"I know how you felt for her years back and how she rode the long way from Myceum with you. Sending her with you that day in Sapesky wasn't meant as a setup, but after hearing what I've heard I wish I could claim I saw it coming. I know there's something beyond loyalty with that woman. I've been around enough people over my life to know people don't go to those lengths without special reasons."

"She probably felt like she had to continue once she started," I say. "Saving me from treachery was loyalty—something everyone would have done if they'd been in a position to know it."

"That was beyond doing the right thing, Chris," Father says. "She loves you. I haven't seen you two together but I can feel it."

"Really? I told her Julek is Branded."

"And how did she respond?"

Trepidation seizes my chest. *How can I tell him everything and still have him respect me?* I venture into the deep waters, with his goodness my only support. "When we were led into Castle Muerthy and Heller first told us, she was devastated. I reversed the day but not my knowledge. Not her disquiet. When I told her after she rescued me, she didn't seem as distraught."

"Heller told you?" the king asks.

I nod. "Julek did also when I confronted him. He really was Branded."

He sighs. "I suppose she had time to come to grips with it. Once she realized he lied about your location and locked you in a secret prison, the next step wasn't far down the slope. Perhaps Claire's initial reaction in Castle Muerthy was the same as June's. Claire had the luxury of another Gifted sparing her the memory and coming to grips with the emotions slowly. June couldn't take the memory from herself. So she tried to save my Eilene by reversing everything up to it. A possibility, but it makes sense."

"A Velvet Breath dagger couldn't have been reversed," I say.

The king nods. "It's easy to forget in the throes of grief."

Could she really love me after snubbing her so often? Weaver and Ann came too, after all. Weaver was grateful for his advancement and beholden to Claire, though I doubt she would have held it over him. It was Weaver... simply doing the right thing. Ann came too. Perhaps she felt she had to come to prove her loyalty.

I suppose none of the three wanted to be the one to stay behind, I think, but... Do I really think that?

"Well what about June?" I ask. "I found a letter she left in Myceum. It hadn't been touched since she placed it. I think she tried to take a whole year back when she found out how Mother died. She tried to age herself by hundreds of years to have a chance at stopping it.

"June's loyalty wasn't built on Julek's goodness," I say. "She found out Julek killed Mother and... what of him?"

The king's eyes turn heavy. He looks a dozen years older in the space of a breath. I feel like a brute for telling him, but someone had to. Neither he nor Captain Pullen move a muscle.

Minutes stretch like kneaded dough in the bakery. Dark-stained wood pillars atop marble foundations provide beauty as well as function in this room; they're carved with heads of the common animals of Elathon: bear, boar, cave wolf, eagle, and others. The richness compliments the glossy tabletop and silver chandelier.

"June's loyalty to Julek was built on his perceived goodness," the king says. I can tell his words cost him. "June saw him as good until the end, when her sorrow overwhelmed her. She couldn't believe what she was forced to confront. The reality of the one action was too much for her, and it drove her into despair. Perhaps a life of ultimate responsibility pushed her to think she had to atone for his crime."

"Her loyalty—her belief in his goodness—it drove her to death in the end," I say. "How can a false belief ending in an innocent death be called loyalty?"

The king sighs and moves to the partially-open window. He throws it open; the bright light dazzles from the veined-marble floor.

"Those we love most can hurt us the worst," he says.

I stare around the room and down to the floor. Gold swirls in the marble look like inlaid rivers on a permanent map. I look up to the mounted animals and see the boar. Courage. I can do something harder than that.

"I think that's what I've done to Claire," I say. "She's given me plenty of signs she loves me. Maybe I'm too late."

"I doubt that."

My mind is spinning. I expected to tell the king a litany of secrets, but I'm here learning as much as he is. In fact, little of what I say seems to surprise him.

"Why didn't you do anything to Julek?" I ask.

"He was my friend—years ago and today I did do much for him."

"What?"

"I forgave him. Then, when it was only a suspicion of guilt, and now. It's the best thing I can do for him and for me."

A gentle breeze caresses through the room. Bitterroot and columbine sway in the packed vase atop the table. Mountain wind refreshed by recent rain is a smell to die for.

"Julek is gone yet that clearly wasn't you atop the tower," the king says. "Who was it?"

"I don't know."

"But you saluted him," the king says.

I shake my head. "I can't explain that," I say. "It felt right at the time. Like I had to thank him for something I couldn't bring myself to do."

Moments pass while he considers. "The Shadow Kings have always had their own honor code," he says. "I think the one on the tower must have come across a chance. Maybe learned something that confirmed their suspicions."

"Like a revenge-killing?" I say.

He takes a deep breath through his nose. "Perhaps. Perhaps they sold him a Velvet Breath dagger and he lied about its use. We might never know." The king shifts. "I'm proud of you for showing mercy. People think revenge heals wounds, but it doesn't; it heals egos, but at the same time it digs wounds deeper. It's like an itchy scab rasped open."

I recoil at the image, struck by the poignancy. Never before have I thought him more worthy of his crown.

"You're more than a king, Father. You're a good man."

He smiles, holding my gaze.

"So you think Claire would give me a final chance?" I ask.

He shakes his head. "Not a final chance; it doesn't work that way. Eilene gave me hundreds of additional chances, but never a final one."

"Another chance, then. You think I have a chance?"

"Always, but your trial may interfere with it."

The king looks aside at Captain Pullen, who flattens his mouth to a line.

I could run and live a good life away from court drama. Claire could come with me; Julek can't sway her anymore, especially with how he ran before he died. Desire pumps my heart ache near bursting. My whole life I've wanted to run, get away, leave it all behind. So many times I've had the opportunity and now here's another one.

I don't run because I can't. It isn't who I am.

"What are you thinking about?" the king asks.

"Doing the right thing."

He smiles.

"The crown looks light, but learning to carry it is backbreaking. I've been preparing you your whole life so you won't bow to vices like so many in high positions do. Once you're prey it's hard to become the hunter."

This isn't the conversation I want now. I shake my head. "I've too many insecurities."

"Oh?"

"Yeah. Haven't you noticed how moody I am? Nothing like you; you're calm and... and happy and always confident."

"When were you last moody?"

"When I..." I think back, wondering when I changed. What was the event?

"You are right now, for instance," the king says. "But that's not my point. It's been less even the last few months. There wasn't a point you changed; it was slow. You've been changing your whole life, only you've been too close to see it. From afar, I've seen you growing into a prince by more than birth.

"And you'll continue to change. You'll continue to get better at everything you care about. You care for the people even though most of them don't realize what you've given them. You'll continue to make things better for them. You care about Claire, so you'll get better at loving her."

"I haven't been that great with her the past decade," I say.

"No, you really haven't; you haven't always been a stunning example of someone who cares either." He smiles through the affront. "But you've been changing. Even then you had many great qualities; now you have more. You'll continue to get better since you care. Same way with Claire—you clearly love her, so you'll grow. Sure, you'll make mistakes—lots of them—but if she loves you as much as you love her she'll grow with you."

My heart feels light at the possibility of her loving me while my mind tries to stifle it. Fear worse than rushing toward an enemy grips me. I stumble through a few moments of silence.

"I'll ask her for another chance next time I see her," I say.

Then I turn and speak to Captain Pullen.

"You said the kingdom would have fallen if the Guldeth hadn't attacked the exact moment they did. Why?"

"The commander threatened the king with death if he didn't hand over his son. The effect of Velvet Breath weapons cannot be reversed with the Gift, so the threat was real even if you arrived. Thankfully for the kingdom, the Guldeth arrived through the rainstorm. Commander Brayler came to tell us and it was enough of a distraction to let us get the king to safety—if only for a while."

"Don't look so peeved, Captain," the king jokes. "When have I not fought beside my people?"

"Never when you have had a chance," Captain Pullen says. "And *I* have the scars to prove it."

The king stops mid-sip, looking over the rim of his glass. His eyes look wider from this angle. With years melting away, I marvel how the concerns of leading the kingdom haven't been able to prematurely age him. "Well... thank you."

Captain Pullen straightens himself. "Just my duty, Your Majesty. I should have said nothing."

"So Commander Brayler relinquished his old grievance before Julek arrived," I say. "And now he won't allow me to face Shutt's charge?"

"Not entirely true," the king says. "I prevailed upon the Commander—Brayler, that is—before either you or Julek arrived. He was still upset you didn't attempt using your Gift for Luis, but said he knew the cost was too high."

The king looks at me for a long moment. "The Gift is a wonderful burden. I watched June bear it for years. I'm sure I have no idea what it cost her—likely Julek didn't either."

"If he's done accusing me of keeping Luis dead, what's keeping me from facing Shutt? As ridiculous as his charge would be, he's not a man to let doing the right thing get in his way."

"Constable Shutt would have you in the dungeon and executed before noon tomorrow." The king takes a drink from his wine, smiling at Captain Pullen. "Thankfully you're the prince, and thankfully I'm the king."

"And where is he now?" I say.

"Probably assessing his forces. I imagine he'll head back for Sapesky tomorrow."

I wrinkle my forehead. "You mean you're going to let him go free after trying to create another rift?"

"Being upset about seeing your family die in war isn't a crime." The king drains his glass. "If it were, we'd have far too many traitors on our hands." A short look at Captain Pullen makes me recall his story.

"There's a difference between being hurt and going after revenge," I say.

"We have nothing against him."

"You know he's going to be a traitor," I say. "Stop him —"

"He's not guilty—"

"He will be guilty for a thousand deaths if you don't stop him from instigating another revolt." My face is hot; I can feel my temper rising even thinking about the possibility. "They'll be after us both if word gets out. Me initially, then you once they even suspect you're sheltering me. It's not just the people. The soldiers see the enemy we're holding back, but they feel the same to an extent; they feel the Gift and see their friends fall."

"If that's how the gods wish our reign to end, then so be it," the king says. "Some of the people think we have innocent blood on our hands but I will never make it so."

He turns in a flourish of blue brocaded fabric.

A slam echoes from the far wall of the room, and an officer of Lorganrule runs in. "Your Majesty," she says, dropping to one knee and giving a full salute. "Smoke. Smoke above the mountains by Toldulgur."

The king and Captain Pullen regard each other, then the king turns to me, announcing, "We ride for our friends." He turns, fast steps expanding his cloak to wave like a flag in wind. When he's almost reached the door, he calls, "Come if you're able."

I've slept at least an hour each of the previous nights, and feel good despite the privations. There's no way I'm staying behind while others ride north to provide aid. Claire would berate me for throwing my health away, but I guess I'm not utterly debilitated like on our journey to Myceum, so maybe she won't say anything.

Chapter 24.

◆◇◆

Another ride through the night stiffens my joints. The few hours of sleep we're allowed only serves to underscore the pain when we set off by starlight. As the sun rises, the smoke, an unseen presence during the night, returns. There was some speculation that the fire was even further north at Mt. Cabrae, but the Oruvian forces in the area aren't strong enough to attempt taking it back. Now through the clear brightness of morning, we see it emanating from a declivity between distant hills.

Leaving Lorganrule without the full garrison is a risk Father and Commander Brayler think worth taking; after all, Jahkay's reinforcements should have arrived within an hour after we left. With a weakened enemy, and fresh soldiers joining, a large force was dispatched for Toldulgur. Constable Shutt is coming with us, so I don't fear for the soldiers staying on.

Late the following afternoon, after another day of hard riding on fresh horses, we reach the outskirts of the fortress. Toldulgur was expanded after the Divide since it protects the largest town other than the capital itself. What it lacks in natural defensibility, the engineers made up for in size. Towers every hundred feet soar twice as high as the wall between them. In the Reconstruction, the town was divided into three sections. The original keep surrounded with short walls rests in the center section, while the other sections mimic wings as they stretch for distant peaks. Eager families built new houses to occupy those areas while over years the city morphed into using the central section as the merchant quarter.

Those houses, once so promising with their thatched roofs and giggling children, provided the fuel for a fire as sure as any beacon.

"I don't suppose trying to dissuade you from joining is worth my breath," Captain Pullen asks the king.

I look over at the same time the king smiles in his direction. He kicks his horse into a trot.

"I daresay it isn't," the captain mumbles.

I wait beside the captain and watch the king ride across the front ranks of his soldiers. Heartening them, rallying them to their country's plight, and receiving cheers in return enlivens him as well.

"Trebuchets," Captain Pullen says as we urge our horses to a downhill trot. I look over and see the weapons—some functioning, some destroyed. Those functioning are focused on the Oruvian trebuchets inside the walls, while our soldiers work their fastest to fire shot after shot. As we look, a massive stone hits the supporting timbers and crumbles a Guldethian siege weapon.

"Yeah!" I yell, losing all sense of tiredness again.

Our goal, since the garrison managed to resist the first part of the attack, is to enter the city. From there, though fire ravaged the southern sections, we'll take up position along the walls.

"It doesn't appear they breached the walls," Captain Pullen yells to me over the thundering of horses. "Fire trebuchets must have overwhelmed the citizenry's bucket brigades."

We crest the ridge close enough to the southern section so the enemy doesn't have time to redirect their strategy against us. There's a rear defense, but we'll cut through it easily if we're quick.

"Stay together and make for the gate," the king bellows.

A lead captain either doesn't hear, or makes a hasty decision and pulls left, using the soldier's momentum to seemingly try and reach the middle gate.

"No!" yell a dozen voices.

"For the gate! For the gate!" the king yells. "It's opening."

The next companies wrestle with their horses, pulling on rein to force the animals for the gate. They break from following the foremost company and hooves boom toward the lifting gate. The enemy's token defense crumbles from behind, and we streak into the fortress. We enter the midst of a ruin; smoldering coals still belch smoke with each gust of wind.

As the horses inside quiet, I join the other soldiers in listening over the wall. Metal on metal, hoof on stone, screaming and despair: the noises of battle reach our ears. New soldiers look around in terror at the sounds, as if they've realized for the first time that horses really can scream. Their screams intermingled with the soldiers die away—fainter from distance and fewer in number.

Occasional whirs and crunches from trebuchets punctuate the disturbance. The king rides around his dismounting soldiers, announces, "Follow orders and live." He looks around amid the fire-lit sunset. "Get on those walls and send them into the pit."

Captains and officers look detached while the soldiers do their best to emotionally separate themselves from the fated company. Soldiers release their giddy animals and rush to join the garrison. I see Claire rush for a staircase with a quiver full of arrows bouncing on her back. At least she has her flawless hair bound tight.

The final volley of arrows speeds through the open gate before it closes with a boom. I follow the king and Captain Pullen to the central section. The king rips his helmet free. His face and bearing are enough to let us enter.

The king stops atop the first height and discerns the battle. "Chris—take two companies to the north section and hold the walls."

I don't even stop to salute. I lead my stallion back through the gate and turn my cheek to the smoldering city. From mere seconds of standing beside the king, I realize the Guldeth are giving Toldulgur a respite. Plenty of fighting, especially from siege-engines, has taken place over the past several days, but for now it appears they've held them off. Soldiers from Mt. Cabrae seeking shelter bolstered the garrison, and I'm sure that's what helped them last; maybe we'll save a second mountain fortress.

A handful of soldiers chase horses through the coal-glowing wreckage. Above on the walls, a few soldiers have sunk to their knees. Some are vomiting over the rear edge. They must see their dead companions over the walls.

"Mariana!" She looks around, and I call again.

She was the first officer I saw, and I need a few to help me gather forces.

"Gather your soldiers; we're going to the north section," I say.

She gives a curt nod, then disappears amidst the surging soldiers. I spur my horse along the back of the wall. From the other side of a fractured wall section, I hear the enemy building for another attack. Our soldiers riding into their teeth must have whetted their taste for blood.

"You there," I yell to someone riding toward me.

"Captain? Your Highness." He reins his horse to slow beside me.

"You're an officer?" I ask.

"Yes, Your Highness."

"What're your orders?"

"Hold this wall," he says with a gesture.

"Change of plans—gather your soldiers and join me for reinforcing the north wall."

He salutes, then kicks his horse into a gallop.

"Captain," a soldier shouts as I ride back toward the interior gate. "Where do you want the horses?"

"Just contain them," I call over my shoulder.

A loud crash erupts as a trebuchet splinters in the central section. Beams fall amidst fleeing soldiers, a few screaming in death-agony as bits crush them. The main arm held a hollow log filled with burning charcoal. The projectile was intended to launch at a siege tower, but instead showers the area with embers.

Shouts on both sides of the walls announce more than the successful hit: they mean another wave of attacks is beginning. I've got to get more soldiers to the northern section.

Mariana Brown and Kelley Broadwine bring their soldiers within a minute. We send the stream through the open gate. Garrison soldiers with knowledge of the city lead us the quickest path to the other gate, where we emerge onto a similar scene of destruction. Fires have touched this area much less, making me think the southern quarter was abandoned to concentrate efforts elsewhere. Hysterical citizens lined the interior walls, little knowing their losses provided the call for help.

I wish we could have taken a different path through the town, but it was too full of terrified families to avoid them. Even seasoned soldiers can't help but be affected by such displays of feeling. I stumble one footstep through blurring eyes, then catch myself. Not here, not now; I push the Gift's beckon aside, race forward.

Atop walls again, I look around to the rest of the fortress. Towers fluttering proud pennants strike a lighter hue against the night sky. The area around the ruined trebuchet swarms with soldiers trying to contain the blaze from the scattered charcoal. Other of our trebuchets defy the enemy's advance, with a projectile scattering sparks across the sky like so many fireflies before crashing into an advancing siege tower.

Dozens of towers advance, and I call words of courage to the soldiers. They're as much to have the soldiers know their prince stands beside them as to impress the behavior on officers.

I'm borderline-relieved Claire's in the southern section. I'd love to have her by my side to protect, yet she doesn't need it. Right now I need a clear head.

Bows twang from the higher towers and the original section of the city. The outer wall was reinforced during the Reconstruction. Originally merely around the castle, defensive engineers lengthened it across the whole valley. They made it stand as another bulwark before the main gate which allows another rank of archers to fire down on attackers.

The siege towers and soldiers split between the two newer defensive wings. Discussions over years have let me know that's what the engineers wanted, but nobody could predict enemy actions. If the Guldeth breach either wall, they'll still have to confront another stronger one on the way to the keep.

Plucked bowstrings sound constant as soldiers on the regular walls join their efforts to those stationed higher. I rub sleep from my eyes and wait with readied sword.

"Captain," cries a voice from below. I ignore the first call, but turn around when it comes again.

"The king has a message for you in the Grand Hall."

The messenger rides away once I nod. I grumble yet sheathe my sword and look around for another horse. There isn't one, and they'll probably lower the gate any second anyway, so I run across the wall-walk. Occasional arrows hiss past me or thud into soldiers lining the openings between battlements. A few crossbow soldiers must have reached firing range with their oblong mobile shields. For the most part, the attackers seem to be focused on moving their towers into position.

The sound of gears clicking into place precedes a boom echoing from every wall and rooftop. I glance at the clock, and see it's four hours until midnight. I hope I survive tonight.

The higher wall around the main section confronts me and I call for a ladder. Soldiers lower one as soon as they hear me and immediately drag it up behind. I run down the wall-walk amidst soldiers hauling sheaves of arrows to the front. Reaching the Grand Hall means I have to enter the keep. Since defensive measures mean it isn't connected to the outer walls, I descend to the trampled dirt at the base of the walls. A figure leans against a series of projecting stones around the gate. He's hiding in the shadows with drawn sword, talking to the messenger, who looks into the northern bailey as I rush past behind.

Groups of citizens cower in corners where buildings meet; few acknowledge me rushing by. The tolling bell dominates all other sounds but between each bell, quiet moaning replaces the louder screams.

I near the keep and though the battle's begun, it's far enough removed where the drawbridge is still across the gap to the ramp. I charge up the ramp, then thud across the elevated planks. Four sentries either trust my Oruvian armor or recognize my face as they let me pass unquestioned.

Familiarity with the castle's layout from years of service lets me rush straight for the Grand Hall. My shallow gasps of breath remind me to walk the last hallway so I'm not winded for my audience. What he could want with me specifically, I don't know.

The Grand Hall is empty, or nearly so; I stride toward a group of soldiers milling about near the center.

"Captain," says one. He snaps to attention. "Any new orders?"

"I was told the king wanted to see me here."

The officer looks beside him at the other soldiers. "The king was never here, Captain. Least not during the battle. Did you want Captain Flamex?"

"No." I crinkle my brow. "Isn't this the Grand Hall?"

"It is."

"Then where did he go?"

"The captain went to help with the trebuchets."

"I mean the king," I say.

"I've been stationed here for hours and haven't seen him." He turns to the others. "Have you?"

The other soldiers shake their heads.

"My mistake then," I say and turn to go.

Muttered curses cross my teeth. I exit, eager to see how the battle's progressed in my absence.

I backtrack through the city and watch the soldiers atop the distant walls of the central section to see what they're doing. Archers rain arrows at the crossbow soldiers below. Beside me and above, a trebuchet creaks with the pressure of slinging a massive stone toward the north section. Splintering wood and cries of joy and disappointment mingle to let me know it was an indirect hit.

I move toward the gate again, passing it with momentary surprise that it's still open, but I want to reach the upper wall to gain a vantage. Something drips on the edge of my nose. I roll my eyes.

Stupid crow.

I wipe the wetness from my face, then halt in mid-step as I draw my hand away. It shines more than it should, and my disgust shifts to wonder. A large drop of blood hit me, but there's no fighting for a hundred yards in front of me—and by the sounds of it, they're still held beyond the walls. I chance a look upward, and see a shining streak dripping down the arched opening.

I reach the source of blood in mere seconds. It's an Oruvina soldier, dead near the edge of the wall. I draw my sword to prod the gatehouse door open. Once my eyes adjust, I move faster, and see nobody in the second-story room. The stone stairs for the third floor look dangerous, but I proceed to crawl up until my head is ready to peek over the floor above. Springing up, I wheel around to scan the room. Nobody.

The ladder leading a story higher looks too dangerous for me to ascend alone. I'm on the point of going for help when the jumble of gears, cranks, and levers catches my attention. Boyish curiosity led Rafael and me to operate Sapesky's gates from time to time. It shouldn't distract me, but something seems wrong.

The windlass is in place, the wooden log around which the chains roll looks free, and the pulleys are undamaged. Even the counterweight for raising it is there. Then I see what unconsciously drew my eyes: the ratcheting lock's handle is missing. There's no way the gate can be lowered with that jammed shut.

I surge down the stairs and onto the wall-walk. A soldier is running toward me; I glance at the bleeding body.

"He's dead," I say. "And somebody disabled the gatehouse—get others to unjam it."

She hurries back toward the front, then returns a minute later with more soldiers. I help carry the dead soldier from the path, then join the north wall.

Drawn where the fighting is heaviest, I look for an officer. "What's the feel here?"

It's Mariana Brown, blood making a motley of her clothes. She's upright, so most of it can't be hers.

"We're pressed hard. One tower's made it here with more coming if the trebuchets can't hold them off." She ducks as an arrow whizzes by. "We held them off long enough to torch the first one, but it cost us dear. It's the towers that're the real risk. The crossbows are only annoying."

A boulder skips across the top of our wall, taking a battlement and several soldiers to the ground beyond.

"That was new," Mariana says, eyes wide.

"They've adjusted since we're not firing at their positions anymore," I say. As bad as a trebuchet battle is, this is more devastating.

"Usually it takes hours to range those," Mariana says.

I grimace. "They got lucky."

"And we didn't." She swallows hard.

I can't let a sour mood spread.

"Keep at it," I shout to everyone, "and warn each other when the next shots come. Fifteen minutes between."

I move down the line to the heaped wreckage from the siege tower. A daring look over the wall makes my jaw drop as I see three more towers roasted into uselessness.

My position along the wall lets me glimpse our trebuchet towers. One is destroyed; another has soldiers swarming around, but it doesn't fire.

"What's up with that one?" I ask, directing a soldier's gaze.

"Joint broke yesterday," he says. "At least they stopped firing on it."

Bad time to have a joint go out. Another trebuchet creaks to life, and I watch the arm fling the stone with increasing rapidity. When it snaps loose, my eyes lock onto it and I see it sail toward a tower. My heart dips the second before it should reach. It looked like it was going to hit, but it slams to earth feet before the front wheels, rolling to a stop in the tower's path. At least it'll slow their advance.

"We've got the blacksmith here," the first soldier I see in the central section says. I recognize her as the one I sent for help. "He says he'll be able to break it free by morning."

Not good enough. "Get soldiers to help him. Everything is at his disposal."

The northern bailey suddenly looms large in my mind. If those towers break the defenses, they'll have a straight path to the central section. Focusing on the problem won't solve it, so I throw myself into the worst fighting along the northern wall.

Hundreds of Guldeth pour from a tower, and we battle them through the night. Hours of effort to light it results in flames reaching exposed areas under animal hides. Scores of our Oruvian soldiers die in the onslaught before flames urge the surviving enemy to retreat.

We're spent from the desperation, and my mind threatens each moment to make me sit now that I'm still. I force my body forward through will alone. My mind rebels, swirling my vision in a burst of possibility—go back a day and choose a different path. I've earned a bed and rest.

I shake my head to clear the temptation and stumble toward the next tower. They advanced nearly to the wall while we fought away the other one. They've already exchanged hundreds of arrows by the time I rush on the scene with another squad of soldiers.

Enemy leap from above, arrows punch holes through armor, and our tired defenders give way before the fresh soldiers. They follow us down the wall-walk where we put up a token resistance. A glance behind shows the gate is still open. As glad as I am it's ready for us, I want to see through the stones above to know if it's working. Will it close once we're through?

It does.

Dropping our defenses to rush for the opening felt like a desperate move, and perhaps it was, but we needed a break after such heavy losses along the wall.

Blood courses through my veins again like rivulets of rain on parched ground. That'll buy us some time. Bows twang like a requiem above me. Our soldiers are driving the pursuers back. They won't retreat far enough for us to counterattack; just enough to regroup before assaulting the inner wall.

Hours pass with our soldiers attempting to retake the northern wall several times. The attempts flail against the hastily-constructed wooden beams piled for protection, and the equal casualties will serve only to bring the battle to a head faster. Ladders replaced siege towers so we're doing a better job protecting the interior gate, but they move closer down the wall with a haughty superiority. They know they have more fresh soldiers than we do, and it begins to show. Our archers can pummel them from above and the side, but their shields bristle like growing porcupines.

I rush to see how I can help when screams break out in the city. I look down and see flashes of dark green between buildings. Green, with bits of red and the shine of steel.

It can't be.

I change my path as screams escalate. The few soldiers amidst the people put up what resistance they can, but their calls for help overpower the shrilling citizens, sounding of desperation.

Stairs are too far away. I rush around to them, slam to the stones, and duck while arrows whistle past my head. Soldiers are pouring in from the north.

They must have slipped in through a sally-port, the narrow door for emergencies. It must have been sabotaged by the same traitor who destroyed the gate.

I scramble to my feet and run bent double to the top of the stairs. Green-clad soldiers swarm through the once-secure entrance. They cut down everyone in their way and overpower the main gate.

"West gate, west gate," I yell.

Their smash through the northern section was an elaborate diversion, a means to access the traitorously-opened sally-port.

The next hour passes in a blur. All vestiges of my fatigue vanish with the effort of holding them from the main gate. Forces clash in showers of sparks. Citizens lie in the streets, hacked by passing Guldeth as they form into a horde.

Fights along the outer walls descend into chaos as they realize our plight and send companies—weakening themselves when they need the strength the most.

Our defenses waver, then break under relentless onslaught. I scream the order to regroup in the keep; the officers repeat it until we're moving in a chaotic mob to the yawning gate.

Many of the soldiers never reach halfway; focusing on the northern gate made us overlook the sabotaged sally-port, and focusing on the western gate made us forget about the northern gate in turn. Green surcoats wink to us like dragon eyes as soldiers pass between battlements atop the gatehouse. Arrows fall like hail and we break and run. Between houses and over corpses—anywhere safe.

It's all the traitor's fault. The northern section may have still fallen, but it was a weakened segment anyway. All the citizens had been evacuated to the safer areas, but walls are no good to them since someone let the enemy in. Betrayal hounds my mind with an intensity mere fighting never does. I want to go back, find the traitor, and end the madness that's been following.

No. I clear the Gift from my mind, knowing it would be useless. There's no way I'd find the turncoat.

We can still win the fight, though. I grit my teeth and push away the jaded feeling of betrayal.

Survivors of the arrow storm follow me to another layer of resistance. My heart leaps free of fear I didn't know I was holding when I see the king leading the defense. Hastily-constructed of wagons, wooden beams, and shields, the palisade will help slow the invaders.

"Chris," my father yells, "to the keep."

Captain Pullen holds his arm stiff, and I see blood dripping from a gap in his armor.

Ignoring him doesn't feel like a slight; I simply do what he would have done.

"They're coming between the houses," I yell.

My soldiers form up behind the barricades. The Guldeth run from their cover, then falter when they see us. Our arrows punch holes in their armor and harry their flesh like killer bees' stings before the stragglers can lurch back. The easy part is over; now they'll know we're here.

Every inch we give costs them a life. In the end, it's enough to rouse us from the shelter. We run up the ramp.

"You shouldn't have stayed behind after your father's explicit order," Captain Pullen says.

"He could have come himself if he was worried about making sure one of us survived," I say.

He snorts. "The king has a man to take blades for him."

Chapter 25.

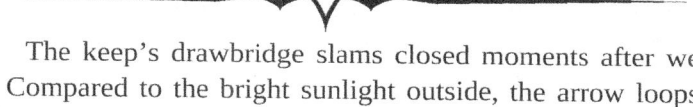

The keep's drawbridge slams closed moments after we enter. Compared to the bright sunlight outside, the arrow loops provide a subdued outline of figures moving through the hall before us. We push our way into the foyer.

A candelabra hanging from the second-story ceiling illuminates the room a mite better then the arrow loops alone. Throngs of soldiers and citizens try to move past each other, making it a constant shoving match. Families elbow to stay together and soldiers jostle to reach defensive positions.

Captain Pullen draws in a breath and I momentarily think he's going to draw everyone's ire by demanding they clear a path. Instead, he groans it out as he adjusts his arm.

"How bad?" I ask.

"I've had worse."

"That's man-talk for bad, isn't it?"

He snorts, then shoots me a grimace. "If you could use your Gift," he says, "now would be a good time."

My head snaps to the side. "What did the south section look like?"

"Three towers coordinated their efforts when we were sending soldiers to help with the central gate. We couldn't have held even if we'd retained everybody."

"My Gift won't help with that," I say softly.

He knows it. The silence coming from him, like he somehow absorbs everything, deadens my perception of the grand foyer. It's so unlike him, this moodiness. He had to have seen more.

Captain Flamex steps before the king, bows. "I wish I could be offering you better hospitality. I hope our need doesn't dampen efforts elsewhere."

He clearly meant to say he hopes the king survives.

My father acknowledges him with a mild bow of his own.

The reeve opens a set of double doors, and citizens filing down a hall makes space for us to enter. After the clatter of battle and murmur of grieving people diminishing to the distance, the silence of the large room feels oppressive.

"It's the trebuchets," I say. "They're not firing."

"Overrun," Captain Flamex says.

"But that means..."

"It means the Guldeth will move their own within range of the keep," the king says.

My father's face is set. He's known every design consideration of Toldulgur since it was built, and understands the ramifications of losing each bit of ground. I used to overlook his strong countenance during times like these; now they make me admire him even more.

My eyes glaze while I stare into the distance.

He reads the question on my face and answers what I didn't ask.

"There wasn't a choice. We had to—now we make the most of the remaining options."

"Can we expect anyone to know of our plight?" Captain Pullen says. His face is unreadable despite the pain that must be radiating from his arm.

The king's slow subdued response says as much before his words reach their meaning.

"Our nearby friends are in no position to help us. What's to be done is up to us."

"We can ride to clear the city," I say.

"We were holding the horses in the southern section," Captain Pullen says. "They're now inaccessible."

"Rush out to free them."

The king sighs. "Doing so would leave the central section and all the people close to defenseless."

I throw my hands in the air. "Then do something," I say. "It was my fault, after all—call me a coward, hit me, strip me of rank—just—something."

The king's eyes remain steadfast through my tirade. "I've lost a city, hundreds of soldiers, their horses, a Commander," he says. "There's no way I'm losing a son if I can help it."

Captain Pullen smiles.

The king strides across the room. "Come on; we're saving this fortress."

"What's the plan?" I ask after I reach his side.

"They'd least expect a counterattack minutes after we take refuge. They'll be moving lines closer for a siege. With them in flux, I'd expect an attack now to do more damage."

Captain Pullen salutes when the king looks at him, then rushes up a set of stairs, shouts, "Captains and officers to the entrance."

Minutes later every ranking soldier stands in a circle around the king while they wait for his words. Ordinary soldiers weren't barred from the perimeter, so the group extends down every hallway as far as I can see.

The king's orders are short and to the point; qualities that endear him to his soldiers.

"We're not in here to hide. We're here to regroup while they huddle outside like a swarm of cowardly wasps. Their stingers are attached by a thread, and our fallen are waiting for vengeance. They better be enjoying the respite we're giving them. Everyone have steel?"

Smiles and soft cheers fill the foyer. The king waves his hand above his head with fingers spread apart.

Five minutes. Leaders depart to ready their soldiers.

I salute. "Thank you for the forgiveness."

He smiles. "Even if it was your fault it was nothing—ask me about Edward Raven sometime."

He clatters from the room with Captain Pullen, Captain Flamex, and a dozen guards around him. Since my authority becomes secondary in the king's presence, I await orders.

He returns minutes later. "You won't be content to remain behind, will you?"

One corner of my mouth lifts.

"I didn't think so. You're growing up to be like me. Alright, then—things will happen fast out there. Lead soldiers north as soon as there's an option; I'll take north; Captain Flamex will work for the trebuchets."

It's the sort of plan I like, if it can even be called a plan. I agonized over a perfect plan far too long before leading my first battle. The enemy disrupted it from the first encounter, and a senior Captain stepped in to salvage a hard-won victory from the chaos.

Everyone knows what to do and how to compensate for failures.

One final check through the upper windows shows the moat is clear.

The king is standing inside the closed drawbridge. He turns around and issues one final command. "Hit them hard and strike where it hurts."

Hands tighten on grips. Chains rattle in the rollers. Noonday sun streams through the opening.

Per the king's instruction, nobody shouts a war cry until the Guldeth scream their confusion. Then ranks erupt.

We're upon the first of their defenses in moments. Besides a stiff-moving middle-aged captain and a few soldiers, only their screams make it back to warn those behind.

Tactical devastation follows until we've retaken half the central section. Their soldiers flee from the initial rush; some even refuse to come through the gate until their comrades stop our advance. The few defenses they've erected become ours, but most of the fighting happens in the street or house to house between individual soldiers rather than large opposing bodies.

I reach as far as the temple when the enemy press us hard. Dozens join me to barricade ourselves in the stone building. We deliver more arrows than we take from the tall narrow openings. We were part of the forward thrust, and with the counterattack we're left alone, on an island in a sea of green uniforms.

I draw a bow and throw myself to a window. I mean to loose it instantly so I can regain shelter, but I meet Berlee's eye and pause. I never considered her my friend, yet it's hard to even see her in the enemy ranks. What she said about wanting the war over skirts through my mind. I draw back with the arrow still nocked and rush for the opposite side.

We hold out for hours. The fight moves farther away, our friends pressed closer by reinforced ranks. The trebuchets we'd freed upon first rush fall silent again.

A soldier starts coughing, but it's not a bloody cough, so I turn. I've been so busy holding the door barricade together I forgot about the rest of the temple. Sunlit smoke filters in from high windows.

"Hold it," I say, then run toward the altar.

The curved walls are warm, and I hear the sharp crackle of dried wood taking sparks. A rug on the ground starts to move, and my instant attention goes to this new threat. Above, around, and now below. I kick the rug away to reveal wooden slats. They bounce again, and I grab a handle to rip it back. Someone stands in the opening, coughing like with lungs full of smoke. Light hair wrapped close about the small head lets me know it's a woman. She coughs a final time and tilts her head to face me.

"Claire!" I yell. "How—how?" *Why'd you come to the worst fighting?* I think. *You should stick with the king where it's safer. You know I'd want that.*

"It goes to the granary," she says. I help her from the hole then look for others.

"Just me," she says. "You've gotta go"—she coughs —"the fires will collapse this end any minute."

It takes me a second to comprehend her meaning. "Go, go, go," I say to the soldiers around me.

"And you." I try to push Claire back through the hole.

She doesn't move. "I'll go once they're out."

My eyes scan wildly across the temple and I see the soldiers still holding the barricaded doors in place.

"We have to leave," I say over the din.

They rush through rows of benches. A resonating crack echoes through the temple and makes me jump. Walls start to crumble in on themselves. What began as a single break ripples through the curving walls of the apse. A stone falls to the white marble floor and shatters. The mosaic ceiling starts to crumble. Ten stones follow a heartbeat later, a hundred a blink after.

"Back," I say.

It's unnecessary, and nobody could hear it anyway. Rubble buries the opening and slides down steps toward the main nave. Roils of smoke and stone dust invade my lungs.

"Back to the"—cough—"entrance," I say. "The narthex. Climb."

The barricade still holds the doors in place, but the enemy battering will smash through them in moments.

An officer leads them up a staircase to the clerestory level. Once there I pause and pull Claire to the side while others seal the opening. Gears and rods from the clock above spin from their weights and decorative pendulum.

"Claire I—need to talk to you." I feel like an idiot since I pulled her aside for that obvious reason. My hands go clammy. "I should have said this sooner. I... years ago. That's how badly I've been delaying. It's that—you're always here in my darkest moments. When it would be so easy to sit back and see what becomes of me, you're always here."

It's everything I can do to hold my gaze off the floor.

"You're always with me even when I don't deserve it. When I shove you away you somehow know it's—" I take a deep breath. "It's me passing my pain on to you. You don't deserve it." She's smiling, so I finish. "I want a life with you. I hope you'll have me."

"You're rambling," she says.

I let my smile grow. When Clarie does the same, mine broadens into a full grin, belying that we're trapped atop a clock tower and surrounded by an army. I fold her into my arms and crush her to my mouth.

She tastes like salt and world-ending goodness at the same time.

A final boom descends into splinters as the door below gives way, and we break apart. The twenty of us remaining rush for the belfry. I insist I'm the last one up the ladder in case they break through. Claire perches on the edge to pull it up behind me. We ascend another and find ourselves in an open-air belfry. Slender stone pillars hold up the spire the bell hangs from. We move around the bell, through the pointed archways, and onto the lip of stone around the tower.

An evening breeze, unfelt below, caresses our faces now that we've reached the highest story. Below, the sounds of a one-sided battle echo in the distance. Motionless patches of blue dot the ground behind enemy lines.

Smoke blankets the near horizon, proof of our loss. The Guldeth have pushed the line of battle so far from the temple we can't see it from our vantage. Screams and cries reverberate through the tight streets. The screeching cries of civilians mixes with the frustrated agony of soldiers.

Nobody is spared.

Citizens stream for the eastern gate, but it's narrow so few make it out. Far in the distance, a horse carrying two people canters along the road. I've only seen one horse saddled since our arrival.

"That's the Constable's messenger," I say. "And Shutt. They tried to kill me earlier."

Tears well in my eyes and I'm so focused on the rout below it takes me a while to hear Claire behind me.

"You see it now? You see it? Most of the citizens were killed. I think they're using this as an example of what'll happen if people keep resisting. Your Gift—you've got to try again. Take us back and we'll do something different, get the people out, soldiers different places. Just move us back and give them another chance."

I stop listening and stare over her shoulder. The giant clock face looms; the whole day has passed and it's again four hours until midnight. As I look up, the hands snap into place and an ear-splitting crash surrounds us. Inside the tower, the hammer strikes the bell.

I try to use my Gift, but it doesn't come. Earlier I shunned it—now I grasp for the least tendril.

Nothing.

Not a glimmer, not an inkling. I try to dive deep to find emotions but find apathy. I've shunned the exact emotions I'm now trying to access.

Again and again, I think my head can't rattle any worse. Soldiers rushing to kill us stop in their tracks; some even drop their swords to cover their ears. All screams atop the tower and from the city wither at the overwhelming sound.

I try to tell her I can't. I can't use my Gift.

Claire has her hands over her ears. Her mouth is moving in silent shouts, but she could be miming words for all my ears register.

From her tears I think she's given up for the first time ever.

Claire raises her hands while I stand mute. I'm too stunned to even cover my ears.

Before I know it, she's pushed me square on both shoulders and I stumble backwards over the low railing. My hands convulse for a saving grip but close on air. Breath forsakes my lungs and I feel like I'm suffocating from losing Claire. That thought, more than losing my own life, drives a dagger of terror so deep into my heart I try to scream in pain. No thought of the nearing ground twists the blade; only the loss—the loss I suffered when she pushed me.

I pelt to the ground and close my eyes when it's a second away. A complete wave of loss overtakes me. Nothing left to live for. Let hope fade.

I jump from the ladder and alight on the central wall section. After a few moments to orient myself, I duck to see if I recognize soldiers. I've passed over this section a dozen times, but the timing matters. Sounds rage all around, and I remember my summons to the king. I stand to rush for the southern section this time, then stop.

This can't be right. A false messenger the first time and a disabled gate distracting us to ruin?

Instead of heading for where I know the king fights, I rush down the steps and toward the gate. I draw my sword as I approach the figure hiding in the shadows.

"Shutt!" the false messenger says.

The constable whirls around to avoid my blade. It swings wide. The instant warning saved his head.

"It was you," I say. My eyes burn. The need for sleep presses even harder as if I'm yet another day behind. Tears take the place of sleep and I blink my vision clear. "You sabotaged the gate. You killed the soldier on guard. You opened the sally port and let a thousand die."

I slice at him with each accusation. He steps back with narrowed eyes.

"I've done nothing," he says. "You let my family die at Giant's Ballroom. I saw them die after I felt relief the first time."

"I didn't know they were there," I say. I swing at him. "The war needed it."

"Needed it. More like *you* needed it. Convenient how it's not your family's blood dripping down enemy blades. I've done nothing—but I should."

He strikes against my sword. It slams into the stones and vibrates so I release one hand. I snatch the dagger from my belt. My hand still thrills from the impact but I palm it. I render Shutt's sword ineffective by stepping inside his guard. I draw the dagger up across his chest, skittering across armor, then slash sideways before stepping clear.

The dagger's blade disintegrates in my hand. Shutt stands a second longer before he goes to his knees, then falls sideways. His young friend, the false messenger, precipitates from his horse. He kneels beside the already-dead man, realizes it, and looks at me in terror.

"You're far from guiltless," I say while I drop the hilt. My arm feels like it's burning; shock from the impact must have rattled my nerves.

The wide-eyed messenger turns and runs without bothering to take his horse. Where he goes isn't my concern; I'm certain he was only a cog in the wheel, not dangerous unless wielded by another.

I stow the bladeless dagger hilt and rush back up the stairs. *Best not leave that around.*

"You there!"

The officer looks around.

"Seal every gate," I say. "Trebuchets support the southern section."

"Yes Your Highness." He bows.

I stop the officer before he can leave.

"Do that then you personally check the sally ports. I want guards on each one. Guards to ensure the gates stay functional, too."

He looks like he's going to tell me the guards are unnecessary, but he swallows, dips his head once, and rushes to pass words to the trebuchet engineers.

I descend the ladder to the northern section and have the pleasure of hearing the gate rattle to the ground.

Hours pass, each one setting upon the life of hundreds. We fight through the night as before, and hear soldiers cheering each time the trebuchets strike a siege tower. When constant hammering brings down a section of our north wall, we retreat behind the stronger sealed inner wall.

Civilians stay safe from harm's reach by gathering in or around the keep. Each time exhaustion threatens to overwhelm me, I look down and notice I'm not having to pick my way between fallen innocents.

Claire reappears toward morning—a hundred paces distant in the southern section. I run to the next knot of soldiers, and lose my thoughts in the fight. Anger or betrayal should have risen in my heart at seeing her, yet it didn't. I don't want it to, yet it not overwhelming my mind startles me.

The battle ends with no clear call for retreat. Individual companies seem to lose heart after the night's fighting and peel away. Cheers that rise from our battered ranks sound pained, on the verge of tears. Any battle is alot to go through; a battle with this many casualties, though, is far worse. Soldiers' never completely forget what they see and might walk around like ghosts for hours.

My own mind isn't much better. I saw almost everyone in the castle slaughtered hours before, and some of them again since.

I wander, doing what I can to help. Several officers take charge and organize survivors into teams; some soldiers are sent on patrol; the rest join civilians in caring for wounded or dying. Even children rush back and forth with buckets of water for cleansing wounds. Nowhere do I see a bright face. It's a victory, but a terrible one, and only I know how much worse it could have been. How much worse it was.

My mind urges discontent. After minutes of repetitive thoughts I shake my head and go toward the temple. There's no fire damage, and the doors aren't beaten in. A few bodies are stiffening around broken statues. I enter, afraid of what I'll see lest people used it as an unbarricaded refuge.

Nobody, thank Xulbris.

Officers must have roused the supplicants to help outside. Beseeching the gods for mercy on the dead and dying is necessary, but their bodies need help too. Better to pray while working.

Since nobody's here, I amble toward the altar. The winged statues are mostly the same as in Sapesky's temple. A mosaic on the domed ceiling drips a tile to the floor at my feet. Clear; the faintest swirl of dusty blue. I slip it into my pocket. It could have fallen from anywhere, but when I look up, my eyes first alight on Lesasil as if it was his tear. I stare into his eyes for a long while. If willpower could force him to blink, to cry again, I would now. I'd give anything to see something. To know it's true. My soul swirls with anger and gratitude; I feel like a hypocrite.

If Nymunia beside him could so much as lift her finger or smile, or Xulbris on Lesasil's other side would even grimace at me, then it would feel worth it. It would feel possible. As it is, I believe, but it feels like a forced belief.

I want to leave, yet the stir in my heart which brought me here won't let me turn away. I go to the rug and kick it aside. There's the door. I half-expect Claire to look at me when I draw it open, yet only a black chasm meets my eyes. I sigh and lower it. She's the reason I came here; I realize that now.

Claire didn't try to kill me. She didn't give up hope. She kept hope to the end, and shoved me in a final attempt to save me. I'd repressed the very emotions I'd needed to use my Gift, and doing so locked them out. She must have realized we were going to die anyway, and that she needed to give me an emotion so powerful I couldn't have felt it before.

I recall falling from the tower, pushed by the woman I planned to spend the rest of my life with. We were together for mere minutes before she shoved me to what I thought was my death. I didn't even care; didn't want to live, yet the Gift saved us.

She came to the realization the same time I discovered another moment would be too late to stop the castle—and the kingdom—from falling. I despaired at my inability to use the Gift, and she pushed me, plunging me deeper into hopelessness.

I thought she'd be here; I need to go find her.

"Hey?"

I turn around and see Claire. She's still in armor from the battle. It's torn and discolored from sweat and blood.

"Did you—you're a year older, aren't you?"

She noticed. Somehow before she saw me, or anyone else noticed, she did.

"How did you know?" I ask while I walk toward her.

She shrugs. "I—felt something." Then she screws up her face and drops her eyes. "I don't know. I felt hopeful all of a sudden, then a rush of desperation. When the battle ended I didn't want to come talk to you. I don't know. Don't know why."

A lump twists free from my stomach. I slow to a stop.

"You came to me. Again."

She moves closer. "So did you."

"And..." I say. "Why?"

"It felt like everything would work out somehow. Last night as the sun went down, I would have sworn the battle would go our way. Then the complete opposite. No reason for it, just a surge of emotion."

"You saved everyone," I say.

She rubs sleep from her eyes. She's been running on as little as me.

"You don't remember anything else from last night?" I ask. "Nothing beyond the feelings of being okay, then despair?"

She smiles shyly.

"I—" I begin, then stutter. "I told you you're the one I want to spend the rest of my life with. I'm done running. I've treated you so poorly the past decade, and there's no excuse for that. It's just when mother and Rafael died, I swore I'd never get that close to another person again. I blamed them for being taken from me. It was their fault, and I know it wasn't—I just—I wanted someone to blame. But you're the one—you said you'd have me and be happy. I hope you'll say it again."

Claire lets me run myself to a standstill. Though I know she shoved me over the edge to save the kingdom, the hurt lodged itself deep in my chest. She came, yet my mind won't let me believe she sought me out.

She takes a few steps toward me. The exhaustion spread in every line on her face hides what I hope is a smile. I reach to hug her, and she allows it. I embrace her, and she melts to match my shape. We're touching all the way from our intertwined necks to our hips, and she hugs me back. We both smell of iron, smoke, and sweat.

Just like last night—or I suppose it's tonight—I pull her to me again and taste everything. Without even a second of resistance, she wraps her arms around my neck and kisses with the force of something ten years too late.

I grab Claire's shoulders and hold her at arm's length.

"Don't push me off the clock tower this time."

Her eyes widen while my smile tugs the corners of my mouth.

Chapter 26.

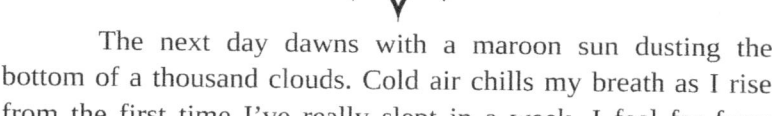

The next day dawns with a maroon sun dusting the bottom of a thousand clouds. Cold air chills my breath as I rise from the first time I've really slept in a week. I feel far from refreshed, but the rest will help me push through another day.

Gangs of men and women volunteered to dig holes, and every unruined wagon was hitched to a mountain pony for transporting bodies a mile into the mountains. A meadow, rather than the usual rocky soil, receives the corpses.

"I hope you realize they're not so against you," the king says.

We watch two women lead another cart down the dirt track. Others are spread out into the distance, dotting the trail into the mountains.

"How can I feel anything different?" I ask. "Isn't everything bad that happens leadership's ultimate responsibility?"

"It's not quite like that. Certainly we spill our blood alongside everyone else when possible. They saw us come to their aid. They saw us fight the whole time. As bitter as a victory can be, it's better than a loss."

"We didn't make it the first time," I say. "There's a reason Commander Shutt didn't survive."

Time stretches between us.

"I thought you looked a year older," he says. "Tell me how it happened."

I relate everything, starting with the false messenger's summons. Mostly I relate Shutt's treachery and how Claire and I realized our one final hope atop the tower.

"I killed Shutt right when I took the day back. Used a—a —"

Fear grips my chest, but the king doesn't seem to notice; he wrinkles his brow.

"I think I had died," he says. "I remember something about a deep sorrow. For others' sake. It's a strange feeling. I can't imagine how your mind must work to arrange the pieces of time like that."

"You'll be proud of me for asking Claire to spend her life bound with mine."

"Did you now? Wonderful."

He beams at me.

"You realized she loves you despite mistakes, huh? Now if only you'd realize the people love you more than you'd like to allow."

I smile. "You didn't hear what the Nealy's said about Giant's Ballroom? Don't you have advisors telling you anything about Eraseam? I imagine Myceum isn't much better."

Another wagon rattles into view. It's uncovered. There's been too many bodies to shroud individually, so the workers grab a cloth from another group and drape it over before proceeding.

"If you stood in their place," my father says, "you'd realize they have reason to be angry with a poorly-used Gift. Even if they know it wasn't your fault, their family dying after surviving the first time around makes it hard."

His words hurt because they're the exact ones I'd say to myself. I know they're true and I can't pretend anything otherwise.

"Each use wasn't always bad," he continues. "Here it sounds like you saved everyone—even your king. Every single one who remembers the emotion of dying still feels it's part of them. Like when they could only point to you for their loss, now they can only point to you for preserving their life."

I so desperately wish I could be like him. Calm, confident, able to rise to any diplomatic situation. "Do you still wish to abdicate the throne?" the king asks.

Nothing comes to me for that. Since I've been in line I've wished for little else. Now after the last months of experiences, I don't know anymore. The least I can do is try. For his sake and mine. I owe it to us both.

"Can we walk?" I say.

We turn away as another cart stops for a shroud. The full sun hits us across the face when we start to walk back toward the southern gate. A dusty sturdy wagon fills the gap—probably a repurposed marble-cart halted when hostilities began.

Scuff marks on the stone show the heavy fighting the king's forces battled before their last push for victory. Soldiers flung thousands of arrows and tons of stones both ways over these walls, and I marvel at the man beside me; strong enough to hold himself together after holding the kingdom together.

"I've wanted nothing more than a quiet life away from all this," I say. "Now that I'll have Claire I want that more than ever. I want a quiet life, a bit of land outside a small village, and a happy family."

He remains silent. It shames me to know he'd give it to me.

"I want to stay in the war at your side," I continue. "I'm the best captain in the field and Elathon can't spare me. As for abdicating"—I pause, torn between worlds—"I could find everything I want in life—even as a prince. A family, leisure, joy—it will take more effort to achieve, but I know you've instilled me with enough courage."

The king smiles. "It takes a wise man to recognize that at any age. Most need experience."

"And many times that experience comes with corruption," I say.

We pass through the crowds easily. We cleared bodies from the castle first lest we need to shelter a second time. As it is, I still gawk at everything. The visceral experience of seeing the ruined city from atop the clock tower holds me like a vise.

"Keep the nobility from making you too power-drunk to care," the king says. "A former king slipped down that path as a young ruler and fought for decades to claw himself back. In the end, he confided he never felt the chains fall."

Its a sobering realization. A lifetime of effort has kept me mostly clean, yet I know some of what he's talking about. Thankfully it hasn't ever been as bad as some of the nobility I've heard about. Heller, or rather the ones Heller told me about.

"You're far from that path—I only warn you to be aware of it," the king says, breaking my reverie.

"They'd really do that?"

He smiles. "Not with intent, at least not most of them. The wealth we allow the nobility isn't always well used. Everything they do is exaggerated by it. When they descend into vice, it can consume them. They think they're strong enough or noble enough to control it, but in the end it controls them. It's not all vice; virtue extends further, too."

"Where does Julek fit in there?" I ask.

"That's in the past. I doubt I'll ever really let it go, but I'm going to try. You should also."

I roll my shoulders to crack stiffness away. It's also a shrug and Father notices it.

"After all he's done to us," he says with a sidelong glance. "Yes, even after that. Especially now since he's dead."

"I don't know if I'll feel he ever deserves forgiveness."

"You don't need to feel it. I know I don't. Feeling makes it easier, but you don't need it."

Cobbled streets replace word stones as we near the merchant quarter. Pennants are still flying, people work at erecting tents, and trebuchets stand ready.

"The feeling you're strong enough to skirt the line around temptation rises stronger the higher position you occupy," the king says. "I suppose that's a lot of the reason I've admired the man you've carved yourself into."

"It wouldn't have happened at court?"

A rueful smile bubbles up. "It could have. I was afraid something would happen to you like happened to Weaver. I suppose having you two grow up entitled and indulgent would have been worse for the kingdom than your deaths."

We arrive at the temple without pushing our way much. Guards surrounded us as soon as we entered the city, but with the last day's chaos it's few enough. Normally we'd be surrounded by the King's Guard. Captain Pullen isn't even here; he's in the infirmary.

The way the people stare from a distance disturbs me.

"What is this?" I ask.

The king chuckles. "I'm surprised they're not swarming you. Everyone knows something strange happened, and you're the only one they can point to."

"And that doesn't terrify them?"

"Evidently not. Remember you saved almost everyone here. They don't know it, but rumors circulate and they're probably nearing the truth."

"Bad rumors circulate easier than the truth," I say.

"But deep down everyone knows what happened. People see you as their hero."

We enter the temple and stop before Lesasil's statue. A shiver flutters up my spine from hearing myself called a hero in front of a god, if only his statue.

I start to unwrap my arm. I've kept armor and gloves on since the battle, even when asleep since I was so drained. "I don't suppose this is necessary now," I say.

Father stops me before I fully remove it. I look into his wide eyes while he checks the temple. Other than our guards waiting at the entrance, there's nobody here. Relief flickers across his face.

"Don't. Leave it covered."

I do, and he asks, "Where did that come from?"

"Killing Shutt. I used the blade I took from Julek."

He doesn't look relieved. If anything, fear shivers through his whole body for an instant. At least he doesn't pull away from me, so I'm spared that ultimate pain.

"What?" I ask. "It was right when I brought the day back, and we needed a new strategy that instant. He was the traitor and needed to go."

His usual behavior returns as quickly as it fled.

"I imagine we'd both be better off if you keep that secret," he says.

"But I'm the people's hero. If I'm to reveal it, best to do it now when they're committed to the cause."

"The victory feels good," he says. "But the rest of the kingdom is far from stable. We've weakened the eastern reaches by drawing upon their resources. Even Toldulgur is far from secure. We don't know if the people around Mt. Cabrae and Myceum are actively hostile."

"But they—" I start.

"We can't fight a civil war on the very front we're fighting a defensive war."

I nod and we turn as one to retrace our steps to the doors.

Outside, dozens of people clear a path. They're staring in the wrong direction. After a moment, the two figures riding up the makeshift path register in my mind. Commander Sandy Nealy and her son Captain Kimbr Nealy.

They dismount and walk to the steps. I stand beside the king, doing my best to mimic his demeanor and act like I'm comfortable here. They kneel on the bottom steps, and I see reason for my father's haughty attitude.

A hush falls across the crowd. Different than the joyless silence of removing bodies, sounds outside the walls make this feel more like secrecy than melancholy.

"We wish to apologize publicly for a private offense," Kimbr says. "I won't waste words of excuse on Your Majesty. I was weak and fell. Please forgive us for another chance."

A driver calls to his team outside the walls, and children run along the inside. Sounds reach my ears like I'm listening through water. A dizziness, separate from fear of people finding my Brand, seizes upon my mind, and it feels like I'm going to black out.

"Rise," the king says. "You are forgiven."

Relief floods Sandy's face as they get to their feet. She looks chagrined from having to kneel where dozens of people could see her. I felt the same, though I don't know why.

"We didn't know Your Majesty would be here," Kimbr says, abashed yet happy. "We wanted to reach Jahkay for this very purpose. The assault here pained us but we are grateful to find you alive."

The king inclines his head. "Did you pass close to Mt. Cabrae?"

"Yes. The enemy hold it though they appeared weak."

"Does Myceum now share the weakness?" the king asks.

Sandy speaks for the first time.

"No Your Majesty. My daughter Captain Searle came from Miluta." She breathes deeply, as if the words are a physician pulling a knife from her gut. "My son and I wanted to find you, and her arrival let us."

The king looks over the crowd. "This storm is behind us. A united kingdom stands strong against its foes."

"She brought a strong force," Sandy says. "Some of it came in our retinue and is even now helping dig in your mountains. I assure you they are and have always been at your complete control."

I regard her red-splotched face. Words like this cost her far more than Kimbr.

"The forgiveness is complete," the king says. "Here's my hand in acknowledgement."

He salutes the way a subject would greet him.

The growing crowd doesn't know half of what has passed, yet the front rows mimic the Nealys and return his pledge. The pledge ripples outward to the gate and draws a shiver from my covered arms.

The crowd disperses when the king rides with the Nealys. I slip into the temple and find reilef in the solitude. Guilt pricks my conscience at resting while the others toil. I tell myself they didn't ride across the kingdom on a survival-level of sleep.

Hopefully Claire and Ann are finding quiet.

Weaver will never find anything else. I look into Lesasil's face. A prayer seems appropriate, and I reach out with my heart. Words simply don't come.

I awake with short shadows recessed on the floor. I don't remember slumping sideways to lie on the bench, nor a hand resting on my shoulder.

My heart stops.

"I've been sleeping in the granary since yesterday afternoon," Claire says. "I didn't want people to know I left my duties for that long, so I thought coming out here would look better." She laughs. "Guess I needed it if I almost slept the clock around."

I yawn and stretch as I rise.

Claire's eyes snap to my wrist. I move to cover it, but her eyes on mine show me she's seen in.

"In the battle?" she asks.

"Yes. The—I'm sorry. He needed to go."

Pain infects her eyes. "But... people said a Shadow King killed him."

I must have sounded heartless. I laugh to cover my relief. "No—not Lorganrule. This was yesterday with Captain Shutt. He opened the gates and sabotaged the castle. I used it on him."

Hope blooms like a spring crocus, bold in its delicacy.

"Oh." She lets out a sigh of a laugh. "I feel like I remember that now."

I stand and move to her. "He wanted to fight to the death. If it's worth anything, I went out of my way to leave him alive. I didn't know the Shadow King was watching us."

The words relieve her taught shoulders more than I expect. Now she looks... huggable. I reach in and she mirrors me.

"I take it you're alright with the Brand?" I ask into her cascade of hair.

"It's another scar." She loosens into a distant hug and strokes my face with the back of one soft hand. "We've both got a few of those already. I'm glad you didn't cut me deep by being the one."

I smile into those deep brown eyes. Never before have I accepted myself so much as I do now, standing with her, a piece I've been missing forever. It's as if I can feel the future radiating in blooms of hope.

I lead us from the temple and we stop on the landing. The noonday sun casts a harsh light, making the city look even more grim.

It's too hard to think of the future now, so I resign myself to living for the day. Repairing the stone walls will take an enormous amount of work. The other ruined fortresses will have to be recaptured before work can even begin on those. And yet we'd tear them down to the bedrock if that's what it takes to reclaim them.

So much to do, so far to go.

I feel like I've won, though the war is far from over.

"You still want to be queen of this one day?" I ask.

Claire tightens her grip on my hand, and I look at the only woman in the world who's received a first kiss twice.

.

About the Author.

Mark has lived in South Dakota his entire life. When not writing, he can be found reading medieval fantasy, building with Lego, gardening, woodworking, and watching movies. All with his growing family.

Please leave a review on both Goodreads.com and Amazon.com. It helps authors more than you know.

Made in the USA
Monee, IL
20 June 2025

19559651R00229